Deception of Magic

Magic

I0525354

Book one of the

Lord of the Stars

By Joel Bouriaque

Deception of Magic

Special thanks to my beautiful wife Sommer for her love and support throughout our whole marriage. A special thanks also to my children Daniel and Diala for character inspiration throughout the story.

A very heartfelt thank you goes out to my Mom and Dad for having a Christian home that taught the Bible. My mother is with our Lord now, but her writing really inspired me.

Thanks to Pam Willard for her editing, advice, corrections, and overall support. This book could have never been done without her.

Thanks to Georgia Willard, for giving me ideas and improvements. Significant areas of this book are from suggestions she made.
Thanks to Mimi Fencil Row for her help and inspiration. She is a great friend who has greatly helped me with my Theology.
Thanks to Santuck Baptist Church in Santuck, AL.

Cover by digitelldesign.com
Extra editing and artwork inside by Peggy Wilmeth Carr. She is a very dear Christian lady I am happy to call my friend.

Library of Congress Control Number: 2011918132
ISBN-10:   0615549020
ISBN-13:   9780615549026
            978-0-615-54902-6
                    Deception of Magic is on Facebook.
                    Deceptionofmagic@hotmail.com

Inside the Elven Throne Room

"You say with your lips what is right and good, yet in your hearts you think it is foolishness. You claim you know me, yet I deny knowing you. Repent, or I will destroy the elves. Every tree shall be cut down and consumed with fire, and the river will overflow with the blood of the elves before the fullness of the greater moon. Humans will refuse to farm this land for seven generations, and the gorm shall call it cursed for three. Dwarves shall cast lots, with the loser entering this land with great trembling."

"Yet, because of the love your kings had for me in times long past, I will grant one last chance. Search and understand, seek wisdom. What turns aside the wrath of God? Did I not say *draw near to God, and he will draw near to you. Cleanse your hands, ye sinners; and purify your hearts, ye double minded. Be afflicted, and mourn, and weep: let your laughter be turned to mourning, and your joy to heaviness. Humble yourselves in the sight of the Lord, and he shall lift you up.* Judgment is upon you, for who can escape my wrath? Yet to the humble will I show mercy, to the weak will I give strength. Heed the words of my maiden, for your time is short."

It was deathly silent in the throne room when Lily finished speaking the word from the Lord of the Stars. She hung her head and looked at the floor in front of her feet, golden hair hiding her face.

"Read every word she said back for everyone to hear," the Elven King said while pointing to an elf that was documenting everything in a large book. The king's face looked very troubled. An elf with glasses stood up, holding his large book in front of his face. His voice boomed out through the throne room.

"Your majesty, I know this dream because the same dream was shown to me. This is what your dream...."

When he concluded her testimony, the elf with the long purple robes began to speak. "The true God has spoken to me, and He has called this human female a liar and a blasphemer." His large staff that had a tip of a silver cross was pointing directly at Lily. Extreme anger showed in his face and eyes.

Standing strong in her faith, Lily lifted her head, locking her eyes on the elven priest. "Your church of idolatry is no more," she said in a low, meek voice. As soon as she spoke, the ground shook. For several long seconds, the throne room swayed back and forth. A loud, crashing noise reverberated through the throne room, followed by a thunderous boom that echoed throughout the Elven City.

Table of Contents

Chapter 1 6

Chapter 2 22

Chapter 3 37

Chapter 4 46

Chapter 5 57

Chapter 6 65

Chapter 7 77

Chapter 8 87

Chapter 9 99

Chapter 10 112

Chapter 11 121

Chapter 12 131

Chapter 13 145

Chapter 14 158

Chapter 15 170

Chapter 16 182

Chapter 17 193

Chapter 18 200

Chapter 19 208

Chapter 20 224

Chapter 21 231

Chapter 22 248

Conclusion 262

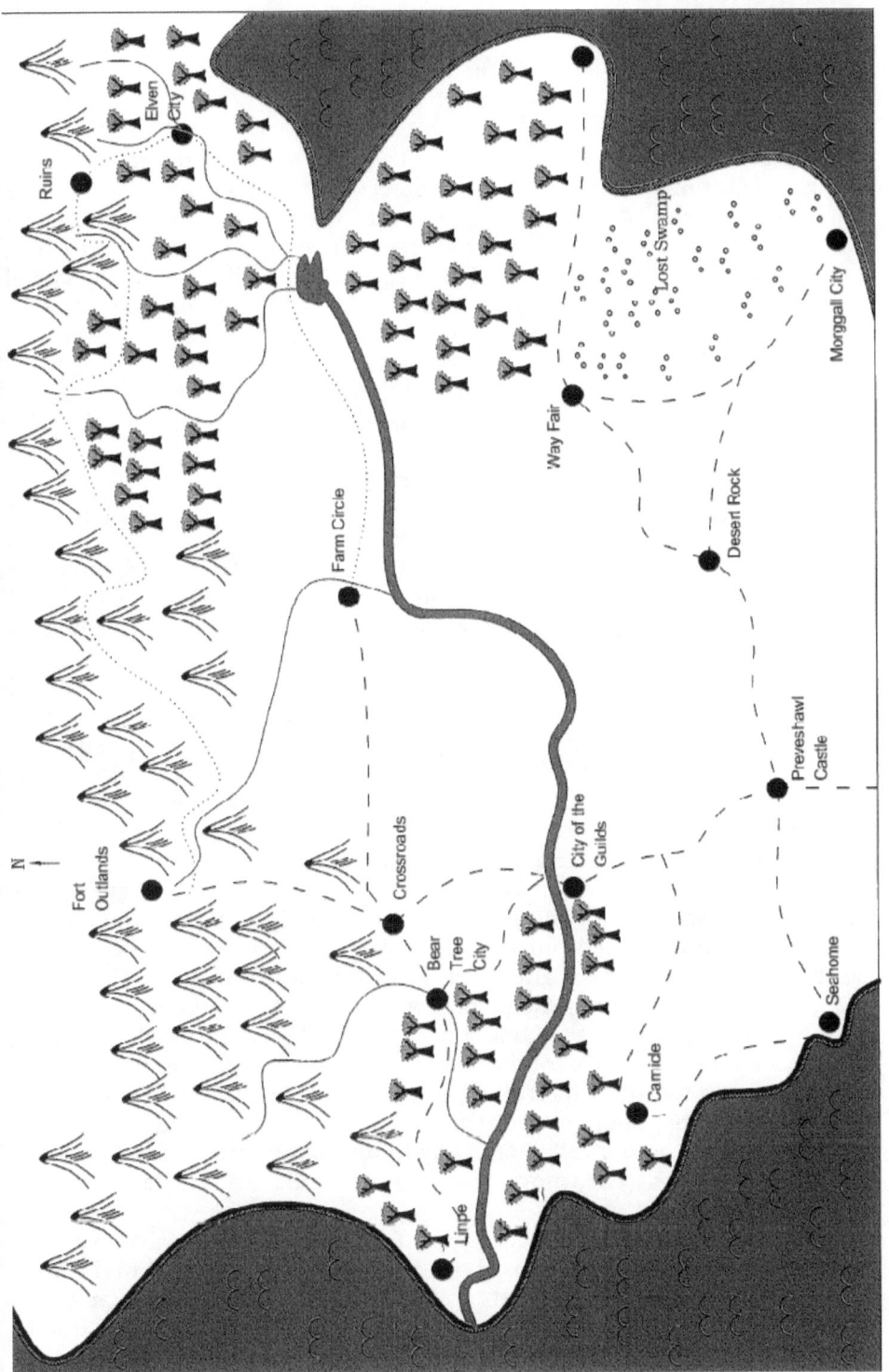

Chapter 1

Train up a child in the way he should go: and when he is old, he will not depart from it. – The Guide

Javin's short sword slammed with super speed into a tower shield held by a giant of a man. The clang of steel striking steel rang through the overcrowded arena, drowning out the enthusiastic cheering. Javin's feet danced back, barely in time to avoid the wild swing of a long sword that came inches from his stomach. His flat, dark eyes lit up as the sword swished through the air past him. Small, but powerfully packed muscles flexed in both his arms, while short swords spun in each of his hands. Lunging forward in a cloud of dust spurred up by his ever dancing feet, two short swords whistled through the air at lightning speed. They were aimed at the huge right shoulder of Javin's now unbalanced opponent.

Merion managed to twist his massive six-foot tower shield sideways, intercepting both Javin's short swords. Even though Javin was easily a foot shorter than him and not nearly as muscled, Merion still felt the power of Javin's blows into his shield. His shield rang like a drum as short sword strikes rained down at unbelievable speed from every direction imaginable. Merion fought to restore his balance thrown off by his wild and desperate sword swing, while at the same time moving his tower shield to deflect Javin's swords.

With a move Merion had never seen done before, Javin jumped high into the air. At the same time, Javin's body twisted with swords extended out away from his body. Whipping from right to left, two short swords now raced toward Merion's unguarded left side. Merion tried to use his long sword to block Javin's swords, while lunging sideways away from Javin. His sword was too slow. Air exploded from his lungs from the force of two short swords crushing into his armored side.

The arena erupted in ear-shattering applause as a bright yellow flag waved to and fro, swung overhead by the judge. "Strike one against Merion," the judge called out as he pointed the flag toward the gigantic fighter. Merion raised his right hand, acknowledging the strike that Javin had given him. The roar of the packed arena grew even louder.

"I will spot you this one hit, Javin," Merion growled. Spinning around, he marched back to his seat at the corner of the arena. Taking a cloth, Marion carefully wiped away the large yellow streak, removing the evidence of his opponent's sword from his upper chest. Javin, Merion's opponent, turned and strolled casually to his seat located on the opposite side of the arena. His movement was smooth and agile, radiating confidence with each step.

Unlike Merion, who stood seven feet tall with impressive muscles, there was nothing spectacular about Javin, in looks or in build. Javin stood an inch below six feet with a slight, but powerful, muscular build. Though slight in build, the muscles on his arms were like steel, due to years of hard training with the swords, and a life of work on the family farm. He had short-cropped brown hair, with dark-brown eyes. He was young, a few months away from his eighteenth birthday. Nevertheless, the Kingdom of Preveshawl had not seen a fighter the likes of Javin for nearly two hundred years.

Grabbing a water skin, Javin sat down on an old wooden bench. Exhaustion showed on his young face as he tried to relax. Parched lips eagerly sought the water from the water skin. Half the water was sucked down within seconds. Muscles starting to cramp warned him that this match was one of the toughest ones he had ever fought.

The warm mid-day sun beat down on him, causing beads of sweat to form on a clean-shaven, boyish face. Brown dust mixed with sticky sweat formed a yellowish mud, covering his arms and face. Taking another swig of water, Javin scanned the surrounding stands. Thousands of wildly cheering fans, mostly teens like himself, filled the arena.

Panic started to rise up in Javin, which he fought down by taken deep, measured breaths. Crowds always did this to him. He had learned to combat the panic that rose up in him anytime he was forced to be around large groups of people. Deep breathing and focusing his mind on something other than the crowd were his main tools to fight the panic.

Each fighter was allowed a ten-minute break between strikes so that they could rest and formulate their fighting strategies. While resting with his back against the hard, cold stone that made up the arena walls, Javin's mind wandered from his opponent. A rueful smile spread across his face as his mind traveled back to the time he first came to the guilds and this arena---a time he was to leave behind him forever.

It started for Javin four years ago at the age of thirteen. He had entered a fighting tournament held by the Guild of Warriors in the City of the Guilds. In fact, the fighting tournament was held at this very arena he was fighting in. The scrawny farm boy paid the entrance fee and declared himself from the town of Farm Circle.

Farm Circle was located in the grasslands of the northern parts of Preveshawl. The town was so small and insignificant that almost no one had even heard of it. Nearly all the young teens eagerly entering the tournament came from the more populated southern parts of Preveshawl or from the capital city named Preveshawl Castle. The top three winners of the tournament received their expenses paid for four years to the Guild of Warriors. Several hundred thirteen-year-old boys and girls competed in the tournament in hopes of winning the prestigious contest. Most were privately trained by the best fighters their families could afford.

Javin instantly got the attention of the thousands of spectators gathered at the arena to watch the tournament because he fought with two short swords, a style nearly unheard of among fighters. The crowd was stunned into silence during his first match, when Javin came out with both swords spinning in each hand. The blades spun through his hands so fast that the short swords were a blur to the amazed crowd. Javin's opponents were hard-pressed, trying to guess which direction Javin's spinning swords were going to come from. The swords would rapidly break out of their spin and stab or strike toward the body of Javin's opponents from unimaginable angles.

Javin's first match was over in seconds. Using a more common form of combat, his opponent stabbed straight at Javin's chest once they closed in on each other. Dodging sideways to avoid the two-handed sword, Javin's right sword struck his opponent's helmet while his left sword crashed into the shoulder. The backwards flip Javin performed to avoid the wild counter swing caused the crowd to go utterly crazy.

The crowd wildly cheered with unfettered abandon as the scrawny farm boy advanced through the tournament, never taking a single hit. Famous and renowned fighters watched their young students whom they had trained for years get defeated in seconds by the completely unknown thirteen-year-old boy. They had never seen anyone twist, roll, and move while spinning two swords like Javin did. Feet and body were constantly in motion while swords came out of their spin to strike opponents or to deflect opponent's weapons.

In the final fight, Javin defeated an extraordinarily tall and muscular boy, hitting the boy twice in under a minute of fighting. That boy was Merion. Javin was the first in recent memory to go through the whole tournament without being touched by a single blade. After the final fight, they held an award ceremony. The winner of the tournament was awarded a gold-plated trophy along with a specially made silver-plated sword belt. Much to the dismay of a large number of fans who had watched the tournament, Javin was nowhere to be found for the award ceremony. He quietly slipped out of the City of the Guilds, returning to his family farm near Farm Circle.

What the spectators did not know, was that Javin had barely made it through the tournament. The crowds and cheering fans caused overwhelming panic in him; panic that he fought down each fight. His breaking point had been reached with the last fight. Standing in the middle of the arena to receive the awards was more than he could take, so he quietly left the city. The mystery fighter remained an enigma to everyone for the next several months, until autumn caused the leaves of the great oaks to turn bright red and fall from the trees a few months later.

Javin, along with an attractive young woman named Chellell, also from Farm Circle, arrived the following autumn to the City of the Guilds for their first year of school. They joined the thousands of students attending the ten guilds. Both Javin and Chellell were among a fortunate few who had scholarships to attend the guilds for free. Chellell had won one of three scholarships to the Guild of Philosophy.

The City of the Guilds was a large, compact city situated right on the southern side of the only bridge in Preveshawl that crossed the Great Henjum River. The Great Henjum River was over a mile wide through its entire length from one end of Preveshawl to the other. Its crystal blue, sparkling waters were one of the great sights in all of Preveshawl. However, these waters held horrors that prevented any human from stepping a single toe in the river. Pherio Fish would strip flesh from bone in seconds. If you somehow managed to avoid the Pherio Fish, giant river serpents averaging fifty feet in length, patrolled the length of the whole river. No boats ever went out on this river for fear of these great river serpents.

The ancient bridge spanning the river at the City of the Guilds was another wonder of Preveshawl. Dwarves with their great machines and superior technology helped the humans build this bridge two centuries ago. The bridge was over a mile long and wide enough for four wagons to ride side-by-side.

Besides the capital city, the City of the Guilds was the largest city in Preveshawl. The hopes and dreams of Preveshawl were housed in this great city. Ten large marble buildings housing each guild was located along the banks of the massive river. Young men and women came from every corner of the kingdom in order to learn everything from art and philosophy to science and magic. Around the ten guilds were numerous cafes and small parks where students gathered to study and discuss the courses they were studying. To the north of the guilds was a massive tower that reached several hundred feet into the air. This great tower was the Library of Preveshawl. All the knowledge gathered over hundreds of years was housed in this library. Thousands upon thousands of scrolls on every subject imaginable filled the shelves and vaults of this tower.

Not only did the City of the Guilds house the guilds, but it was also the major center for the trade businesses in Preveshawl. Leatherworkers, blacksmiths, woodworkers, along with engineering and architectural houses were on nearly every street. Smoke constantly filled the air, and the streets ran with filthy water. Crowds of people filled the streets night and day.

Coming from the farm, Javin felt claustrophobic in this city. The overcrowding and the smells were nearly enough to drive him insane. Fortunately for Javin, the city was compacted into a small area that was surrounded by ancient oak and elm trees. The forest gave him the quick escape from the crowds that he needed. The forest soon became his best friend, giving him the peace and solitude he yearned for. Without the comforting embrace of the ancient forest with its magnificent trees, Javin would have never survived the four years of schooling at the guilds.

The first year was extremely difficult for incoming students. New students had to take one class from each of the ten guilds. Each student was required to master all ten courses, or they were forced out of the guilds. Only half of the first-year students managed to pass the courses and stay a second year. Of those that remained, a quarter would survive the rigorous training of the guilds and reach graduation three years later. The ten guilds were: Guild of Warriors, Guild of Science, Guild of Healing, Guild of Nature, Guild of Philosophy, Guild of Engineering, Guild of Elements, Guild of Arts, Guild of Religions, and the Guild of Magic.

The Guild of Magic was the newest of the guilds. Magic was strictly forbidden throughout Preveshawl up until two decades ago. Unfortunately for Javin, he had serious problems with the introduction to magic course. For some reason, being around magic made Javin ill. Nausea and severe headaches always came over him whenever he was near magic or magic users. Even though first-year students were only indoctrinated with magical philosophy, being in the building and around the magic user instructors overwhelmed him. He would have flunked the course cold and been thrown out of the guilds if Chellell had not helped him get through it. Javin ended up barely passing the introduction to magic class, but his relationship with Chellell ended up failing. Chellell's new-found love for magic combined with Javin's growing hatred of magic and the sickness that overwhelmed him whenever he was near it destroyed their relationship.

A roar from the crowd snapped Javin out of the past and back into the present. Merion was standing on his side of the arena, waving his sword overhead in order to get the arena cheering. Javin sighed as he took another sip of water. He searched across the arena and instantly spotted Chellell's long, fiery red hair in the crowd. Her hair, bright blue eyes, small slim figure with pale white skin made her a very attractive young woman. Javin sighed again as he looked away from Chellell and back toward his opponent. A sharp pain stabbed into his heart. He really missed her. He and Chellell had been together since early childhood. She had been his one and only friend all those years. Their families had farms right next to each other where they had spent their childhood playing together.

Every student that did not fail had to spend a total of four years at the guilds to graduate. The first year consisted of introductory courses taken at each guild. After that, students were required to spend a total of three years taking classes in the guild of their choice. Students were only allowed to switch guilds at the beginning of each year.

At the start of the second year, Javin officially joined the Guild of Warriors. His days were filled with learning weapons such as the pike, sword, bow, and mace. He also had to take courses on battle strategies and how to lead men in combat. Chellell joined the Guild of Magic. Even though she enjoyed her first-year course at the Guild of Philosophy, Magic had become her first love. Within months, Javin was getting violently ill every time he was around Chellell and her new familiar that every mage summoned. Desperate, he tried everything to convince her to switch guilds once the second year ended. Instead, Chellell ended her relationship with Javin. Chellell flatly refused to speak a single word to Javin for the next two years. Looking back, Javin regretted his lack of tact in his dealings with Chellell and her love of magic.

This year, their last and final year in the guilds, Javin had put major effort into reestablishing their friendship, but Chellell had completely ignored his efforts. The memories of the great times they had together always came with the heartache; like the time they built a fort out of old wood from a fallen barn and pretended that she was a queen, and he was her knight. Another fond memory he had was the times they sat side by side in church and the times they spent studying together for school. Basically, Javin was conflicted in his heart. He was either physically sick being near her and her magic or heart-broken being apart from her.

Javin's thoughts of the past were interrupted once again because the crowd came alive with an even louder roar. Glancing up, he saw the judge waving a green flag. Bowing his head, Javin said a quick prayer to God for his safety and for the safety of his opponent, Merion. Tossing his water skin aside, he stood up and walked toward the center of the arena. Both short swords came out, slowly spinning in each hand.

The sword spin was a trick that had taken Javin years of practice to perfect. As a child, he was amazed at the way the girls spun batons through their fingers. Observing them closely, Javin starting applying what he saw girls doing with batons in his sword practices. Working with his father, Javin modified the handles of his swords and re-balanced them. Years later, he perfected the sword spin.

"One strike," the judge called out loud enough for the audience to hear while pointing at Merion. "Are you ready?" Merion nodded to the judge. Merion's arms were nearly as big around as Javin's legs. His heavily muscular frame carried a huge six-foot shield in one hand and a long sword in his other hand. He growled at Javin while the judge inspected his sword to make sure it had the protective covering on it. The judge quickly applied yellow grease to the sword covering. He then turned toward Javin. "No strikes," he shouted while pointing the green flag at Javin. "Are you ready?" Javin nodded toward the judge while holding his swords out. The judge quickly inspected both the short swords and applied the yellow grease. "To your corners," he ordered. Both fighters turned and trotted back toward their earlier seats. However this time, neither sat down. "Fight!" the judge shouted while slapping both hands together.

Moving back toward the center of the arena, Javin tuned out the noise of the crowd that had gathered at the arena to watch the final fight featuring the number-one and number-two ranked guild fighters. Last time, Merion had been cautious with his fighting style against Javin. That tactic had only earned him a strike. The victory was awarded to the first opponent to win two out of three matches. Javin had won the first match. From the determination showing on Javin's face, he meant to win the second match as well.

Once the two combatants closed within ten feet of each other, Merion bellowed like an enraged bull and charged right at Javin. Javin rolled sideways as Merion's long sword crashed into the ground where he had been a split second before. Ripping his sword out of the dirt with incredible speed, Merion whipped his sword horizontally through the air. Javin rolled back to his feet, but was forced to jump backwards as Merion's sword sliced through the air right in front of his chest. Once Merion's long sword went past him, he leaped forward. Both of Javin's short swords whistled through the air to crash into Merion's giant shield. Javin's swords flew in six times, but Merion caught them all as he furiously moved his shield side to side. Merion recovered and swung his sword back around, forcing Javin to disengage and nimbly retreat backwards.

The two combatants warily faced each other again. Merion's shield almost completely covered his massive body. Knowing he would have to find a way around the shield while avoiding the long sword, Javin studied his opponent's movement. Last time he got Merion to swing the shield too far to the right, which had cost him. Javin doubted that would work again. The other problem he had was that Merion was so strong that he could not block Merion's sword. He was forced to either deflect the long sword or completely dodge away from it.

Both fighters slowly circled around each other, their feet kicking up dust. Fast as a striking snake, Javin lunged toward Merion. His right short sword swinging down toward the head while his left cut in hard sideways toward the giant man's chest. Merion's sword flashed upward while his shield moved sideways. Both of Javin's swords were blocked. Javin expected the big man to step backwards or to try lashing out with his sword. Instead, Merion surprised him for the first time ever in their many matches through the years. With his mighty strength, Merion rammed Javin with his six-foot shield. The shield smashed into Javin with so much force that he flew backwards. Javin arched his back while his feet shot skyward up into the air. His swords barely scraped the ground as he back flipped, landing cleanly on his feet. He instantly dove sideways while flashing a sword at the charging Merion. The sound of Javin's short sword striking the massive shield rang throughout the arena. Javin rolled back to his feet to face his snarling foe.

To Javin's dismay, Merion charged a second time. His sword pointed straight out like a spear behind his tower shield. Instead of backing off or dodging sideways like Merion would likely expect, Javin lunged right toward the big man. Shock registered on Merion's face because of Javin's sudden aggression. He stabbed his long sword toward Javin, only to have both of Javin's short swords bang into his long sword, deflecting it toward the ground. When Merion's sword hit the ground, Javin spun his body sideways around the big man whose momentum was still carrying him forward. With his swords now free, Javin slashed them repeatedly into the back of the large fighter. Merion crashed into the ground hard, a cloud of dust blowing upward around him. He quickly rolled sideways and leaped to his feet, much faster than a man his size should have been capable of. A big yellow 'X' was etched into the armor covering his back.

"Strike two," yelled the judge while pointing the yellow flag toward Merion. Javin heard the crowd roar with approval, but his eyes were on Merion. He was nervous about how the notoriously bad-tempered Merion would react to another defeat. Javin cautiously watched while Merion angrily flung his shield to the ground and approached him. Once he reached Javin, he seemed to have a change of attitude. Instead of fists like

Javin feared, Merion extended a single open hand out toward his smaller foe. Javin reached out and locked hands with Merion. Merion did not release Javin's hand. Instead, he raised it up over his head. Dropping his sword to the dusty ground, Merion used his free hand to wave the crowd to silence. A hush fell over the arena.

"Everyone here tonight has witnessed history being made," Merion shouted in a deep bass voice that echoed through the arena. "Javin is the only fighter since the legendary Lord Gray, two hundred years ago, to go through every tournament for four years without anyone touching him." The crowd roared again, even louder this time. Merion circled around the edge of the arena, dragging an embarrassed Javin with him while holding his arm high overhead.

Javin's shyness and reclusive nature were well known to those at the guilds; almost as well-known as his skill with the swords. While fighting, Javin's concentration on the fight overrode the fact that thousands were watching him. After the fight however, the weight of the adoring and cheering fans focusing on him was almost more than he could handle. A deep panic was overwhelming him as Merion circled him around the arena so everyone could acknowledge his accomplishment.

Merion finally released him after taking him in a full circle around the arena. A bear hug followed, forcing the air out of Javin's lungs. "I am proud that it was you I lost to," he said before letting Javin go. The chant of "Javin, Javin, Javin," reverberated through the arena. "You caused me to practice day and night for four years. Four years I practiced, with dreams of pulverizing you. I may have lost again, but I know I am ten times the fighter I would have been had you not challenged me." Javin bowed his head toward Merion, but no words came from his mouth. As the noise of the crowd slowly died down, Merion put his arm around Javin's shoulder. "Come on, let's go to graduation and get our apprenticeship assignments. If we are blessed, then we will be apprenticed to the army." Javin gave a wave to the screaming crowd, before walking with Merion through the exit tunnel and out of the arena.

****

The second moon's pale light slowly rose above the top of the giant trees, casting ghostly shadows down on a small clearing in the middle of the woods. The clearing was covered in thick, green, knee-high grass. Through the edge of the trees, the Great Henjum River reflected silver moonlight into the darkness of the night.

A lone figure stood quietly with head bowed and a short sword held loosely in each hand. Javin started to move once the pitch blackness of the clearing was replaced with faint moonlight. Slowly, both swords started turning and spinning in each hand. His arms started moving faster and faster, causing the spinning swords to gain speed. Both swords weaved left to right in front of his body while he slowly turned in a tight circle. Javin started moving around in a dance that took him around the small clearing. At times, a sword would flash out straight into a stab or a cut before

13

returning to their spin. He moved gracefully to the edge of the clearing where both swords sliced in and out of their spin to make contact with a training bag hanging from one of the ancient trees. Every two to three seconds a sword would strike the bag as Javin's body spun, rolled, or flipped, while swords lashed out at an imaginary enemy.

Continuing his attack on the bag, Javin did not noticing a ball of light coming towards him through the thickening mist that was slowly invading the forest of ancient trees. Within minutes, another figure stepped onto the edge of the clearing, a ball of light floating inches above the fingers of an outstretched hand. The individual stepped further into the clearing, causing the ball of light to abruptly vanish. As soon as the ball of light disappeared, a miniature creature flew off the individual's shoulder. Wings carried the tiny creature smoothly through the gnarled tree limbs until it found a branch near the clearing where it could land. Javin turned to face the woman, the moonlight illuminating her pale white face. Curly, flaming red hair circled her face, hanging down to the middle of her back. Bright blue eyes seemed to glow in the pale moonlight. Her pencil-thin body stood several inches above five feet tall. A blood-red mage's robe covered her. Chellell paused briefly at the edge of the clearing; her gaze on the small creature that left her shoulder to seek the protection of the trees.

"H-H-Hello Chellell," Javin stammered. He started to stammer something else, but stopped. He was not sure what to say. Chellell hardly noticed Javin's stammering; she had become used to it as a child. When they were growing up, he primarily communicated with writing or sign language because of his fractured speech he had been born with. The exception was Chellell; he always talked with her. It was not until he won the Guild of Warriors fighting tournament in a spectacular way that he got the confidence to talk to other people. With sadness, Chellell remembered how proud he had been after winning the championship, and how proud she had been of her friend.

With his fractured speech, came an extreme shyness around people. Even with his fame, shyness still hung on him like a thick winter cloak. It didn't matter that he had gone undefeated, with no weapon touching him in four full years of tournament fights; Javin was a loner with almost no one he could call a friend. Once he and Chellell started fighting, Javin had retreated into a world no one else could penetrate. Several of Chellell's female friends had tried, but Javin simply ignored their advances and offers of friendship. Every evening he would come to this clearing, spending hours alone practicing with his swords.

Chellell was the only person that knew this clearing, but Javin was still surprised to see her, since she had not visited him these past two years. Both short swords spun in his hands before going smoothly back into the sheaths buckled around his waist. A stab of pain shot through his heart at the sight of her. Javin could not imagine anyone taking the place in his heart that Chellell had occupied for so long. Still, he could see no way for them to ever be close again. He also realized that the pain was a whole lot less than it had been two years ago. A chill came over him, making the hairs on his arms stand on end. Nausea and a slight headache soon followed the chills. Javin, again, was reminded of the real reason he and Chellell could never be as close as they once were.

Chellell had no idea that Javin reacted so badly around magic, thinking only that he strongly disliked it. It was one secret he kept close to his heart and away from her. She never understood why Javin had demanded she give up magic, and then spent less time with her. In her anger, she had refused to hear any explanation he tried to give. The hurt and pain that he had caused her years ago could still be felt. Chellell had learned a lesson that she had promised herself never to forget. Under no circumstances would she ever allow anyone, especially a man, to get emotionally close to her. The end result was always the same, pain and abandonment. Every man she had ever loved and trusted had abandoned her like Javin, and like her father when she was nine years old.

Even so, Javin tried hard this year to be civil. This night, their last night at the guilds, Chellell decided to part ways as friends again. She knew there was no reason for them to spend the rest of their lives despising each other.

While walking to the middle of the clearing, an audible sigh escaped Chellell's lips right before she sat down cross-legged in the green grass. "I still can't understand why magic will not work around you, Javin," Chellell said, referencing her magic ball of light vanishing as soon as she entered the clearing. "You can be so frustrating at times."

"I have no control over that," Javin stuttered, unsure whether he should stand there or go to her. She answered his unspoken question by patting the ground next to where she sat. Magic not working around him was another secret he kept. Chellell knew because her own magic failed anytime Javin was near, but none of the others in the guild had figured it out. The combination of familiars, mysteriously refusing to tell their magic users why their magic failed, combined with Javin's reclusive nature, helped keep that secret.

"I really need to speak with you before we leave on our apprenticeship assignment," she said, patting the ground beside her, again. "Even though you fought Merion in the arena today, I knew you would be out here practicing." Javin walked over and plopped down next to her, pushing back the waves of discomfort that came from being so close to the magic that radiated from her body. "It is such a lovely night, with the stars and the greater moon. The air is so fresh, and these trees..." Chellell threw a glittering smile toward Javin. "It is almost like the grove of trees near your farm we built our play castle in, except we were never allowed to stay out late enough to see what it looked like at night."

Chellell went silent, memories of her past childhood with Javin rushing through her mind. Finally, she broke the silence, "So, where is your assignment at?" she asked while gazing off into the trees that were lit up by the pale moonlight.

"Actually, I am not sure yet," Javin stuttered. "I haven't opened it to look. I was going to wait until I got back to the dorm later tonight."

Chellell turned her head to look at him, a big smile on her face and her eyes barely holding back the laughter. "That is just like you, Javin; too scared to open it and see a horrible assignment." She then lightly punched him in the shoulder, a teasing gesture from their youth. "You would wait and put it off forever, if you could. Come on, hand it over, and I will open it for you."

"All right, I'll open it. I wouldn't want you to die right here from curiosity," Javin replied with a laugh, his constant stuttering easing a little as Javin grew more comfortable with Chellell's presence.

Reaching into his pouch, Javin pulled out a rolled scroll. His eyes scanned quickly through the scroll which was congratulating him on making it this far. He read how he was now expected to uphold the honor of the Guild of Warriors and obey the laws of Preveshawl. Finally, he got to the part that told him his future assignment. It read:

Name: Outlands Weapon and Armor
Location: Fort Outlands (see attached map)
Job Description: Guard, Blacksmith apprentice
Note: Approved by General Franks, Preveshawl Army

"Very northern edge of Preveshawl," Javin commented with a stutter while examining the map. He then passed the scroll over to Chellell. "In a very dangerous part of the kingdom; this should be an interesting experience." Javin flicked a small caterpillar off his leg. He watched the insect for a few seconds as it crawled through the grass. "I am not sure why a blacksmith shop. I know nothing about blacksmithing. Maybe my Dad is behind it. He was at Fort Outlands years before I was born. So, where are you going?"

Chellell reached into her robe pocket and handed him her scroll. Her eyes though, stayed on Javin's assignment. Javin went straight to the bottom of her scroll to find:

Name: Ministry of Magic
Location: Preveshawl Castle
Job Description: Chancellor Assistant
Note: Requested by Chancellor White, Advisory Council to King Logan XII

Javin gave a low whistle, impressed with her assignment. "Wow Chellell, the capitol city, right in the middle of the power. You must have really impressed somebody to get this assignment." He handed her scroll back to her. Chellell continued to closely examine Javin's scroll for several more minutes before finally handing his assignment back to him.

"They are sending you to the northern border," she whispered to herself, but Javin heard. Chellell looked up into the sky, slowly lying back onto the lush grass while staring up at the stars. "No matter what we do or how hard we try Javin," a faint trace of sadness was barely audible in her voice, "our worlds are heading in opposite directions."

Javin remembered when they had fought over her decision to enter the Guild of Magic. He had tried everything to convince her to choose differently. Later on, he regretted the things he had said and how badly he had handled the whole situation. This time, Javin was determined to say the right things, and to behave like a friend.

"Looks like a once-in-a-lifetime opportunity for you," Javin stammered. "I know you will make Chancellor White a great assistant. It seems like it is everything you wanted, a dream job for someone from the Guild of Magic." Lying back in the grass beside her, he too stared up at a sky full of stars. It was times like this that Javin wished with all his heart he could talk normally. He had so much he wanted to say. He knew if he tried, his speech would let him down, as it always had in the past.

"Maybe," replied Chellell. They both continued to stare at the night sky exploding with stars. "You know how much I love magic, but I..." Chellell sighed audibly, "Never mind. It's something you wouldn't understand." Unseen by Javin, a tear slowly slipped out of her right eye and down her cheek. She quickly wiped it away while taking a deep breath. "So, when do you plan on leaving?"

"Well, now that I know where I am going, I guess I will leave tomorrow, after church services. I can spend a couple of days with my family before traveling on to the fort. The farm will only be a half-day out of the way; how about you?"

"I might leave in a couple of days; I almost have a new fire spell memorized. After that, I guess I will take the coach over to the capital. Hey... since you are going to the farm, can you drop off a letter to my mom? I have been meaning to send it for weeks and never got around to it." Chellell rubbed her hands through the lush grass.

"Sure, you can give it to me at church." Javin instantly regretted saying that. "Sorry, Chellell, that wasn't nice of me; I really am sorry. I will swing by your room and pick it up after church."

Chellell sighed, "I'm fine Javin. I actually miss church, especially the singing. It's because... well, you know how I feel."

Her heated words came pouring back into his mind. "Church was for the young to learn morals and to control the uneducated. Since I am no longer a child and have been educated, I see no need for church. Besides, how can an educated person possibly believe that the Lord of the Stars is the Son of God, and that he died on a cross for our sins?"

Through their childhood, Chellell's mother had always taken her to church, where she would usually sit with him. Now, Javin understood that Chellell had never really believed, while his own faith had manifested and grown stronger. It was something else that had driven them apart.

Chellell interrupted his thoughts. "Javin, I know we did not want any of this, but maybe it will work out in the end." She paused and looked sideways at him. Chellell stretched out in the grass, enjoying the feel of the soft grass on her skin.

They continued to lie in the grass, side by side. Chellell talked about her dreams and her concerns with the future. Javin stared at the stars and the greater and lesser moons while Chellell talked. Hours passed, with Chellell talking, and Javin listening. Without warning, Chellell sat up. To his surprise, she started laughing. "Javin, you have changed so much. You know exactly how to make a girl feel better, by listening and keeping your mouth shut." She put her head down between her knees, still laughing.

"I'm sorry Chellell," stuttered a very confused Javin, who sat up as well. "I was trying to think of something to say, but nothing came to mind. I am sorry that..."

"Shhhh" She whispered, placing her finger on his lips. "I meant it. You did what I needed; you listened. I should not have talked so much. I am in a strange mood today, I guess." She slowly got up and ran her hands through her red hair, pulling grass out that stubbornly clung to it. "Tell you what, I will meet you by the big oak near the Guild of Nature at noon, and give you the letter for my mom. I better get going now, and leave you to your robbers and goblins." She threw another beautiful smile at Javin, winking at the same time. A smile spread across his face as he thought back to the time they had pretended to be defending their play castle from goblins and robbers.

"A week from now, it will no longer be pretend, except I seriously doubt I will be defending a princess and a castle." Javin said laughingly as he slowly rose from the ground to stand beside her.

A shadow of worry quickly crossed Chellell's face, "Promise me, Javin, that you will be careful. It is the border area they are sending you to."

"Don't worry," he stuttered, "I will be as careful as I can. Besides, I know the Lord of the Stars will be with me." He held his hand out toward her. "Truce? Friends again?"

Chellell looked at his hand. Then she looked into the eyes of her childhood friend. She gently brushed his hand aside and stepped forward to embrace him. "Friends? You are very special to me Javin. Please, never forget that," she whispered in his ear. With that, she pushed away from him. "You need to stop ignoring all the girls; and stop breaking their hearts." Chellell said with a sly smile on her face.

"I never..."

"Oh stop that, Javin," Chellell said with a huff. "You are the greatest swordsman the guilds have ever seen. Girls have been trying to get your attention since you came here. You ignored all of them." Chellell playfully punched his tightly packed, muscular shoulder, before walking back toward the edge of the clearing. "I'll bet you a home-cooked dinner that the next time I see you, some beautiful farm girl will have you wrapped around her finger," Chellell called back over her shoulder.

"I'll take that bet; remember that mince pie is my favorite," Javin called back toward her.

"Sugared fruit bread is mine," she yelled back.

Javin continued to watch her as she walked away, noticing the small creature flying out of the trees, landing on her shoulder. A ball of light again appeared in her hand as she disappeared back into the forest. He sank to his knees and put his head down on the ground, waiting for the waves of sickness washing over him from her embrace, to leave his body.

****

Lamar, Javin's father, was plowing in the fields when he spotted Javin coming through the gate. Dropping the reigns to the horses, he ran toward his son, picking him up with a bear hug. As soon as he let go, Javin's three little sisters nearly took him to the ground in their rush to greet him. Annba, Javin's mother, came out of the house, smiling ear to ear.

"You are just in time for dinner," Javin's mother said as she gave him a big hug, once his little sisters were finished with him.

"Let me put the plow horses in the barn, and I'll be right in," Lamar said as he gave Javin a last pat on the back. "I'll get your horse as well." He grabbed the reigns of Javin's horse and headed for the barn. Javin's three little sisters took that time to jump Javin. He let his younger sisters take him to the ground. Little girl giggles sounded as they wrestled with their big brother.

****

"I am pleased you and Chellell are friends again," Lamar said to Javin as he deflected a short sword coming down toward his head. Lamar and Javin were dressed in practice padded armor; each held practice short swords in their hands. "I know the situation with her was very hard." Javin stepped back as he furiously deflected his father's swords that came raining down repeatedly.

"She has completely forsaken the church, and God," Javin stuttered as he countered one of his father's swings and stabbed his right sword forward. Lamar knocked the sword aside. "God convicted me of the fact that I would not reach her and be a witness to her, until we were friends again. I will never agree with her following magic and rejecting God, but I can still be her friend."

Lamar stepped back, hanging his swords by his side. He looked proudly at his son. "That is very wise of you, Javin. Remember to pray for her as well. I do want you to know something, son. Your mother and I both know how much this hurt you. Keep your focus on God. He will heal your hurts."

Javin gave his father a small smile. He doubted anyone knew how badly the whole thing really hurt him. He was glad the pain was less than it was two years ago, and having Chellell as a friend again also helped.

19

"So where is your apprenticeship?" Lamar asked as he sat down on an old stool near their practice ring.

"Fort Outlands," Javin stammered, "at a blacksmith shop. Didn't you live for a while at Fort Outlands when you were in the army?" Concern showed on Lamar's face, but he hid it quickly. "Yes, son, I was there before you were even born. I'm sure it has greatly changed since then." Lamar stood back up, trying to change the subject. "I want to show you a disarm move. It may come in handy if you ever find you need to disarm an opponent instead, of going for a kill shot."

****

"He is going to find out someday anyway," Annba said to her husband. The two were sitting together on the front porch. The three girls were fast asleep and Javin had gone to deliver Chellell's letter to her mom. "It would be better to hear it from us. That way, he gets the truth instead of some fairy tale."

"The truth could put him in danger," Lamar replied with a sigh. "One thing I learned from a career in the army is that you can't tell the enemy something you don't know. If our son where to slip up one time and say something he shouldn't, then his life could very well be in danger. For the time being, I think it safer to let him think I am just a retired soldier, who is now a farmer."

****

Reaching over into his duffle bag, Javin pulled out a large, thick book with bold, white lettering across the front, *The Guide*. The fire crackled and sparked in its small ring of rocks, pushing back the darkness around his campsite. He flipped *The Guide* open to a bookmark, and held the book so that the fire illuminated the pages. *Keep on, then, with your magic spells and with your many sorceries, which you have labored at since childhood. Perhaps you will succeed, perhaps you will cause terror. All the counsel you have received has only worn you out! Let your astrologers come forward, those stargazers who make predictions month by month, let them save you from what is coming upon you. Surely they are like stubble; the fire will burn them up. They cannot even save themselves from the power of the flame. A flame that is not coals for warmth; nor is it a fire to sit by!*

Javin leaned over and carefully stuffed *The Guide* back into his duffle bag. Thoughts of how this section of *The Guide* talked about God's strong dislike for magic raced through his mind. God even mocked them for the power they claimed to have, but it could not save them. Javin knew that the people of the Kingdom of Preveshawl were fast becoming lovers of magic, with witchcraft and magic spreading like wildfire through the grasslands on a windy day. He wasn't sure how long God would withhold his judgment, but he feared time was very short.

The day before, Javin had returned to his farm after delivering Chellell's letter to her mother. His parents were on the porch waiting for him. His mother had talked to him about things going on in the Kingdom of Preveshawl, and how people were turning away from God. Afterwards,

20

Javin's parents prayed for him, that God would keep him safe while at the fort. They also all prayed for Chellell. For some unknown reason to Javin, his father had again warned him to never talk about his family life. It was a warning Javin had gotten from his father every time he was back home from the guilds. This morning, Javin said good-bye to his family, and rode his horse toward Fort Outlands.

The fire hissed and sparked in front of Javin, bringing him back to the present. He stood up and walked beyond the firelight of his campsite. As he walked, he thought about his childhood with Chellell. A light went on in Javin's mind, and the puzzle pieces started to fall into place. When Chellell's father had left her and her mother, Chellell had prayed. She even had Javin pray for her father those many years ago, yet nothing happened. At some point, Chellell must have become angry that her prayers had not been answered. She finally must have reached a point where she decided there was no God. Even as young teenagers, Chellell would often ask him "How do we really *know* there is a God?" He understood now that he had never given an answer that satisfied her. He continued to walk out into the night, alone in the darkness with his troubled thoughts.

Along with his concerns for Chellell, another discussion he had that same night with his parents bothered him. The people of Preveshawl no longer had any relationship with God. Javin went to church every seventh day, but among the guilds only three other students, from the Guild of Healing, regularly went to the last true church left in the City of the Guilds.

According to history, people of great faith had originally founded the Kingdom of Preveshawl. The founders believed in the Word of God, *The Guide,* which was written by men inspired by the Holy Spirit through history. However, everyone he knew at the guilds was like Chellell; they did not believe in God. The rest went to The Enlightened Church, where *The Guide* was rarely cracked open. The Enlightened Church was the largest church in Preveshawl. This church believed that *The Guide* was good for past generations, but that it did not fit into the new, modern world. They taught that *The Guide* was written by men without any inspiration from God. Therefore, they claimed that it contained many fallacies.

The Enlightened Church accepted magic, even though God strictly forbade magic in *The Guide.* Preveshawl had followed God's directives concerning magic up until two decades ago, when the king overturned all laws forbidding magic. He also had the Guild of Magic added to the guilds, so that young people could learn and practice magic. This act by the king started the kingdom down a road supporting magic, while forsaking God and His word.

Yet, Javin thought, *The Guide* says *"Then they cried unto the LORD in their trouble, and he saved them out of their distresses."* Under the light of the greater moon, Javin bowed his head and prayed for his family, Preveshawl, and for Chellell.

Chapter 2

Study to show thyself approved unto God, a workman that needs not to be ashamed, rightly dividing the word of truth. – The Guide

Before the sun had risen in the eastern sky, Javin was awakened by the smell of breakfast being cooked. Sleep instantly left his body as he leapt to his feet with both swords drawn.

"I got eggs, meat strips, and biscuits," said an older man, cooking over the fire a few feet from Javin. A loud braying noise caused a confused Javin to spin around. Tied up next to his horse was a donkey. The donkey's back was loaded with all types of old leather bags and leather pouches. "You wait your turn, you old, stubborn donkey," the old man said from beside the fire. "You know the rules. Humans eat before donkeys." The old man turned toward Javin, "Old Milbur loves biscuits, but he needs to learn patience." The donkey let out an obnoxious "Hee Haw" as the old man finished speaking.

Javin was normally a light sleeper. He could not understand how someone could walk into his camp with a donkey and start cooking without waking him up. "What are you...?"

"Fine, I'll work on teaching you patience later." The old man tossed three biscuits toward the donkey. "If he doesn't get what he wants, he will bray until I give in. How are we supposed to talk with a stubborn donkey constantly braying?"

"Who are you? What are you doing in my camp?" Javin asked with a stutter so bad he could barely be understood.

"Why do you stutter like that? Can't you talk normally?" The old man was now staring at Javin with piercing eyes. "Those swords of yours can go as well, unless you think an old man with a donkey is dangerous." Promptly scooping some of the breakfast he had cooked on to a plate, the old man held it out toward Javin.

Javin hesitantly returned both swords to his belt and took the plate from his uninvited guest. "I stutter because I was born this way." He looked down at the plate of food handed to him. The eggs and meat strips looked and smelled delicious. "Now--answer my question! Why are you in my camp, cooking breakfast?"

"Born that way, you say?" The old man sat down a few feet from where Javin was standing. He had a plate of food as well, but he was not paying it any attention. "Why don't you see a healer about that condition? I knew a healer once that could..."

"My mother is from the Guild of Healing. She is the best healer north of the river. She tried everything known, when I was a child."

"She prayed for your healing, yet God saw fit to leave you as you were", the old man said as his voice changed, becoming serious in tone. "Understand this, Javin, God decided to raise up a warrior for these troubled times ahead."

"How do you know my name?" asked Javin. Alarm, mixed with

confusion, showed on his face as he hurriedly put his plate down.

The old man completely ignored him. "To be a strong warrior for God, you must be weak. Does not God say in *The Guide, My strength is made perfect in weakness?* Without your stutter given to you by God, pride would have prevented you from being the warrior God needs to lead His people in the days ahead. Your weakness has allowed God to strengthen you."

The old man stood up, looking at his plate with disgust. "I need to learn to cook! Now my wife, before she went to be with God, she was a cook. I need to get on with my travels. My donkey is getting anxious for home." The man sat his plate down by Javin's feet and proceeded to walk over toward his donkey. He abruptly stopped and spun back around, again facing Javin.

"Two weaknesses were given to you at your birth. One will be fully healed. Your mother has prayed for you daily since the day you started talking. God has decided it is time to answer her prayers. On the day you put on the full armor of God, and swords of flame devour the enemy that God has stirred up to judge Preveshawl, then you will stutter no more."

Javin stood in complete shock and confusion while the old man untied his donkey. This meeting had to be the strangest thing that had ever happened to him. "I see you are wondering why I said two weaknesses, but you only know of one. For your second weakness, only a partial healing will be granted. A barbarian princess, known as the slayer of giants, will be given the power from God to give you partial healing. In turn, you will lead her people into war."

The old man had his donkey on a rope, leading the animal out of Javin's camp and down the road, in the opposite direction Javin was traveling.

"Who are you?" Javin called toward the departing man.

"Remember Javin, pride will make you weak. Humility will keep you strong." The man continued leading his donkey down the road as Javin watched in confusion.

****

Three hours later, Javin arrived at a branch in the road known to the locals as the Crossroads. The Crossroads was a major junction point for Northern Preveshawl. The south fork eventually crossed the Great Henjum River, leading travelers to the southern parts of the kingdom. This area included the City of Guilds, where Javin had spent his last four years, and the capitol city where the king ruled Preveshawl with an iron fist. The east road took travelers back into the grasslands, to Javin's farm and the small town of Farm Circle. The west fork led to the only major city north of the river, Bear Tree City. It was a major trading hub for farmers and miners. The north fork was a road Javin had never been on. It took you to the wild northern border of Preveshawl and Fort Outlands. Two great mountain ranges were separated only by a narrow mountain pass. In the middle of this pass sat Fort Outlands, guarding Preveshawl from the war-like Northern Races.

Javin flicked the reins against the neck of his horse, turning the animal up the north fork toward Fort Outlands. He was on the road for only a few minutes, when the sounds of fighting filled his ears. The noise was mixed with strange, high-pitched squeals that he had never heard before. Metal, banging against metal, echoed through the hills.

Javin could see nothing immediately up ahead because the road curved, winding through the small evergreen trees and rock outcroppings. Kicking his horse in the side, he galloped through the curves until he came around a large bend. Clearing the bend, he saw the cause of the commotion. Stopping his horse almost instantly, Javin took in the scene before him, while trying to fight the cold fear, spreading through his body.

Two large wagons were stopped in the middle of the trail, next to a wide rock face. Four humans stood in the space between the rock face and the wagons. Two men were wearing chain mail armor with a shield and sword. Stamped on the front of the shields was an eagle, the symbol worn by Preveshawl army soldiers. Another man was covered in brown leather armor, with a wicked-looking long sword drawn and ready. The three men were protecting a woman.

Walking around the wagons, were a dozen vicious-looking humanoids armed with sharp daggers and short spears. They were three feet high with sharply pointed ears that poked out above the top of their heads. Pale, greenish skin could be seen through the rags that they wore for clothing. One soldier and at least three of the little creatures were down on the ground, either badly injured or dead.

"Goblins," Javin realized. He had seen pictures of them in classes at the Guild of Warriors. Goblins were a humanoid creature, distantly related to elves and humans. They were also known for their evil and cruel ways.

Javin sat glued to his saddle, paralyzed with fear and uncertain about what he should do. While frozen to his saddle, he watched the woman point her staff toward the goblins. Lightning sizzled from the end of the staff, blowing into one of the more aggressive goblins that had climbed onto the back of a wagon. The goblin flew backwards through the air, hitting the ground with a thud. Smoke rose from its body. An ear-splitting boom echoed through the hills.

Squealing loudly, the goblins charged the humans. Now unfrozen, Javin was off his horse, legs pumping as hard as they could go. Both swords flew from his belt and into his hands. Rapidly approaching the back of the first wagon by the rock face, Javin veered toward the back of a gang of goblins exchanging blows with one of the soldiers.

Javin hesitated, having never been in real combat before. Raising his sword, he tried to force himself to strike the creatures from behind before they overwhelmed the soldier they were fighting. To Javin's surprise, one of the goblins spun around. Dancing back from a spear tip that barely missed impaling him through the stomach, his reflexes took over. When the goblin pulled the spear back for a second lunge, Javin's right sword came down across the spear, driving it to the ground. At the same time, Javin's left sword streaked in to cut a deep gash across the chest of the goblin. The goblin squealed and leapt backwards into the back of his two friends, who were battling the human soldier. All three goblins ended up in a pile right at the soldier's feet. The soldier's sword began chopping down into the pile of goblins.

Out of the corner of his eyes, Javin glimpsed a goblin flying off the wagon towards him. One of his swords stabbed upwards while he fell to his knees. The sword stabbed into the goblin as it flew over his head. Squealing, the goblin crashed into the ground, rolling into the rock face.

Javin ignored the goblin and its squeals, knowing his sword had critically injured the little creature. Leaping on top of the nearest wagon, he glanced around. Seeing no goblins near him, he ran and leaped over to the back of the second wagon. Weaving through the boxes and pallets loaded onto the wagon, he spotted a group of goblins engaging another soldier, near the left front wagon wheel.

A blinding flash appeared at the edge of his vision along with a deafening boom. A goblin flew backwards into the side of the first wagon he had vacated. Sparks crisscrossed over the body of the now dead goblin.

"Be careful with that thing!" Javin heard someone yell through the noise of fighting. Leaping off the wagon, Javin landed behind three goblins fighting another Preveshawl soldier. As his feet touched the ground, the soldier twisted sideways and fell backwards, an audible groan escaping his mouth.

Two swords flashed down from Javin, finding the back of the neck of two of the goblins. They collapsed to the ground in a heap. The third goblin spun back around with a snarl. Javin's blades flashed forward again, dropping the goblin on top of his two companions with fatal chest wounds. Rapidly spinning his body with both short swords whipping through the air, Javin's swords crushed into the side of another goblin that had come up behind him. The tremendous force of the spinning blow sent the goblin flying, dead before the unfortunate creature met the ground.

Another goblin, with a dagger, now faced Javin alone. Terror filled the goblin's face as it slowly backed away from Javin, dagger waving frantically in front of him. Both swords started spinning in Javin's hand as he advanced on the goblin. The goblin's eyes blazed with pure terror, for only a second, before the life faded from them. Javin's swords had stabbed three times through the goblin's weaving dagger, dropping the creature where it stood.

Three goblins exited from under the wagon, running toward the trees opposite the wagons. Putting on a burst of speed, Javin rapidly closed on them. All three turned in unison before he reached them. Hissing in their strange language, they faced Javin, who had slid to a stop. A shrill, high-pitched squeal from the center goblin caused the three goblins to charge. Javin's swords spun in his hands at super-human speed. As the goblins reached him, he leapt high into the air in a forward flip, right over the three surprised goblins. His right sword slammed down from above onto the top of the head of the center goblin. Before his feet hit the ground, Javin twisted his body so that he was facing the backs of the goblins. The two remaining goblins spun around, only to have Javin's swords stab forward into their chests.

Looking around, Javin saw goblin bodies littering the ground and three humans staring with amazement at him. It was eerily quiet. He sprinted back toward the wagons, stopping by the man whom the goblins had injured. Javin stood by the man, not sure what he could do to help the injured soldier.

The woman continued to stare at Javin, until a groan came from the man by Javin's feet. Glancing down at the soldier, Javin saw the injured man was using the rock wall to brace himself, trying to regain his feet. Blood was pouring down his side from a nasty cut on his rib cage.

"Mac, get the healing elixir," called out the woman before hurrying over to the injured soldier. The young lady helped Javin force the man back to the ground, his back against the rock wall. The man in brown leather armor, Mac, jumped up into the back of the first wagon and started frantically digging through a chest. A tiny flask was in his hand as he leaped back off the wagon.

"Help me get his armor off," the woman said to Mac as she took the flask from Mac's hand. The two moved quickly, but gently. She tore a piece of cloth off the bottom of her dress before carefully pouring some of the blue-colored liquid directly onto the cloth.

"Put him on his good side and hold him tight." Mac did exactly as the woman asked, gently putting the injured man on his side with his wound facing upward. He wrapped his arms tightly around the man, pinning his arms to his chest. The woman held the cloth soaked with healing elixir over the wound, and squeezed the cloth.

When the elixir entered the wound, the man started screaming insanely, while thrashing around. After twenty to thirty seconds, the injured soldier went totally limp. In fact, Javin noticed he was either fast asleep, or unconscious. To his amazement, the man's side showed no sign of the wound, except for a bright-red line that ran through the middle of where the injury used to be.

"Where is Vavicavian?" The woman called out, looking at the uninjured soldier in chain armor, who was standing toward the back of the second wagon.

The man looked back at the woman and slowly shook his head. A sad, distressed look covered his face.

Silence hung heavy in the air. While Javin took in the horrific battle scene, littered with dead goblins, he felt something running down his arm. Glancing at his arm, he noticed a small amount of blood trickling down and dripping to the ground. Following the trail of blood upward, he saw the source, a small cut on his upper shoulder. He had not even felt the cut in the heat of battle.

"Thank you, Stranger," Mac said while raising himself up from the ground. He held out his hand to shake Javin's hand and saw the blood. "Gevi, you better look at this young man's cut," Mac called out while vigorously shaking Javin's hand.

"Come here. Let me see what you got," Gevi said to Javin. She sat up from where she had been leaning back against the rock wall. "Sit right here," she said with a shaky, tired voice, while patting the ground beside her. As soon as he was on the ground by her, Gevi lifted his sleeve to get a better view of the cut. "By the way, I'm Gevi."

"Javin," he murmured barely above a whisper. His shyness with people, especially girls, controlled the volume of his voice. While she examined his cut, he looked at her through the side of his eyes. She was close to his age, around eighteen. She had to be near the same height as he was, a shade less than six feet, with a medium body build. Coal-black hair hung down to the middle of her back. The face was really different, having eyes that were more slanted than round and eyebrows that curved upward away from her eyes. Even though her hair hid her ears most of the time, Javin did briefly see small ears that ended in a slight point, instead of the normal rounded ears. She had to be elven; or most likely part elf. The eyes though were what really grabbed his attention. They were bright green, like the color of emeralds. Her eyes had to be the brightest, greenest, eyes he had ever seen.

Gevi took out the flask and started to pour a tiny amount of the elixir onto the cloth that she had earlier torn from the bottom of her dress.

"Wait!" Javin stammered with alarm as he pulled away from her. Embarrassed, he pulled out a pad he always carried and quickly wrote, "It's only a scratch; it will heal on its own. I have had worse than this, many times."

Gevi glanced at the note, but quickly turned back to her work. Javin watched her nervously as she poured several drops of the powerful healing liquid on the cloth. She was completely ignoring his written comment. "Goblins stick their spears and daggers into dead animals, and only God knows what other unclean things. Any cut from a goblin weapon will almost always lead to a nasty infection, or so I have heard. I really would hate to see you lose your arm over a small cut like this."

Something that was bothering Javin gradually came to his mind, something he had to know. He quickly wrote, "Can I ask you a question, first?" He then held the pad of paper out for her to read. Unconsciously, he scooted away from the half-elf girl. He was uncomfortable with a stranger being so close, especially a woman.

"Make it quick; the elixir will start to evaporate if it exposed to air for too long," Gevi replied to his hand-written note.

"Well, I, hmmm, feel very uncomfortable around magic and people that use magic. However, I feel nothing right now," he stammered, forgetting to write down the message. Javin's face turned red in embarrassment, realizing what he had done.

Gevi smiled at him, ignoring his stuttering. "I'm not a magic user, and the staff is not magic. Now hold still, while I put the healing elixir on your cut." Grabbing his arm at the elbow, she pulled him with surprising strength back beside her. The cloth, soaked with healing elixir, hovered right above the cut.

"But I saw..."

"Shhh, let's get this over with. I will explain the staff to you later, if you wish." A warm smile radiated from Gevi's face toward an apprehensive Javin. "Now if you do not know already, the first law of healing is that great pain must come, before healing can begin. The second law is that rest begins, after healing ends." Remembering the screaming and thrashing that occurred; Javin glanced over at the man sleeping on the ground, before pulling his arm out of her grasp. Gevi clamped down on his elbow, pulling his arm back toward her. Her bright green eyes locked onto his brown eyes. Javin stared, mesmerized by her eyes. "The third law is that the amount of healing and the amount of pain following, are equal. I won't lie to you; this will really hurt, but it won't be like what he went through." She glanced quickly over at the sleeping man whom she had healed with the elixir. Javin made sure, this time, not to stare into those emerald-green eyes when her attention came back to him. "His wound was very serious, even life-threatening. Now, hold still and try not to scream too loudly." A teasing smile spread across her face, "it won't hurt that badly, and will be over quickly."

Fiery, burning, pain penetrated deep into his shoulder as soon as a single drop of the liquid hit his skin. Javin closed his eyes and gritted his teeth in pain. It felt like his arm from the elbow up was on fire. Through sheer force of will he clamped his good arm on his leg, determined not to grab at his burning arm. All of a sudden, the pain was gone. A comforting, cool, feeling was now spreading through his shoulder. Javin felt weariness overcome him. He leaned against the wall, thankful that it was over.

"See, it's over already. Now you can have confidence you won't be getting an infection in that cut. Sit here and relax until you fully recover." Gevi carefully slipped the bottle of healing elixir into a pouch on her belt before releasing Javin's arm and standing back up.

Javin kept his eyes shut. He felt completely exhausted. It felt so good to sit back against the rock wall and rest. He wondered why she said, 'not magic'. Seeing two goblins blasted with lightning from that staff made that claim seem impossible. Even though he had taken a basic course in every guild, he had never heard of anything able to do that without magic involved. He believed Gevi though, because he felt no sickness like he did anytime he was near magic and magic users.

Healing elixir he had read about in his studies at the Guild of Healing. He remembered it was something very rare, made by the dwarves. Only the very powerful and wealthy in society had access to it. Nevertheless, this little group in the very northern end of the kingdom, that almost nobody ever visited or even cared for, had healing elixir! It was known that dwarves lived in the very northern mountains outside of Preveshawl, and rumored that they had a fairly large underground city. No one was really sure, because dwarves rarely interacted with humans and were rarely seen in human towns. Javin had only seen two dwarves his whole life. They had come to see his father many years ago.

"Do something with these dead goblins!" he heard Gevi scream out, interrupting his thoughts.

"I need to catch the horses before they get too far away and something happens to them," Mac yelled back from down the road.

"Get back here, now!" Gevi yelled toward Mac, "Help Kevinan dispose of these stinking goblins, or you will be looking for me. I am not spending hours sitting around with a bunch of nasty, dead goblins while you're out searching the hills for horses." Javin smiled and started laughing, unable to control himself.

"Since you think it's so funny," Javin peered out of half-opened eyes to see Gevi standing in front of him. She had her hands on her hip, green eyes flashing with a look of agitation, mixed with annoyance. "You can get yourself right on up and help. It's plain as a wart on the end of a goblin's nose you've rested enough."

Javin managed to stop laughing. He did feel better, so he went ahead and stood up. Dizziness overpowered him for a split second, but it vanished within seconds as he gained his feet.

"Your highness," said Mac dryly as he stomped back into camp, pausing only to give a mock bow at the waist in Gevi's direction. "What do you propose we do with the goblins without our horses? Slinging them over my back and carrying them out into the woods is not an option. Surely, your majesty can wait an hour or so for me to get the horses and use them to drag the bodies away."

The two continued to argue heatedly, but Javin tuned out the argument and took in the details of this man called Mac. He was tall, probably six and-a-half feet and moderately muscled. Scars covered both his arms, complimented by a long scar that ran down the right side of his face. He had graying brown hair with a steel grey mustache. Javin guessed his age as mid-forties. Across his back, he wore a long bow with a quiver of arrows. Brown leather armor completely covered his body. Hanging from his belt, was a well-used long sword.

Pushing himself away from the rock face, Javin approached the arguing pair. "Hold on," Javin cut in on the argument, an idea coming to him. Out came his writing pad. Mac and Gevi stopped arguing and stared at him as he wrote. He handed the pad to Mac.

"I have my horse. If you help me make a gurney, then I and the other man (I do not remember his name) can take care of the goblin bodies. Meanwhile, you can look for your horses," Mac read out loud so Gevi could hear. His eyes then fixed on Javin. "Kevinan. His name is Kevinan."

"Give me that," growled Gevi as she ripped the pad out of Mac's hand. "You speak fine. You are among friends, so no more of this silly writing." The pad flew through the air right back at Javin. Irritated from arguing with Mac over the goblins, Gevi stood there with arms crossed, glaring at the two men.

Mac stared at Javin for several seconds before turning and walking toward a thick gathering of trees. "Come on then, friend. I saw something we can use to make a gurney, if that will work for princess Gevi."

****

The five companions sat around a large campfire in a clearing, right off the main road. The air was pleasantly cool. Smoke from the fire was twirling straight up into the night sky. A creek with water pouring over rocks bubbled a short distance from the camp. Rocks and boulders littered the ground. Medium-sized evergreen trees surrounded the campsite, casting moonlit shadows off into the night. The sound of owls calling to each other echoed through the air on a clear, cloudless night.

After the goblins had been taken care of and the horses found and returned, Javin had followed the wagons until the sun was nearly set in the western sky. Initially, he tried to set up a little camp away from the others, but Mac forcefully insisted that Javin camp with them. Even though Javin preferred the solitude of the night away from strangers, he heeded Mac's demands and set his bedroll near the fire.

Everyone was silent as they sat around a blazing fire, sipping on cups of a hot drink called Maka that Mac had made. The soldier who had been severely wounded was completely recovered from the fighting and even the painful, rapid healing. He went to bed early, curled up under one of the wagons.

"Javin, I want you to know that we are very grateful to you for saving our lives," Mac said, breaking the silence. Kevinan nodded at him while Gevi gave him a sparkling smile from across the fire. "I have been fighting a long-time, and you have me curious. Where did you learn to use swords like that?" Mac spun his arms, pretending to spin two swords in his hands. "And that twist flip you did over those goblins is like nothing I've ever seen before."

Javin thought about getting out his note pad, but the memory of Gevi's glare as she tossed it back to him stopped him cold. "Well," Javin answered with a trembling stutter. The others had to carefully concentrate to hear his words. "My Dad really is the one who taught me everything I know; that, and ambidexterity runs in my family as well. I really am not that good yet; my father's skill with the swords is still superior. Before I went to the guilds, Dad and I practiced almost every night for as long as I can remember." Javin turned his head, looking out into the darkness of night. An uneasy feeling was growing in his stomach, caused by having to talk to people he hardly knew.

Mac raised one eyebrow, "You're humble I see; so who is your father?"

Javin hesitated, realizing he may have said too much. He really did

30

not know a lot concerning his father's past, but his father had warned him never to talk about the family. Mac saw his hesitation and the silence that followed.

"I think I may know who your father is," Mac said while looking directly at Javin. "I used to know a soldier who fought with two short swords." Javin looked down to the ground, his stomach turning. "And if I am right, you are wise to keep silent." Mac paused in obvious thought. "When I was a young soldier fresh out of the guilds, I was assigned to Fort Outlands. It was during the time of the Ogre Invasions. The great hero who ended the Ogre Invasions fought with two short swords, like you. His name was Lamar Sental, or General Lamar."

Javin heard Kevinan chocking on his drink. The shocked expression on his face was clear to Javin. Gevi seemed not to know that name; or she didn't care. Javin could not tell from her flat expression. The name was correct, but the family went by a different last name now. Javin did not learn that Sental was his true last name until he accidentally overheard a conversation late one night between his parents. He had always gone by the last name Tamaner for as long as he could remember.

"I learned about the Ogre Invasions at the guilds and how a special operations unit of soldiers and dwarves killed the chieftains, but I never heard anything about this general." Javin mumbled. He was telling the truth. History professors had not mentioned this general in any of his history lessons.

"Well, there is a reason he is not mentioned. I was a really young soldier at that time, but I was at the fort. I know a lot about what really happened." Mac reached over and grabbed the pot of Maka, pouring himself a fresh cup of the hot drink before passing the pot over to Gevi. Mac started the story as the Maka made its way around the campfire.

"It started twenty years ago. Ogre and giant attacks had been increasing for several months. The fort was stretched thin, trying to protect the outlying farms. One day, scouts reported a large army of ogres mixed with giants forming in the north outside our borders. Raiding parties started to increase, attacking farms and soldiers on patrol. In response, the capital city sent a regiment of a thousand infantry soldiers. One of them was a brash young captain named Lamar. Captain Lamar was in command of a small unit of special operation soldiers, maybe twenty or so in number. They were called the Wolf Troop." Javin recalled how his father's short swords had a wolf etched into the blades. His interest in Mac's story piqued.

"The General over the fort at the time ordered his special operations unit, along with a scout troop, to go behind enemy lines. No one knew what their orders were, but we sensed it was something really important."

Sipping on his steaming hot Maka, Javin excitedly listened to Mac's story; this was the first time he had ever heard anything involving his father's past.

"I remember watching as Captain Lamar, with the special

operations unit, a scout troop, and a chaplain, left through the gate. Somewhere in the mountain areas outside Preveshawl's border, Captain Lamar joined with a small band of dwarves. Dwarves live somewhere in the mountains a few days east of the fort. Messengers started coming back to the fort with reports of a larger army than was first thought. There was no doubt that the army was marching toward Preveshawl. Estimates gave us two weeks to prepare the fort for what seemed like an un-winnable siege. It takes roughly two and a half weeks to get troops from the capital, and that is if they really rush it. We were going to have to fight this army with only the soldiers we had."

"One week passed. We were working, preparing for a battle that was sure to come. Our plan was to delay and hold until reinforcements arrived. Instead, scouts started reporting large numbers of ogres and giants, breaking apart from the enemy army and heading north away from the fort. Within a week, the whole army of ogres and giants had vanished."

"Shortly after that, Captain Lamar, the chaplain, five men from the special operations unit, along with a handful of scouts, returned to the fort. Word quickly spread that Captain Lamar's special operations unit, known as the Wolf Troop, along with a band of dwarves, infiltrated the invading army's camp during a dark and moonless night. In one night, they eliminated the five ogre chieftains leading the army, along with a Giant Commander over the giants. The unit suffered great losses. Only five of the twenty special operations unit survived that night. Most of the dwarves involved died as well. To this day, no one I know is really sure how or what went on that night. Ogres are extremely tribe-oriented; so challenges and fighting over selection of the new chiefs probably broke the army up. What we do know is that the ogres returned to their home tribes and have never reunited again."

"Wow," said Javin with a look of complete astonishment on his face. "But when we study this at the guilds, why is Captain Lamar never mentioned? With the exception of the Captain's involvement, this is what the professors told us."

"Well, what you have been taught is not the end of the story. When the story was told to the King back in the capitol city, he sent a military commission north to Fort Outland. They presented Preveshawl's highest Medal of Honor to Captain Lamar, along with a promotion to general over the Northland Armies. The current general was reassigned to the South, replacing a retiring general there. As I am sure you know, the king died a few years later and King Logan XI started ruling Preveshawl. One of his first acts was to remove all references to the Lord of the Stars from official documents. The duties of the Guild of Religions were greatly reduced at the same time. To this day, it is only through discussion of ancient myths that instructors are allowed to mention the Lord of the Stars."

Javin nodded, having experienced this for himself in his only required class at the Guild of Religions.

"The Guild of Religions' name should be changed to the Guild of

False Doctrine, because that is all they teach anymore," commented Mac. "Anyway, a year later, laws were passed that outlawed any school from teaching about the Lord of the Stars. *The Guide* was no longer allowed in any school. You would not remember, but *The Guide* used to be the backbone of our education system before that time. It wasn't too long after that, maybe a few months, it was decreed that anyone on the payroll of the Kingdom of Preveshawl could not advance the teaching of the Lord of the Stars, have *The Guide* on Preveshawl property, or pray during times working for Preveshawl."

"That is why I'm home schooled," Gevi interjected. "Daddy said no child of his would be brainwashed with nonsense and evil." She threw another beautiful smile at Javin. He gave her a brief, nervous smile back.

"I'm from a small farm town; the parents controlled the school and didn't allow certain things to be taught. It was..."

Mac interrupted Javin, "Hold on, let me finish. I am almost done. The last decree affected the army. They are public servants on the payroll of the king. An official from the capital showed up at the fort and read the new decree. After the official read the king's decree, he asked the chaplains to come forward. When they had gathered up front, the official told them that if they could not follow the decree from the king, then they were hereby dismissed from the army. They were to turn in their weapons and armor and be out of Fort Outlands by noon the following day."

"General Lamar, standing at the very front where the general always stands, walked forward. He took the Medal of Honor off his chest and tossed it to the official who caught it in his hand. In a loud voice so that everyone on the parade ground could hear, he told the court official that an army without the true God, is a defeated army. He then turned around and walked out the gate of the fort. That, Javin, is why no one mentions Lamar's participation in the Ogre Invasions."

"When the king found out, he was so angered that he ordered that the name Lamar Sental never to be mentioned again. Mentions of him were removed from official documents. They never did anything else to General Lamar, at least not that I know of. I figure it was because he was popular enough that the people would be angered, combined with the fact that General Lamar kept a low profile and for the most part, disappeared from public sight. The rest, as you know, is modern history. The king passed away last year and his son, King Logan XII, now rules over Preveshawl. Almost everyone has forgotten General Lamar and how his name was removed from the histories of the Ogre Invasions."

All was quiet around the fire. The creek bubbling in the distance and an occasional hoot of a nearby owl was the only noise out in the night. The air was still, with not even a hint of a breeze.

"So Javin, like Mac, I am curious, about something," Gevi said, finally breaking the silence. "Now that we know that your father was some legendary figure that taught you swords, what are you doing up in this end of the world?"

"I never said that this general was my father." Javin raised his head, looking around the fire at everyone staring back at him. Mac gave him a sly smile, nodding his head toward Javin. Taking a deep breath to calm his nerves, Javin replied, "I finished my final year at the guilds and..."

"Ah ha," cut in Mac. "You have to do your apprenticeship at Fort Outland for the Guild of Warriors."

"Not quite," stuttered Javin. "I am doing my apprenticeship with Master Smith Thunderfall, at the Outland Weapons and Armor."

Mac burst out laughing while Gevi rolled her eyes. "Oh quiet it up! I don't think this is a bit funny. Besides, Javin has no idea what the joke is."

Mac completely ignored her. If anything, he laughed even harder. Gevi reached over and smacked him playfully on the shoulder, causing him to fall backwards to the ground, laughing.

"Master Thunderfall is my Father." Gevi said as she looked directly at Javin, now completely ignoring Mac. "And one of these wagons is loaded with supplies for his shop."

"Sorry Javin. I must be there when old Thunderfall finds out he owes you a debt for rescuing his daughter and his supplies." Mac was smiling ear to ear. "His kind takes debt very seriously, so, the master will be in debt to his apprentice." Mac started laughing again. Gevi's eyes started to flash with annoyance by the time Mac finally got control of himself.

"Come on Gevi, you have to admit, that the Lord of the Stars has a sense of humor. Besides, when was the last time your father requested an apprentice from the guilds?"

"Never," whispered Gevi, barely loud enough so everyone could hear. She looked at Javin with curiosity. "He has never requested an apprentice."

Javin tossed Gevi his assignment paper, making sure he missed the fire.

"It says Outlands Weapon and Armor. Fort Outland's General Franks approved request," Gevi said, reading the assignment paper to Mac, before tossing it back to Javin. "Strange; extremely strange," Gevi said as she stared at Javin. Javin nervously moved his gaze to stare once again into the comforting fire.

They talked another hour or so before everyone started getting out their bedrolls and getting ready for bed. As soon as Mac started snoring, Javin sat on up on his bedroll and pulled out *The Guide*. He spent nearly a half hour reading by the dim light of the dying fire, before bowing his head and praying. Once finished, he lay down and closed his eyes. He never noticed Gevi watching him from her bedroll.

****

Excruciating pain pounded through Chellell's head. Her eyes were closed tight, trying to will the pain away. "Sanatarial, can't you teach me some spell to take this horrible headache away?" A small creature, the size of a cat, stared at the girl with glowing red eyes. It had two large wings with a tail that curled around its body. An elongated, skinny, neck extended from the torso. The head was very similar to the head of a snake; diamond shaped with a red, forked tongue. The red dragon stood perched on the bed's headboard, right above Chellell's head.

"Remember the rules of magic, my lady. Magic cannot be used to heal anything or anyone. That is a different type of magic we do not possess," The dragon hissed. "When your body gets used to magic, the body will stop fighting against it, and then the pain will be no more. Remember what you have been taught, pain only makes you stronger. It is the strongest that survive."

The young woman reached up to the headboard behind her and grabbed a handful of pills, quickly swallowing them down. She closed her eyes before lying back on the bed, knowing that the pain would greatly reduce. Eventually, it would disappear.

"Don't worry, Chellell. The more you meditate and let me fill you with power, the less pain you will feel," hissed the little red dragon. Chellell moaned in response.

****

A small band of humanoids was lying flat in the grass deep in the pitch-black darkness of night; only the twinkling stars shown overhead. These humanoids stood four to five feet high, with legs, arms, and a body much like a small human, but that was where the similarities ended. Their skin was a dull brown color with scraggly bits of black hair covering their bodies. Their noses were so small they could hardly be seen, and were overpowered by large, round eyes with black pupils. Scruffy, black hair covered their heads. Bones from different animals were displayed proudly in their hair. The Kingdom of Preveshawl called these humanoids "gorms".

Gorms were driven out of Preveshawl early on in its history. The gorms had originally lived on the lands between the Great Henjum River and the Northern Mountains. They were a tribal race that lived in tents and hunted the massive herds of elk that filled the grasslands. When the gorms weren't fighting among themselves over tribal leaders, they were fighting with the elves in the Elven Forest, or raiding humans on the south side of the river. The gorms were an evil race, with no respect for life. In fact, gorms believed that the souls of anyone they killed entered into their own bodies, making them stronger. This belief had them constantly on the war path, looking to kill anyone they encountered.

Five hundred years ago, the people of Preveshawl had reached a point that the raids from gorms on their villages had to be stopped. They had a problem though, and that problem was the Great Henjum River. The gorms crossed it on boats by throwing weaker gorms or captured slaves over the side of the boats to distract the great river serpents that infested the river and attacked any boats in their waters. The God-fearing humans were unwilling to practice such a brutal sacrifice of life, to cross the river.

The answer to their problem came when a boat of elves successfully

35

crossed the river. The elves had thrown small roots into the water as they crossed. The foul smell of these roots, found only in the Elven Forest, drove the great river serpents away from the boat. The elves were seeking a treaty with the humans. They too were tired of the constant fighting with the gorms. Over the next decade, humans could cross the river with the aid of the foul-smelling roots provided by the elves. Human fighters and elven fighters combined to drive the gorms North beyond the mountains and out of Preveshawl.

The gorms had resettled in the Frozen Wastelands, where their blood-thirsty way of life continued as fought against the Northern Barbarian tribes. Through the centuries, in-fighting and battles with the barbarians kept them out of Preveshawl. Recently though, a giant had raised the banner of war, offering the gorms a chance to kill humans and reclaim their ancient home. Gorm tribal leaders eagerly joined with the giant. Now, they were on a hill with several goblins outside Fort Outlands, scouting the area around the fort.

In a guttural language that few humans understood, the gorm leader spoke. "You, you and you," he pointed to the three goblins in the group, "take this report on the fort back to the Grand Leader." He reached over and grabbed the nearest goblin by the throat, lifting him off the ground. "Do not be seen, and do not engage any of the locals, like your friends did. They were fortunate that the humans finished them off, before I got my hands on them!" The gorm snarled at the little squirming goblin he held up in the air, showing the goblin his razor-sharp teeth. "Do not fail me." With that, he tossed a terrified goblin to the ground.

Chapter 3

Defend the poor and fatherless: do justice to the afflicted and needy. – The Guide

Fort Outland was an undersized fort sitting right where two large northern mountain ranges met at the northern most edge of Preveshawl. The fort was split between military buildings and small shops that supported the soldiers and the few farmers who braved farming in this dangerous part of the kingdom. Large stone walls stretched east and west from the fort for two miles, where they blended in with the cliff faces from the mountains. These massive cliffs reached skyward like giant skeletal hands breaking out of the ground.

The fort itself was enclosed with thirty-foot high walls. Four to five hundred soldiers at any given time lived in the fort. North of the fort was beyond Preveshawl territory, with very few humans daring to venture into that hostile terrain.

The two wagons entered Fort Outlands through a narrow gate on the south side of the fort. The inside of the fort was old and run-down, with the exception of a large, new, wooden northern gate and a newer thirty-foot wall, facing north. Shop owners were busy pulling outside wares back into their old brick stores, locking them up for the evening. The only thing Javin saw that was really beautiful was a small park, full of green grass, flowers, and trees. It stood in sharp contrast to the rest of the fort. Aged shops surrounded the charming little park on all sides.

After dropping off Kevinan and the other soldier with the wagon full of fort supplies; Mac, Gevi, and Javin headed east out of the fort, turning onto a trail winding its way Southeast. The fort was barely out of sight, when Mac stopped the horses in front of a modest, white, farmhouse. Horses and cows were scattered in the pastures beyond the farmhouse, along with fields of various crops. Pens full of birds used for eggs and meat were off to one side of the house near a large barn. A creek wound around like a giant, blue, snake, behind the farm house. Colorful flowers surrounded the farmhouse in neatly trimmed flowerbeds.

The door of the old, wooden farmhouse slowly creaked open. A woman came out of the house with an enormous, cat-like creature following lazily behind her. They stood on a covered porch that held several chairs and tables. Together, the woman and the large cat left the porch, strolling casually down a rock path that meandered through the dozens of fruit trees spread around the front yard. The path ended at the dusty road where Mac had parked the wagon.

"Hey Honey. I'm home!" Mac waved to the woman as he jumped out of the wagon. Javin saw that the cat-like creature behind the woman was actually some kind of tiger, with visible fangs protruding out of its mouth. It was sleek, yet muscled, standing four feet high at the back. The tiger was pure white, with the exception of four or five black stripes that ran around its back and belly.

"I would hate to run into that thing out in the wilds," thought Javin to himself. Before he could even blink, the tiger leapt forward, running straight at Mac.

"Bad Kitty, bad Kitty!" screamed Mac who was swinging his arms wildly. The tiger hit Mac squarely in the chest with its two front paws, knocking him to the ground.

Javin had both swords out, which he quickly re-sheathed once he saw a long, slobbery tongue going all over Mac's face.

"Stop it! Stop it, you mangy old house cat!" Mac was sputtering and squirming around, but the massive cat's tongue continued to cover his face. The front legs of the tiger sat on him, pinning him to the ground. "Blah! I'm having cat steak tonight, you giant hair ball! Ledia, get your sorry excuse for a cat off of me!"

Gevi was roaring with laughter from the front of the wagon when a shrill whistle sounded. Instantly, the massive tiger leapt off Mac, prancing confidently back to Ledia. The tiger fell right in step beside her. A loud purring came from the tiger as its tail wagged side to side. Jumping off the wagon, Gevi ran over to Mac's wife, giving her a hug. Javin dismounted and walked over to Mac, offering him a hand. Wiping tiger slobber off his face and out of his hair, Mac finally stood back up. The two joined the women, though Mac kept a careful eye on the purring tiger.

"Javin, this is my wife, Ledia," Mac said as he put his arm around his wife. Ledia turned her attention toward Javin while Mac kept talking. "And this sorry beast with no self-control, is Kabbiyr, a Great Northern Tiger. Gevi called him Kitty when he was a cub and she was a child, so everyone around here just calls him Kitty."

"Ledia was my teacher growing up; She taught me daily, right in this house," Gevi commented, her face beaming with pleasure. It was abundantly clear that Gevi and Ledia were close friends.

Ledia smiled fondly toward Gevi before focusing again on Javin. "Hello, Javin. Nice to meet you," Ledia said in greeting. Javin saw that Kitty was rubbing himself against Mac's leg. Mac was gently scratching the tiger behind his pointed ears.

Javin pulled out his pad to start writing, but as he glanced toward Gevi and saw her rolling eyes, he changed his mind. In a low, nervous voice, Javin responded, "Nice to meet you as well, Ma'am." Ledia was close to the same age as Mac, mid-forties, but not nearly as tall. She wore solid green clothes, a custom among the individuals from the Guild of Nature. Dirty-blond hair was cut below the neckline. Her skin was deeply tanned from spending a lot of time in the sun. A miniature red jewel, gleaming in the sunlight, was on her forehead, held in place by a green bandana. Javin recognized the jewel instantly as a Communication jewel worn by naturalists. The sister jewel would be on an animal, allowing for limited communications and control. Looking closely at the tiger, Javin saw a similar red gleam on the tiger's forehead.

"This is going to be Thunderfall's new apprentice," Mac said, smiling at Javin. He continued to pet the tiger that was purring and rubbing up against him.

"Well, I am not sure if 'new' is the correct term, considering I have never known Master Thunderfall to have an apprentice. You have no need to worry, Javin; he is a good person and a devoted disciple to the Lord of the Stars. Not only is he a one-of-a-kind blacksmith, but he is very wise as well." Ledia looked away from Javin and fixed her gaze upon Gevi. "I see you already met the blacksmith's lovely daughter."

Gevi blushed and Javin started to stammer a response, but nothing came out. Javin nervously moved his feet around while Gevi continued to converse with Ledia over the next few minutes. Finally, Mac spoke up. "Come on Ledia; let's allow these kids to get on home. Javin, you see that big building, where the creek crosses the road?" Javin looked where Mac was pointing and saw the building he referenced. "That is Master Thunderfall's shop. His house is over to the side a bit. Don't let Gevi get you lost. She has a bad habit of doing that."

Gevi glared at Mac, "It was years ago I got lost," she retorted. "And besides it was you who…"

"Leave the girl alone dear," interjected Ledia with a frown, "or I may lose control of Kitty again." Kitty gave a particularly loud purr, causing a concerned look to cross Mac's face. "The way you are talking about poor Gevi, Javin's going to think she's completely daft." Gevi threw a grateful smile at Ledia before grabbing Javin's arm and pulling him back toward the wagon.

"Bye Gevi; bye Javin! Feel free to stop by anytime," Ledia called out before she turned and started walking back toward the house with Mac.

"It's the same every time he comes home after a long trip, but I still find it funny," Gevi said while walking beside Javin. "I think Mac actually enjoys this greeting from Kitty, but he has to act tough and surprised every time it happens." Javin was getting set to mount his horse, but Gevi beat him to the reins. She quickly tied his horse to the back of the wagon. Much to her dismay, Javin jumped into the back of the wagon instead of sitting up front with her. She couldn't believe he had to be convinced to sit in the front wagon seat with her.

"I don't bite, and he better not think I smell," snorted Gevi to herself, once he was seated up front. Out loud, she asked him, "so what did you think of Mac and Ledia?"

Javin was extremely nervous. There had to be only three or four feet between him and Gevi. He was so nervous, that he said the first thing that came to his mind. "Kitty, good name," stammered Javin, causing Gevi to start laughing again. Waving to Mac and Ledia, the two headed on up to the blacksmith shop. As they approached the blacksmith shop, Javin saw a creek flowing over the cliff into a spectacular waterfall, falling thirty feet until it hit a huge waterwheel sitting on the edge of the creek. The force of the waterfall caused the wheel to spin, driving a large, wooden shaft that went into the side of the shop.

The shop was made of a gray stone that matched the color of the rock cliff it stood against. Massive piles of charcoal, iron and various other materials were stacked neatly in bins around the shop. Carefully manicured flowers and shrubs surrounded the shop and the house. Up the hill from the shop sat a two-story log house. Off to the side of the house was a bright-red barn. A single horse with a couple of cows was eating grass in a fenced pasture adjacent to the barn.

Gevi pulled the wagon up to the shop. While she unhitched the prancing horses and took them to the barn, Javin started unloading the wagon. He stacked boxes and sacks on a rock pad next to a door, as Gevi had instructed him to do. He was struggling with a heavier crate when the door to the shop opened. A dwarf stood in the doorway. The dwarf was four feet tall, with a long, black, beard that flowed down a colossal, muscular chest. The dwarf's body was covered, top to bottom, in mammoth-sized, rippling muscles. In fact, this had to be the strongest person Javin had ever seen. The massive muscles covering the dwarf's body were absolutely unbelievable. Once Javin managed to get his attention off the muscles, he saw that the dwarf's head was completely bald. A large leather apron used by metal smiths covered his chest.

"I am Javin Tamaner, Master Thunderfall's new apprentice." Javin stammered nervously. It was quiet for a few seconds while Javin and the dwarf stared at each other.

"I see that you decided to hitch a ride in with the supply wagon," grumbled the dwarf in a deep, gravelly voice. "Go ahead and set the supplies there, but some of them will have to go up to the house. Set your belongings next to the..."

"Daddy!" screamed a returning Gevi, who flew into the arms of the dwarf. The massive dwarf barely had time to put his arms out and catch her. Kisses started raining down on top of his shiny, bald head. Javin saw that the dwarf's face was turning bright red behind his bushy black beard.

"Girl, can't you show an old dwarf any respect?" the dwarf sputtered while he gently pushed Gevi back at arm's length, "and what in black rocks are you doing here? Aren't you supposed to be learning how to make that fancy nonsense stuff at Bear Tree City?"

"I'm on vacation," she replied before jumping back into his arms and giving him another hug. "Arialian closed the shop for a couple of weeks. She wanted to go South and spend some time with her aging parents." Gevi was bent over, squeezing the dwarf as hard as she could while she talked.

"Humph, couldn't trust you to run the shop by yourself, I see," grumbled the dwarf. "I bet you pestered her half to death with your rambling talk and crazy ways, so she took a vacation. Arialian is probably laughing herself silly, knowing this poor old dwarf, who can't get any work done, because he's being pestered to death."

Javin stood silent and observed their reunion. He felt awkward and did not know what to do or say. He was curious how a half-human, half-elf, could have a dwarf for a father. He would have to ask Gevi about her parents when he got the chance. He also reminded himself to ask her about her staff. He started nervously shuffling his feet while looking at the two from the corner of his eyes.

"Well Daddy, I really missed you too!" she exclaimed in a huffy voice. She gave him a final big smack right on top of his bald head before stepping from his embrace, though she kept one arm draped around his shoulder. "I see you have met your new apprentice, Javin. We met him on the road, and he helped us with our journey." Javin was relieved that Gevi left out the goblins. He did not want to make a big deal out of the battle with the goblins.

"I know girl; we met. He was trying to be helpful, before you ran over here and started acting silly." Javin noticed that the dwarf had slipped a big arm around her waist, giving her an affectionate squeeze while he was talking. "Since you're here, why don't you check each item and see if it should go into the house or into the shop. Have Javin carry it, if he can. If not, then I will get it after I put the forge down. I doubt you two will let me do any more work tonight anyway." With that Master Thunderfall turned and went back into the shop, only to pop his head out a second later. "Javin, remember your manners. A real man will not allow a lady to carry anything."

Javin struggled, but managed to get the boxes, sacks, and pallets, to either the house or the shop as Gevi directed, with the exception of one pallet. Try as he might, he could not budge the final pallet; so he left it on the wagon, as Master Thunderfall had directed. Gevi came back out from inside the shop, where she had learned from her father, where Javin was to store his clothes and personal things. Grabbing his two duffle bags, he followed her to a little building connected to the outside of the shop near the waterfall. Inside was a bed with a small chest at its foot. The new twin bed took up most of the tiny room. Against the wall was a fireplace with cooking wares and utensils hanging beside it. An open window, facing the spectacular waterfall, filled the wall opposite the fireplace. He threw his bags on the bed and went back outside to Gevi.

"Come on; let's get over to the house and get supper going. Dad should be done any time now," Gevi said. Walking beside her, Javin noticed that the pallet he could not get off the wagon was gone.

He spent his first supper with Thunderfall and Gevi eating burned fish, pretending nothing was wrong with it. Thunderfall never said a word the whole meal. Threatening to throw the stove into the creek and buy one that actually worked, Gevi seemed awfully upset with herself over the blackened fish she had cooked. She carried on with ideas she had to improve the functions of the stove.

Later on that night, Javin finished reading a portion of *The Guide*. The passage he was reading contained these words:
And whatsoever mine eyes desired I kept not from them, I withheld

not my heart from any joy; for my heart rejoiced in all my labor: and this was my portion of all my labor. Then I looked on all the works that my hands had wrought, and on the labor that I had labored to do: and, behold, all was vanity and vexation of spirit, and there was no profit under the sun.

He put *The Guide* down on his clothes chest. Then he buckled on both his swords and went outside. As was his habit this time of night, he walked over to a spot by the creek and started his dance of swords. As usual, he thought over what he had read, while his weapons weaved around in the dance.

This portion of *The Guide* made Javin realize something very important. Everything in life you did, no matter how base or how glorious, was a complete waste of time, if it was not done for the glory of God. Javin moved in circles, going from one fighting stance to another. Blades flashed in and out in cuts and slashes while spinning in his hands. His body flipped, spun, and rolled while swords attacked imaginary enemies. He thought about his life of swords. Was he really doing this for the glory of God, or was it for selfishness and pride? Why did he spend so much of his life, working the swords?

After twenty minutes of warm up routines, Javin started trying to incorporate the new disarm move his father had taught him into his routine. With jerky movements, his right sword flew out of his hand and fell to the ground. Javin picked up the sword and repeated the moves he had been taught. Sometimes he succeeded, but more often than not, one sword, or the other, would fly from his hand.

Finally, he sheathed both swords and returned to his room. When he got a chance, he planned to hang a bag of sand like he had back at the guild; that way, he could practice hitting a target. Before falling asleep, Javin prayed to the Lord of the Stars for God to use him and his swords unconditionally, for God's glory, and not for his own pride. Little did he know, how soon his prayer would be answered.

Thunderfall stood at the window of his upstairs bedroom, watching Javin practice with his swords. His night vision allowed him to see Javin clearly, as if he practiced in broad daylight. After Javin went to bed, the dwarf left the window to lie down in his own bed. "Debts must be paid; debts must be paid," he thought to himself. "After twenty years, the debt can finally be paid."

****

From sun up until supper, Javin spent the next week working for the dwarven smith. He hauled charcoal for the forge, fetched tools, brought bricks and nuggets of metal to the smith, and worked the bellows, as needed. Basically, Javin did a lot of manual labor with a little bit of actual smith work. At times, Thunderfall would instruct him on the art of blacksmithing, letting him work the tongs and the hammer. Javin quickly learned that as long as the dwarf was grumbling and complaining, he was doing fine. It was when the dwarf went silent that Javin knew he had made a mistake.

Another job he worked on was sharpening and grinding, which he did on various wheel stones that were mounted on the spinning shaft from the waterfall wheel. The same shaft also worked bellows for the forge. Sometimes, Javin had to add extra air to heat the forge, by manually working a bellow, but most of the time it was a matter of engaging or disengaging bellows from the turning shaft.

The most important job Javin did, as far as Thunderfall was concerned, was shop housekeeping. Tools were hung on pegs around the walls of the shop. Every tool had a place, and Thunderfall insisted that if a tool was not being used, that it was to be hung in its proper place. An hour was spent every evening, before supper, cleaning the shop. First thing in the morning, Javin had to water plants that were in pots. Green plants and flowers filled the outside of the shop. Thunderfall insisted the plants were Gevi's, but he made sure they were well taken care of.

There was, however, one exception to the clean shop. One corner of the shop contained tables stacked with equipment Javin was not familiar with. Gems, rocks, colored glass, along with multiple tools, lay on the tables and in piles on the floor around the tables. It was pure chaos in this one corner. On his first evening in the shop, Javin asked the smith about cleaning that cluttered area, but Thunderfall had told him to leave it alone. He learned why the next day, when Gevi spent most of the day working in that messy corner. It was her work area. Thunderfall's only comment, which got him an angry glare from Gevi, was that at least it was cleaner than her room at the house.

Thunderfall refused to work on the seventh day. Instead, he, Gevi, and Javin, went to a little church an hour's ride from the shop. The church was a small, white, wooden building, on the edge of a farm. A large oak tree sat near the front door, with a children's play area built under the old branches of the tree. Very few people attended services, but Javin did see Mac and Ledia. Though filled with devotion, Master Smith Thunderfall's singing at church was something that Javin thought he would never get out of his head.

After the seventh day, Javin got back to work, concentrating more of his efforts into sharpening and grinding. He knew he was getting better, because the old dwarf grumbled more and more. One morning in the middle of his second week he got to work as usual with sharpening an axe when Master Thunderfall stopped him.

"Go get the horses and hitch them up to the wagon, I need you to take a load into Fort Outlands. Gevi will go with you and show you what to do." Thunderfall pulled one of his hammers off the wall, inspecting it, while continuing to talk. "Since you will probably be too tired from loading and unloading to be any use to me this evening, you might as well stay and let Gevi show you the stores at the fort." Thunderfall set the hammer down and picked up a tiny leather bag. He tossed the leather bag to Javin. Javin snatched the coin bag out of midair. "Apprenticeship wages; everyone should be paid for their work. Now go on and get the horses."

Gevi arrived at the wagon right as Javin finished loading it up with everything from swords and armor to hammers and nails. Javin actually had spent part of a day making nails, though it took some time before Thunderfall accepted his work. Hopping up into the wagon beside him, Gevi allowed Javin to keep the reins and drive the horses. Thunderfall came out of the shop and handed her a list. "Swing by Albert's place and give him this list of molds I need him to make, and be sure you two are home before sundown. You know how grouchy I get when I have to come looking for you."

"No problem, Daddy," replied Gevi. "I'll be back in time to tuck you in and kiss you good night." She blew a kiss at him from her seat in the wagon.

"Get out of here!" roared the dwarf, the top of his head going bright red. Holding back a laugh, Javin started the horses down the road. Laughter did erupt from his mouth when he heard the dwarf's parting words, "This is what an old dwarf gets for not spanking a little girl enough when he should have."

"Love you too, Daddy!" called Gevi back to the dwarf as the horses pulled away. Javin looked over his shoulder to see the heavily muscled dwarf stomping into his shop.

As they passed Mac and Gevi's house, another cart with three soldiers coming up from Fort Outlands met them on the road. Kevinan was on one of them. He stopped and talked for a few minutes with Gevi. Being too self-conscious about his speech, Javin refused to join the conversation. Kevinan told them they were taking a load up to the shop, mostly weapons to be sharpened. They parted ways, one wagon heading toward the shop, the other to the fort. As they approached the gate, Gevi grabbed Javin's arm.

"Oh no, we forgot to warn Kevinan not to say anything to Dad about the goblins on the road!"

Javin leaned back in his seat, his mind swirling for an answer that did not come. Finally he said, "Nothing we can do now except hope and pray Kevinan doesn't bring it up."

"I guess you're right; let's go and have some fun," she replied. Gevi was pleased to see that Javin did not seem as edgy about being in the front of a wagon with her. "I guess it takes him time to get used to people," she thought to herself.

****

Chancellor White was reading through the glowing praises from the Guild of Magic instructors about his new apprentice, Chellell. He flipped through another page before setting it to the side of his neatly organized desk. He took a deep, measured breath before connecting with his familiar. Magic flowed into his body. Reaching across his desk, he grabbed a small mirror, placing it in front of him. Concentration showed on his face for several seconds before he reached out and touched the mirror. The grimacing face of an old man filled the mirror.

"You are late, again, as usually," the older man said.

"My apologies, arch mage Ambrissan," the king kept me in council longer than I expected."

"And?" Ambrissan asked.

Chancellor White leaned back in his chair, a chuckle escaping his lips. "The king is approving every law you proposed. Proclamations will go out in a couple of weeks."

Ambrissan smiled a wicked smile. "As I have told you and all the magic users in Preveshawl that I trained decades ago, my power is a thousand times greater than yours, because my magic is no longer muffled by the followers of The Lord of the Stars. You eliminate them; then your magic power will grow as well."

From the mirror, Chancellor White could see the excitement on the old man's face. Inside, he felt the same excitement. "I want to talk more about the council of mages that will rule Preveshawl once we...."

"Next time," replied Ambrissan. "I have urgent business that needs attending to. Keep on your king with these laws. The rest of our plans then will fall into place."

Chancellor White did not get a chance to respond. His mirror abruptly went blank. He leaned back in his chair, deep in thought. After several minutes, he slid the paper work on Chellell in front of him. "She will work into our plans perfectly," he thought to himself.

Chapter 4

For he hath made him to be sin for us, who knew no sin; that we might be made the righteousness of God in him. – The Guide

Gevi showed Javin each shop to stop at and what to unload. Each shop owner, in turn, gave them a list for goods they wanted Thunderfall to make, or items they needed to have repaired. Gevi collected the coins which she kept in a small, iron box, attached to the floor of the wagon. The largest delivery was to the fort armory, where Javin had to unload several crates of weapons and armor. Afterwards, they parked the wagon and walked around the shops. The streets were filled with a mix of farmers and off-duty soldiers. Smells of cooking meat filled the air. Fruits and vegetable stands lined the road, with merchants calling out sale prices on their wares. Gevi spent a lot of time in various specialty shops doing more looking than buying. The antique stores especially fascinated her. Javin followed along, pretending to be interested when Gevi got excited over some item or antique that Javin saw absolutely no use for. He tried to hide his anxiety with crowds and people. Gevi noticed, but thought he was extremely shy.

Finally, Javin used some of his own wages to buy some ice cream for himself and Gevi. In the small nature park in the middle of the fort, they sat on the grass, backs against a large tree. Together, they watched the people going shop to shop and children playing while parents did business. It seemed like everyone waved to Gevi or said hello to her. Some even stopped to chat a few minutes with her. Javin realized that she was very popular and well-liked by the people in and around the fort.

"Hey girl, why don't me and you...," a soldier yelled toward Gevi from a group of soldiers across the street from the park. Javin turned in time to see fists flying as other soldiers in the group knocked the soldier who called out to Gevi to the ground. One of the soldiers jumped on him, covering his mouth with his hand.

"Sorry Gevi," another soldier yelled back. "New kid."

Gevi waved toward the soldiers. She glanced over at Javin and saw his puzzled expression. "The soldiers are scared to death of me," she explained with a big smile.

Astonished, Javin watched the soldiers drag their fellow companion that had dared to call out to Gevi down the street. "Why are they afraid of you?" he asked. Gevi continued to watch the people meandering around the shops, before answering Javin.

"When I was sixteen, I came to the fort with Ledia to do some shopping. I was resting here in the park while Ledia was in that store over there," she pointed toward a store that was selling various fruits. "A group of five soldiers came out of nowhere and surrounded me. They were saying stuff about me being pretty and other things a polite man would never say. They scared me to death. One of them was really obnoxious and very big. Ledia came running out of the store and chased them away. They continued to yell lewd things back at me and Ledia as they left. I was scared and embarrassed. Ledia angrily marched me straight back home and told Thunderfall. Daddy left me with Ledia and went straight to the fort. When he came back that evening, he assured me something like that would never happen again. And it hasn't."

Still curious, Javin stared at Gevi, but she was obviously done speaking. "What did Thunderfall do?"

A small smile slowly crossed Gevi's face as she watched a group of young children laughing and kicking a ball down the street. "I found out what happened, several weeks later. Daddy picked up Mac. Together they asked around and found the group of soldiers at a local tavern. Dad put the big, obnoxious soldier head first through a wall. The other four soldiers were terrified, after they saw what he did to their leader. Besides, if you haven't noticed, Daddy's looks are a little intimidating."

"That's an understatement," mumbled Javin.

Gevi laughed, "Yes, I guess you could say he is extremely intimidating, if you don't know him. Anyway, he made the other soldiers sit down at a table with him, where he informed them if they tried to run, that he would find them and not only break their arms, but their legs, as well. Then he lectured them on how real men were to treat women, especially under-aged girls like myself, at that time. After he was finished lecturing the wide-eyed and terrified soldiers; Daddy informed them that because they had acted like snotty-nosed teenage boys with his daughter, he was now going to treat them like little boys. To prove his point, he ordered the first soldier to bend over a chair. Daddy paddled the soldier's behind so hard that the screams could be heard outside the tavern. Everyone in the tavern was laughing and jeering at the soldiers."

"They didn't draw weapons on Thunderfall?" Javin asked.

"Almost no chance of that ever happening," explained Gevi. "If a soldier draws a weapon on a civilian or another soldier in the fort, they can be executed. Since neither Dad nor Mac drew weapons, the soldiers did not draw weapons. Fighting with fists is tolerated, but punishable, within the fort. Using weapons in fights is taboo." Stretching her arms, Gevi paused. "Besides, would you draw a weapon on Daddy?"

Javin had to agree with her on that one. Someone would have to be insane to pull a weapon on Thunderfall.

"After Daddy finished with the first soldier, he ordered the second one to bend over the chair. He tried to run, but Mac grabbed him. Because he tried to run, he received a harder spanking than the first soldier. All four had to bend over a chair and take a paddling from Daddy. I heard they couldn't sit for days. After he doled out his lesson in manners, Daddy grabbed the big man he had put through the wall and woke him up with a pitcher of ice water. Daddy bent him over his knee and paddled him as well. I heard he screamed louder than the previous soldiers. Daddy paid the owner double for the damages to the wall, and left."

Gevi paused for a second, "Since then, I have no problems with soldiers when I come to town. They have behaved as perfect gentlemen towards me. In fact, I can't think of a single woman in this fort who has had a problem with rude soldiers."

Javin started laughing so hard, his sides hurt. Images of Thunderfall paddling a soldier in front of everyone went through his mind. Finally, he stopped laughing. Catching his breath, Javin decided it was a good time to ask her about her parents. "Gevi," started Javin, then he paused. Gevi looked at him sweetly, encouraging him with her eyes to continue. Taking a deep breath, Javin blurted out his question with rapid stutters. "You don't have to tell me if you don't want to, but how is it that you are obviously part elf and part human, but your father is a dwarf? I bet that it is one interesting story."

Gevi laughed while running her hand through her long, silky hair. Hair black as midnight covering her face was swept away by a delicately smooth hand. "Not as interesting as you would think, but I will tell you what I remember. You know where you fought the goblins? There was a four-way in the road; you remember that, right?"

"Yes, the Crossroads," answered Javin

"Right, but if you had gone down the West Road you would have entered a small city with a castle called Bear Tree City. That is where we were coming from when you met us and where I am currently working. That is where my story starts."

"Bear Tree City," commented Javin, no longer feeling so shy. "My family and I would go there every other year or so. It's the closest city to Farm Circle, where I am from."

"Good to know; now let me tell my story." Gevi lightly punched him in the shoulder as she said this. The gesture instantly brought memories of Chellell flashing back through Javin's mind. He suppressed the memories quickly.

"Sorry; go ahead," Javin said, as he glanced over at Gevi.

Gevi's Story

"I am not sure how it happened; I was too young to remember, but probably around the age of four or five, my birth parents died in Bear Tree City. I can hardly remember their faces, so I know I was very young. I am fairly sure we did not live in the city, but that we were only visiting. I have memories of my parents and me living among a lot of trees, like a forest somewhere. I also remember walking for a long time before we arrived at Bear Tree City."

"Daddy does not think it was the Elven Forest south of the Dwarven Nation, because I remember lots of snow. He did check with the elves in the Elven Forest, but they knew nothing about me. After my parents died, someone found me, wandering around the streets, and took me to a house with lots of little children in it. At night, we would be given one ragged blanket and a sleeping mat. We had to find a space on the floor among several rooms to sleep. In the morning, we were given a loaf of bread or a piece of fruit and put out of the house. As I said, I don't remember how long, but I know I lived this way, for several years."

"Cold and hunger were my constant companions while wandering around the streets by day and sleeping on the floor of that house, by night. Out on the streets, I would have to beg and steal food to survive. Actually, I only stole a few times. I felt so bad when I stole, that I would rather beg. To beg, I tended to go far away from the house where the orphaned children slept. Deep inside, I always hoped my parents would show up and get me out of this nightmare. They didn't. They couldn't."

"The struggle to survive went on for years. Around the age of nine, I saw Thunderfall arguing with a shop owner. Having never seen a dwarf before, I was extremely curious. He was small in height, but the most massive person I had ever seen; bulging muscles, with no fat at all. His shoulders were nearly as wide as he was tall. I had never seen a long beard like that either. After attending to his business at the shop, I saw him leave and stomp off down the road. You know how he does it, that stomp he does. I followed him, until he went into this little outdoor café. I watched him for a time, sitting and eating, complaining about the food, the weather, and everything in general. Finally, I got up the nerve to approach him."

"Since I was so young, the only thing I could think to say was, "Sir, what are you?" He looked right at me, seeing a very dirty little girl, dressed in rags, with slippers that were coming apart. Believe it or not, I remember clearly what I looked like. I used to sneak into a house a couple of times a year if I knew the people were gone and look at myself in a mirror; then take a bath. I could only bathe a few times a year, so I must have smelled awful. He looked at me for what seemed like hours, but was probably only a few seconds."

"In his gruff voice he said, "I am a dwarf." Now tell me; what are you?" Given the circumstances, it was a good question."

"I thought that was extremely funny, so I replied while giggling, "I'm a little girl." He was the first person to make me laugh about anything since I was orphaned."

"Looking at me from head to toe, he said, "Well, little girl, you know that little girls should not be out talking to strangers they do not know. Get on back to your mom and dad." He then turned away from me and started eating again. My hunger and begging instincts overwhelmed my curiosity."

"With what had to be a sad look on my face, I replied, "I don't know where my mom and dad are. Sir, can I have a piece of bread. I'm very hungry." I locked eyes with him as I spoke with my innocent, pleading, voice that had successfully gained me food in the past."

"He handed me a piece of bread. "Where did you last see your parents?" he asked me in a voice less gruff than before."

"I don't remember," I replied, "It's several years since I've seen them."

"He sat there silently and watched me as I ate my bread. When I finished he handed me some meat, a rare treat for me. He had stopped eating and continued to stare at me while I eagerly gobbled down the meat. It didn't bother me though, the staring. By now, I was used to people staring at me. Then he waved his hand for the server, and a man came over to us. "Bring me another chair," the dwarf told the server, "and another platter of food, looks like I will have a guest joining me."

"I got all excited, and then very sad because the server replied, "No sir, we don't serve her kind here." I remember the server looking at me and saying, "Go away girl, and leave our customers alone." I noticed that everyone in the café was looking at me, but Thunderfall was glaring at the server."

"I turned to leave when I heard, "stay put." I turned back around and saw every muscle in this massive dwarf start to bulge. On his face was a scary look I had never seen before. It froze me in my tracks. I was very afraid, absolutely terrified. "Bring a chair, and a platter of food, right now," the dwarf ordered the server in a very quiet voice."

"No sir, we don't serve..."

"Before the server could finish his words, I heard a roar from the dwarf louder than any lion you have ever heard. His roar was like nothing I had heard before, and honestly Javin, I have never heard anything like it since. The whole table flew through the air and crashed into the server, knocking him to the ground. I turned and ran as hard as I could. Scared and alone, I spent the night in an alley. I was so scared."

"Oh wow!" exclaimed Javin, "wow."

"For years I didn't know what happened at the café after I left. I never asked, and Dad has not discussed it. As an adult, I heard a story about a dwarf completely demolishing an entire café at about that time, leaving the whole place a pile of broken wood and busted brick. The magistrate had, for some reason, pardoned the dwarf within days of the guard taking him to jail. I suspect that the server survived, but Thunderfall tore the whole place down in his rage. I believe the magistrate pardoned him because the army is in extreme need of his services. I am also suspicious that Daddy is a very important person amongst the dwarves. He won't discuss it, but visiting dwarves treat him with a lot of respect."

"I guess the old tale about never making a dwarf angry is true," stammered Javin.

"Yes. Believe me, it is something you never want to see. The only good thing is that it is very hard to get a dwarf truly angry. They are so good-natured, once you get to know them and get past the surface grumpiness. Dwarves are also honorable and dependable. Honestly, since that one time, I have never seen Daddy lose his temper." Anyway, back to my story."

"I spent my days getting back into my normal life of sleeping on the floor in the house at night and begging for food during the day. Two weeks after the café incident, I felt a huge hand come gently down on my shoulder. I turned around and saw Thunderfall. He started talking very gently the instant I turned around."

"Holding out a large piece of bread, he said, "I've been saving this for you."

"You know what? I took the bread from him. For some reason, I was not afraid of him. Even after the café incident, I was not afraid. He may seem grouchy and sour to others, but I have always sensed a deep love in him, even as a little girl."

"I also found something else for you while we were separated." He reached into his pack and pulled out new clothes and new shoes."

"I will never know why, but I did not reach for the dress. Instead, I flung myself at him and hugged him. I squeezed him as hard as I could while I cried and sobbed. I don't think I had cried so hard since I lost my parents. I refused to cry. That day, all my pain and anguish came out. No one ever cared enough to give a poor, homeless little girl a new, expensive dress. I held on to him, I know, for over an hour. He simple stood still in the street while people walked by staring at us, letting me squeeze him as hard I could. Finally, I stopped crying and he asked me if I could take him to the house where I stayed during the night. I held his hand and walked to the home."

"When we got there, the lady there handed me an old blanket, but Thunderfall asked me to stay right where I was. He walked with the woman into another room. After several minutes, he came back to me and asked me if I wanted to stay at another house, with a nice lady who would let me take a bath. I happily agreed and he took me all the way across town. It was deep in the middle of the night, and I was so tired that he ended up carrying me. I fell asleep in his arms while he carried me. I remember waking up in a house where a nice lady put me straight to bed. The next day she gave me a warm bath and helped me dress in the new clothes Thunderfall had given me. She did my hair too, which was a long and painful experience, I still clearly remember. After I was bathed and dressed in my new dress, I saw the massive dwarf sitting in a chair in the living room. Again, I don't know why, but I ran and jumped in his lap."

"What's your name?" I asked him.

"You can call me Thunderfall, and what is your name?"

"Gevi. I think it used to be bigger, but I don't remember the rest of it."

"Gevi it is then. Well, Gevi, how would you like to come home with me?"

"The rest, Javin, is history. I spent the remaining years with Thunderfall as my father, making him an even grumpier dwarf than he was before he met me."

"Gevi, that is a great story; thanks for sharing it with me."

Gevi quickly responded, "Don't you ever mention to him that I told you how he adopted me." She pointed her finger right at Javin's face. "I mean it! Not a word. He is very sensitive about that time. To this day, he refuses to go back to that city. That is why I have to come visit him, and he hires the soldiers to get supplies for him in the city on their days off. Not a word or hint that you know anything better ever come out of your mouth."

"My lips are completely sealed." Javin ran his finger over his closed lips, signaling his lips were sealed.

"Gevi stood up and stretched, trying to get the stiffness out of her body. "Those lips better stay sealed, or I will make a staff that turns you into such an ugly frog no princess will ever kiss you." Javin couldn't help it; he started laughing. Gevi smiled and offered her hand to help him stand up. "We better get the wagon and head back. Dad wasn't joking about how grumpy he gets if I am not home by sunset."

Once they were back at the wagon, Javin asked her about her real parents. Gevi's gaze went skyward, toward a very blue sky, full of puffy white clouds. Javin was instantly sorry he asked; the sadness plastered on her face was heartbreaking. He started to stammer an apology but Gevi cut him off. "It's fine," she sighed. She threw a forced smile sideways at him. "As I said, Daddy tried, but the elves in the Elven Forest knew nothing. They do know there are other tribes of elves, the nearest, is way north beyond the lands of the gorms. However, they have not been in contact with them in over twenty years. Surprisingly, they know little about their northern cousins. One day, somehow, I will find this tribe of elves."

****

"It is so nice to finally get to meet you. Have a seat, Young Lady." Chancellor White waved his hand towards a chair across from his desk. Chellell quietly took a seat as directed. Her familiar, Sanatarial, flew off her shoulder to join a similar creature on a perch near an open window. Chancellor White's familiar looked the same as Chellell's, except it was shiny black, instead of red. "I saw your grades; it seems to me you have a very bright future ahead of you."

"Thank you, Sir," replied Chellell, who was squirming in her chair with barely concealed excitement. "I hope I can be a big help to you."

"Oh, you will. I actually have an interesting assignment for you." He handed her a scroll. Chellell took it and quickly read through it. "Your assignment will be teaching and demonstrating magic throughout Preveshawl." Looking up from his desk, Chancellor White noticed the look of alarm on Chellell's pale face. "Don't worry. You will do fine. Herana will be training you all next week. If you need more time, then we can be flexible. You will love it. Herana has been doing similar work for several years in the southern part of Preveshawl. I however, feel that we need a new face, with new enthusiasm."

"I see you have me visiting the northern castles and forts, giving demonstrations for soldiers." Chellell said in a voice that was asking a question more than commenting.

"Yes, and for a lovely young lady like yourself, I think you will find this assignment a lot of fun," he replied with a smile on his face. His words caused Chellell's face to blush a bright red. "Seriously, Chellell, we have a big need for the army to accept and see the usefulness of magic." Chellell sat up stiffly in her chair, her mind whirling with thoughts of doing magic in front of crowds of people. Children she might be fine with, but towns and soldiers made her stomach churn. Chancellor White got up from his desk and crossed over to her. "Chellell, you will be fine. You won't be by yourself. I have a whole team of people going with you. Remember, you will be helping to spread the knowledge of magic. Think how much good you will be doing our kingdom."

Drawing a deep breath, Chellell looked up into the eyes of the Chancellor. "I will try my hardest, and do my best, to make you proud."

****

Chellell stretched out her hand. A ball of fire flew from her hand into a practice dummy dressed to look like a soldier. The dummy exploded in a spectacular tower of flame, joining other objects already a-blaze that were made to look like various creatures known to Preveshawl's people. Chellell spun around and faced her instructor. "All enemies have been neutralized. How much time did it take?"

"Thirty four seconds," replied a man standing off to the side of the stage by a large curtain.

"Excellent, excellent," Chellell's instructor commented, clapping her hands in applause. "All right, Chellell, follow me outside and I will introduce you to your team." Chellell smiled as she leapt off the stage. She felt the power link between herself and Sanatarial disappear, causing the magic power to drain from her body. With her familiar on her shoulder, she followed her instructor through the seemingly endless castle hallways and out a large gate into a courtyard. Seeing a group of nearly a dozen wagons loaded with crates and boxes, the two women approached the wagons.

The instructor stopped in front of them and called out, "Everyone! Front and center." The group working around the wagons ceased their work and gathered in front of Chellell and her instructor. "I asked you to meet here so that we can get to know each other, even though I know a lot of you already have met each other in our practices. After introductions, we will head over to Azure Hall, where I have a banquet waiting for us. You will be spending the whole summer together as a team, so it will be vital that you learn to work together. Guards, step forward." A group of men with a couple of women stepped forward. They were eighteen in number. Each of them gave their name to Chellell.

"Thank you. You may step back now. Chellell, these soldiers are highly trained and will act as guards. They will do the stage setup and tear downs at each stop. Licheaon, can you come forward?" A finely dressed older man stepped forward. "Chellell, this is Licheaon, the director of operations. He is in charge of everyone and everything involved with this show." Licheaon gave Chellell a bow.

"Chellell, it is nice to have you with us. If you need anything at all, or are unhappy with anything, feel free to talk to me," he said in a whiney voice. "My door will always be open for you, day or night." They knew each other quite well already, due to the fact that he had been to almost every practice.

"Thank you Licheaon," the instructor said. "Lily, come here please." A gorgeous young woman, Chellell's age, stepped forward. She had long, flowing blond hair that went down past her waist. Long bangs were swept sideways, covering one eye. Chellell thought to herself that this had to be the most beautiful girl she had ever seen. Her face looked like it was perfectly chiseled out of marble. Her complexion was soft and smooth, with bright blue eyes. "Chellell, this is Lily. She will do your hair, makeup, and wardrobe. She is a great artist and will make sure you and everyone else on stage look their best." Chellell hoped the girl could make her look half as good as she looked.

"You are so pretty; I see my job will be easy." Lily purred.

Chellell blushed, but before she could say thank you, the instructor cut in. "Actors and actresses, please step forward." A group of six stepped forward. There were two men and four women. They were young and almost as good-looking as the makeup artist. Each of them "introduced" themselves to Chellell, even though she already knew them from practices.

"And last, Kyle and Draden, come forward." Two men, whom Chellell had only met once before, during a full rehearsal, came forward. Each had a familiar riding on their shoulder.

"As you know, Chellell, these are your backups. They will be doing the extra magic effects, like we have practiced." The instructor then addressed the group. "Finish up the loading and then meet at Azure Hall in one hour. You must be back here at five-thirty in the morning; you will be leaving by six. Licheaon will go over your upcoming schedule at Azure hall. Thank you for your hard work." She reached over and grabbed Chellell's hand as the group broke up and started back toward the wagons. "Come with me Chellell, Chancellor White wants to talk to you one more time, in private, before you leave." Together, the two walked back into the castle.

****

Mikelsheck the gorm walked among the rows of tents and campfires. Seeing an especially large tent ahead of him, he veered and headed straight for the doorway. Two giants, each twelve feet tall, guarded the entryway. Ignoring the guards, Mikelsheck walked through the entryway. Inside, he saw a huge giant, several inches over sixteen feet, sitting in an oversized chair made of pure, white ivory. Red jewels covered the legs of the chair. Several gorms and goblins were at a table. The giant saw the gorm and waved him over to the table, where a map showing the Kingdom of Preveshawl and the areas north of the kingdom, was displayed. A large red dot marked their current location.

"You know the area around the human fort by now, I assume," The huge giant spoke, causing the whole tent to go silent.

"Yes, Grand Leader," Mikelsheck replied. "Our scouts know every landmark within a day's ride of the fort."

"Excellent," rumbled the giant. "Take ten squads of your best and cross the border on the eastern high trail. When the greater moon is dark and the lesser moon is a quarter, five days from now, I want you to raid as many outlying human dwellings as you can. You are to take as many slaves as possible. Kill only as needed, but bring me back the humans. Make it look like a single gorm tribe is raiding." The giant pointed down at the map on the table. "Follow this trail up through the mountains after the raid, and circle back toward the army later. That should throw off the humans that try to follow you, for a while."

The giant stood up from the table, his head nearly reaching the top of the tent. "My father was assassinated by cowardly humans and dwarves, and his army failed," he roared. "I WILL NOT FAIL!" His voice echoed through the tent and the camp. The giant sat back down with a thud, the chair barely containing his weight. "Go, Mikelsheck! I want to see at least one hundred human slaves we can use for our farms and mines while we are at war. You have one night, split your gorms up and have them meet you back at this high mountain meadow," the giant explained as he pointed to a spot on the map. "The more confusion you create, the less killing you will have to do, and the more slaves you can bring me.

Mikelsheck bowed and turned toward the entrance, but a sharp command from the giant made him spin back around. "I know how much you gorms love to kill," the giant growled in a low, ominous voice. "If you cannot control the blood lust of those under your command, then I will make sure your death and the death of your soldiers is so slow and cruel that gorms will be talking about it for a hundred years. Do you understand me, Mikelsheck?"

"Yes, Grand Leader," squeaked the shaking gorm. He bowed his head again and rushed out of the tent.

Mikelsheck had only been gone a few minutes when one of the giant guards stepped into the tent. "Grand Leader," the giant said in a deep, calm voice. "A group of goblins riding strange two-headed wolves, along with some kind of flying monster, has been spotted. They are fast approaching the north end of our camp."

"Looks like my special guests have arrived," the Grand Leader replied as he raised himself out of his ivory chair. The giant ordered his generals to continue their planning, before he left the tent. Once he reached the north side of the camp, he saw gorm soldiers scrambling to get into defensive position. Several hundred feet out, two-headed wolves, bearing goblins on their backs, were lining up in formation as a circling gryphon slowly came down for a landing. The gryphon screamed toward the Grand Leader, its beak snapping in the air. Wings twenty-feet long folded smoothly against its body. Riding on the gryphon's back, between folded wings, sat a human male holding a long staff.

"What is that monster?" asked one of the Grand Leader's guards. He nervously fingered the sword hanging from his belt.

"A gryphon," responded the Grand Leader. Body of a full grown male lion, with wings and beak like an eagle; they are only found on islands in the South Sea. Besides the dragons of the Rhamnon Desert, very few creatures are as vicious or as powerful as a gryphon. As for the two-headed wolves the goblins are riding, they are known as Fenris wolves. They range north of the barbarian tribes, and are the most ferocious of all the wolves." A smile slowly spread across the face of the Grand Leader. "Let's go meet our new friend and ally."

****

"It is agreed then, Ambrissan. You will act as my second in command and provide whatever magical services I need. Your Fenris wolves and their goblin riders will stay as a unit under your command. In return, I will pay you twenty pounds in gold." The Grand Leader leaned back in his chair, eyeing the arch mage.

It was hard to believe that the five-foot, eighty-pound man in his mid-fifties was such a feared man; a true psychopathic killer, afraid of absolutely nothing. The Grand Leader wanted Ambrissan for his skills with magic, which was reputed to be beyond any of the magic users living in Preveshawl. In fact, Ambrissan had been one of the principal players in bringing magic to Preveshawl. He had started the Guild of Magic and presided over it for nearly a decade, before being forced to flee Preveshawl over the murder of several administrators at the guilds who had angered him. Ambrissan had fled past the northern borders of Preveshawl, where his magic powers continued to grow, along with his evil.

The Grand Leader had first met Ambrissan when the arch mage had approached him for the use of giants to help rebuild an old castle the arch mage had decided to take up residence in. Seeing the potential of having such a powerful ally, the Grand Leader agreed to help with the castle. Now, Ambrissan controlled one hundred goblins on trained Fenris wolves, along with a gryphon. It was an established fact that his castle dungeon held captives from nearly every race, many sold to him as slaves by the giants. Why Ambrissan wanted slaves from all the races, the Grand Leader did not know, nor did he care.

"Agreed," responded Ambrissan. "Twenty pounds of gold, and I am your mage." Ambrissan planned to play along, for now. This giant and his army was the exact tool he had been waiting ten years for. This army would break Preveshawl, making it easier for him to accomplish his plans.

Ambrissan knew what few others knew. In ancient times, Preveshawl had been ruled by a race known as the Linkrins. This race had made Preveshawl the greatest nation known on their planet. Its borders had extended to the great northern ice caps. He knew this because Ambrissan had more than one familiar. Everyone could see the familiar on his shoulder, but they could not see the infinitely more powerful familiar whose spirit lived inside his body. This familiar Ambrissan had sought out. In a ritual evil beyond description, Ambrissan had contacted this ancient, powerful spirit and invited the spirit to possess him. This ancient spirit had once been the familiar to the last living chief arch mage of the Linkrins. All the memories and knowledge of this race that became extinct two thousand years ago, now belonged to Ambrissan.

56

Chapter 5
In the beginning God created the heaven and the earth. – The Guide

"Have a seat," Thunderfall said to Javin as he came into the shop at his usual time, very early in the morning. Since leaving the guilds three weeks ago, Javin was quickly learning the art of being a blacksmith. Javin nervously tapped his foot on the ground, wondering what mistake he had made that was so horrible that Thunderfall wanted to sit him down for a talk. "I know dwarves can be a tad bit grumpy at times." Javin raised an eyebrow and forced himself not to smile. "Don't worry; this is not one of those times."

Thunderfall looked around the shop, before finally fixing his gaze on Javin. He placed an iron hammer on the table, between them. "See this hammer?" Javin nodded and looked toward a wall covered with various sized hammers. He was always amazed at the amount of tools the dwarf blacksmith had. "Hammers shape metal, after the metal goes through the fire of the forge. The metal is shaped on the anvil until it cools down, then back into the flames it goes. So it is with our lives. The Lord of the Stars knows what he wants us to be, how best to shape us into the image of God. Some of us are more stubborn than the oldest dwarf on the mountain, causing God to continually put the fire to us and pound us into shape. Like the metal, eventually we yield to the Great Blacksmith." Thunderfall paused in thought. "Blacksmithing is an honored profession amongst the dwarves. We see God as the Great Blacksmith that shapes our lives."

"Dwarves have many traditions, with blacksmithing being one of them. Another tradition we hold above all traditions, is that debts must be paid."

Javin's stomach jumped and a cold lump settled in his gut. "Yes sir, but..."

"Hold on; I didn't ask you to interrupt. Young people have no manners and no respect for their elders. Where was I? Oh yes; debts must be paid. It's an ancient dwarven tradition, based on an actual event. You already know how we were all created in the image of God. In the beginning, when the first man and woman sinned, they incurred sin. That sin became a debt now owed to God."

Seeing that Master Thunderfall was very serious, Javin listened. "By definition, sin is willful disobedience to God. God, by His eternal Nature, can only accept perfection. Only a perfect person can come into His Presence. When the first man and woman sinned, they passed on to their children a nature that has a desire to sin. Their children passed it on to their children, and so on. Ultimately, every person fails God and sins, creating a debt to God that can never be paid, but of course God knows this. So, God sent his one and only Son to this world to die for our sins. The Lord of the Stars came and died, paying the debt we owed. As *The Guide* says, *having canceled the charge of our legal indebtedness, which stood against us and condemned us; he has taken it away.*"

"With the condition we believe," stuttered Javin.

"Yes," Thunderfall replied, "*The Guide* says that we must confess with our mouth that the Son is God, and believe in our heart that God has raised him from the dead. If we do that, we are saved. We will never reach a point that we think we need God to save us, unless we realize we are sinners. We must also accept that we are sinners who can never make it right with God. We are in debt, and debts must be paid. When we realize that and accept the Lord of the Stars as our Savior, then God accepts the payment that He has made on our behalf. Our debt is now paid to God and we can be with Him forever."

Thunderfall looked around the shop in thought for a minute. "To put it simply, everyone living has sinned against God. God is willing to forgive us our sins. His only requirement is that we believe in His Son. If we believe, and ask him to forgive our sins, then we are forgiven our sins. One day, we will be resurrected into eternal life.

Thunderfall went silent for a minute while Javin waited, getting more nervous as time went by. "In honor of the debt the Lord of the Stars has paid, we dwarves have a tradition that through their lives all debts are paid. It seems I owe you two debts."

Javin's face paled, but to his surprise Thunderfall started laughing. It was a deep, booming laugh. Javin had never heard him laugh like this before. "By looking at your face, you would think the end of the world had arrived, but you really don't understand." Thunderfall had a big smile on his face, "In memory of the Lord of the Stars paying our debt, it is a dwarf's greatest joy to pay a debt. It is our custom and an honor we hold dear."

"I guess you found out about the goblins, but it really was not a big deal. Mac and Gevi would have stopped them without me. So really, I do not think that..."

"Not according to Mac, or Kevinan. Both claimed they were way outnumbered and did not have a chance. I thank you for saving my daughter's life. For that, I will repay you before the end of the apprenticeship. The second debt..."

"What second debt?" Javin asked in confusion.

"The second debt is owed through your father. The dwarves never had a chance to repay him. Now that you are here, we can honor that debt. All debts must be paid and that debt has been on the books way too long."

Thunderfall shoved two scrolls across the table toward Javin. One was a map; the other contained strange, flowing script in a language Javin didn't recognize. "The map shows the way to an ancient dwarven mine. You will only need it if Gevi forgets the way, because she will be going with you. I would go with you, but this order from the fort must be finished by the end of the week. Besides, as my apprentice for the summer, I am going to need you to make a trip to this mine every month to get needed materials from the dwarves. Now, the note is dwarven. There are always dwarves guarding that entrance because it connects to the Dwarven City. Show the dwarves the note, and they will help you fulfill your mission. It is the first step to paying the debt."

"I'm ready to go, if you boys are done chitter-chattering," Gevi said as she pranced into the shop. She was dressed in brown leather armor with a bow across her back and staff in hand.

"I think I may owe a third debt, making you put up with her for two days," mumbled Thunderfall quietly. Javin smiled, hoping that Gevi had not heard Thunderfall's comment.

Gevi walked up to their table, "Now Daddy, I am sure Javin would rather travel with fun old me instead of having to listen to a grumpy dwarf all day." Javin smiled again, realizing she had heard Thunderfall's comment. Thunderfall ignored his daughter.

"You two will arrive at a little meadow up in the mountains after traveling for four hours, if you don't get yourselves lost. It's another two to three hour hike on foot from there to the dwarves and the mine. The dwarves will take you into the mine; you can get the metals I am sending you for in under an hour's time. Stay the night with them then come on back in the morning. The dwarves will help you get back to your horses with your load." Thunderfall got up from the table and walked over to his tool shelf.

"What are we getting out of the mine?" Javin stuttered; his curiosity piqued.

"You are going to bring me back a rare metal, that is the lightest and the strongest metal known to dwarves," replied Thunderfall. "What I do with that metal will really help you in battle. Go ahead and get ready; you will be out two days. Follow the map if this girl here forgets..."

"Oh Daddy, I know how to get there. I've made the journey with you several times," said an indignant Gevi, her face going into a pout.

"Yeah Girl, I know," replied Thunderfall with an indulgent smile. "I also know I am too old to have to spend several days hiking all over the mountains looking for two lost kids! Now come give me a hug, and go get your horses."

****

Javin and Gevi staked their horses in the meadow that Thunderfall had marked on the map. They transferred supplies and weapons from the horses to their packs before hiking up the mountain trail. The sun was shining and the temperature was just right for a mountain hike, not too hot and not too cold. Climbing steeply upwards, the trail twisted through vast mountain rocks, mixed with small, mountain, Evergreen trees. On a trail barely wide enough for two people to walk side by side, the pair talked about events going on around them. Gevi was extremely pleased that Javin was finally coming out of his shell. Before this trip, she had wondered if anything or anyone could draw him out of his solitary world.

After they had crossed a mountain brook by jumping rock to rock through the gentle flowing waters, Javin decided to ask Gevi a question. "Gevi, how exactly does your staff work without magic? That was quite a blast it put out on those goblins!"

59

Gevi spotted a nice rock, wide enough for two people right next to the bubbling brook. She sat down on the rock and dropped her pack to her feet. Javin took the spot next to her, while she laid out the staff across their laps.

The crisp, clear water sparkled from the bright noon day sun reflecting off the water's surface. The view was breathtaking. You could see all the way into the plains below, including the start of Maarcave River, which fed into the Great Henjum River. The river twisted like a bright blue snake through the great grasslands, before disappearing into a deep green forest at the very end of their vision. Small farms dotted the plains, with dark green squares, marking the crops being grown. Javin could even see the road heading east from the Crossroads toward Farm Circle. Large white, puffy clouds were zooming across the sky, promising rain either later that night or early the next day. The warm breeze was blowing Gevi's hair around, causing her to constantly have to tuck it behind her pointed ears.

"You would really love the staff, now. I increased the power of the lightning threefold last week." Gevi said with a smile. "The staff works in three parts and is really quite simple, if you know what you are looking at. It actually combines three of the guilds into one device. First is the Guild of Elements. Look at the head of the staff; you see these two gems?" Gevi pointed over to the head of the staff, where two large gems were set, one rose red and the other a pale blue. The two gems were separated by a deep black material that ended in a point four inches above the gems. "The first part involves the red gem. Go ahead, you can touch it. It won't bite," she told Javin while looking at him with a smile on her face.

He ran his hands over the gems, noticing the red gem was warm, while the blue gem was at ambient temperature. "The red gem absorbs the rays of the sun. A small, thin, material we call Bhovan, connects to the bottom of the gem. The Bhovan runs inside the staff down to the bottom. Branching off it every inch is small crystals, the size of a pea. They are called battery crystals. These crystals are actually very common. They convert the sun's solar energy into electrical energy found in lightning, and store it. The Bhovan material transfers the sun's energy straight to these crystals. There is a drawback to using this type of energy. The staff can only store enough energy to fire three shots per day."

"Three powerful shots," mumbled Javin. He cleared his throat before continuing. "You know how to make stuff like this? Where did you learn how to do that?" Javin asked while running his hand along the wood of the staff in amazement. By touch, he could feel the seam going all the way down where the two halves of the staff had been glued together.

"I guess it's my elven blood. I learned about gemstones and various other materials from Ledia. Then, designs come into my head and over time, I have learned to make what I see. Ledia was my teacher; I never went to the guilds. She is an amazing woman. Before she married Mac, she was a teacher at the Guild of Elements. While teaching, she completed all the course work at the Guild of Nature. She is one of the rare people that is a member in two guilds.

She looked off down the mountain, enjoying the view of the landscape below. A few minutes of silence passed between the two while Gevi enjoyed the scenic view and Javin looked over her staff. "You see those buttons in the middle of the staff?" Gevi asked.

"Yes," Javin said as his hand starting towards them. Gevi grabbed his hand before it reached the buttons.

"Don't push them, or we will be dodging lightning," she laughed as she let go of his hand, which quickly moved away from the buttons. "You probably would not do anything; they have to be pushed in combinations. That insures I do not accidentally shoot someone. Anyway, the right combination causes a copper wire to connect to the battery crystals which in turn allows the electrical energy to move to the blue gem. The gem briefly stores the energy. This process comes from the Guild of Engineering. Believe it or not, Mac came from the Guild of Engineering, though you would think he is from the Guild of Warriors, like you are. Mac was my engineering studies instructor."

"Now, the Guild of Science comes into play. Lightning seeks the easiest path to ground. I have loaded into that black point between the gems small stones, called ground stones." She touched the very end of the staff, showing him the black point. "They come from the dwarven mines and are known to attract lightning during storms. Next, I pack three small ground stones with three explosive powder charges." Gevi unscrewed the top of the staff, showing Javin the three small chambers with pea-sized rocks in each chamber, resting on a black powdery substance.

"I press a different button combination to ignite the black power, which also opens the point of the staff. The powder ignites, causing the ground stone to fire out of the staff toward the target I am pointing at up to fifty feet. After the stone is launched, I charge the blue gem as I described earlier. It can be done in a few seconds. Once the stone makes contact with any target touching the ground, the lightning discharges from the blue gem, hitting the target."

"Impressive," Javin commented while looking over the staff.

Gevi laughed, "The shop I work in makes all kinds of neat things for people that have the money; though we rarely get into things like this staff because my boss dislikes doing weapons. I am learning so much from her; she is really the smart one. Things Ledia, Mac, and my Dad, taught me when I was younger, play a part in helping me put the puzzles together. I have a very creative and active imagination, if you have not noticed by now."

"This is absolutely amazing," was the only thing Javin could think of to say.

"Thank you, Javin," she said, looking him in the eyes, "it is really sweet of you to say that." Gevi rose up off the rock, putting her pack back on her back. "We had better get going, before we lose our sunlight. Remind me to get more ground stones and powder from the dwarves once we get to the mine."

****

"We are not lost!" Gevi declared with agitation in her voice. "Temporarily misplaced, maybe, but not lost!" She continued to lead along an overgrown trail. Javin was trying to simultaneously follow her, and read the map.

"Nobody has been on this trail for centuries, Gevi!" Javin stuttered. He dodged another sticker branch that was reaching for him from the side of the narrow path. His agitation grew as he glanced at the scratches on his arm from his previous fights with these thorny vines. "If we had turned right, instead of left, as I suggested, then we would not be lost." He nearly ran into the back of Gevi as he finished speaking.

The trail abruptly stopped. Directly in front of Gevi was a large square of pure white marble, six feet across, and six feet deep. On top of the marble base was a statue that stood ten feet tall. The statue looked like a creature that was half-man and half-monkey. Thorny vines and green algae covered the whole statue. They both stared at the strange statue for several minutes. Finally, Gevi turned her attention to the base.

"Can you remove the vines from the base?" Gevi asked. "There seem to be writing and pictures on it." Javin stepped around Gevi, happy to at least get some revenge on these thorny vines. Once it was cleared, he stepped back in amazement. Three very colorful pictures with flowing script covered the side of the marble base. It was surprising how well preserved it was, considering the old age of the monument. Words were written with letters Javin was familiar with, but none of the words made any sense.

"It's very ancient writing," commented Gevi. She brushed a strand of hair out of her eyes with one hand while examining the writing. "Ledia had me read several ancient books on plants and animals with this style of writing, when she schooled me. Our writing today came from this form of writing. They are actually similar, if you know what you are looking at. I think I can read most of this." She studied the writing for several minutes, before slowly reading aloud. "It says, '*This oh man, is your beginning.*' It seems like each script is referencing the picture above it."

Above the writing was a picture of a jagged circle, with dots inside the circle. Small lines protruded out around the circle. It blazed with color; primarily red, yellow and blue. Javin stared at it, completely puzzled.

Looking back at the script, Javin saw a line with text over it going to another group of text. The text above this line was something he recognized, a bunch of ones and zeros with strange text mixed in with it. "Do you know what this means?" he asked Gevi, pointing at the numbers.

"Let's see," she said while examining the numbers and text. "It is a math formula. The numbers are ten thousand times ten thousand times twenty, followed by the word years." Javin's mind could not even fathom that amount of time. He looked at Gevi in puzzlement. Gevi simple shrugged her shoulders and drew his attention over to the next picture. This picture was similar to the first one, except it was filled with distinct, multiple shapes instead of dots. "This one says, *'Through fire and gas, complexity arises'*. The line moving from that text to the next one is similar to the first; it says, *'Ten thousand times ten thousand times fifteen years'*."

The third picture was the most beautiful picture yet. Fish of many colors and shapes swam in a clear blue sea. Javin continued to admire the painting while Gevi struggled to figure out the text. Finally, she read. "*Natural selection, those that improvise prevail.*" Another line, with numbers over the line, went around the corner of the white marble slab. Javin drew his sword and cleared the side of the monument. Once cleared, they again saw many fish. This time however, some of the fish had legs. It showed them on a beach with trees in the background. The text under the picture read, "*Change over time, adaptation arises.*" The line with numbers above it moved to the next quote and painting.

As far as Javin was concerned, the fifth picture was absolutely gorgeous. It showed many kinds of land animals mixed with trees and plants. The pair recognized some of these animals, although most they had never seen before. The text underneath read, "*Constant struggle for existence breeds superiority.*"

"I can't begin to understand what this thing is trying to tell me," Javin said as he moved around the base of the statue to clear out more vines. Curiosity had overruled the fact that they were supposed to be finding their way back toward the dwarven mine.

Gevi watched Javin clear the remaining vines from the base of the statue. The next drawing was different from the rest. On the left side, stood a monkey, hunched over, with its hands on the ground. To the right was another monkey taller than the first, and only slightly hunched over. Next was a third monkey, taller still and not hunched over at all. Javin glanced at the third monkey. He realized then that it was the same as the statue: half-man, half-monkey.

Next, on the drawing, were three humans in a row. Their posture was similar to the drawings of the monkeys. Each human was taller and less hairy than the one before it. This painting took up the whole side of the marble base. Instead of a single quotation, there were two quotes. Gevi really struggled with the first quote.

"I am going to have to paraphrase this one. It seems to say that man comes from a hairy-tailed something. It's a word I have never seen before."

Shock showed on her face. "Javin," she explained, "I think it is saying man descended from a monkey." She moved on to examine the other text, before looking back up at the picture. "That is exactly what this horrible, blasphemous, statue is saying! The second quote reads: "*Look, oh man, at your forefathers, bask in the evidence that man was not created by any God.*"

Javin moved around to the last side of the square monument while

Gevi glared at the half-man, half-monkey statue. He cleared the vines and growth away. A huge picture of a tombstone with a human male standing beside it filled this side of the monument. The man looked like a normal, professional, human you would see today at the Guild of Science. He was wearing a white overcoat and holding a glass bottle in his hand. It was obvious to Javin that this man was some kind of scientist. Writings covered this side of the monument. Gevi slid in behind him, alarm growing on her face. "This is getting worse, Javin. The text says, '*the wisdom of man using science has proven there is no God*'. Another text in the upper right says, '*religion is the crutch of the simple, science is the strength of the wise*'. The words on the tombstone claims, '*God is declared dead, by science*'."

Javin grabbed Gevi's hand, pulling her away from the monument. "Let's go! I cannot take any more of this!" Gevi let him drag her away. Twenty feet back down the overgrown trail, she abruptly jerked her hand out of his grasp. She whipped her bow from her back and grabbed an arrow from her quiver. The arrow was unlike any Javin had ever seen. The tip was large and blunt, while the shaft seemed to be abnormally thick. Gevi gave the feathered shaft a firm twist before notching the arrow to her bow.

Gevi's arrow exploded upon contact with the half-man, half-monkey statue. The explosion threw shattered bits of the monkey-man in all directions. Javin's reflexes threw him into Gevi, taking both of them to the ground. Bits of exploded marble pelted Javin's back as Gevi angrily struggle to get out from under him. Javin jumped back up and helped Gevi regain her feet. Glancing over his shoulder, he saw that the monkey-man statue was obliterated.

With no other explanation, Gevi coolly said, "I needed to test my new exploding arrows." Blood trickled down her chin from several small cuts caused by flying pieces of marble. "Great target to try them on, don't you think?" Pushing his hand off her shoulder, she marched back down the trail. "Come on Javin; we need to back track and find the right trail. Try to read the map correctly this time, so you don't get us lost, again."

"You're the one who..." Realizing Gevi was nearly out of his sight; Javin stopped speaking and glanced back at the ruined monument. Releasing a sigh, he hurried after Gevi.

"I knew I should have trusted my womanly sense of direction above a male with a map," Gevi huffed. Javin rolled his eyes. He started to point out that she was the one who had insisted this was the trail they should be on. Instead, he kept his mouth shut, following her back down the overgrown trail.

Chapter 6

For thou art not a God that hath pleasure in wickedness: neither shall evil dwell with thee. - The Guide

After more wrong turns from Gevi, corrected with the help of Thunderfall's map, they finally found the correct trail to the dwarven mine. The sun was starting to set, when Gevi informed Javin that they should almost be at the mine. As they came around a curve in the trail, they spotted several small rock buildings set up against a cliff. A cave entrance, covered by an iron gate, set against the face of a solid rock wall.

Without any warning, a dwarf stepped out from behind a rock to stand in the road right in front of them. "And where are the two of ye going?" asked the dwarf, behind a long, brownish colored beard. A double-headed war axe was resting comfortably in his hands. "And before ye think of trying anything, me brothers have crossbows trained on ye."

Javin quickly looked around, but saw no one. He was going to respond to the dwarf when Gevi said, "Good Sir, we come in peace, bearing a message from Master Smith Thunderfall, my father."

"Well Lass, Gevi ye must be then. Ye fit the description me brothers have given of ye." The dwarf lowered his axe to the ground. "What be yer message, Lass?"

"My companion has a note from Master Thunderfall." As she spoke, Javin reached into his pack and pulled out the message written in flowing dwarven script. He walked forward and handed it to the dwarf. The dwarf spent half a minute looking through the note, before looking up and staring at Javin.

"Who be ye then, and who be yer father?"

"I am Javin, son of Lamar," Javin stammered to the dwarf, who continued to stare at him. After reading the message again, the dwarf lifted his arm and waved it over his head. As soon as his arm came down, ten dwarves stepped out from both sides of the road, cranking down and unloading crossbows.

The dwarves were between three and four feet tall, with long flowing beards. All wore shiny, metallic chain mail armor. Besides the crossbow, every dwarf carried a battle axe or a large war hammer.

"Follow me," said the dwarf as he turned and walked back toward the cave mouth. Gevi and Javin followed him to a campfire located between one of the buildings and the cliff face. Two other dwarves joined them. "Welcome and be seated, Gevi and Javin. I be Ironhand, and this be Smeltdown and Chiselrock." Ironhand pointed to the two other dwarves sitting with them. "Smeltdown will be taking ye into the old mine here in a wee bit."

Javin took out his note pad and started writing, ignoring the stares from the dwarves and the frown from Gevi. He wrote: "What are we going to be doing in the mine? Thunderfall gave me the note, but did not really explain anything else." He then handed the note pad over to the dwarf, named Ironhand.

"Sorry lad, I may speak yer language, but I cannot read it. Is this mountain air bothering yer throat? Smeltdown, go get the lad a..."

"Javin has a speech problem; that's all," Gevi cut in dryly, continuing to frown at Javin. "He seems to think people look down on him for it, so when he is nervous or anxious, he prefers to write." Gevi reached over and took the note pad from the dwarf, ignoring an embarrassed Javin. "He wants to know what Thunderfall's note says." The note pad went spiraling through the air, landing right in the fire. "I will buy you another one at the fort, if you really think you need the silly thing." Javin stared anxiously at his pad as flames covered the pages. "Believe me Javin; you are better off without it."

Javin sighed, "Your right, Gevi. I will try not to be so self-conscious of my speech from this day forward."

Ironhand gave a cough, causing Gevi and Javin to focus again on him. "Well lad, I can tell ye what the note said, but I am not sure it will help ye much, even though it tells us what we must do," Ironhand replied, ignoring the whole note pad thing. "It says; the boy is the dwarven nation's chance to pay its debt due his father, and personal debt owed by me, to Javin. Take him to the black rocks, 20 lbs. worth. DEBTS MUST BE PAID."

Javin sat quietly, until Ironhand broke the silence. "Whether ye know it or not, it is a great honor for me to represent the dwarves in clearing this debt; a great honor. Since yer the son of Lamar, the debt will be cleared that we owe yer father." He smiled beneath his bushy beard. "Chiselrock, go get everyone out of the bunkhouse. We have a lady staying the night with us." Chiselrock got up and walked around the building. "So Gevi, tell me what that old dwarf Thunderfall has been up to, as well as any news from Preveshawl."

Gevi briefly watched Chiselrock nervously, as he headed toward the doorway of the building behind them. She then cleared her voice and started filling the dwarves in on the news going on around the kingdom. Ironhand sat silently and listened, only occasionally asking questions. He leaned forward with interest when she got to the goblin attacks, exchanging looks with Smeltdown who was sitting by him. Finally, Gevi went silent.

"What is this debt owed to my father?" Javin asked. He could no longer contain his curiosity. The dwarves exchanged glances between each other again.

"Ye really don't know," Ironhand replied. Both Javin and Gevi shook their heads. "Well, I will tell ye then. Do ye know anything about the Ogre Invasions?"

"We heard the story a few weeks ago," responded Gevi.

"My story will start where Thunderfall and Lamar met up north of the..."

"Daddy was involved in the Ogre Invasions?" Gevi asked with astonishment.

"Aye Lass, he was leading the dwarven scout patrol that encountered Lamar and his scout patrol." Gevi was real interested in the story now. Thunderfall had never mentioned this part of his past to her. She motioned for Ironhand to continue with the story.

"Lamar learned from Thunderfall that the army of ogres and giants were not really interested in Preveshawl. The giant commander planned to go through the human fort so that his army would have an easier march, straight east to the dwarven homelands. They wanted the dwarven mines and its extensive wealth of metals for their own. The army planned to take the year digging out the dwarves, and then go for the elves the following year. It would be the third year before Preveshawl would be in any danger."

Ironhand paused for a second to make sure he had the young people's attention. "An argument broke out among the group that was with Lamar. They recognized that all they needed to do was retreat from the fort, allowing the ogres and the giants to advance east through the mountains to the dwarves. Preveshawl would then have three years to prepare. During that time, the dwarves and elves would kill many of the ogres and giants. By the third year, a fully prepared human army could meet the depleted ogre army."

"And the dwarves would have to face a full army at full strength, had they been allowed to march through the fort without a fight," commented Javin.

"Ye are right about that lad, and the dwarves knew this as well. Still, Thunderfall is typical of most dwarves. Tell the truth and let the consequences fall as they may. Expecting the humans to run from the monster army and leave the dwarves to face its full might, Thunderfall prepared his dwarves to start attacking supply lines, without help from the humans. However, Lamar had different thoughts. He called for quiet amongst his men and in a low, commanding voice; he informed them that while he was in command, they would fight with and for the dwarves. Their orders were to scout the area and cause havoc to the monster army, and that was exactly what they were going to do."

"That sounds like my father!" Javin said with a smile. "But how could an army of ogres stay together for three years? They are notorious for fighting among themselves."

"Right ye are; Preveshawl might never have been in real danger, with the exception of the fort guarding the pass. The army could have easily broken up after fighting either the dwarves or the elves. Lamar knew this as well. Instead of dwarves and humans going their separate ways, they joined as one force. The rest is history. Thunderfall and Lamar spied and planned for several days. After locating where the giant commander and the ogre chieftains slept, Thunderfall and his dwarves, along with Lamar and his men, infiltrated the camp."

Closing his eyes to the memories dancing in the flames, Ironhand continued. "Thunderfall slew the giant commander, while Lamar and the humans killed the five ogre chieftains. Most of the dwarves and many of the humans died that night in vicious fighting as they tried to sneak back out of the camp."

Ironhand went silent. For several minutes no one talked. Finally, the dwarf spoke up again. "The dwarves owed the humans a debt, for surely we would have lost thousands, along with our city and mines, if Lamar had not helped us. The debt to the humans has been paid in full with Thunderfall's duties as blacksmith at their fort. The army received ten years free services from Thunderfall. He only charged for material. The debt to your father, Javin, has never been repaid to our satisfaction." The dwarf gave a big smile, "That will be fixed tonight."

"Since Daddy satisfied the debt to the humans, why did he stay at the fort?" Gevi asked. As soon as she asked, her bright green eyes lit up and a "oh" escaped from her mouth. A shocked look covered her face. Gevi knew the answer as soon as she had asked it.

"The underground city is no place for a non-dwarven girl to grow up," Ironhand replied in a low voice. Several minutes of silence followed. Gevi struggled within herself with her thoughts.

"Javin, time ye get going to the old mine; Smeltdown will have everything ye need. Do exactly as he says. The metal you are getting is very fragile in its natural state. It has to be removed carefully from the stone. We will have a bit of a late supper for ye when ye get back." Smeltdown and Javin got up and headed for the mine entrance. "Gevi, I will show ye where ye will be staying. We have private rooms where a lady can stay in peace."

"You don't have to do that," Gevi replied. Javin paused, turning to look at Gevi. He could hear a strange touch of fear in her voice.

"Nope, won't have it," replied Ironhand. "No lady on my watch will be camping outside while the dwarves get bunks. Ye will have ye own private place tonight, unless ye and Javin are married..."

"No, we are friends; he's Dad's apprentice," Gevi cut in, her face turning bright red.

"Then ye get your own place; it won't kill the boys to sleep on the ground one night, now will it?" stated Ironhand. As Gevi came to the front of the building with Ironhand beside her, she saw two dwarves burst out the door. Fists were pounding on each other while they rolled around on the ground. The dwarf called Chiselrock finally broke away from the other dwarf and leaped to his feet.

"I said out, and I mean out!" Chiselrock yelled at the other dwarf. Javin had stopped over by the mine entrance, watching the two fighting dwarves. The other dwarves completely ignored the fight, including Smeltdown, who was busy unlocking the iron grill that covered the mine entrance. Both dwarves started to square off again until they saw Gevi and Ironhand standing a few feet from them. "Sorry miss," said Chiselrock, looking sheepish as he knocked dust out of his beard. "Flashfire and I were discussing what supplies we needed out of the house, before you move your stuff in. Right, Flashfire?"

"Humph," said Flashfire. He stood there glaring around.

"I think what Chiselrock is telling ye is that ye have thirty seconds to get yer stuff out," commented Ironhand with a frown on his face. "If ye aren't out in thirty seconds, oh second son of mine, I will drag ye out by yer beard and paddle yer posterior right in front of this lady. Thirty seconds starts now."

Flashfire glared at his father for a second before quickly running back into the building. Chiselrock looked up at Gevi, face red with embarrassment. Gevi started laughing, joined by Javin, standing by the cave entrance.

"We better get going," grumbled Smeltdown. Javin waved goodbye to Gevi before disappearing into the mine.

With his arms full of clothes, Flashfire came running out of the small building. At his appearance, Gevi covered her mouth to muffle the laughter. She looked back at Ironhand, whose eyes were flashing with anger, a stern look on his face.

"Ok me lady, go ahead and set yer stuff in yer room," the dwarf mumbled. "We will be over by the campfire, should ye wish to join us."

****

"We better get on back to the surface," Smeltdown said to Javin. They were standing in a large, open cavern, full of white stalagmites and stalactites. The whole cavern was lit up with a faint, greenish light, provided by glowing mushrooms that covered the floor of the cavern. Hairless creatures that looked like rabbits without the ears hopped around the seven-foot tall, glowing mushrooms. Their tongues constantly flicked in and out of their mouths, grabbing insects that buzzed around the mushrooms.

Javin enjoyed the mine and caves. Having walls close in on him with just enough light to see, along with the deathly silence, was strangely comforting to him. The only thing he did not like was the stagnant air that filled the cave.

Javin had chiseled out of the wall twenty pounds of a smooth, glass-like black rock. The rock was fragile as glass in its natural state, not hardening to the hardest metal known until it was introduced to fire. Following Smeltdown's directions on how to remove the rock from the wall without shattering was difficult, but Javin caught on fairly quickly.

"We dwarves can see fine in the dark without torches or these Illuminator Mushrooms, but let me show you a trick, in case you ever end up in one of these caves on your own." Smeltdown grabbed Javin's extinguished torch and walked over to one of the mushrooms. The dwarf proceeded to rub the end of the torch across the surface of the mushroom. He returned the torch to Javin. The end of the torch now glowed green, just like the mushrooms. "The Illuminator Mushroom secretes oil, which causes this greenish glow. Rub anything on it, and it will glow for several hours." Javin took the torch and followed Smeltdown back down the tunnel that led to the surface.

Smeltdown came to a stop at an intersection of tunnels. "See that dwarven mark on the upper right wall of that side tunnel?" Smeltdown was pointing to a dwarven mark that was a triangle inside a circle. "That mark means danger. Never go down a tunnel if you see that mark. A lot of tunnels and caverns down here are not controlled by the dwarves. Many strange creatures, nastier than anything on the surface, can be found down here. This tunnel is considered safe for a mile or so, but past that, it gets dangerous."

The words had just left his mouth when the dwarf flew backwards, crashing into the tunnel wall. Both swords flew from Javin's belt and into his hands. Smeltdown was covered by milky, white strings, which had him stuck fast to the wall.

"Run, Javin!" screamed Smeltdown as he struggled in vain to free himself. Javin took a step toward the entrapped dwarf, when a gigantic spider crawled out of the intersecting tunnel. Its hairy face, with beady black eyes, turned to face Javin. Mandibles like two swords, clacked together hungrily. The spider spun and fired a web from its posterior toward Javin. The web splattered against the wall, missing Javin who rolled sideways.

With Smeltdown trapped in the spider web, Javin did not have time to think. Rolling back to his feet, he charged right toward the giant spider that had spun back around to face him. Two claws from the monstrous spider reached toward him. Both of Javin's swords flashed forward, cutting deep into the claws. Mandibles clacked as the spider shrilled in pain. Icky, black blood sprayed out from the damaged front claws.

The spider hissed and rushed at Javin. Mandibles above his head came down hard towards him. Javin saw his chance, probably the only chance he would get with this monster. He slid feet first under the spider as razor sharp mandibles bit toward his head. Both swords flashed upward into the soft underbelly. Moving forward underneath the spider, Javin ripped his swords through the spider's belly. Icky, foul liquid sprayed all over him. He quickly exited his position under the spider before the body could fall on top of him. The spider squealed, twisting and turning several times, before falling to the ground, dead.

****

Later on in the evening, Javin joined Gevi and the dwarves near the fire, after cleaning up from the spider fight. Smeltdown had just finished telling the story of Javin and the spider for a second time as he sat down. Gevi shook her head while giving him a smile. Ironhand had apologized over and over to Javin, embarrassed about putting his guest into harm's way. Javin learned that these giant spiders were called Kilk Spiders. Before now, the dwarves had no idea they were up in this part of the mine. Ironhand promised that the dwarves would eradicate the spiders over the next couple of weeks.

Javin sat a little more than five feet from Gevi, but while eating supper, he started slowly moving closer toward her. Once he was three or so feet from her, Gevi slid over to sit right up against him.

"You don't have to be so terrified of me. I only bite early in the morning." She gave him a pat on the knee with her hand before facing a dwarf telling the tale of Thiacon, the giant scorpion rumored to live deep in the underground caverns. Javin felt his face go flush with embarrassment. He moved his hands behind his back, hiding the fact they were shaking like a leaf in the winter wind.

The dwarves were a very rowdy group, at times arguing to the point of an all-out brawl breaking out. Ironhand would resettle the group, only to have them laughing and hugging minutes later. To Javin, the dwarves seemed to be a spirited and fun-loving bunch. Finally, Ironhand stood up and waved for silence.

"The dwarves have a custom, to do a reading of *The Guide* before going to bed. As our guest, would either of ye like to do the reading? Our Guide is in dwarven, so ye would have to read out of *The Guide* ye have."

Javin looked at Gevi sheepishly, hoping she would do the reading. Public speaking only made his stammering worse. It was something he avoided at all cost. Gevi caught his gaze and rolled her eyes, "I will do the reading. Do you have *The Guide* on you?"

Javin got up from beside Gevi and removed *The Guide* from his pack. Returning to Gevi, he plopped back down on the ground beside her, handing her his copy of *The Guide*. "Didn't bring yours, I see," he said while smiling nervously at her.

"Quiet, or I will make you do the reading," she replied with a hint of agitation in her voice.

"You know you should never go anywhere without..."

"Here you go; read away," Gevi snapped. She put the book forcefully in his lap, and crossed her arms.

"Are ye sure that ye aren't married?" interjected Ironhand. "Ye act like old, married, dwarves."

Gevi jumped to her feet, anger clearly showing in her flashing eyes, "Stop your teasing, Master Ironhand," she said in a calm voice, pointing her finger right at the dwarf sitting across the fire, "before I put ye over me knees and give ye a spanking ye will not ever forget, right in front of yer second born son. Ye have thirty seconds to apologize. Thirty seconds starts now!"

In absolute silence, the dwarves stared at Gevi, while her finger pointed at Ironhand and her eyes flashed. Silence turned into snorts. Then, all the dwarves started hooting, hollering, and rolling around on the ground. Javin started laughing too, so hard his sides started hurting. Gevi glared at the dwarves around the fire before sitting down in a huff.

"And what do you think you are laughing at?" She asked, fixing her glare on Javin. She grabbed *The Guide* from his hands, demanding an answer from him with her eyes. Though he tried not to, Javin met her gaze and started laughing even harder. He did however; notice a smile cross her face, which she quickly hid.

"Whoa, Lassie," said a gasping Ironhand, "ye made yer point." He burst out laughing again. "I won't tease ye or the lad anymore." After several minutes of Ironhand being teased by the other laughing dwarves, Ironhand finally got them to quiet down. Gevi let the smile on her face show once again. She started reading from *The Guide*. Her crystal clear voice brought to life the words of *The Guide*.

"In the beginning was the Word, and the Word was with God, and the Word was God. He was with God in the beginning. Through him all things were made; without him nothing was made that has been made. In him was life, and that life was the light of all mankind. The light shines in the darkness, and the darkness has not overcome it."

****

It was hard for Javin to fall asleep that night. Not only was the temperature cool up here in the mountains, but the dwarves snored like bulls. He couldn't understand why Gevi had opened the window facing him and the dwarves, or why she had pulled a bed up to the window. It would seem with the snoring and the cold air that she would want the window closed. After several hours of dwarven snoring keeping him awake, he finally fell into a deep sleep.

"WAKE UP," spoke a voice to Javin, bringing him instantly wide awake. Completely confused, he lay there for several minutes staring up into a night sky full of stars. With only a quarter of the lesser moon giving off significant light, the darkness felt very deep, and an uneasy feeling was growing in Javin. Jumping to his feet and clearing his mind, Javin knew what he had to do.

****

On stage in front of the audience of school children, Chellell held out her right hand, slowly lifting one of her dancers off the ground with magic as the dancer moved in a rhythmic dance. Her hand then spun in a circle, spinning the dancing woman out above the audience of school children. The children's eyes looked skyward at the beautiful woman moving and twisting in the air above them.

Alone, Chellell actually could not do this for very long, but one of her magic assistants, Kyle, was hidden behind the side of the stage. He was providing the extra magical power needed to move the dancing lady around above the children. Chellell could hear the "ooh's" and "ah's" coming from the children. She used her magic to help circle the dancer around the outside arena a few times, avoiding the far back left side of the arena as instructed by Licheaon, the director of operations. The actress swung back above the stage, going into a blur of twists and spins off to the side of Chellell's out stretched hands. As soon as the actress's feet touched the stage, a bright explosion flashed above her head, booming out into the audience. The second magic assistant, Draden was doing the lights and fireworks. The children absolutely loved it. Clapping and shouting filled Chellell's ears.

"You children are so sweet; thank you so much," Chellell said, using a minor air spell to carry her voice across the arena where she was performing at the City of the Guilds. The curtains came down behind her, leaving her alone in front of the audience. Even though most of the children looked excited, she couldn't help but notice that several children looked like they were sick. A guard had even picked up one child that had passed out. Chellell brushed any concerns that came to her mind away, deciding that some minor illness must be going around.

"Please welcome Master Magician Kyle and his lovely assistant Dryana. Keep an eye on him, boys and girls," she whispered, her magically enhanced voice carrying the whisper to the audience. "Some of the things he will show you, you too can do with a little bit of meditation and practice. I will be back once he is done." Suddenly, an earsplitting bang filled the air, with smoke rising up in a column around Chellell, or where Chellell used to be. Everyone gasped. Chellell vanished, in a puff of smoke, right in front of their eyes.

Chellell felt her magic connection with Sanatarial vanish and the magic power drain from her body after she reappeared behind the curtain. Weariness overcame her, and her head started to ache as it always did when she used magic. Her headaches always came with a feeling that something extremely evil was nearby. She brushed this feeling away, blaming it on nerves. Besides, she thought to herself, there really is no good or evil. Like the headaches, she thought, it must be her body trying to get used to something foreign to it.

"Come on, Chellell. You need to get your make-up and hair fixed for the finale," said Draden, who was standing right next to her. He had helped her teleport back behind the curtain. "Lily will be waiting for you." Chellell was exhausted and her head hurt. Still, she rushed out the back of the stage, to a tent where Lily worked her own kind of magic.

****

At a small table in a tent he used as his personal office, Licheaon barely glanced up as a guard walked through the door. Licheaon continued his work of sorting through a pile of cards, ignoring the guard. After several minutes, he took all the cards and placed them in a large envelope along with a note. "Take this to Captain Janisk in the palace," Licheaon told the guard while holding out the envelope. "He will be in the north guard tower and is expecting you."

"Yes sir," replied the guard as he took the envelope from Licheaon. As he was about to step out of the tent, Kyle walked in through the entrance. The guard let Kyle pass before going out into the night, heading for the palace.

"How many names did we end up with?" asked Kyle while pulling up the only other chair in the tent. He sat across the table from Licheaon.

"A couple of dozen children, a handful of soldiers, but only three civilian adults," replied Licheaon who sat back from the table and focused his full attention on Kyle.

Kyle lazily looked around the tent before speaking. "The adults are old enough to know the effect magic has on them. The soldiers as well, but

73

they were ordered to attend the show. The children were easy to reach; the schools forced them to attend the show, without informing the parents. They do not yet realize that the sickness they feel is from magic."

"Chancellor White's idea to use the children to find the parents was brilliant," commented Licheaon. "The new school is already set up, so that we can re-educate them. While he does not have much hope for the adults, Chancellor White thinks most of the children can be properly re-educated."

Thoughtful for a minute, Kyle asked, "What about Chellell?"

"The only thing Chellell knows is that the magic detectors are making sure that no one with magical aversions gets too close to the stage, and that they are separated out to our predetermined spot in the back of the crowds. That explanation makes sense to her. She is aware that magic does not work around certain types of people."

Kyle paused again in thought. "You know Licheaon; I think we should let her in on everything else. She has proven she can be trusted with..."

"The girl knows enough already and is certainly not ready for more." The words appeared in both their minds simultaneously. Sanatarial flew in through the entrance and landed on the table. He proceeded to curl up on the table, resting comfortably. "She is fast asleep." His words again appeared in their heads, letting them know where Chellell was before they could even form the question.

"I have more work to do on her," hissed the dragon, not using the mental communication anymore. "The longer someone is influenced by the ancient religion of the Lord of the Stars and its writings, the longer it takes for that person to give themselves over to our truths. Some get so indoctrinated, that they literally radiate a spiritual defense that magic cannot penetrate. That is the aversion to magic that you see. That is why, for the good of Preveshawl, humans must get rid of *The Guide*, and with that, their beliefs in super powerful, fantasy gods, that live in the sky. This show was designed to find those that are indoctrinated."

Licheaon nodded, he discussed this very thing with the Chancellor White months ago. Plans for this show and for what was to come, were laid in motion then, with the king's full support. "Soon, we will see *The Guide* and followers of the Lord of the Stars removed from Preveshawl," thought Licheaon to himself.

****

The farmer jumped out of bed, the loud crashing noise coming from the common area waking him up instantly. He ran into the room, thinking the old tree near the doorway must have fallen on the house. He froze upon entering the common area, where all five children slept. Several creatures he knew to be gorms, stood in the doorway. The door was on the floor in several pieces. On their sleeping mats, the children were staring up at the gorms, frozen with fear.

"Get dressed. Get family dressed. You go with us. You go, or you die. You choose," grunted one of the gorms, struggling to speak the language of the humans. Gorm weapons were drawn. The farmer saw that the gorms meant business. He felt his wife behind him, her hands trembling with terror on his shoulder.

"Kids, do as he says," the farmer told his children, his mind searching for some way out of this. "Get your outdoor clothes on, and your shoes, also..."

"Try anything human, and you die. Five minutes you got." A few minutes later, a farmer, his wife, and five children were being led by two of the gorms, up into the mountains. Every hour or so, they were allowed to stop and rest for a few minutes. During one such rest, they were joined by more people, being led by gorms, up into the mountains.

****

Ledia woke up in the middle of the night. Mac was in the bed beside her, snoring away. Kitty was not on the floor at the foot of the bed, the place he typically stayed at night. She grabbed her red jewel headband off the bed's headboard. A graduate from the Guild of Nature, Ledia was tuned in with Kitty, and she used that power now to reach the Great Northern Tiger. She could sense that Kitty was close by, in the main room. A rush of agitation and anger came to her from Kitty, causing Ledia to sit up in the bed.

"Mac, Mac," she whispered while repeatedly hitting him on the arm, "Mac, get up."

"Huh. What? I'm not snoring," he groaned while opening his eyes barely enough to see her sitting up beside him.

"Wake up! Something is..."

A noisy crash came from the living area, followed by an ear-splitting yowl of a tiger. Screams could be heard as Mac leaped out of bed and grabbed his sword hanging on the wall. He was in the main room within seconds. A gorm was laid up against the wall, thrown there by the Great Northern Tiger. It would never bother anyone again. Another gorm was on the floor, dead at Kitty's feet. Two more gorms stood in the doorway. One was wildly stabbing a spear at the tiger, while the second held a long, and wicked looking, two-handed sword. As Kitty jumped back from the spear, Mac leaped forward, bringing his sword down hard across the shaft of the spear. An audible crack could be heard as the spear splintered in half. He quickly reversed his sword swing back up, blocking the gorm's sword just inches from his head. His foot kicked straight out, into the stomach of the sword-wielding gorm. Pain showed on the gorm's face. The second gorm dropped his broken spear and ran out of the house, leaving his companion alone to face an enraged tiger, and an experienced fighter.

Mac started mixing swings and thrust, which the gorm fought to deflect while it backed out the doorway, and onto the porch. When the gorm went to block a thrust at its stomach, Mac shifted his sword left in a sudden swing. The tip of the sword cut into the gorm's arm at the wrist,

75

slicing all the way up to the elbow. The gorm screamed, its sword falling to the floor at its feet. Mac's sword flashed in, stabbing into the gorm's neck. When the gorm fell, Mac felt Kitty brush by him, as the tiger leaped out into the night, quickly disappearing. Within a few seconds, a gorm's scream, mixed with a tiger's roar, filled the night.

"Kitty got the runner," thought Mac, spinning around to head into the house to check on Ledia. Instead, she was standing on the porch behind him, bow resting in her arms.

"Kitty is searching the area for more of them," Ledia said to her husband, knowing what he was going to ask. "So far he has not picked up the scent of any more gorms." Ledia embraced her husband for several long seconds, shaken by the gorms attacking her home and relieved her husband was not hurt in the fight.

"Get your gear on, Dear; we need to check on Thunderfall and Gevi." Mac said as he gently released his wife and started to head through the doorway.

Ledia quickly stepped in front of Mac, stopping his advance. "Get those dead gorms out of my house," she said in a shaky voice. "I sent Kitty over to Thunderfall's place. We will know if they are in trouble in a couple of minutes." She turned and headed for the bedroom.

In astonishment, Mac stood watching Ledia disappear down the hall toward the bedroom. "So that's where Gevi gets it," he thought angrily to himself, remembering the goblin attack. Realizing he had better hurry, he quickly dragged the gorms out of the house.

"She will probably make me clean up the mess as well," he thought while rushing back into the house. In the bedroom, Ledia had his armor and weapons belt lying on the bed.

"You can clean the mess up later," Ledia said to him. She was putting on the last of her green leather armor. Mac rolled his eyes and made his way to the bed, quickly getting into his armor. "Kitty says Thunderfall is on his way to our house, but neither Gevi nor Javin are with him. He has not smelled any more gorms. All is clear."

"Why would gorms try to come into our house?" Mac asked while strapping on his weapon belt. "There haven't been gorms on this side of the wall in over a decade."

"In the past, they have always attacked in huge numbers. Four would never attack a single house on their own," replied Ledia.

"Very true," thought Mac. He reached up and took a large bow and a quiver full of arrows off the wall. Out loud he said, "Ready? Let's go meet Thunderfall."

Chapter 7

Fear thou not; for I am with thee: be not dismayed; for I am thy God. – The Guide

A bleary-eyed Gevi stood with the door cracked open. "The building better be on fire," she mumbled half asleep. She had one of the worse cases of "bed head" Javin had ever seen. Her hair was sticking out in every direction.

"Sorry Gevi. We have to go, now!" Even half asleep, Gevi could see he was on edge, over something. She stared at him for a second, her mind confused from being awakened from her deep sleep.

"Be out in a minute," she finally said as she closed the door.

"What's wrong?" Javin nearly jumped out of his skin, he was so tense. Turning around, he saw one of the dwarf guards standing a few feet behind him.

"Something is wrong. We have to leave now." The dwarf nodded to Javin before walking over to the dwarves that were sleeping around the campfire. Javin paced and circled around in front of the door. Finally, the door opened and Gevi walked out, staff in hand and ready to go. Javin saw that her hair had been fixed and was back in place.

"You could have woken me up through the window you know, instead of beating the door down." Gevi said with agitation.

"I know, it's just I was..."

"What's going on, Lad?" interrupted Ironhand. "I was having me a right beautiful dream, till the guard woke me up."

"We have to go now. We can come back later for the black rocks," stammered Javin. "I want to thank..."

"Tell me what happened, Lad. Did one of me brothers..."

"No sir," stuttered Javin, "It is strange, but a voice in my head woke me up. Something is wrong. I strongly feel that we need to go, and go quickly."

Ironhand looked at Gevi, who shrugged her shoulders at him. "Give me five minutes." He turned and walked back to the campfire without waiting for Javin to agree. "Everybody up," he roared, "full armor, full weapons, marching in five." Javin watched in amazement as every dwarf sprang up. It seemed complete chaos while a dozen dwarves ran around grabbing supplies, dressing in armor, and getting their axes or hammers. In slightly less than five minutes, they were standing in a square formation in front of the building, with Ironhand in front.

"Smeltdown, get the black rocks for Javin. Carry them with ye at the rear of the formation." Gevi moved out of the doorway to let Smeltdown enter and get the sack of black rocks. "Chiselrock, ye and Smashgum scout ahead on the trail going to the meadow the kids came up on." Both dwarves left the formation and ran down the trail. Ironhand called out two other dwarves, ordering them to stay and guard the old abandoned mine. "March," he commanded. Dwarven feet pounded the trail as dwarves started marching in perfect unison down the trail. Gevi and Javin fell in behind the dwarves with Smeltdown marching behind them.

"I hope I am not wrong about this," Javin told Gevi.

"Actually, I hope you are wrong." She said, looking at him and seeing the tenseness in his body.

****

After two hours, one of the scouts came back up the trail and whispered something to Ironhand, who dismissed him, back down the trail. "They found two gorms back-tracking ye up the trail." Ironhand said as he came to stand by Javin. "They took them both out, but we are going to slow down a wee bit. Looks like ye were right, something is wrong. I haven't seen gorms on this side of the mountain in decades."

"How far are we from the meadow?" asked Gevi.

"Maybe an hour," replied Ironhand. "Stay as quiet as possible from this point on."

Close to an hour later, one of the scouts returned and again, whispered something to Ironhand. After a brief discussion with the scout, Ironhand and the scout disappeared down the trail. Taking a much needed rest, Javin and Gevi sat down. The rest of the dwarves fanned out in a small circle around the area. Half an hour passed before Ironhand abruptly appeared. He gathered the group together on the trail, squatted down in the middle of the group, and began drawing a circle shape in the dirt at his feet.

"Ok boys, here is what we got. This here be the meadow, and it is full of gorms. Close to a hundred, I would guess. Don't look like they be staying long either, they're not set up to camp. On the edge of the meadow here," he made two marks with an X on the edge of the circle, representing the meadow, "is a group of humans, close to the same number as the gorms. They be men, women, and children; whole families. Women and children here, and a hundred or so feet away are the men. A dozen gorms be guarding the men, with half that, for the women and children."

"Why would they..." whispered Gevi, but Ironhand cut her off.

"Not sure why they have captured the humans, or why they be separated, but we have no time to discuss it if we want to help them. Now, here is what we are going to do. There be only ten of us dwarves and two humans. We will not be able to take the gorms, so we must try to free as many of the humans as possible. We will have to use a combination of confusion and subterfuge."

"Javin, Gevi, I would like ye both to return to the mine," Ironhand said as he fixed his eyes on Gevi. "This is going to be extremely dangerous."

Javin shook his head "no", as Gevi stepped up beside him. "I could not live with myself, knowing I ran while others needed my help." Javin said. Gevi nodded her head toward Ironhand while grabbing Javin's arm, showing her agreement with Javin.

"Spoken like a true dwarf," Ironhand replied. It was clear in his expression that his respect for Javin and Gevi had just increased. "With this many gorms, we are going to need all the help we can get."

"Tubnose, stay by Gevi at all times, and protect the lass. I don't need to remind ye she is Thunderfall's daughter." Ironhand gave a hard look at one of the more powerfully built dwarves. Tubnose pulled a steel war hammer off his back that was as long as the dwarf was tall, before moving over to stand behind Gevi. Gevi started to protest, but Ironhand cut her off. "Ye can be a big help, Gevi, but I will not risk Thunderfall's wrath. If anything happens to ye, your dad will have me hide." Ironhand fixed his gaze on Gevi's staff.

"Is that the marvel of engineering lightning staff, we dwarves have heard tales of?" Ironhand asked. Gevi nodded her head in affirmation. "Good, here is the quick and dirty plan. Gevi, Javin, and five of me brothers, will go around the meadow like this, till ye reach the edge where everyone is being held."

Ironhand proceeded to point out five dwarves. "Ye will try to rescue the humans as quickly, and most important, as quietly as possible. Start with the women and children. Get them going down this trail," he drew a little trail near to where the holding area was. "That's the trail that will lead back to Thunderfall's shop. Take the guards out as needed, but do it quietly. Darkness will be on our side. Chiselrock will be in charge of this group."

"The second group, I will lead. We are going to sneak around to the other side of the meadow. At some point they will notice that guards are missing, or humans are missing. Then, Gevi will blast a gorm with that staff. When we hear the blast, we will attack from our side of the meadow. Once that happens, the confusion should draw most of the gorms toward us. Once my group engages the gorms, you will only have a few minutes before we will be forced to retreat. That should give you enough time to take out any gorms in your way and get the remaining humans to safety. Any questions?"

It was silent for several long seconds. "Ok boys, a quick prayer, then we go."

"Girls too," piped in Gevi.

Ironhand gave her a smile. "Lasses too, he agreed." Everyone bowed their head in prayer.

****

Javin hid behind some large bushes, with Gevi and Chiselrock beside him. Clouds had rapidly rolled in, causing a light sprinkle of cold rain to fall. The lesser moon and most of the stars were hidden behind the clouds, making the night nearly pitch black. Javin could see nothing, but neither could the gorms. The dwarves were at a great advantage now, being able to see clearly in the dark of the night. Out of the darkness near Javin, a dwarf appeared, dragging a gorm behind him.

"This is not how dwarves fight," Chiselrock whispered toward Javin with disgust. "We crush our enemy with strength and force. Only because of the captive humans do we kill quietly." As Chiselrock finished speaking,

79

two gorm guards disappeared into the grass. "That's the two guards on this side; we need to start rescuing the women." He turned his gaze toward Javin. "Go ahead; we will cover your back."

Javin came out from behind the bush. Under the cover of darkness, he quickly slipped in among the women and children. Spotting a woman holding two children by their hands standing a few feet from him, he reached out and tapped her gently on the shoulder. She turned and saw him, eyes growing big. He quickly signaled her to be silent. "Stand over by that bush," he whispered to her. "We are getting everyone out of here. Stay quiet and don't do anything suspicious." The women nodded and led the children over by the bush Javin had pointed out.

Javin quickly moved three more mothers with their seven children over by the same bush. Others had noticed him, so he took the time to tell one of the women to have everyone else wait and not do anything suspicious. He would come back for them in a little bit. An idea came to him. He whispered further instructions to one of the women. She nodded her agreement. Javin had everyone he gathered slip behind the bushes and out of the meadow, one family at a time.

"Follow me," he stuttered quietly to them once they were together behind the bushes, "and be as quiet as possible. Try to keep the children from crying." He then took off for the trail that led down to Thunderfall's house. As soon as he started for the trail, a wailing and screaming came from the area behind them where the women were held. Smiling to himself, Javin knew the screaming from the woman would cover any sound the children following him were making.

Reaching the trail that Gevi and Javin used from Thunderfall's shop, Javin stopped the group he was leading. "Follow the trail down as quickly as you can. I know it will be hard for the children, but move as fast as you can. We will be getting everyone, including the men. They will be following you down. It took me four hours with a horse to get here, so it will be well into the morning before you reach Thunderfall's shop. May God's blessing be on you all." After several grateful hugs and questions about their captive men folk, the women quickly disappeared down the trail. Turning around, he went back to the meadow.

"We had to take out another gorm. Better hurry and get a second group," Chiselrock commented as Javin slid in beside him and Gevi. "Nice move, getting the woman to scream; I could barely hear the crying children you had with you." Javin had asked her to stop after ten minutes, and she had. Javin smiled over at Gevi, and she promptly returned it. Her dazzling smile showed her confidence in him, melting the terror away Javin felt inside. Turning back toward the meadow, he slipped back in among the women. A few minutes later, he led another group of fifteen out toward the trail.

"One more trip, then we are going to have to start taking the rest of the guards out, so that you can get the last of the women moving," Chiselrock said as Javin returned. "Thank the Lord of the Stars for this rain and clouds; this darkness is absolutely a God send."

"What about the men?" Javin asked, looking over to where the men were being held. He could see nothing but pitch black darkness.

"Good point." The dwarf sat back in thought. "Get the next group of women started. Then I will have one of my brothers take them to the trail. We will have you get the rest of the women quickly after that. Then we go for the men."

Javin nodded his understanding and slipped back in among the women. The rain started to come down even harder, making it even more difficult to see anything. Javin was leading the third group of women with children into the bushes when one of the gorm guards walked over close enough to see them escaping. A crossbow bolt streaked through the blackness of night, hitting the gorm dead center in the neck. He dropped before a sound could be made.

"Change of plans. Get all the women; now!" Chiselrock said urgently once he was beside Javin. "We are going to take out the last of the guards any minute now. It is too dangerous to wait any longer."

Javin saw the last of the gorms go down as dwarves jumped them from behind. He quickly got every woman and child together and led them behind the bush and out of the meadow. One of the dwarves led them away as he, Chiselrock, Gevi, along with her bodyguard Tubnose, silently crept over to the men's captive area. They joined two other dwarves lying flat on the ground, concealed in darkness a few feet from the men.

"Javin, I want you to sneak in with the men. Have all of them ready to run when they see lightning from Gevi's staff." Chiselrock motioned for Javin to go. He jumped up, joining in the middle of a small group of captive men, sitting down several feet from the hiding dwarves.

"Everybody quiet," he whispered as he lowered himself to the ground, sitting with them. All eyes instantly fixed on Javin. "We are here to rescue you. Pass the word to every man that as soon as you see a lightning blast, get moving in that direction." Javin pointed off toward the bushes he had come from. "A dwarf will guide you and set you on your way. Tell everyone to stay together."

"They counted us," hissed a man in a low whisper, "and informed us a human female or child would be executed for every male that turned up missing."

"All the women and children are moving down the mountain as we speak," Javin stuttered back. "They can't execute anybody now." Hushed, excited whispers started spreading through the captives. Javin waited a few minutes so word could spread, before slipping back out to join Gevi and the Dwarves.

"Ok, brothers, get your crossbows ready. We got a dozen guards to take out as fast as possible. I want you to get as close as you can to the guards without being detected. However, stay at least ten feet from the gorms so you don't get blasted by Gevi's lightning staff. As soon as the lightning goes off, fire crossbows and then draw axes to attack." The two dwarves crawled out into the meadow, disappearing into the darkness. They waited, giving the departed dwarves a chance to get into position.

Above them, the clouds uncovered the moon, letting its light shine down on the meadow. Javin and Gevi could now see further into the meadow. Meanwhile, a gorm ran up to a group of guards now illuminated, pointing excitedly over to the area where the women used to be. At that moment, the dwarf that led the last group of women to the trail returned.

"You get to guide the men now," Chiselrock said to the returning dwarf, as he leveled a crossbow on the gorm guards. "Fire at will, Gevi."

Gevi stood up, pointing her staff at the group of five gorms gathered together. Javin came up behind her, drawing both swords as Gevi's fingers danced over the buttons on her staff. Lightning flew from the staff, lighting up the meadow. It was followed instantly by a deafening boom that echoed through the mountains. The gorm in the middle of the group took a direct hit, but all five gorms were blown several feet through the air. Javin and Chiselrock ran toward the gorms that Gevi had blasted, but several captive men beat them there. They took the gorm swords, finishing off the only two that had survived Gevi's blast. Javin looked around and saw the rest of the men disappearing out of the meadow. At the same time, he heard dwarven battle cries from across the meadow, mixed with the high-pitched screams of the gorms.

"Get going!" Chiselrock yelled at the men who had taken up the gorm swords as he pointed toward the area where the rest of the men were leaving the meadow. The men shook their heads, preparing to stay and fight. "There are too many gorms to fight; we are only going to distract them until you have a chance to escape. Then we are going to retreat back up into the mountains." The humans acknowledged their understanding to the dwarf before running across the meadow toward the last of the escaping men.

Javin turned and sprinted toward a gorm that was closing in on the escaping men. Before he could strike, the gorm stumbled and fell to the ground. Chiselrock's crossbow bolt was sticking out of the middle of the gorm's back.

Javin continued to search the area, looking for gorms. In the darkness and the rain, he had a difficult time seeing anything. The dwarves across the meadow were really making quite a racket, drawing most of the gorms their direction. Suddenly, three gorms with swords drawn came out of the darkness into Javin's field of view. Before he could even think, he charged toward them with both swords spinning in his hand. The front gorm deflected Javin's left sword with his own sword. Javin's right sword went right into his side at the armpit, a place not protected by chain mail armor. Javin's left sword spun away from the dying gorm's sword to deflect a stab from another gorm. He twisted his body, causing the gorm sword to continue its momentum past him. The twist continued, bringing his right sword full speed into the side of the creature's head. The gorm's helmet cracked in half from the force of the blow, dropping the gorm straight to the ground. Javin finished his spin by crossing both swords in front of him, catching the sword of the last gorm.

The whole meadow again lit up with a flash, allowing Javin to see the utter hatred on the face of his opponent. While the boom filled the air from Gevi's second lightning blast, Javin stepped sideways, allowing the gorm's momentum to push both his swords to the ground. Both of Javin's swords parted and flashed upward, before the gorm could react. Two short swords whacked the gorm in the chin. The impact sent the gorm's helmet spinning up into the air. The creature was on the ground dead before its helmet came back down, bouncing across the grassy meadow.

Javin could not see any more gorms in the blackness, but he could hear the sounds of screams and fighting everywhere. He quickly decided to head toward the closest sound of fighting.

"I'll cut you up and use you for fish bait," Javin heard Chiselrock taunt. Within seconds, Javin came upon Chiselrock and another dwarf fighting at least ten gorms. They were backing up while ferociously deflecting gorm swords. The two dwarves were being surrounded. Sprinting forward, Javin lunged with both swords, stabbing into two gorms from behind. He felt one sword go in, fatally injuring the gorm. The second sword bounced away, deflected by the gorm's armor. Feeling the blow to his armor, the gorm spun with his sword coming around hard at Javin. He managed to leap backwards, but his feet tripped over a gorm body. Javin crashed hard, flat on his back. Air flew out of his lungs, and for a split second, he lay on the ground stunned.

Realizing the danger he was in, he willed his arms to move. One sword he flung across his body, the other sword he stabbed upward. A gorm sword slammed into his sword that was across his chest. Pain exploded into his chest. Javin heard the audible crack of his ribs. His sword had blocked the gorm's sword from cutting into him, but the sheer force of the blow had cracked his ribs. A great weight fell on him, dragging his second sword from his hand, and causing excruciating pain to shoot through his chest. A gorm body was now on top of him with Javin's second sword that he had stabbed upwards, driven all the way through the creature.

Trying to twist free, he realized that two gorms stood over him. Flashing a wicked smile, one of them raised his sword, preparing a killing blow. Javin could feel his heart trying to beat out of his chest. Trapped beneath the dead gorm, Javin knew that this was the end. He could not escape.

Suddenly, both gorms flew backwards. Something massive flew through the air, right over Javin's prone body, smashing into the gorms. A tiger yowl erupted through the darkness of night. Javin thanked the Lord of the Stars while rolling out from under the dead gorm. While straining to pull his sword out of the gorm, another flash filled the meadow. In the light, Javin saw a vicious tiger flinging a gorm through the air.

"Havel, havel, havel," the gorms screamed from every direction.

Javin pulled his sword free, but was almost bowled over when a gorm rushed by him. The gorm continued to run full speed into the darkness. A tiger's roar filled the night air again, followed by the scream of a gorm. Javin gingerly started to move back toward the area where he last knew Gevi to be. He heard gorms screaming "havel", mixed with tiger yowls echoing through the mountains.

"They are retreating. 'Havel' is gorm for 'retreat'," a dwarf told Javin. Behind the dwarf, Javin saw Gevi walking towards him, her staff slung across her back and bow in hand. Tubnose was beside her, scanning around for gorms. Javin gave a sigh of relief once he saw that she was unhurt.

"I hope that blood is not yours, "commented Gevi with a worried expression. Javin looked down, only to see gorm blood covering his shirt.

"Thanks to Kitty, none of it is mine," replied a grateful Javin.

Relief showed on Gevi's face. She turned, looking around the meadow. Fast moving clouds were covering and then uncovering the moon. When moonlight did show, Gevi saw that the meadow was rapidly clearing of gorms.

"Kitty! Here Kitty," Gevi called out. She continued to call for Kitty as a torch light appeared in the middle of the meadow, lighting up a group of dwarves.

"Everyone, gather over here," Ironhand yelled. Kitty picked that moment to show up, bounding toward Gevi.

"Good Kitty! You are such a good tiger," Gevi cooed to Ledia's pet while he rubbed against her and purred. She rubbed her hand lovingly over his head. "Good Kitty."

Javin gave the tiger a pat on his muscled back. Tubnose didn't say a word, but he kept a careful eye on the Great Northern Tiger. They started carefully walking toward Ironhand and the dwarves gathered in the middle of the meadow.

Nursing a slight limp, Gevi saw Javin holding his chest as he walked. "Are you hurt?"

"I'm fine. It's just a badly bruised chest," he grimaced. Talking made his chest hurt even more. She didn't say anything else to him until they joined Ironhand and the dwarves.

"I have some healing elixir," volunteered Gevi as she and Javin joined the dwarves.

"Already taken care of, but thank ye lass," replied Ironhand pointing absently toward the ground where two other dwarves were already fast asleep. His eyes however, remained fixed on Kitty. "What in the world you got there girl?"

"This is Kitty; he lives with a family next to the smithy." Kitty fell to the ground, rolling onto his back with paws in the air. "He loves a good belly rubbing." She knelt down by the tiger and proceeded to rub his belly. A loud purring came from the tiger, who was obviously enjoying himself.

Ironhand shook his head in disbelief, staring down at the tiger.

"That thing scared me to death. I never heard anything like that before. It froze me blood right in the middle of combat."

"If he is here, then Mac and Ledia must be nearby as well. Thunderfall may be with them," stammered Javin; wincing as he talked.

"What's wrong with...?"

"He took a blow to the chest," Gevi said, interrupting Ironhand. "Get your shirt off and let me have a look." Javin obliged, wincing while she poked him and felt along his ribs. "A couple of cracked ribs, but none are broken. The healing elixir should work since nothing is broken. I think we should wait and have Ledia check you out. She is a better healer than I am." Once again, the clouds cleared, allowing moonlight to flood the meadow.

As if on cue, Thunderfall and Ledia walked into the meadow. Gevi jumped up and ran to Thunderfall, hugging him tightly. They stood there, holding each other, while Ledia continued on toward the group of dwarves. As soon as she arrived, the rain slowed down to a misty dribble. Kitty stayed on his back, paws in the air.

"Sorry we couldn't get here sooner," she said with a sad expression on her face as she glanced at a single dead dwarf under a cloth. The dwarves had paid a high price to rescue the humans.

Ironhand noticed her looking at the deceased dwarf. "Aye, he was a good dwarf. He is now with the Lord of the Stars, free from the worries of this life," the dwarf said sadly. He took his eyes off the body, and looked again at Kitty. "Ma'am, Is this yer cat here?"

Ledia smiled at the dwarf. Her gaze scanned around the meadow full of dead gorms. She put her hand in a comforting manner on Ironhand's shoulder. "He lives with me and my husband, but I would have to say Kitty thinks that we belong to him." Kitty picked that moment to roll back up to a sitting position, promptly cleaning himself with his tongue.

Ironhand snorted, "I believe ye on that." He paused for a second. "That tiger saved our hides out here, and for that we owe ye a debt. He put the fear of God into those gorms. They are now either dead in this meadow, or scattered across this mountain, running for their lives."

Ledia started laughing as Thunderfall and Gevi joined the group. "The debt is not owed to me, good dwarf, but owed to Kitty. He would take a nice deer, or a good belly rub, for payment of debt."

Ironhand looked over at the tiger that was contentedly cleaning himself. "Deer it is then," he mumbled, shaking his head. "Brother, how be ye?"

"Good, considering I'm an old dwarf running up the mountain like I was young again," grumbled Thunderfall. He looked into Ironhand's eyes. "I am sorry for the loss of the brother, and I thank you deeply for taking care of Gevi and Javin. I will repay the debt. I will also repay the debt the humans you rescued owe."

"There can be no debt between us," Ironhand replied, a very serious look on his face. "Javin and Gevi fought beside the dwarves voluntarily, therefore incurring no debt. As for the humans, they can give a basket of grain per person if they wish. We will not accept ye covering their debt, since ye did not ask us to rescue them."

Thunderfall nodded toward Ironhand, "It will be as you say then. My deepest thanks then to you, my brother."

"Ledia, can you look at Javin's ribs? I think they are cracked and not broken, but you better make sure," Gevi said while looking around the meadow. "By the way, where is Mac?"

"Mac is guarding the people you rescued," Ledia replied. She started examining Javin's ribs. "I sent Kitty on ahead since he could reach you long before Thunderfall or I could. We should be able to catch up to the slower families with the younger children tonight; Mac will be with them."

Ledia reached the same conclusion as Gevi; cracked ribs. "By the way good dwarf," Ledia said to Ironhand, once she finished with Javin. "Kitty wants to pass on the deer and take the belly rub." Everyone started laughing at the expression that crossed Ironhand's face.

****

"So, your little magic show is finding all these ideological, brainwashed humans," Ambrissan sneered at Chancellor White through the mirror in Chancellor White's office. "How many have you killed so far?"

"Oh, well... actually none, yet," Chancellor White stammered.

"Ambrissan frowned through the mirror toward Chancellor White.

"The king's proclamation was held up. It won't be announced throughout the kingdom for another week." Chancellor White saw Ambrissan's face start to show anger. "We are taking names of everyone who sets off the anti-magic detectors at the magic show. The day the law is proclaimed, I have special soldiers that will arrest every name we have."

"Arrest?" Rage could physically be felt in his voice, and seen on Ambrissan's face in the mirror.

"The king insisted on jail and fines only," Chancellor White replied. A slow, evil smile covered his face as he leaned back in his chair. He stayed silent.

Ambrissan instantly knew Chancellor Whites was not saying something.

"Finish it," he curtly ordered, barely controlling his rage.

"The king assigned me the task of hiring and training the guards at the new prison and re-education facility, built for the followers of the Lord of the Stars. The guards are under my command. The king knows what will happen. What the law says, and what will happen, are two different things."

Ambrissan broke out with diabolical laughter. Chancellor White started laughing as well. Pleased with how things were going, Ambrissan's image vanished from the mirror.

Chapter 8

How art thou fallen from heaven, O Lucifer, son of the morning! How art thou cut down to the ground, which didst weaken the nations. – The Guide

Chellell sat in the back of one of the show wagons, her legs dangling over the edge. The sun was bright and warm, helping Chellell really enjoy one of her rare times alone. She gazed at the farms and ranches on both sides of the road. A farmer with a team of horses was cutting hay in one of the fields. Smiling to herself, she enjoyed the memories the farms brought up. She had promised herself years ago never to live on a farm, but seeing the scenery around her and the working farmers made her remember the good times she had as a child, before her father left her. Chellell willed the bad memories of her father away from her mind, concentrating instead on the farmer cutting hay.

Within hours, they would be in her hometown of Farm Circle. Her family farm and Javin's farm were both a couple of miles east of the small town. A mix of nervousness and excitement made her stomach churn. Her family and her friends would be seeing her show, tonight. Chellell had not returned to Farm Circle since she left for the guilds four years ago. So, except for a handful of people from this area that had come to the guilds, she had not seen any of them. She was really nervous about seeing her mom and Javin's family. Even though she had been too busy studying magic to come home through the years, her mother's love and approval meant the world to her. She continued fighting mixed feelings, all the way into Farm Circle.

****

Licheaon was sitting down for a quick snack before the start of the show when Kyle, along with two guards and the guard captain, strolled into the tent. Licheaon looked up in irritation, his mouth full of a juicy fruit.

"We got a problem, a big problem," commented Kyle. As he started to sit in the only other chair in the sparsely furnished tent, he noticed a cat curled up in sleep right in the chair. Kyle brushed the cat off the chair and sat down. The cat gave him an indignant look, before it curled up in the corner of the tent.

Licheaon delicately wiped the fruit juice off his chin and stared straight at Kyle. "Solve it. Do you need me to hold your hand for everything?"

Ignoring the snide remark from his boss, Kyle leaned forward across the table. "Almost everyone coming to the show is setting off the magic detectors. The quarantine area is the whole stinking field. And I mean stinking! The guards had to remove a lot of cow and horse manure from this pasture so we could use it for the magic show."

Surprise crossed Licheaon's face, but he quickly hid it behind the stone-cold business demeanor that he was known for. He leaned back in his chair, his mind rapidly working. "How many are there? This is a small, backwoods farm town; there cannot be too many people. I considered not even bothering to come here."

"Several hundred, most likely; many are children. The school has to bring the children to the show as decreed by the king. The guards went to the school and made sure this happened. Many of the families were trying to pull their kids out, but the guards did not allow it. Right now, half my guards are assigned to keep parents from leaving with their children."

"Any fighting?" asked Licheaon.

"No," replied Kyle. He had a puzzled expression on his face. "The people are actually very polite and kind." Kyle shifted in his chair, his uneasiness showing in his body language. "Look Licheaon, my familiar is going crazy. I think we have stumbled upon a hornet's nest of Lord of the Stars' followers. Strangely enough, this is where Chellell is from." Kyle ran a hand through his hair, his stress showing. "That explains why her old boyfriend had a strong aversion to magic. He is from this town as well."

Thoughts quickly went through Licheaon's mind, until finally he smiled. "Go to Chellell; have her do everything with the show on the stage. Tell her, under no circumstances, is she to do the normal magic above the audience." He looked over at the guards standing in the doorway of the tent. "Let everyone in. Block the stage, so no one can get within twenty-five feet of the stage. Call it a safety precaution. Captain," he said, still looking at the guard, "please stay a minute." The guards and Kyle left the tent, leaving the captain with Licheaon.

"Captain, you understand what has to be done, don't you?" The captain nodded, but with a troubled look on his face. Licheaon noticed his troubled look and sighed. "Look, we cannot take this many people captive. I tell you what; I will have them try to save as many children as possible. This sickness will have to be removed from Preveshawl, or it will spread." He saw the captain relax a little when he mentioned the children, but he still looked troubled. Licheaon frowned at the captain. "You have a job to do. As a military officer, I expect you to obey orders. Am I understood?"

"Yes sir," snapped the captain. He was making an effort to wipe the troubled expression off his face.

"Good. Have several of your men scout the area discreetly. Map the town and the farms as far out as you can. Fortunately, they are lowly farmers, so we will only need two or three squads to clean up this mess."

"Yes sir," replied the captain. He abruptly marched out of the tent. The cat lazily got up from the corner and followed the captain out of the tent. A brief red gleam flashed in the moonlight from the forehead of the cat as it strolled away from Licheaon's tent.

****

Chellell sat in a chair in front of a large mirror while Lily busily worked on her hair during the intermission. Chellell was totally and completely exhausted. For some reason, the connection with Sanatarial was strained, making the magic show a lot more difficult than usual. The same strain showed on the face of her magic assistants. To make matters

88

even worse, her cantankerous familiar was in an extremely foul mood. For the first time ever, Sanatarial had refused to show himself. He had always reveled in the attention from the crowds in the previous shows. This performance he did, invisible.

Lily finished with her hair, and moved over to work on her face. "You seem worn out, Chellell. You must be working hard to impress your home town," Lily teased as she carefully applied makeup around Chellell's eyes.

"My mom is here along with Jav..., I mean my neighbors. My school friends are out there as well. I can't wait until this final act is over." Chellell commented while Lily worked on her. She could feel her excitement growing. "I plan on staying the night at my house. Do you want to come?"

"Why thank you, Sweetie. I may take you up on that. I've never been to a farm before. City girl, you know. It should be fun. You did say you lived on a farm, right?"

"Yes, I grew up on a farm. I will swing by here after the show and pick you up. But I warn you, farms are boring, especially for city girls."

"I'll be here. There, you're now prettier than ever. Go on back out there and show your old boyfriends what they missed by breaking your heart," Lily smiled, still trying to tease Chellell. Chellell frowned, her thoughts going straight to Javin.

"Oh Sweetie, I'm sorry," Lily said, when she noticed the expression on Chellell's face, "I was just teasing. I did not mean to..."

"I'm fine, Lily. There was only one ex-boyfriend, and he is not here. I'll see you after the show." Chellell got up out of the chair and gave Lily a quick hug. She walked out of the tent and back toward the stage.

Lily sat down in the chair Chellell had vacated. Taking a comb, she ran the comb several times through her waist length blond hair. Finishing her hair, she spent several minutes working on her make-up, concentrating on bringing out her bright blue eyes. Lily stared hard into the mirror, not liking what she saw. She never did. Sighing, she wondered why so many thought she had the perfect face and hair. "There has to be more to life than this," Lily thought to herself while she reddened her lips with a rose red lipstick. There was an empty feeling inside her that wouldn't go away.

"I've got five minutes before I have to go out again," one of the actresses said as she ran into Lily's tent.

"Have a seat, Beautiful," Lily replied with a perfect smile that flashed ivory white teeth.

****

The dancing lady gave Chellell an irritated look as she fell to the stage. Chellell had dropped her the last two feet as her connection with Sanatarial broke, again! She looked over to the side curtain that hid her assistant. There had been no sparkling lights or boom like there was supposed to be.

"End the show," her magic assistant mouthed to her. Chellell

89

turned back around to face her hometown audience. Children with their parents were the only ones present, besides a few of her childhood friends, and her mother. They were all backed away from the stage as far as they could get, with guards all around them. Many looked very ill.

"I better end this before I embarrass myself even more," Chellell thought bitterly to herself. This had to be the worst performance she had ever put on. A grouchy Sanatarial had stayed around for the first half of the show, but now he kept disappearing and reappearing which caused magic spells to abruptly end. He was in the foulest mood Chellell had ever seen. Her magic assistants were having the same problems.

"That concludes our show, Ladies and Gentleman. We have been having extreme technical difficulties, so I want to thank you, for your patience and kindness." The children and parents politely clapped, causing Chellell to smile. She had to admit that they were being very respectful, considering how badly everything was going. They had clapped as she finished each magic act. Giving them a curtsy, Chellell strained and drew on every last bit of magic she could. Smoke surrounded her, as she vanished into thin air. She reappeared right behind the curtain, before collapsing from exhaustion.

****

"Your home town is so friendly," Lily said to Chellell as they walked down a dirt wagon trail. "The general store gave me half-off a new blouse because I was a special visitor. The manager of the store gave me a hug to welcome me to her town. She was so nice."

"Small town life," muttered Chellell who was still thinking about everything that went wrong with her show. It was obvious to Chellell that the children and parents were only at the show because of the king's decree that all school children attend. Even though the show was terrible and half the people attending had some kind of sickness, her audience had been very polite.

"Maybe," replied Lily. "But this place feels different. I cannot explain it, but the air just seems peaceful." Lily looked deep in thought as the two walked on down the trail with two guards following behind them. "Love," Lily finally said. "That is what is different. I think these people genuinely love each other. They are showing love to us big city strangers as well. There is a general aura of peace and love covering this whole place."

"It's only small town life," Chellell replied. She turned off the trail and led Lily through a gate. The two guards stopped at the gate. The guard captain had ordered them to stay at the gate and not interfere with Chellell's family reunion. "This is my neighbor's house. Mom told us to come by here first; they are planning a big cookout to welcome me home."

"Lots of love," Lily whispered wistfully.

****

Javin's mother was halfway recovered from her anger at having her daughters forced to watch the magic show. She and her husband had decided this was the last day any of their children would attend a kingdom

90

school.

Food was ready shortly after the girls' arrival. Lily was introduced by Chellell to her mother and Javin's family. Everyone was laughing and having a good time visiting and catching up on news. Javin's youngest sister had fallen asleep on Chellell's lap, causing Javin's mother to put the younger girls to bed. Afterwards, she returned and rejoined the group.

"Lamar, it is way past time for you to put the cow in the barn for the night," Annba, Javin's mother, said as she sat back down next to her husband.

"All right, I'd better make sure the chickens are in the hen house as well, and close it up for the night. I saw some fang hopper tracks a week or so ago. Those creatures really love chickens." He got up and buckled on his sword belt. He noticed Lily staring hard at the swords. "It's for snakes or other critters, if they show up," he said, smiling at her.

"Can I go with you?" Lily asked. These were the first words she had said all evening. "I've never been on a farm before, and I would love to see some of it." She wiped long, blond hair out of her face, looking hopefully toward Lamar.

"Come on then. But I warn you, it's boring."

"That's what Chellell keeps saying," murmured Lily, so low that only Lamar heard her.

"I'll go with you; I need to stretch my legs anyway," Chellell said as she stood up from the table.

"Have fun girls," Annba said. "Come on, Kelley," Annba put her hand on the shoulder of Chellell's mother, "let's get the dessert out. The pies should have cooled by now."

****

"I got the last chicken," yelled Lily, as she carefully put the flapping chicken through the door of the hen house. Lamar shut the door. Lily and Chellell were leaning on each other, laughing. Having never done anything like this before, Lily was having a lot of fun. They followed Lamar over to the cow, which was standing patiently by the barn door, waiting to go inside. Opening the door, the cow calmly strolled into the barn. She walked straight into a stall and started chewing on some hay. A howl of laughter from Lily made Lamar turn around. Chellell was holding up a shoe, with a sour expression on her face.

"Now I know why I left the farm," growled Chellell; but a smile was on her face. She wiped the bottom of her shoe on the straw that covered the ground.

"You better watch where you step on a farm, especially in the barn," commented Lamar. He started pumping water into the water trough by the cow's stall. Next, he put grain and hay in another trough, shaking his head because the girls were nearly fallen over with laughter.

"Come on, ladies. We need to let old Bretta here get some sleep, or we won't have much milk come morning."

After they left the barn, Lamar turned and sat on a long log that he

91

had set up as a bench years ago. He gestured and the two girls joined him. They were in full view of the porch, where Annba and Kelley were deep in conversation.

"Can I help you milk tomorrow?" Lily asked. Her face was beaming with happiness.

"You're staying at my house tonight," Chellell replied.

"And you have to be up before the sun comes up to milk the cow..." started Lamar.

"And there is no way I am getting up that early, walking all the way over here, to milk a cow," Chellell said with exasperation in her voice. She couldn't believe what Lily was asking to do.

"I would. One of the guards can bring me over. We will be back at your house before breakfast. I won't even wake you up," Lily said to Chellell. Lamar and Chellell looked at each other, before shrugging agreement. They were silent for the next several minutes.

"I cannot believe how beautiful the night sky is with all these stars," commented Lily, "I don't remember seeing so many in the city."

"You will never see stars in the city like you do in the country," replied Lamar. He proceeded to point out different constellations in the sky. Finally, Lamar decided to address the real concern he felt in his heart. "You know, Chellell, that was an impressive show you and your friends put on. I could tell a lot of hard work went into it."

"Why thank you," she said as she leaned over and gave him a sideways hug, her face beaming proudly.

"I wonder though, do you really comprehend what magic is?"

Chellell sat up straight, her face going into a serious expression. "Of course I know what magic is. I have been studying it year-round, day and night for four years." A frown was on her face while she struggled for words. "Magic is hard to explain to someone who has never used it, almost impossible, I would say."

Lamar turned to face her and smiled, "Let me guess what you know. Correct me, if I am wrong. By the way, where is your familiar?"

"He did not come. He is not happy in this area. He gets like that in some places and around some people." Her mind went back to her familiar's reaction to Javin.

"Well, I have always wondered. How does magic work?" chimed in Lily. "Maybe the two of you can tell me. I've been around it quite a bit lately." Lily smiled while leaning her head on Chellell's shoulder. "And Sweetie, you are quite good with this magic stuff."

"Magic takes two willing parties, a familiar and a person." Chellell nodded as Lamar started explaining, signaling her agreement. "The magic itself is a flow of power from the familiar to its mage. The mage then has to learn how to control the power, to harness it to do what the mage wants it to do. This takes years of study and practice. However, the use of power is so different and unnatural to a mage that it is extremely difficult to accept and control. Often it makes the newer mages violently ill as their body tries to reject it."

Chellell thought of her headaches, "I would say reject is not the correct term. Body adjustment would be closer. The use of magic gets easier, as time goes by."

"Adjustment then," agreed Lamar. "As the body adjusts and learns how to deal with the power flow from their familiar, the mage learns more types of magic and grows in power. However, it is limited, it..."

"It is not limited; anything is possible, as long as you believe. Your belief is the key." Chellell interjected, her voice getting a little hot with indignation.

"You know it has limits, Chellell," Lamar said softly. "It can never heal, and it will not work around certain people, is that not true?"

"True," sighed Chellell, giving in to that point. "But outside that, there are no limits, except how you limit yourself."

"Ok, except you will probably find out someday there are more limitations, but that is not important right now. Have you ever wondered what a familiar is, and why their magic is limited in certain ways and around certain people? Understanding a familiar's limitations is the key to knowing what they really are."

"Familiars are creatures from another dimension, another plane. Using magic is as common to them as breathing air is to us. They have a strong desire to help people learn more about themselves, to help them to discover what they are capable of. The familiar's desire is to help the mage find the god that is in all of us."

Chellell abruptly stopped, realizing she had probably said too much. These truths offended Javin, and she was sure those same truths offended his father. Instead, she was surprised when she heard him start to chuckle. Lily sat very quietly, listening intently.

"Let's just say we will disagree on that; I do believe, one hundred percent, that familiars teach about discovering the god in all of us. It is something they would do because of their nature, and because of what they really are."

"What they really are does not matter as long as..."

"Hold on, Sweetie," said Lily. She lifted her head off Chellell's shoulder and put her arm around her, giving Chellell's shoulder a squeeze. "I am really curious about this. Aren't you?"

"Not really," huffed Chellell. "I heard it all from Javin already."

"Who is this Javin?" asked Lily. "I heard Chellell ask about him earlier while we were eating."

"Javin is my oldest son and Chellell's childhood friend. But I doubt Javin really knows anything about familiars. Neither I, nor his mother, told him about our experiences and dealings with them, though we probably should have." These words got Chellell's attention, even though she looked skeptical.

"I encountered them when I was in the army a long time ago, out in the wilds north of Fort Outlands. My wife had a different experience with them, long before I met her. Because she came from the Guild of Healing, she has helped heal several people that had familiars turn on them. To understand what a familiar is, you have to go back to the beginning, to the creation of everything. When the Lord of the Stars created..."

"I knew this conversation would have to get into religion; it always does. We learned all this in church." Chellell said in disgust.

"I've never been to church," whispered Lily as she stared up at the stars.

Chellell looked at her in astonishment, never imagining someone had not been to a church. She was literally speechless.

"Almost nobody went to church when I was growing up in the city of Preveshawl Castle." Lily wiped a stray strand of blond hair out of her face and turned to face Lamar. "Keep going; I have never heard about this creation."

"Well Lily, that is really no surprise to me," replied Lamar, "Teachers were forbidden to teach creation in the schools around the time you were born, twenty years ago. They replaced God's creation with the teaching that a magical explosion without cause created everything. Familiars introduced this teaching to Preveshawl."

"To understand what a familiar really is and what magic truly is, you have to go back to the beginning. In the beginning, the Lord of the Stars created everything, including the stars we are looking at tonight. He also created powerful servants known to us as angels. They have many jobs and functions, but let it be said that they have access to our creator, to God Himself."

"The most powerful of the angels one day decided he was entitled to be like God, and rebelled against God. One out of every three angels joined this powerful angel, in a full-out rebellion. The leader of the fallen angels is known as the Great Dragon, as well as several other names. The angels that fell with him are known to us as demons." Lamar looked at the two girls. Lily was listening and interested. Chellell had a look of fear, mixed with rebellion, on her face. Lamar sighed internally; knowing what had to be said next would cause trouble.

"Unexplainable power can only come from two sources. One source is God Himself. God only grants it to mankind on a case-by-case basis, and typically only to those who have accepted his Son as their Savior. An example would be healing someone. Some in the Guild of Healing know this, and they are powerful healers who heal others through prayer. People can be healed in an unexplainable and miraculous way, demonstrating the power of God. Prayer can be used to ask things of God, and if he sees fit to grant the prayer, then great things can happen. This form of power, called miracles, always glorifies God and can help those who ask for his help."

Lamar was actually surprised that Chellell seemed to be listening intently now. "The other form of unexplainable power is called magic. Its source is not from God, but from fallen angels, or demons, or, as we say today, familiars. These extremely evil beings give magic to willing humans, but only to expand their evil interests. Their only desire is to see mankind suffer the same eternal fate that is due them, for their rebellion, on judgment day, at the end of this world."

"I had a feeling this was where you were going. You are correct; Javin never said anything like this," Chellell commented, acid in her voice as she spoke. She took a deep, shaky breath. "I sat in church for years. I prayed. I sang. I listened to *The Guide* being taught. I begged for my father to come back with daily prayers. Nothing happened. I was so confused my whole childhood, wondering why God did not listen to me. I wondered why God did not love me."

"The Guild of Magic finally showed me the truth. I was praying all those years to something that only existed inside me. If I wanted power, then that power had to come from me. The familiars teach us how to get our own power. They connect to us, enabling us to use our power. Magic could have changed my life as a child. One spell, that would take seconds to cast, would have made my father love me. Compare that, with years of unanswered prayers, and you know why I chose magic."

Chellell stopped speaking. She hung her head, fighting all the confusing emotions raging through her. Deep inside, she was scared that possibly, Lamar was correct about familiars.

Lamar reached over and gave Chellell a big hug, though she was stiff as a board. "Magic can never be used to make someone love you, but I want you to know, with or without magic, I love you. God loves you as well. You are a very smart girl. One day, I know you will discover and acknowledge the truth. Always remember one thing. Look me in the eyes; I want you to remember this." She did as she was told. Lamar saw tears in her eyes. "If a familiar ever turns on you and tries to hurt you, no power on earth can stop it. You have to call upon the Lord of the Stars; only He can stop a familiar. The power of the Lord of the Stars is more powerful than the magic of familiars." Lamar paused for a second. Turning her head, Chellell stared off into the darkness. "Have you ever heard a familiar tell you something was not allowed when you asked them a question, or asked them to do something?"

Chellell's head whipped around toward Lamar, a shocked expression on her face. Lamar accepted that as a "yes" from Chellell. "That is because familiars are under the power of their creator, the Lord of the Stars. They can do nothing he does not allow them to do. So whose power is greater?" Lamar paused, thinking carefully on what to say next. "The other clue, Chellell, in understanding what a familiar really is, involves the ritual to summon your familiar when you first decide to become a magic user."

Chellell's face turned red with embarrassment. How much Lamar actually knew about the Ritual of Summoning was a mystery to her, but she figured he probably knew everything. That was one thing about Lamar; he really had a lot of knowledge. He was right though, if you looked at the ritual through the eyes of a churched person, instead of through the eyes of an educated person, the Ritual of Summoning would seem extremely evil and wicked. You had to be educated enough to understand the truth and the symbolism behind the ritual.

Chellell sat silently for several minutes, tears welling up in her eyes. "My father never bothered talking with me. As I said, all the praying and begging I did to God never made my life better; he left me. God never listened to me. Sanatarial, comes anytime I ask. God did nothing I asked Him to do. With magic, I decide what I want, cast a spell, and it happens." With that, she pushed herself up and away from Lamar and walked back toward the house.

Lamar started to get up to leave, but Lily stopped him. "I will go and talk with her." Lily said as she got up. "Chellell just needs some time to think about everything you said. I know I sure do." Lily started to walk toward the house after Chellell. "Don't forget, you are teaching me how to milk in the morning," Lily called back over her shoulder.

****

Annba shook Lamar's shoulder, "Wake up! Someone is knocking on the door." Lamar was instantly awake. He was on his feet when he heard the knock again.

"Annba, Lamar, it's me Jewla, I have to talk to you." Lamar visibly relaxed. After he opened the door, he saw a very upset and nervous older lady. Jewla was one of the oldest and most respected naturalists in the farming community. He motioned for Jewla to come inside, curious as to what had her out in the middle of the night. Annba came into the room and all three sat at the kitchen table.

"I saw you at the magic show," Jewla said to Lamar, "so you will know what I am talking about. The entire production made me edgy. I decided to send one of my cats into the back areas where the tents and wagons were. As you know, we can direct our animals and receive everything they see and hear. Through the cat, I overheard a conversation in one of the tents." She then proceeded to repeat everything the cat had seen and heard in Licheaon's tent.

Finally the naturalist left, but not before Lamar cautioned her to tell no one else. He assured her that he would take care of things in the morning. Afterwards, Annba and Lamar sat together on the front porch, arm in arm.

"What are we going to do?" Annba asked. Lamar sat quietly, listening to the sounds of the night, deep in thought. "No wonder they were forcing the children to attend; and anti-magic detectors!"

"I think we should get with the elders first thing. We will need a call to go out for fasting and prayer." Lamar was looking at the stars that filled the night sky. "Then, I am going to call my old special operations unit, the Wolf Troop, back into action."

"Are you sure? I know they are loyal to you, and most of those that survived settled in this area to be near you, but it has been decades."

Lamar smiled, "I think they have stayed sharp. The training I put them through and the selection process lends itself to never forgetting. Besides, they were the best soldiers in Preveshawl at one time. I doubt Preveshawl has many their equal to this day."

"Why? Why would our beloved kingdom turn on us? We love our country. We haven't done anything wrong." She put her head on his shoulder. Tears started running down her cheeks.

Lamar squeezed her tight once Annba began to sob loudly. "I do not think they are turning on us," he whispered, "I think they are turning on God, and when they look at us, they see the light of God."

****

Lamar and Annba got the shock of their lives the next morning. They went out to the barn before sunrise, only to see Lily standing patiently by the barn door with an extremely irritated guard. Annba taught Lily how to milk a cow because Lamar had to go to town to gather the elders. Lily kept asking Annba questions about God and creation while they milked. As Lily was about to leave, Annba gave her a book, *The Guide*.

"Thank you," said Lily, but there was sadness in her voice. Sighing deeply, she held it back toward Annba. "I can barely read."

"No, it's yours," replied Annba, "I think you will find you will understand more than you think." Lily smiled and pulled the book back to her chest. After helping with barn chores, Lily left, so she could be with Chellell for breakfast.

****

Mikelsheck the gorm stood before the Grand Leader in the command tent. His hands and his feet were shackled. His whole body was visibly shaking while he finished relating what had happened in the meadow. Hanging his head, the gorm stood, shaking with fright, while he stared at his feet, waiting for his fate to be decided.

"So, you and your troop decided to run like the cowards you are?" screamed the giant, rage in his voice so strong the tent shook. "Then, you thought you would flee from me? Kill him! Kill every gorm that was on that mission." The guards at the tent entrance came forward toward the pathetic gorm.

"I have an idea that will take care of several problems and make this coward wish he were dead, Grand Leader," a man with a green dragon on his shoulders spoke from the table where he was seated.

"Hold," spoke the giant, halting the coming guards. "What do you have in mind, Ambrissan?"

"We needed slaves; why not make him and the other cowards the slaves we need? Let me show you a spell that will make them the perfect slave." Mikelsheck squealed, his eyes moving around wildly.

"Proceed," said the Grand Leader. "If I don't like it, I will kill him anyway. Mikelsheck's terror grew once he saw the cold, evil look on the Grand Leader's face."

The mage stood and closed his eyes, stretching out one of his hands. After several seconds, an oily, blackish smoke started forming

97

above his hand. Then, he opened his eyes and pointed straight at the imprisoned gorm. The smoke flew from the mage's hand and struck the gorm in the head, disappearing into the creature's skull. The gorm fell backwards, hitting the floor with a thud. Ambrissan walked over and forced the gorm into a kneeling position. Not moving, the gorm stayed silent, with a dazed look in his eyes.

"You will never do anything to hurt, harm or kill any creature, unless I or the Grand Leader orders you to do so." Ambrissan said while looking directly into the eyes of the gorm.

"You will do what anyone and everyone tells you to do. You will do it instantly and without question. Never verbally complain about anything or act against your orders. From this day forward, you will answer when addressed, as slave."

With that, Ambrissan touched the gorm's head. The smoke came out, disappearing into the air. Ambrissan pointed to one of the guards standing at the entrance, "Do not rise. Clean his shoes with your tongue." With his legs chained, the gorm crawled on hands and knees to the guard. At the guard's feet, the slave's tongue quickly touched the guard's boot and started to work.

"Here's the best part about my spell. The slave understands everything. In his mind he fights, but his physical body cannot resist the compulsion to do as ordered. Every gorm here will see what happens to cowards. When they go into battle, they will have to choose between this," he pointed down to the gorm, still licking the boots of the smirking guard, "or fighting to the bitter end. I think they would fight. Do you not agree, Grand Leader?"

Ambrissan smiled wickedly at the Grand Leader. "Unchain him. Have him drive a slave ring through his own nose. Prepare a coward's brand. Have him brand his own forehead. Take him to the mess hall and order him to clean from sunup till sundown." The Grand Leader was pleased with Ambrissan's order and followed his torturous example by giving his own order. "Bring the rest of the cowards to the center square at two hours past noon. Ambrissan will cast the spell on them. They will also do their own rings and brands in front of the assembly that meets during that time. Assign half of the cowards to the mines and farms. The other half is to do camp clean-up." A self-satisfied smile spread across Ambrissan's lips as he thought about how easily the Grand Leader was influenced.

"Yes, Grand Leader," said the guard. He led the ex-gorm officer out of the tent and into his new life of slavery.

"Now," said the giant, bringing his attention back to the table. "Let's finish our plans for Preveshawl."

Chapter 9

Hear, O earth: behold, I will bring evil upon this people, even the fruit of their thoughts, because they have not hearkened unto my words, nor to my law, but rejected it. – The Guide

Javin put his hammer down and wiped the sweat off his brow. He was working on a smaller forge and anvil toward the back of the shop. Arrowheads filled his schedule for today. Tomorrow, he would work on sharpening the arrowheads he had completed. After that, his days would be filled with making horseshoes.

Two weeks had passed since the battle in the meadow. Thunderfall took the black rocks Javin had retrieved from the mine, and curtained off his work area, so that Javin could not see what he was working on. Gevi had been involved the first two days. The two constantly argued behind their curtain. Whatever it was they were working on, Javin knew it was to be given to him when it was finished, to repay the debt the dwarves felt they owed.

The third day there was no arguing. Javin had given Gevi a ride down to the fort, dropping her off at the wagon compound. Gevi had to return to work in Bear Tree City and would probably be there the rest of the summer. Javin still tingled from the good-bye hug she had given him. He was really going to miss her. She had made him promise to write her a letter every week and drop it off at the fort for delivery every sixth day. Gevi had become a true friend, someone Javin truly cherished.

***

Late one night, a week after Gevi had left, Javin was going through his sword practice routine. He did worse than usual because his mind kept going back to Gevi. What really was bothering him was that he was no longer thinking about Chellell, who had been relegated to fond childhood memories. Their fights from their time at the guild were replaced with recollections of time spent with Gevi. He smiled as he thought back to a few weeks ago, when some bread she was baking caught on fire. She had blamed the stove, the bread dough, and the spices; never acknowledging that she forgot about the oven because she was thinking about a new invention.

He had become accustomed to, and dearly missed, their early morning walks before the shop opened. They would talk the entire time. After supper, they would read *The Guide* together before Javin's sword practice and prayers. Gevi often watched his practices. His extreme shyness around people, especially women, was no longer evident when he was around Gevi. He was just getting comfortable being around her, and then she left. The two short weeks he had with her between the battle in the meadow and the time she left for work, had created a lifetime of pleasant memories for Javin. She was the first person his age that he had really gotten to know that held the same beliefs in God that he held.

Breakfast the following morning was unusually quiet. Thunderfall had hardly complained or grumbled since Gevi had left. Javin made several attempts to draw him into conversation, but eventually he ended up eating in silence, like he had every meal since Gevi left. After breakfast, he got to work on sharpening arrowheads.

Around mid-afternoon, Ledia and Mac showed up at the shop. Javin kept on working while Thunderfall went outside to talk with them. With a sharp command, Thunderfall stopped Javin from his work and had him come outside with Ledia and Mac. Walking over to a little picnic table set up by the house, Javin started chuckling when he saw Kitty sleeping on the grass. The tiger was flat on his back, four paws waving in the air, as usual. When he sat down at the table, he noticed that everyone else had concerned looks on their faces.

"Read this," Thunderfall grumbled. He passed a pamphlet over to Javin. Javin picked it up and started reading.

Proclamation of Law by King Logan XII
Office of Law and Enforcement

From this day forward and forever, ownership, sale, and distribution of a book called The Guide *will be strictly prohibited within the borders of Preveshawl. All churches and citizens are to cease and desist from all teachings related to* The Guide. *Penalties for above stated law will include fines, not to exceed one quarter pound gold, and imprisonment, not to exceed ten years.*

I, King Logan XII, proclaim this law to be true and just, and from henceforth and forever, the law of the Kingdom of Preveshawl.

Statement of clarification
The Office of Law and Enforcement encourages all citizens to turn any and all copies of this book in to the nearest office of law or fort.
It is heavily encouraged that preachers and teachers get the book, Modern Truths and Thoughts, *by Guild Master Philosopher, J. M. Lasunty. This book has been used successfully in place of* The Guide *by many churches.*

With a look of disgust, Javin slid the pamphlet across the table back to Thunderfall. "We actually expected something like this," Ledia said. "We have spent over a year making preparations. The king made it obvious in several speeches last year that something like this would happen."

"What do you mean by getting ready?" asked Javin in confusion.

The three exchanged looks, before Thunderfall cut in. "A lot of lives depend on what we are about to tell you. You must promise to keep this secret."

Javin nodded agreement, so Thunderfall continued. "Long before the Lord of the Stars came to us as a man and died a sacrifice to pay for our sins; a race grew in strength and in power. They built great cities and were very prosperous for several hundred years. However, through the years, they had stopped following the true God, worshiping nature and science instead. God's anger grew. Through a series of great natural disasters, followed by invasions from other evil races, this race was almost completely destroyed. There were a few that held to the belief of the true God. These few escaped. Some hid in the mountain caves, while others escaped to the great forest. Another group escaped to the swamps, near the southern coast. Because of that, we now have dwarves, elves, and humans."

Thunderfall paused and looked straight at Javin. "When I was a young boy, I always heard legends of an ancient castle that had belonged to these ancient people. As I became a young man, I got curious and researched it in the dwarven archives. Eventually, I found a general location and began to search. It took me three trips, a week each, over a year's time, but I found it. It was located between the Elven Forest and the Dwarven Mountains. The castle itself was nothing but a heap of stones, but many of the surrounding buildings were for the most part intact. I even found an old blacksmith shop nearly intact."

"But how does that help us now?" Javin asked, concern clearly showing in his voice.

"As Ledia said, we expected this," chimed in Mac. "Working together, our church started slowly storing seeds, tools, and everything you could think of that you might need to turn those ruins into a home. A couple of the houses have been completely restored and some of the pasture area fenced. There are fields around the ruins, and plenty of water. Every month, somebody takes a turn to gather up supplies brought to the church and take it up to the ruins."

"Another important thing," interjected Ledia, "is that the ruins are outside the Kingdom of Preveshawl's border. Their laws will not apply to us. Did you notice that the king's proclamation said 'inside' the kingdoms borders?"

"What will happen to Gevi?" asked Javin. "How do we get her to safety?"

Thunderfall sighed, "I will send her a coded message on the next wagon out of the fort. She was in on this, so she knows how to get to the ruins. She will probably return home before we leave. We will stay as late as possible, to see if she sends word back about whether she is staying in the city, or coming to meet us. It took me way too long to accept it, but she is no longer my little girl. She is a little too free-spirited at times, but no longer a little girl."

"Come on, Honey. We need to get back home, so I can feed the cows." Mac said while standing and stretching. "Tomorrow, I will meet Thom and his family. I am going to go ahead and move my livestock and his livestock up to the pastures by the ruins. Half the church families will be coming with me. Ledia will help with coordination of the other families until I return. There are only a dozen or so families involved, so the move will be easy. Surviving on our own will be the difficult part."

"Surviving on our own will be tough, but God will be our strength," commented Thunderfall as Mac and Ledia got ready to leave. Javin also stood up, but Thunderfall signaled for him to sit back down. The two watched Mac and Ledia walk hand-in-hand back towards their farm.

"I know you have your family and your guild," Thunderfall said as he handed Javin some papers. "These are the forms the guild requires for completion of your apprenticeship. You have earned a passing grade. You are free to leave anytime, to go back to your family and school, if you wish. Turning this form into the Guild of Warriors means you passed, and forever will be a member of the guild. If possible, I would like you to give me a couple of days to finish what I am making, before you go."

Javin sat silently, his mind swirling in thought. "Thank you, Master Thunderfall. I will think on it; I am not sure what I should do."

"Good answer," replied Thunderfall, "A wise man always thinks and prays before he acts." Thunderfall stood up and stretched his muscular arms. "I am getting too old for all this. Come on. Let's get back to work."

Javin continued to work at the smithy the next two days, though his mind was very troubled because of the events going on. He knew, without a doubt, his parents would not follow the king's decree. Once again, he did not sleep well that night, worrying and trying to figure out what he should do. Graduating from the guilds meant the world to him, but not if he had to give up everything about God he knew to be true.

The next morning, Thunderfall came into the shop, whistling a tune. Javin was in total shock. Thunderfall either grouched or complained while working, or was silent. Whistling a tune was not something he ever did. Javin was so shocked by Thunderfall's whistling that he was not paying attention to his work. The hammer in his hand came down, not on the shield he was working on, but on his thumb. Javin was dancing around in anguish with his thumb in his mouth when Gevi walked into the shop.

"My boss saw the king's decree, and shut the shop down," Gevi explained when she saw the look of surprise on Javin's face. "Aren't you a little old to be sucking your thumb?" she asked with a sly smile. Javin jerked his injured thumb out of his mouth. Shaking her head, Gevi continued, "My boss is moving back South, to the farm her parents have. As a loyal follower of The Lord of the Stars, she has no intention of giving up *The Guide*."

Javin didn't know what to say or do. He felt better knowing she was safe, and he really enjoyed having her around.

"I have something for you." Gevi held out an oiled leather cloth she was carrying, putting it gently down by her feet. Javin walked over and examined the cloth. Thunderfall, meanwhile, stopped his work so he could watch what was going on. A rare smile was on his face.

"It looks nice," he stuttered, not sure what she wanted him to do.

Gevi rolled her eyes and grabbed his upper arm.

"Don't be silly. Open it!" Javin started to unroll the oiled leather cloth. "It looks nice!" She parroted. "You actually think I would give you an old leather cloth?" Javin smiled at her mockery, but his expression changed to one of amazement when he pulled out a short sword. It was the exact same size and shape as his swords, but lighter. The blade was midnight black, with a pure silver handle. A dove, flying straight down, was etched in silver on both sides of the blade. Tiny red gemstones, mixed with clear stones, were embedded in the handle of the sword. Javin picked up the sword, speechless while he tested the grip. It was the same as his old swords. The handle and balance of the sword was extremely important to Javin, otherwise his sword spinning would be awkward at best.

"Keep unwrapping. You're not finished yet," Gevi said with a smile. Javin carefully set the sword aside and started unrolling the rest of the leather cloth. Another sword, identical to the first one appeared. It even had the same gem pattern embedded in its handle. He gave the sword a quick spin, and sure enough, except for being a little lighter, they felt the same as his old swords.

"This is fit for a king. I don't know what to say. Thank you, Gevi. Thank you, Master Thunderfall." Javin felt a huge hand on his shoulder. He looked up to see Thunderfall standing right behind him.

"The black rocks you brought me, becomes the hardest metal known, if worked correctly in a forge. It is also extremely light."

"Daddy is being way too humble, Javin," piped in Gevi. "This metal is so difficult to work that only two dwarven smiths alive today can use it to make anything! Daddy is one of those smiths. Those swords will never break. They will always have a razor sharp edge that will cut through normal steel like it is butter. The only thing that can stop these swords is armor made from the same black steel."

"The girl had to put some of her fancy stuff on them, that's where the gems came from. Better take them..."

"Fancy stuff!" Gevi stomped her feet in agitation at her father.

"Just take the swords outside and play with them. I don't want my shop blown to pieces," Thunderfall said, looking at Gevi.

"Fine; come on Javin," Gevi said in a huff as she grabbed his shoulder and marched him outside. Once outside, she drew both swords.

"Daddy knows how to make swords, and these are the best I've ever seen him make. But these swords have some extras. You should love this, but if not, you don't have to use it. Watch this." Gevi hit the base of the sword handles together. Javin's mouth fell open in shock as deep red colored flame flickered and danced across both blades.

Gevi handed him the swords, smiling at his expression. "Go ahead; try it out, unless you're scared you're going to burn yourself. The swords will only flame up if they are held." She gave him a beautiful smile while stepping back. Javin started spinning the swords, stabbing and swinging through the air. Flames flared around the blades in a spectacular display.

After a few minutes, he stopped.

"Thank you, Gevi; you are amazing!"

"You are welcome. Now, there is one other thing they can do, but you have to be careful," Gevi said. She took both swords from Javin. She made the swords flame up again and then pointed the left sword out straight toward the creek. With her thumb, she flicked open a hidden panel on the base of the sword handle. Her thumb mashed a hidden button now exposed. A ball of fire leapt from the point of the sword, exploding as it hit the water in the middle of the creek. Javin jumped back in alarm, completely unprepared for the violent explosion he had witnessed. "You only get one ball of fire per day, per sword; it takes a full day to recharge. The recharge is in the handle of the sword, so try to keep your handles exposed to sunlight as much as possible."

Reaching toward her belt, Gevi pulled out a bottle containing a clear liquid. "This is your flame oil for the sword. I made this specially for your new swords. I will show you tonight how to add the fuel to the swords. Let me know anytime you start to run low, and I will make you a batch of this flame oil."

"What in black rocks are you two doing?" yelled Thunderfall from the doorway of his shop. "I knew you would blow up my shop, and me with it, if I had given you half a chance."

Ignoring her father, Gevi showed Javin how to open the panel on the sword handle, using only his thumb, so that he could still keep a grip on his sword. At that point, the button to launch the ball of fire was easy to push. Javin practiced opening and closing the panel. It was amazing how simple it was to operate.

Javin practiced as Thunderfall stomped over to them, a stern look on his face. As he came up beside Gevi, Javin pointed the sword toward the creek. A ball of fire flew from the flaming sword, exploding violently across the creek. Javin turned to Gevi, a look of amazement on his face.

"I would explain the engineering to you, but it's really quite complicated. Even though you used the once per day ball of fire, the sword can still stay lit with the flames for another hour or so. After that, it will need the full day's charge of sunlight."

"Just be careful where you point that thing." Thunderfall paused, obviously wanting to say more, but instead, he turned back to the shop. "Nice work, Girl," he called back toward Gevi as he disappeared back into his shop. Gevi beamed, happy with the rare compliment from the dwarf.

"Practice for a while and then we will return to the shop. Neither sword has a charge anymore, so we can't hurt anything. After we are done, Daddy has something else for you." They spent the next half-hour practicing, before returning to the shop.

"Daddy, are you ready to give Javin the rest?"

"Let me finish this off first," replied Thunderfall to his daughter. He continued to hammer at something he was working on. After a few minutes, he set it aside and reached down, picking up a small chest.

Walking over to Javin, he set it down in front of Javin, who simply stared at the chest.

"Don't tell me you want me to open it for you as well," grumbled Thunderfall.

"At least we get equal treatment. I thought I was going to have to unroll the oiled cloth for him," Gevi replied as she put her arm around Thunderfall's massive shoulders. Javin leaned over and opened the chest. He pulled out a helmet that was pure black, made from the same black steel that the swords were made of. A silver cross was right on the front of the helmet, where the forehead would be. The helmet was rounded, with small ear holes. A chain mesh, with large eye slits, covered the front of the helmet, and hung down past the neck. Javin put it on, taking notice of how well it fit and how light it was.

"Thank you sir, I..."

"Keep going," Gevi interrupted, "hold the thanks until after you empty the chest. Does it fit?"

"Yes, it's a perfect fit," he replied, still in shock.

"It should fit. Remember me measuring you for those 'new clothes' I was going to get you?" Javin did remember, right after they had come back from the meadow. He protested, but nothing ever stopped Gevi, once her mind was made up. So he had been forced to stand while she used a measuring tape on him. Taking off the helmet, Javin set it to the side.

He reached back into the chest, pulling out a ring mail shirt. It was again, midnight black. It was made of very small, interlocking rings, over black leather. The rings were so small that even an arrow would not go through them. On the very front of the armor, etched in silver, was a crown. Javin put on the armored shirt, with Thunderfall showing him how the clasps worked. The armor was extremely light. What interested Javin was how comfortable and quiet it was; very easy to move around in, without making the typical rattling noise that armor made.

Reaching back into the chest, he removed a leather belt. The leather had been dyed pure black, matching the armor. It had sheathes on each side for his swords, as well as several other pouches for holding various items. The buckle was silver, in the shape of an open book. Javin put the belt on.

Next, he pulled out black leather pants, along with a pair of black leather boots. The leather pants were covered with the same black steel chain mesh that the chest armor was made from. The boots were stitched with a small Lucas Flower, a symbol of peace in Preveshawl. He set both of these to the side. Last, he took out two black leather gauntlets that would cover his forearms. Each gauntlet was black leather, covered with the black steel chain mesh. Each gauntlet had a silver symbol of two praying hands. Overcome with emotion, he walked over to Thunderfall, bent down, and gave him a hug. Thunderfall accepted the hug, for a second or two, before he stepped back.

"You're getting as bad as the girl," he moaned, but he had a smile on his face. Javin took that moment to give a smiling Gevi a hug as well.

"I don't know what to say. Thank you so much." Javin released Gevi. Feeling awkward, he said, "I will never forget this." He looked down at his armor, "This is so beautiful. What do the symbols mean?"

"They are from *The Guide*, replied Thunderfall. "*Stand therefore, having your loins girt about with truth, and having on the breastplate of righteousness; And your feet shod with the preparation of the gospel of peace; Above all, taking the shield of faith, wherewith ye shall be able to quench all the fiery darts of the wicked. And take the helmet of salvation, and the sword of the Spirit, which is the word of God.* You don't use a shield, so your shield will be your bracers. Again Javin, thank you for rescuing my daughter, and allowing me to repay the debt I owe you, and the dwarves owe your father."

"See what happens when you rescue the daughter of the world's best blacksmith?" Gevi said as she draped an arm around Javin's shoulder. "You get that blacksmith to reward you richly. No weapon will get through black steel armor."

Javin felt the heat of embarrassment flood his face. Gevi seemed not to notice that her arm draped comfortably over his shoulder, was making him squirm on the inside.

Without warning, bells started ringing in the distance. "What is that?" asked Javin, looking toward Gevi and Thunderfall in confusion. Thunderfall's face was instantly serious.

"That's a call to arms at the fort. All males are required to go to the fort." He looked right at Javin. "Get your horse and I'll meet you in front of the barn." With that, Thunderfall spun around and ran out of the shop.

Gevi moved her arm off Javin's shoulder. "Put those on," Gevi said pointing to the new armor. She then sprinted for the house, while Javin ran to his room. He quickly put on the pants and boots. Then he grabbed a large shirt which he put on over the mail armor. He put his helmet in a carry bag and slung it over his shoulder. Grabbing his bow, quiver, and placing the new swords in his belt, he turned and raced over to the barn.

Javin finished saddling his horse and was starting on Gevi's horse, when she came into the barn. She was dressed in her leather armor, with her bow slung across her back, and staff in hand. She helped Javin with her horse, and waited for Thunderfall.

Thunderfall came running out of the house, heading toward Javin and Gevi. He was wearing bright, silver-plated mail armor. A massive, two-headed battle axe was slung across his back. The axe was pitch black, made from the same black steel that Javin's swords and armor were made of.

"I thought I heard you getting dressed. Get back in the house. This is a call for men, and no one will mistake you for a man." Gevi actually looked hurt for a second, but then anger overtook her.

"What do you want me to do, stay here and bake cookies? I can go to the park at the fort and wait for you men to have your meeting about whatever is going on."

"You are not going to the fort. The situation could be dangerous. You know good and well the last time they rang those bells was before you were even born! This is not a joke. Now get back to the house, and I am not saying it again." Javin could tell Thunderfall was very serious. Fear began to rise up in him.

"I cannot stay alone, Daddy," Gevi said in a barely audible and shaky voice. Thunderfall stared at her for a brief second.

Thunderfall's tone changed, going from stern to gentle. "Come on then, you can stay with Ledia and that cat of hers." He took a deep breath. "Gevi, all will be well. Do you want Javin to stay with you and Ledia?"

Gevi seemed to think on this for a second, "No, he can go with you." Her voice was still shaky and her head was hanging down, hair covering her face.

"Come on. Let's get going," Thunderfall said as he turned and started a slow run down the road. Gevi and Javin trotted their horses down the road beside Thunderfall. Gevi looked straight down the road, visibly upset.

Javin and Thunderfall headed on to the fort after dropping Gevi off at Ledia's. For all Thunderfall's complaining concerning his age, he seemed not the least bit tired while he ran beside Javin's horse.

"You know, I can be such an ignorant dwarf," commented Thunderfall. Javin was surprised that he could talk and run like this at the same time. "Gevi is not upset about not going to the fort. She is upset because I was going to leave her, by herself. Upset and embarrassed, because you saw her get upset." Thunderfall kept on trotting and talking. "You know Gevi is adopted, right?"

Javin smiled and nodded. "It is fairly obvious, Sir." He managed to stammer while bouncing on his horse.

"Well, she didn't get her looks from me. Because of things that happened before I ever knew her, she is afraid to be alone. Absolutely terrified, beyond belief; I am such an ignorant dwarf for forgetting that. She had vivid, horrible nightmares, the first couple of years after I brought her to my home. More often than not, she would end up in bed with me. As she got older, she managed to stay in her own room and bed, but I have to leave my bedroom door open at night so she can see and hear me. She is alright most of the time, now, because the sound of my snoring helps her feel she is not alone. Occasionally, she still has the nightmares; nightmares of being alone". He went silent after that, causing Javin to remember back to the mine and how Gevi had opened her window, even with the dwarves snoring like bulls. Within a few minutes they were through the gate and into the fort.

****

"The Lord of the Stars was a good man that taught us to have faith, and to give of our wealth." The Enlightened Church preacher stood on a crystal podium, looking out over a packed congregation of nearly a

107

thousand people. "Even though ancient writers changed his sayings to make the claim he was God. We now know that he never really made any claim to be God. If anyone wants to know what is true and what is false in *The Guide*, then come by my office. For a small fee, I can show you what the Lord of the Stars really said, and what ancient writers of *The Guide* added or changed. I will tell you this, for free, that the Lord of the Stars taught us to give in faith, so that we can receive in faith."

"You have to have faith. You have to believe. Pray like you believe, and God will answer your prayers. Ask God to give, and he will give you whatever you ask. You see these brand new boots? I wanted these boots. I believed I should have these boots. God gave me these boots because I had no unbelief in my heart. Are you sick? God wants you healed. You have to believe you will be healed. Come forward to the altar. The more coins you put into the chest, the more faith you show that you have in God. Ask for anything; ask for everything. Honor God with your coin, and He will honor you."

The preacher continued to preach. Visible upset, Lily nudged Chellell on the shoulder. While people were stampeding down the aisle to the altar at the front of the church, Lily and Chellell were leaving through the front door. Sanatarial was riding on Chellell's shoulder, humming contently. The familiar seemed extremely happy.

"Come on Chellell, I meant a real church," explained Lily with obvious agitation. "Something like Lamar was telling us about. I do not think The Enlightened Church is what he was talking about."

"This is a real..." started Chellell, but Lily cut her off.

"Would Lamar attend this church?"

Chellell hesitated before replying, "Lamar would not step a single foot in that building, but it is a church. They have morals and ethics like all other churches."

"You know what I mean, Sweetie. I have never been to any church, I want to go to a real church while we have a free day this seventh day. Isn't there anything around here?"

Chellell sighed, "Alright, just for you, Lily. Whenever my mom and I were in the city on seventh day, my mom would take me to a little church on the edge of town. If we run, we can get there as they start."

"Oh, you're the greatest!" cried Lily as she hugged Chellell. Lily was practically jumping up and down with unbridled joy before she grew serious again. "It's not going to be like this, is it?" She pointed behind her to the majestic marble building of The Enlightened Church.

"No, it is like the church I went to. I least it was last time I attended."

"Come on then," said Lily. There was excitement in her voice. Chellell rolled her eyes and led the way.

Chellell sang along in a low voice, but Lily was singing almost as loud as she could. Chellell smiled as Lily tried to follow the melody from the song book, missing notes as she sang. Lily seemed to struggle with reading the words from the song book as well. She actually had a nice voice, but she didn't know any of the songs.

Chellell glanced at her unoccupied shoulder that was usually filled by Sanatarial. He had refused to come in to this church. The song ended and the two musicians put their stringed instruments down. A man walked up to the front of the church and turned to face the forty or fifty people present in the church. Since Lily had insisted on sitting in the very front, the man was practically standing in front of the two girls.

"Let us pray," the man said as he bowed his head.

"What does pray mean?" Lily whispered to Chellell. "What am I supposed to do?"

"Shhhh, bow your head and close your eyes," Chellell whispered back, her face turning red when she glanced up and saw the man looking at them.

"Hold on everybody. We had a question up front, which needs to be answered before we pray." Chellell's glanced angrily at Lily. She was sure this would go down as one of the most embarrassing moments in her life. She could feel everyone behind them staring at her.

"I am so sorry, Sir," Lily said to the man. She glanced over at Chellell, but Chellell was looking straight down at the floor. "I have never been to a church before, or at least a real one. The other one this morning did not pray. So how do you pray?" She nervously ran her fingers through her blond hair.

The man smiled down at Lily, putting her instantly at ease. Looking up, he faced everyone in the church. "I think everyone here today should be reminded what prayer is. So before we pray, maybe we should explain prayer." He again looked at Lily, giving her another warm smile. "Fortunately, *The Guide,* God's Holy Word, preserved unchanging by the Holy Spirit, has a lot to tell us about prayer. Simply put, prayer is communication with God. You can and should ask things of God, but His answers may not always be what you expect. You can ask for new boots, but God may tell you your old sandals are good enough."

"Some churches falsely teach that your coin has a direct bearing on how God answers your prayers. God gives you everything you have. His services cannot be purchased with coins. *The Guide* teaches us to give, but God is interested in our motive for giving. To give your coin to any church for the sole purpose of having God answer your prayers, is the wrong motive."

"As for faith and healing, your faith should be focused on God and how God knows what is best for you. You should always pray for healing. Sometimes, God will heal you. But frankly, some of us have stronger faith because our bodies are weak and sick. Did not the great apostle in *The Guide* ask God three times to heal him, and God refused? God told this apostle *"My grace is sufficient for thee: for my strength is made perfect in weakness.* The apostle went on to say, *Most gladly therefore will I rather glory in my infirmities, that the power of Christ may rest upon me."* False

109

churches today would tell this apostle that he does not have enough faith to be healed, and that he needs more faith. The fact is, sometimes, God allows this fallen world to overcome us with weakness and sickness, so our faith in Him will be stronger. He wants to be our strength. Often, severely handicapped people have a stronger faith in God, than healthy people do. As far as God is concerned, they are stronger than we are.

The man paused, looking out over the people gathered at the church. "So how do we pray to God? First, you have to remember that you are talking to the Creator of the universe. As *The Guide* says, *God resists the proud, but gives grace unto the humble.* That is why you should always approach God in humility when you pray. You need to remember how great and powerful the God you are talking to is. Second, *The Guide* tells us that He is our Father. As you should always talk to your own father respectfully, so you should be respectful when talking to God. Think of your father, or a man you know and respect, and then think about how you would converse with him. As a good father loves his child and delights in talking with his child, so too does God love his children, and delights in their prayers to him."

Lily's mind went to Lamar while the man continued to lecture the congregation. She rarely had even seen her own father. Her father worked as a wagon driver, who would be gone for weeks or months at a time, delivering goods to other cities. When he was home, he was either at a tavern or sleeping off the effects of the tavern's drinks.

"We need to always remember to thank God for what we have," the man up front said. "Remember that everything, including our very lives, is because God has given it to us. The prayer of the saints is a joy to God, and answering is His delight."

"While God does hear the prayers of His people that believe in His Son, He also hears the prayers of anyone and everyone who acknowledges that they are sinners, and believe upon the work of His Son, and the sacrifice He made for all mankind. Those that pray and ask for God to save them from their sins, have prayers that are always heard. Such prayers are always answered, with a yes."

The man paused again. "Does that answer the question of what prayer is?" He was now looking at Lily and Chellell. Lily stared wide-eyed at the man. She nodded her head enthusiastically. "Good. Let us bow our heads to show our humility, and I will pray. By the way, you can talk to God anytime, anywhere, aloud or quietly in your mind. He will hear you. *The Guide* says to *pray without ceasing.* Now, let us pray." Lily bowed her head as the man prayed.

After prayer, another man came to the front and took out *The Guide.* He began to read from it and explain what he was reading. Lily listened with pure excitement, sitting on the edge of her chair. This is what she had thought church should be like. The man sounded like Lamar. Halfway through the man's preaching, something seemed to strike her heart. Sadness overcame her. The emptiness inside her seemed to grow infinitely. As the preacher talked about sin, the conviction in her grew. Her mind flashed back to the times she had lied to her parents, was selfish, and all the other bad things she had done. Another thing that really struck her heart was how much time and effort she put into her looks, the make-up and the hair. She realized that her whole focus in life was how she looked to other people, yet on the inside, she was unhappy. Worse yet, Lily realized that even though she looked beautiful on the outside to everyone, on the inside she was really ugly. No one could see that, but she now understood that God could.

The man switched and started talking about how *God so loved the world that he gave his one and only Son, that whoever believes in him shall not perish but have eternal life.* Lily came out of the sadness she felt and listened to how God's Son had literally taken the punishment for mankind. How God had poured out His wrath on His only Son, so that those who called upon the name of the Lord might be spared the punishment due them for their sins. He fully paid the debt they owed to God. How He was raised on the third day and eventually, ascended back into heaven, with the promise to one day, return.

Tears started to flow from Lily's eyes. The man talked about God changing your heart and making you clean on the inside. Finally, the man finished reading from *The Guide*.

"As is our custom here," he said, "anyone who wants to accept the free gift of salvation, may come forward and talk with me. Or, they can catch me any time after we are finished." Lily stood up, shaking off Chellell's hand as Chellell tried to pull her back into her seat. With tears rolling down her face, she walked the couple of steps to the preacher, falling to her knees in front of him. She completely lost control and started sobbing uncontrollably, with her head bowed between her knees.

Chellell sat there exasperated. "I cannot believe this," she thought, as she slinked down in her seat, hoping no one was looking at her. Several ladies came up and knelt beside Lily, their arms around her. The man who had prayed earlier came up and knelt with them as well. He started talking to Lily, who was still sobbing. Lily was nodding her head "yes" to the man, while trying to stop crying.

What looked like a small, white, bird came down through the roof of the church and hit Lily, disappearing inside of her. Chellell looked around in complete astonishment, but nobody seemed to notice the ghostly bird. Lily spent a couple of minutes on her knees. Finally, she stopped crying and stood up. With the exception of Chellell, everyone in the church started clapping. Then they were coming forward, taking turns hugging Lily. Jumping up from her chair, Chellell cut through the people and whispered in Lily's ear.

"I will see you back at the show; you can find your way back, can't you?" Lily nodded. Chellell left the church as fast as she could. Sanatarial landed on her shoulder shortly after she left the church. His good mood was gone. Her familiar was glaring with hatred in its glittering eyes at the small church building, but Chellell didn't notice. Her mind was swirling in confusion. As a child, she liked going to these churches. Such visits always made her feel good inside, but in her mind was the reality that if there really was a God, then He had never done anything for her. Anger rose in her as she thought back to her father, and the wasted time she spent praying for his return. If there was a God, then He did not listen to her. As far as she was concerned, she would not have anything to do with a God like that.

Something else really troubled her. Five days ago, the show had started posting the king's decree that outlawed *The Guide*. Having grown up in the church, she knew people would not give up its teaching. People she knew would probably end up in prison. Her mother was one of them, and Javin would be another. She believed that the church was a problem for society, but the king's decree went way too far. Surely education and logical thinking were working, so why take it to this level?

Also, the thing with Lily really bothered her. She simply could not purge her mind of the scene with Lily on her knees, sobbing. What was that strange, ghostly white bird that went into Lily? Troubling thoughts ran through her mind as she walked back to her tent.

Chapter 10

For the invisible things of him from the creation of the world are clearly seen,
being understood by the things that are made, even his eternal power and
Godhead; so that they are without excuse – The Guide

When the bells had rung several weeks ago, the general of Fort Outlands announced that a large army of gorms were spotted by scouts in the Northern Wastes moving toward the fort. The general at the fort had made a critical mistake. He did not initially request reinforcements, assuming the army to be one to two thousand soldiers strong. A week later, the army was estimated to be made up of twelve thousand gorm and goblin soldiers, with several hundred giants. The only reinforcements that could make it to the fort now, were several hundred soldiers from Bear Tree City, not near enough to face an army this size. Still, the general decided to stay in the fort, and fight. He hoped to hold the army until the ten-thousand man army from the capital city could arrive.

Ledia arrived at the shop around noon to look at one of Thunderfall's horses that had developed a slight limp. Shortly after Ledia's arrival, Thunderfall informed Gevi and Javin that he was going to meet with some dwarves and that he should be back late in the evening.

Javin had finished his work for the day, when Gevi walked in carrying a basket. "I was about to go to the house for supper. Is it ready yet?" Javin asked while strapping on his new sword belt. The way things were with the gorms lately, he did not feel comfortable without his swords close by.

"Is supper ready yet?" Gevi mimicked. "Do I look like your personal cook? Do I get a hello, or a nice to see you, Gevi? No! I get, I'm hungry. Feed me now!"

Javin smiled as he walked toward Gevi, who was glaring at him from the doorway. "Burned supper again, didn't you? That's alright; I can grab some fruit and bread." Holding in laughter, Javin waited for Gevi's reaction while he continued to walk toward her.

Gevi stomped her foot in indignation, her emerald green eyes flashing. "Burn something one time and everybody forgets the hundred good meals they had," she said, glaring at Javin. "I should throw this mince fruit pie in the fire and make you eat it, charred!" She waved the basket in front of her, causing the wonderful aroma of the fruit to reach Javin's nose.

"My favorite, and it smells good," Javin stuttered as he came to stand by her in the doorway. The pleasant aroma circulated through the shop, making Javin's mouth water with anticipation. "I'm sorry; you are a great cook." Javin kept his face as serious as he could even though the reality of Gevi's cooking often involved burned meals because her mind was constantly on new inventions and not on food preparation.

"And don't you forget it. Daddy could be the one doing the cooking. After one bite of his food, you would be on your knees, begging me to cook.

Come on. We are going on a picnic down by the creek. The weather is too nice to eat inside."

Both Javin and Gevi were sitting on a red blanket spread out on the sand right by the creek. A nice warm breeze was gently blowing, causing Gevi to constantly flick her rich black hair out of her eyes. In the waters of the creek, two otters were playing. As they ate, it was inevitable that they would start talking about the present events affecting their lives. From their location, the shop and the road to the fort could be easily seen. Neither felt comfortable straying too far away from the shop with the invading army so close to the fort.

Javin had decided to stay, despite the fact that Thunderfall had signed his guild papers. These past couple of weeks had been very pleasant for Javin, and for Gevi. His friendship with Gevi had grown beyond the childlike friendship Javin had experienced with Chellell. His favorite time of day was in the late evening where the two of them studied *The Guide* together. Thunderfall always sat in his chair in the main room of the house, while Javin and Gevi sat on the floor. As Javin and Gevi studied *The Guide*, they often stopped their readings, to discuss its topics. Occasionally, Thunderfall would answer a question or try to settle a dispute between the two, but most of the time, he left them to themselves. In reality, Thunderfall was extremely pleased to see Gevi growing spiritually. In fact, Thunderfall realized that together, Javin and Gevi were both growing spiritually.

"Do you remember that horrible monument we found on the way to the mine?" Gevi asked, bringing Javin's thoughts back to the present. Her slick black hair was blowing gently in the wind. She was sitting cross legged on the red blanket. Javin was lying on his back a few feet from her.

"The statue we found because you got us lost; the statue you blew up." Javin replied with a smile on his face.

"Yes, the one we found because a man can't follow a map; and I can tell you I am not done with that evil thing yet. One day, I will return and turn it into gravel." Gevi threw a beautiful smile towards him. Javin shook his head and smiled back. "I asked Ledia about the monument and she told me some interesting things. You want to hear what she told me?"

Javin nodded his head. "It seems that the Linkrins built the monument. They built many of these monuments throughout their lands."

"Are those the same people who built what are now the ruins the people of your church are going to?" Javin asked.

"Yes, the very same; Ledia told me they were worshipers of science and nature. At what some call the height of their power as a kingdom thousands of years ago, their elite scientists came to the conclusion that scientific laws proved there was no God."

"That is absolutely crazy. Science absolutely proves there is a God!" Javin stammered in astonishment.

"Oh, it gets even better," Gevi replied with a laugh. "Ledia went on to say that in the beginning, almost no one believed these few elite scientists because the majority were actually followers of God. Using their flawed, unproven theories, they called scientific laws, the scientists developed the theory we saw on the monument." Gevi looked down at Javin, who was still lying on his back. Gevi's sparkling green eyes locked onto Javin's brown eyes. Her eyes could barely contain her mirth. "The theory they came up with to explain creation without God is that all the stars we see in the sky suddenly appeared in an unimaginably big explosion, in a time so long ago you cannot even comprehend it."

Javin started laughing, "Come on Gevi, what scientist would believe that? I knew scientists at the guilds. They are very intelligent."

"Those who don't believe in God, have to believe in something. Without God, you can believe anything, no matter how ridiculous. That monument we saw proves that. The first picture we saw, the circle with lines, represented the first life on this planet. It was non-life that mysteriously, somehow, instantly came alive." Gevi started laughing and giggling so hard, she fell down beside Javin. Javin shook his head.

"Gevi, you can't be serious?"

Gevi burst out laughing even harder. "I'm serious!" she said while trying to catch her breath. She rolled over on her side with her head in her hand, facing Javin. "The monument said that this life thing became more complex. After a tremendous amount of time, it became a fish. Some fish eventually decided to grow legs so they could crawl on land." Looking at Javin's astonished face, she started giggling again. "These legged fish changed into land animals, once again, after a tremendous amount of time. Some decided to grow wings and become birds. A monkey appeared and over time it became smarter and less hairy, changing into a human."

Javin couldn't help it, he started laughing. "That sounds more like a fanciful imagination than science. Animals don't become completely different animals, even if given an eternity to change." Javin managed to finally stammer. "What were they thinking?"

Gevi smiled again before sitting back up and crossing her legs. Her expression grew more serious. "Ledia said something about these ancient people that really concerned me, Javin. She told me these scientists got the schools to teach this mess as fact. The kids grew up believing it. Within a couple of generations, very few believed in the Creator, the true God. Monuments were constructed throughout their lands, proclaiming their belief in science—their belief that science had declared God never existed. Ironically, God judged them through science and nature. Within the course of a few years, the greatest kingdom ever known was destroyed by volcanoes, floods, and earthquakes. What was left was destroyed by a great drought. An invasion of goblins followed the drought. Ultimately, the Linkrins became extinct. All that is left of them is a few monuments and some ruins."

"Everyone?" stuttered Javin. "Surely some had faith in God."

"You are correct, some in fact did believe in God. God spared them. Three groups of believers fled right before the wrath of God came down on the Linkrins. They ended up in the Dwarven Mountains, the Elven Forest, and the Lost Swamp in Southern Preveshawl. That is where the races of dwarfs, the elves, and humans come from." Gevi looked off toward the creek. "The Linkrins are our ancestors."

Javin sat up, pulling in close beside Gevi. "History repeats itself. The king is doing the same thing in our schools today," he said in a low voice. "Except his viewpoint claims magic, not science, caused everything."

"Seems to me that the Linkrins really believed in magic as well," Gevi snorted. "Non-life, somehow becoming alive, fish growing legs, animals growing feathers and flying, monkeys becoming humans; that is unexplainable magic, not science."

Javin grabbed a piece of pie out of the basket. They sat there, silently, for several long minutes. Ledia came out of the barn, grabbing some tools from her horse. Gevi waved to her, before grabbing a sandwich. Finally, she decided to ask Javin something else that really worried her.

"Javin, what do you plan to do with the king's decree? I know you are fine for now, but what about your family in Farm Circle?" Gevi took a bite of her sandwich while looking curiously at Javin.

Not wanting to answer her, Javin took a bite of the pie Gevi had made. "This is really good, Gevi. You really out-did yourself baking this."

"Thank you, but you're avoiding my question," Gevi said, pleased that he liked the pie.

"I think the army is too busy to worry about enforcement of the king's decree, for now. I doubt they can spare the time to hunt down those of us who have *The Guide*." Javin took another bite of his pie, "This is really good. To answer your question, I plan to stay and help defend the fort. Then I will travel to Farm Circle and check on my family. My Dad will take care of things there and help the community deal with the king's decree. It would take a small army to arrest him. I am needed here. If the gorms get past the fort, they will be at Farm Circle in a matter of days anyway. I think it best for everyone, including my family, to defend the fort."

Gevi lay back on the picnic blanket, watching the clouds moving through the light blue sky. "I think you are right. But we both know Dad will never put his apprentice deliberately in harm's way. I guarantee you he will order us both to safety somewhere."

"I know; but I will be at the fort fighting, guaranteed."

"How do you plan to pull that off?" She asked with her brows raised in curiosity.

Distracted by something he saw, Javin said, "What is that?" He pointed right past Gevi, "No. Stay down." Gevi had started to rise up to look, but heeding Javin's warning she spun around flat on her stomach. A cloud of dust was coming up off the road near Mac's farm. Knowing a large group of something was on the road heading toward the shop; Gevi reached over and grabbed her staff, pulling it snuggly next to her body. A few minutes passed when abruptly, Gevi jumped up.

"It's Daddy, with a bunch of dwarves." Javin jumped to his feet.

Sure enough, Thunderfall was at the head of a column of dwarves. The pounding of their feet was causing a massive amount of dust to swirl up into the air.

"He better not ask me to cook for all these dwarves," murmured Gevi as she and Javin walked down the road to meet the dwarves.

"He won't, I'm certain he likes his brothers." Javin barely dodged the playful swing that Gevi aimed at his shoulder. He took off running, full speed toward the dwarves, with Gevi chasing after him.

****

"So this is the lovely young lady that threatened to paddle old Ironhand's backside," said the dwarven captain once Thunderfall introduced him to his daughter. "But of course, seeing you chasing that boy and tackling him up the road there; I can see why Ironhand thought the two of you were...friends." The dwarf captain gave Gevi a wink as he said the word "friends". Javin wasn't sure who looked more embarrassed, Thunderfall or Gevi. He decided to pretend he didn't hear a thing while he pulled grass out of his hair and clothes.

"Hey boss," one of the dwarves yelled from the group, "better be careful what you say, or you'll be the one getting the paddling." A roar of laughter went up from the dwarves.

Thunderfall, the whole top of his bald head, red with embarrassment, shook his head. "One day, Girl, you are going to have to tell me what happened between you and Ironhand." His eyes looked around at all the dwarves still roaring with laughter, but came to rest on Javin who was trying really hard not to smile. "Never mind, I probably don't want to know."

"Ironhand deserved it, Daddy," said an incensed Gevi, "and if you were a good Daddy, you would defend your daughter's honor and teach these insensitive hooligans you call brothers a lesson on how to treat a lady." She turned and started stomping off back toward the creek. "I left my staff by the creek," she called back over her shoulder. Thunderfall put his head in his hands, hiding his face while the dwarves roared even louder with laughter.

Javin was in a deep conversation with a dwarf when cold water spilled over his head, soaking him from head to toe. Turning around in shock, he saw Gevi standing with an empty water bucket in her hand. "This is your lesson for the month, never insult a woman's cooking, especially mine," Gevi said with a teasing smile. The dwarves started roaring again with laughter. Sitting down next to Javin, Gevi pulled out a cloth and started drying him off. Thunderfall decided to save himself further embarrassment by pretending he had not seen what his daughter had done.

****

Several hours had passed since the dwarves had arrived. They had set up a camp in front of the shop. Thirty dwarves were sitting around discussing the events coming up. "Besides us and the siege engines we dropped off at the fort, there will be no other dwarves." The dwarven captain said to Gevi. "Our Battlelord has ordered us to stay and fight, but we are to leave the fort when it seems doomed to fall to the gorms. And from where I sit, I see no way the fort will survive."

"Why?" asked Gevi, who was sitting next to Javin, across from the dwarven captain and Thunderfall. "Why are the dwarves unwilling to help Preveshawl, the way they have in the past? Didn't Javin's father help the dwarves?"

The captain started to reply, but Thunderfall cut him off. "The dwarves are wise enough to know that God will not be with Preveshawl. The dwarven Battlelord knows that any kingdom that rebels against God is a defeated kingdom. *The Guide* says: *But if ye will not obey the voice of the LORD, but rebel against the commandment of the LORD, then shall the hand of the LORD be against you, as it was against your fathers.*"

"That is correct," said the dwarven captain. "Our Battlelord is reluctant to defend a kingdom in full rebellion against God. However, he is willing to help Preveshawl somewhat, in honor of Lamar. He sent messengers to your king, asking him to humble himself before God, and to restore Preveshawl back to the worship of the one true God. Only if the king repeals his laws, which have certainly angered the Lord of the Stars, will the dwarves throw their full weight into the fight."

"What was the king's response?" asked Gevi.

The dwarf captain's eyes instantly lit up with anger. "The human king told the dwarven messengers that if any dwarf ever mentioned this God in his presence again, then he would have his guards shave their beards, before sending them back to their holes in the mountains."

Gevi gasped with shock. Everyone knew that dwarves took great pride in their beards. Only as a punishment for running away during battle, or for some other extreme display of cowardly behavior, was a dwarf's beard shaved.

"Wow," said Javin. "It's a miracle then that you are even here."

"We are here only because of Lamar and this fort. To maintain those ties, the Battlelord sent us with several siege engines. However, the Battlelord really feels that defending the fort is a lost cause till Preveshawl repents of its evil."

Everybody was silent after that statement. The mood was now very somber. Javin glanced to his side at Gevi; she had tears in her eyes. "When do the gorms get here?" Javin asked after several minutes of no one talking.

"The gorm army will be at the fort sometime around noon tomorrow," replied Thunderfall. "The general has ordered all able body fighters to the fort by sunrise. My brothers and I will be there. You and Gevi will be with Ledia..."

"You signed my apprenticeship papers; therefore I'm free," interrupted Javin, hoping that Master Thunderfall would understand what he meant. He held his breath nervously, not sure how the dwarf would react. Gevi gasped, staring at him in astonishment. After nearly a minute of nothing said, Javin looked up from the ground at Thunderfall. The dwarf had a calm expression.

"Right you are; I did sign your papers." Thunderfall couldn't look at Gevi, because he had a feeling this young man was important to her future. He spoke again. "Let me rephrase what I said. I think it would be best if you stayed with Gevi at Ledia's. She will need protection. Many men will die tomorrow, Javin. Wars are horrible events. If you go, at worst you will join the dead on the wall tomorrow. At best, you will have memories that will haunt you until the day you die." His words were spoken like a dwarf who had seen many battles.

"Javin, the choice will be yours. You are free from me because I did sign your release from my apprenticeship. Because you are over the age of fifteen, you are allowed by law to fight for the army. Because you are not eighteen yet, the General's order for all able bodied men to be at the fort does not apply to you." Thunderfall paused, taking a deep breath.

Javin was going to speak, but Thunderfall stopped him. "Don't decide now. We leave at five in the morning. I will not say a word if you decide to go with us to the fort. You will be welcomed as a brother in arms. If you decide to stay and guard Gevi, then that decision will be welcomed as well."

Javin nodded his head toward Thunderfall, acknowledging the agreement. He would have to pray about his decision tonight.

"Daddy, can I talk to you a minute, in private?" Gevi asked. Thunderfall stood up and walked hand-in-hand with his daughter away from the group. Javin listened to the dwarves discussing gorms and battle plans. Finally, Gevi and her father returned.

"Slight change of plans; Gevi has convinced me that being at Ledia's house could be more dangerous than being in the fort. If the gorms decide to have soldiers come over the wall and wreak havoc on the countryside around the fort, they would be in trouble. There is an underground shelter in the fort that they have set up as a hospital. Gevi and Ledia will stay there and help with the wounded. There is an escape tunnel that goes from the shelter to a spot a couple of hundred feet south of the fort. If events make it necessary, they can escape through the tunnel. Javin, I would like for you to stay in the shelter, but again, the choice is yours."

Gevi sat down next to Javin. She put her arm around him and her head on his shoulder. "He will listen to what you have to say, and change his mind if it seems like a good idea," she whispered into his ear.

"Stubborn as a dwarf does not always apply then, does it?" he whispered back. Slowly, over the last couple of weeks, Javin had gotten more comfortable with Gevi being closer to him. Gevi smiled and tucked a strand of hair behind her slightly pointed elven ears. She lifted her head and arm off him, but stayed leaning against him. Javin gestured toward a dwarf with a big red beard and short cropped hair. The dwarf came and sat by him and Gevi.

"While you and Gevi were talking," Javin stammered to Thunderfall, "Snarlhair here told me something I think you should hear." Thunderfall and Gevi turned their attention to the dwarf called Snarlhair as the rest of the dwarves broke into a praise song to the Lord of the Stars. Snarlhair spoke above the clamor of dwarven singing.

"I was telling the boy here, that a patrol I was with encountered a group of elves and humans way up in the mountains, north of the dwarven mines. They were looking for the Elven Forest." Gevi and Thunderfall exchanged glances. "The elves looked like typical elves, tall, with long blond hair. Unlike any elf I have ever seen though, they were heavily armed, with the look of hardened fighters."

"The humans looked different. They looked like you." Snarlhair fixed his gaze on Gevi. "They had hair as black as mountain coal and bright green eyes. They wore the strangest furs you ever saw, and were armed head-to-toe with swords, bows, and knives. Tough looking group of humans." Gevi exchanged glances again with her father. Excitement showed in her eyes.

"Where are these elves now?" Thunderfall asked.

"A few days ago, we guided them through the mountains to the Elven Forest. That is the last I saw of them."

Thunderfall thanked Snarlhair for the information. He watched his daughter, sitting against Javin, with her arm around his shoulder. She was providing a beautiful singing voice to the gruff singing of the dwarves. Thunderfall was very conflicted. On one hand, he was extremely pleased to see his only daughter take an interest in someone who was spiritually grounded in the Word. That was an answer to his prayers. However, Gevi was his little girl, and it pained him to see her growing up. The thought of his little girl depending on someone, other than himself, caused him tremendous grief. Yet, he knew it would happen. It had to happen. *The Guide* did say, *therefore shall a man leave his father and his mother, and shall cleave unto his wife: and they shall be one flesh.*

Thunderfall had to admit to himself that these two were doing really well. Without him saying anything, they had drawn boundaries with each other. These boundaries seem to come to them unbidden.

The only thing that worried Thunderfall was that Javin was extremely shy; to the point that he avoided people. He avoided social interaction with people, and crowded places. On the complete opposite end of the spectrum, was Gevi. She craved social interaction and loved being close to people. She was popular among the locals. He wasn't sure how this would work out between the two, if their relationship kept growing.

They stayed up with the dwarves until midnight. Different dwarves would read passages from *The Guide*. At times, they would break into songs praising God. They finally went to bed after a wisecracking dwarf got threatened by Gevi. Thunderfall had to practically drag Gevi back to the house, while the dwarves roared with laughter.

Chapter 11

O God the Lord, the strength of my salvation, thou hast covered my head in the day of battle. – The Guide

Javin and Thunderfall sat impatiently on the wall with twenty-two of the thirty dwarves. The whole morning had been hard on Javin, due to anxiety over the coming battle mixed with boredom from sitting on the fort wall. They had been assigned the far west corner of the north wall. Four dwarves were working with the human engineers to set up the four huge catapults that the dwarves had brought to the fort. Four other dwarves were spotters up on the wall near the gate. Their job was to signal distances and angles back down to the catapult operators.

Javin had on his full armor as well as his two new swords. The chain mail mesh attached to the helmet completely covered his entire face, except for the eyes. Since he had only been to the fort a handful of times, no one recognized him. A lot of stares came his way from the soldiers, but they assumed he was with the dwarves and left him alone.

While impatiently waiting, trumpets started blaring around the fort. Javin's heart jumped into his throat. This was it. The battle was about to begin. Fear overcame him as he wondered about his decision to fight, instead of staying with Gevi, in the safety of the hospital bunker. He pushed the fear away, remembering that this is what he had trained for at the Guild of Warriors.

"Here we go, boys. Get those crossbows loaded," the dwarven captain ordered. Dwarfs started calmly setting bolts into crossbows. After the crossbows were loaded, they stared over the walls, trying to catch sight of the enemy.

The walkway they were on was below the top edge of the wall. It was made so soldiers could fire over the wall from a kneeling position. Wooden ladders were the only method up to the walkway. If the walls were compromised, then the wooden ladders could be knocked down by soldiers on the ground inside the fort. That left attackers twenty-six feet up in the air, on walkways and easy targets for any archer in the fort.

They waited, kneeling behind the wall. Within a few minutes, faint, steady, drum beats were heard. They still could see nothing, due to the fact that the fort was in a pass between two mountains. A mile north of the fort, a magnificent cliff jutted out of the ground, reaching hundreds of feet skyward. The locals called it Sky Cloud Cliff. This wall of rock was part of the Western Mountain Range.

Another defensive advantage to the fort was the fact that it was located at the highest point of the pass. Once the army came around this cliff face, they would have a steep climb upwards toward the fort. Large pits full of spiked sticks were scattered around in the open fields between the fort and Sky Cloud Cliff. Preveshawl soldiers had created many nasty, deadly surprises for the enemy army in the fields, especially in the area directly in front of the walls.

Minutes passed, with the only sign of the enemy army the pounding of gorm drums, growing steadily louder. The only sign, until bands of goblins and gorms began to appear at the base of Sky Cloud Cliff.

"Load the catapults," yelled the general, who was stationed on the wall near the gate, "Anti-personnel shot." More and more goblins and gorms started appearing. They stayed back, way out of catapult range.

"Get ready, youngster", the dwarf next to Javin said. "They will charge the walls shortly. Once they reach us, they will use ladders and grappling hooks to try to take the walls. While we fight to protect the walls, the enemy will attack the gate with battering rams. Finally, they will bring up their catapults. I hope your general knows what he is doing. If you concentrate on the foot soldiers trying to climb the walls, then you will forget the ram that breaks the gate and the boulders that will crush the walls."

As if on cue, Javin saw a large number of gorms and goblins pour around Sky Cloud Cliff in formation lines. Hard drum beats from the enemy army reverberated through the fort.

"On my command, fire Infantry shot, all catapults." yelled the general.

Abruptly, the drum beats stopped. Nervously, Javin waited on the wall. Five minutes went by, with the massive enemy army standing a mile back from the fort in perfect formation lines. A great shout came from the gorms and goblins. The battle cry caused cold fear to spread instantly through Javin's body. Once again, he regretted not taking Thunderfall's advice and staying out of this battle.

"Here we go," murmured Thunderfall from Javin's other side. A rapid, steady, drum beat started pounding. At a fast paced march, the enemy marched toward the fort. Several long minutes passed as the army closed the distance between them and the fort.

"Fire!" screamed the general, once the enemy army had closed within a thousand feet of the fort. Simultaneously, all four catapults fired. Fist-sized rocks rained down on the front lines of the marching army, killing dozens of gorms and goblins.

Another heart-stopping war cry came from the enemy army as goblins and gorms charged toward the fort. Javin ducked back behind the wall, shaking with uncontrolled terror. Closing his eyes, he forced the overwhelming fear out of his mind. Taking a deep breath, he opened his eyes. His hands were still shaking and he was deathly afraid, but he was now in control of himself.

Viewing ports were cut into the wall every four feet. Javin used one to watch the battle unfold. While gorms and goblins rushed toward the wall, catapults fired from the fort. The fist-sized stones smashed into the mass of gorms and goblins, but they kept on coming. The noise of the screaming enemy army running toward the walls was deafening. Hidden pits with spiked sticks along with the catapult shots killed many goblins and gorms, but they did not slow the charging army.

"Wait for my command to fire," the dwarf captain called out. Another barrage of catapult stones flew into the charging army. The goblins and gorms were yelling so loudly that Javin could not hear the screams of those crushed by the catapult stones. They disappeared almost instantly under the feet of the charging army that was behind them.

"Fire!" ordered their captain. Every dwarf rose up and discharged their crossbows toward the gorms. Javin fired his bow toward the mass of creatures. He noticed a multitude of them lying dead across the fields in front of the fort. Dropping back down, Javin quickly put another arrow to his bow. Seeing that the dwarves were busy cranking their crossbows, he peeked out the viewport again. The gorms and goblins had stopped their advance and were firing arrows toward the wall. Javin could hear the arrows as they crashed into the wall and could see them flying over his head. Arrows were bouncing off the protective shield wall, held by the soldiers in the courtyard below. It sounded like hail stones hitting the metal roof of a house.

"Fire!" Javin rose and fired down toward the enemy lines. He ducked back down without knowing if he had hit anything or not. Several arrows had flown right by his head, missing him by inches. The dwarf beside him was not so lucky. He fell back, an arrow sticking out of his neck.

Javin stared at the now dead dwarf, fighting down the bile that was rising in his throat. He glanced down the wall and saw other soldiers down, with arrows sticking out of various parts of their body. He missed the next fire command. Anger mixed with disgust started to overcome him, pushing any fear left out of his mind.

Drawing one of his swords, Javin leaped to his feet and flamed the sword. He pointed the sword out over the wall while opening the hidden panel at the base of the sword handle. An arrow bounced off his helmet at the exact same time as the ball of fire flew out from the flaming sword. It exploded into the front line of the enemy. Bodies flew in all directions.

Javin stood on the wall with flaming sword still pointing toward the destruction he had caused. A cheer went up along the wall. Nearly all the soldiers had turned to see what had caused the explosion. What they saw was a black armored warrior with a flaming sword standing defiantly against the enemy. Several more arrows bounced off his armor before Thunderfall forcefully pulled him back down behind the wall.

"Calm down, Javin," Thunderfall ordered. He stopped Javin from drawing his other sword. "Save it. You will need it later. This is what it is like to experience war. If you want to live, get your emotions under control." With sadness, he glanced down at the dwarf on the ground by Javin. "A lot more will be meeting the Lord of the Stars before this day is over."

Javin took a deep breath before extinguishing the flame on his sword. "Thanks," he said as he grabbed his bow and put an arrow to it. "I'll be alright now. I just got so angry..."

"Fire!" Javin rose up as ordered and fired his bow, dropping right back down. The arrow flew into a large mass of goblins running toward the wall carrying long ladders.

Thunderfall worked on reloading his crossbow. "This is war and this is what happens in war. Keep yourself under control and pray you and your buddies live to see the morning."

Javin nodded and looked out at the battle. The ladders and gorms carrying grappling hooks were almost at the base of the wall. All the arrow fire from the fort was now concentrated on this group. The fire command came again. He rose up and shot directly down the wall toward the group carrying ladders. An arrow again bounced off his helmet. Formations of gorms and goblins firing arrows were behind their comrades that were charging the wall with ladders and grappling hooks. Javin recognized that deadly arrow fire would continue until the walls were taken.

"Every third, take up hook poles," the dwarven captain called out. Every third dwarf dropped their crossbow and took up a long pole with a hook on the end. Ladders started coming over the top of the wall. The dwarves with the poles hooked the ladders, pushing them backwards or pulling them sideways. The fire command came once again and Javin fired another arrow directly into a goblin on a ladder ten feet below him. The fallen goblin body caused every creature on the ladder below him to fall back to the ground by the wall. Ducking down behind the wall, he saw ropes with grappling hooks flying over the wall.

"Every second, axes," was called out. Javin remembered that he was numbered with the axe call, so he drew both his short swords. Deep red flames licked around the blades of the swords as Javin ignited both his swords.

It was amazing how sharp these swords Thunderfall had made him were. One swing with a sword and the ropes were instantly severed from the grappling hooks. He could hear the screams as the enemy fell from the ropes. For nearly half an hour, the struggle at the wall went on. It felt more like an eternity to everyone fighting. Ropes were cut by Javin's short sword. An occasional enemy that managed to come over the wall was instantly sent to his Creator by Javin's spinning swords. However, more and more gorms and goblins were making it onto the wall.

With amazing speed, Thunderfall dropped his crossbow and drew his large, black steel battle axe. A goblin was chopped nearly in half a second later. Javin stabbed a gorm that was at the top of a ladder, not even bothering to watch it fall screaming back over the wall. The enemy was up on the walkway with them now.

"Axes, all," the captain called out. Javin started stabbing and cutting into every gorm and goblin he saw with lightning speed. His body was in constant motion, spinning and twisting with swords blazing fire around him. The menacing black armored figure with flaming swords that seemed to strike everywhere, was freezing the gorms and goblins. Fear could be seen in their eyes, right before Javin cut them down. Bodies started piling up around him and his deadly swords. Javin sliced through the leather armor of another goblin when he heard the noise of wood splintering. The wall under his feet shook violently.

"Off the wall," yelled Thunderfall loudly, as he swung his axe into a gorm. He proceeded to slide down the ladder into the courtyard of the fort. Javin's left sword stabbed into the chest of his current opponent, before he too, jumped onto the ladder. He was down in the courtyard in seconds. The surviving dwarves came sliding quickly down the ladders, rapidly disposing of several gorms in the courtyard. The ladders then were knocked to the ground.

Javin surveyed the chaos of the courtyard and saw that the large wooden gates were splintered, lying on the ground. A massive battering ram was lying across the gates. Human soldiers stood side by side, fighting the mass of gorms, goblins, and now a few giants, that were pouring in through the destroyed gate. The chaotic noise of the wounded and dying, mixed with swords banging shields and armor, was deafening.

No matter how hard they fought, the Preveshawl soldiers were slowly being pushed back. Two of the four catapults were on fire. Frantic fighting was going on around the last two surviving catapults. Joining in the fight, the dwarves ran towards the closest catapult.

Javin however, charged toward the fighting at the main gate, cutting down a goblin that got too close to him as he ran. Jumping onto the back of a wagon, he pointed a flaming sword toward the gate.

A two-headed wolf, with jaws snapping, leaped through the gate. The wolf's goblin rider was armed with a wicked looking lance. Javin could see several more such wolves and riders just outside the entranceway. A ball of fire flew from Javin's sword, exploding into the two-headed wolf. The ball of fire also blew up a horde of gorm soldiers massed around the gate, throwing bodies through the air. The wood from the broken gates ignited in a pillar of flames.

A cheer went up from the soldiers. None of the enemy could come through the burning gate. Preveshawl soldiers started overwhelming the enemy massed against them in the courtyard. The gorms, goblins, and giants had to decide whether to fight to the death, or burn in the fire they were being pushed backed towards. Javin jumped off the wagon, engaging the gorms and goblins that were using ropes to come down the wall into the courtyard.

A large portion of the wall shook, and then collapsed, crushing several gorms near it. Javin was fighting a group of three gorms when another section abruptly collapsed. He disarmed one gorm and killed the second gorm when a third section of the wall violently exploded, throwing rock shrapnel all over the courtyard. The enemy catapults were collapsing the wall. Javin finished off the last gorm in his area, letting the one he disarmed run away. He knew the fort had fallen as more of the wall collapsed under the barrage of boulders hitting them.

A loud explosion with a bright flash of light caused Javin to look back into the fort where most of the stores were located. A mushroom cloud of smoke was rising into the air from one of the buildings. A lightning bolt flew from the sky down into another building. The building exploded. Javin looked toward the sky, his eyes not believing what he saw. A man was riding on a flying monster that Javin instantly recognized from his Guild of Warrior classes as a gryphon. He watched in stunned silence as lightning flew from the hand of the magic user riding the gryphon, disintegrating another building inside the fort.

Loud trumpet blasts rang through the air. The gorms, goblins, and several of the remaining giants, turned and sprinted out of the fort through the collapsed sections in the wall. The gryphon turned and flew back toward the enemy army, its powerful, flapping wings audible to everyone inside the fort. Javin stood there, puzzled, as a gorm ran right in front of him, back toward the collapsed wall. Within a few minutes, the fort was cleared of the enemy.

"Come on," yelled Thunderfall as he ran past Javin. Javin followed him to the wall, where Thunderfall was setting a ladder back up. Climbing up the ladder, Javin stood beside Thunderfall. The fields in front of the wall were littered with the bodies of gorms and goblins. Barely out of bow range, thousands of gorms, goblins and giants, stood in perfect formations. Dozens of flags were waving in the wind at the front of each formation. Over a dozen catapults were lined up at the back of the enemy army. A soldier came up the ladder, joining Javin and Thunderfall. An officer, Javin saw from his torn and bloodied uniform.

Drumbeats started pounding in a steady, eerie rhythm. A giant strolled out from the army with a human walking beside him. A giant, a gorm, and a goblin marched in unison ten paces behind the giant and the human.

"That giant is at least sixteen feet tall," the officer commented out loud, awe in his voice.

"And that is a magic user next to him," said Thunderfall. "I can see the familiar on his shoulder." Javin looked closer and realized Thunderfall was correct, it was a magic user.

"Order everyone to hold their fire," Thunderfall said to the officer. The officer relayed the order back down the wall to his soldiers.

The giant, along with his magic user, continued to walk toward the fort, until they came within fifty feet of the still burning gate area. The giant's massive hand grabbed a flag that the magic user was holding, jamming it into the ground. The pair turned around and walked twenty paces back toward their army, where they again stopped and faced the fort. The gorm, goblin and the second giant moved forward and waited by the flag. In unison, they drew out weapons. The drums instantly stopped. The whole field went deathly silent.

"What in the world?" asked the officer.

"It's a Hero Challenge, a custom amongst the giants," Thunderfall said gruffly. He turned away from the field and faced the officer. "When a giant commander considers the battle all but over, he will stop fighting and offer a Hero Challenge. The best warrior of each race is to meet and fight to the death. There are three races in the army below, so the best fighter from each race is picked by their leaders and brought forward. The extremely tall giant is the general of this army, and those are his best fighters, standing by the flag."

Thunderfall paused a second in order to sling his axe back across his back. "The losing army, which is us, is expected to send our best fighter from each race out to the flag. For us, that is one dwarf and one human. Since we are being attacked, we get to choose which two of their heroes we want to fight. If they win both fights, we are to surrender as their slaves forever, or be killed to the man. No prisoners. If we win both fights, then they have to wait twenty four hours before they can attack again. That gives us time to escape with our lives. If wins are split, the army can attack again, but must acknowledge those who choose to surrender rather than fight. Those that surrender are marked as slaves, to be released after one year. We have one hour to present our heroes. If nobody comes out, they attack, and no prisoners will be taken." Thunderfall paused as he looked again out over the field. "Pride is the greatest weakness of the giant race. It has not even crossed their minds that they could lose."

The officer looked down at the five figures standing on the field waiting. He looked like a man deep in thought. "I am the senior surviving officer now, the general is dead."

"As the most senior leader of the dwarves, I will go out and represent the dwarves," Thunderfall said. "Go find your best fighter, and then both of you meet me by the gate."

Thunderfall wasted no time. He was down the wall in seconds, heading for the section of wall broken down beside the burning gate. Javin wondered why Thunderfall considered himself senior to the other dwarves, even though the dwarven captain was giving orders.

"I know who my human hero is," the officer said as he faced Javin. "You are; I saw you fighting several times. I have no idea who you are, or why you are with the dwarves, but I can honestly say I have never seen anyone fight the way you do. Those magic flaming swords are incredible."

"They are not magic," Javin mumbled, more to himself than to the officer. From the wall, Javin could see the smoke as buildings burned back inside the fort. The courtyard was full of smoke from the burning gate. Soldiers were trying to attend to the wounded and the dead. Javin briefly glanced out toward the field where the enemy waited for an answer to their challenge.

"I am just out of the Guild of Warriors," Javin said to the officer. "This is my first major battle. There has to be a warrior better than me. I only survived because of the dwarves around me."

"You didn't look like a trainee to me," retorted the officer. "I have one hour to get my men moving to safety. I think you are our best chance for winning the challenge. Meet me here before the end of the hour. I will bring my best fighter that I have left in case you decide not to fight. However, anyone I bring won't have the skills you have. My soldiers' survival depends on this challenge. I think you are our best hope."

The officer turned and left, leaving Javin alone on the wall.

Javin slid down the ladder into the courtyard. Troubled thoughts raced through his mind as he strolled over to the dwarves gathered around a pile of smoldering wood that used to be a catapult. A gray, hazy, smoke filled the courtyard, causing Javin to cough and his eyes to water.

Out of the corner of his eye, Javin saw someone flying towards him. He barely caught Gevi as she flew into his arms.

"Where is Daddy? Is he alright?"

"He's fine, Gevi. He's over by the gate." Javin thought the life would be crushed out of him, she was squeezing so hard.

"Thank you God and praise you Lord," she said as she let go of him. Javin pointed over to where Thunderfall was waiting. Gevi turned and ran over toward her father.

Women were moving around, tending to the wounded as best they could. Javin joined the dwarves who were loading up several of their wounded companions onto carts.

"What is going on out there lad," the dwarf captain asked him. "I thought for sure we were all dead dwarves, until the gorms pulled back."

"The giant over the army has issued a Hero's Challenge." Javin replied. "Thunderfall is going to fight for the dwarves."

"That is the way of the giants," the dwarf captain said. "Thunderfall is the best fighter the Dwarven Nation has seen in many lifetimes." The captain paused for a minute, watching the last of the wounded dwarves get loaded onto the cart. "I pray they find a good human fighter. I've seen several gorm and goblin heroes in combat before; they are tough fighters." The captain turned away from Javin and addressed his dwarves. "Clubfist, get what's left of the healing potions over to the humans. Hold the carts for now. I got a feeling Thunderfall will be sending Gevi with us, out of the fort."

Leaving the dwarves, Javin helped the soldiers with their wounded. He was trying to fight the cold fear that was spreading through his body. Finally, the hour was nearly up. He walked over to the gate, hands shaking with fear. The officer was standing by the gate with Thunderfall and Gevi, along with the soldier the officer had picked for the Hero Challenge. Javin felt sick to his stomach, once he saw who the officer had picked. It was Kevinan, the soldier from the goblin fight, where he first met Gevi.

"Don't you do it, Javin," Thunderfall said with a hard glare toward Javin. "This is not the arena with boys fighting for a trophy. These are hardened killers out on that field. They will show no mercy."

"Javin?" Kevinan peered at Javin. "I didn't recognize you with that armor covering your face. Where did you get swords like that? I saw them flaming..."

"Javin is your name then," the officer cut in. "As commanding officer of this fort, I am asking you to take the Hero Challenge. Even though you are fresh out of the Guild of Warriors, your reputation as an arena fighter at the guilds is well known, even this far north." The officer paused for a second. "A lot of lives depend on the Hero Challenge, Javin. If I can have twenty four hours, I can safely evacuate everyone out of this fort. Without the twenty four hours, most of these people will die, or become slaves."

Thunderfall looked pained. He knew deep inside that the officer was right. Javin was the best human fighter, by far, in the fort. However, he could not justify in his mind endangering a young person like this. On the flip side, if Kevinan fought, he certainly would be killed. Thunderfall had seen Kevinan fight several times. Kevinan was good, but not at a level for a Hero Challenge. If Kevinan lost the fight, there would be no chance of evacuating the fort.

Thunderfall's thoughts were interrupted by Javin. "I will accept the Hero Challenge." He took a deep breath, trying to calm himself. "I could not live with myself if lives were lost because I did not accept the Hero Challenge."

Thunderfall looked toward Javin. Finally, he nodded agreement. There really was not a lot he could do because Javin was no longer under his authority as an apprentice. In addition, the officer was correct in his assessment. Javin was the best human fighter.

Gevi stepped forward, embracing her father. "I love you, Daddy," Gevi said, hugging Thunderfall as hard as she could. She held him for over a minute, before letting him go.

"Gevi, you are the best thing that ever happened to this old dwarf. No matter what happens, you always remember that." Tears ran freely down her face. She gave the dwarf another fierce hug and kissed him on the cheek. Letting him go, she wiped the tears from her eyes and turned toward Javin. She put her arms around him and dropped her head to his shoulder.

"Be careful. Be strong. Remember your training. I will be praying for both of you," she told Javin. "I love you," She whispered as she let go of him.

"Gevi," Thunderfall said before Javin could respond to her. "Go to the dwarves, and tell them I said to go to Crystal Cave. I want you to go with them. If Javin and I both win, then we will have time to pick you up. If one of us loses, then the dwarves can get you to safety by taking you to the Dwarven City."

With tears freely running down her cheek, Gevi gave Thunderfall and Javin another quick hug before running over to the dwarves. Thunderfall, Javin, and the officer walked out the gate to meet the enemy for the Hero Challenge.

Chapter 12

I can do all things through Christ who strengthens me. – The Guide

"Stand right here, look proud and important," Thunderfall told the officer. "Javin, walk with me, but stop when I tell you. I will make the first challenge. Whatever happens, I strongly suggest you pick the goblin when your turn comes. Watch carefully what I do, then copy it when it is your turn to fight." Javin walked toward the flag, stopping when Thunderfall ordered him to stop. Thunderfall continued on, approached the flag that was flapping gently in the light summer breeze.

When he reached the flag, Thunderfall pulled out his massive black steel battle axe and pointed it directly at the giant standing a few feet in front of him. This giant stood fourteen feet in height. He wore thick plate metal armor. Long, shaggy hair ran down his back while a large, scraggly beard covered his face. The giant gave an evil smile, with a wicked laugh. He reached across his back and pulled out a six foot, two-handed sword, which he easily held with only his left hand. With his right hand, he held up a massive shield that covered half his body.

The top of Thunderfall's head did not quite reach the knees of this giant, who was more than three times taller than the dwarf. "Today you die, little squirt of a man," the giant spit out through yellowish brown teeth in the language of the giants. The gorm and goblin heroes moved ten paces back from the flag.

Javin swallowed a lump in his throat. Thunderfall looked way outmatched in this fight. The reality of the Hero Challenge was starting to affect Javin as his hands began to grow moist. This was real. One of the two combatants would soon be dead.

"You won't be the first giant this axe has killed, or the last," Thunderfall replied in the same language the giant had used. The giant roared and charged toward Thunderfall, his giant sword crashing downward right toward Thunderfall's head. The only movement Thunderfall made was to lift his battle axe over his head. The crash of the weapons colliding echoed through the battlefield.

The giant's face registered shock at how easily the dwarf had blocked his sword. Arm muscles bulged as the giant tried to push his sword down. Thunderfall held the giant's sword above his head for a few seconds, before twisting his axes and swinging it out sideways. The giant almost had his sword ripped from his hand.

Thunderfall's battle axe abruptly stopped its sideways momentum, coming back around with blazing speed toward the giant's shins. Moving his shield downward, the giant blocked Thunderfall's battle axe. The blow from the axe onto his shield was so powerful that the giant was knocked backwards a step. Pulling his sword back in front of his body, the giant started to slowly circle around Thunderfall. Hate filled his eyes. They slowly circled each other, with the giant on the offensive. His sword would move in quickly, but it was always knocked aside by Thunderfall's battle axe. The giant had to stab or chop downward, due to the fact his opponent was below his knee caps.

Several minutes passed. The giant continued to take quick stabs or jabs with his sword, only to have them continually deflected by the dwarven axe. Thunderfall took no more swings at the giant, causing the giant hero to get extremely frustrated.

"You fight like an elf, little man," the giant hissed after his sword was deflected again. Evil hatred glowed from his eyes. Thunderfall knew that the giant race despised elves above all other humanoids. He also knew that in the giant's complicated system of honor that they rigorously held to, the insult of being called an elf was extremely dishonorable.

"I've had elves hit harder than you, weakling" retorted Thunderfall, who smiled because the giant started swinging and chopping downward without a pause. Powerful blows no normal man could ever stand against rained down. Berserk, the giant was now swinging his sword wildly. Being called a "weakling" was the ultimate insult to a giant.

Thunderfall slowly stepped backwards, deflecting the hail of sword strikes coming down on him. When the giant's sword came down especially hard with the entire giant's weight behind it, Thunderfall lunged toward the giant. Thunderfall's mighty axe swept the giant's shield to the side while his momentum carried him into the giant's shins. The dwarf's great mass won the collision.

The sound of dwarven plate mail armor crashing into giant plate mail armor caused Javin's ears to ring. Astonished, Javin watched as the massive giant flew into the air, landing flat on his face. His two-handed sword flew from the giant's hand, flipping end-over-end through the grass. Thunderfall had swept the feet out from under the giant.

The giant rolled sideways. As he rolled, pain exploded in his lower right leg. Thunderfall's axe shattered the giant's plate leg armor and was embedded into the giant's leg. Roaring in pain, the giant continued to roll sideways in an attempt to escape the dwarf. Finally stopping so that he could regain his feet, the giant looked up to see Thunderfall standing right by his head.

Javin watched Thunderfall's axe fall. The final blow finished the giant. Everything was quiet for a second, when suddenly a cheer went up from the fort behind him. He looked back and saw soldiers standing on the wall.

Fear washed over him in an uncontrolled flood. This was no arena with protective coverings over blades and the loser shook the hand of the winner. This was a fight to the death, with naked steel blades. No shaking hands after this fight. His stomach lurched, and bile rose up into his throat.

Javin came close to throwing up right then. The thought of the soldiers in the fort depending on him crossed his mind. If he backed out of the challenge or lost, the gorms would attack again. What would happen to the soldiers? Would Gevi and the dwarves have time to reach the cave?

Taking a deep breath, Javin steeled his mind to what he must do. Wiping the palms of his hands off on his leather leggings, he started walking toward the flag.

"*Be strong and of a good courage; be not afraid, neither be dismayed: for the LORD your God is with you wherever you go,*" Thunderfall quoted *The Guide* as the two faced each other. He firmly grasped Javin's shoulder in the way of warriors and walked back to the spot Javin had come from.

Taking *The Guide's* words to heart, Javin acknowledged his fear. He walked to the flag and stopped. The gorm and goblin hero walked forward to stand right in front of him. From their facial expressions and posture, Javin could see they were arrogantly confident. Panic began to overcome him.

Before choosing his opponent, Javin glanced to his right, seeing the dead giant lying on the ground. Would he be joining the giant soon? He prayed silently in his mind "Lord, please help me to be courageous and not to be afraid. For you are my God." All of a sudden, a peace came over him and the terror that was making him sweat and shake fled from him. He lifted up his head and looked directly at the snarling gorm and the sneering goblin.

Drawing his right sword, he pointed it directly at the goblin. The goblin pulled a short sword out from a sheath at his hip and gave a wicked little laugh. When the goblin moved forward, Javin drew his left sword and pointed it at the gorm. Freezing in his tracks, the goblin looked sideways at the gorm in confusion. The gorm grunted and pulled a wicked looking axe from off his back. Javin kept both swords pointed at the two creatures. "That's right, both of you," he said, with the hope one of them would understand the human language. He guessed right.

"Are you dazed from a blow to your head, or just ignorant?" the gorm sneered back at him while his off-hand grabbed a small buckler shield, hanging from his belt.

"The Lord of the Stars fights with me this day" responded Javin right back. "Are you ready to meet him?" Javin then flamed both his swords. At the mention of the Lord of the Stars, a gleam of fear appeared briefly in the goblin's eyes.

The gorm nodded his head back toward Javin, staring at the swords. "You are foolish, but brave. Your soul will greatly strengthen me, and two magic swords will be added to my collection." The gorm turned and said something in a language that Javin did not understand. The two then split five feet apart, before slowly coming back toward Javin, intending to trap him between them.

Once they got within a few feet of Javin, the gorm screamed and jumped forward, his axe swinging sideways. Javin slammed his right sword down on the gorm's axe blade while jumping backwards. His left sword connected with the goblin's short sword that was coming straight down toward his head.

"Attacking at the same time will never work boys," Javin said while his left sword did a complicated twist like his father had showed him and he had been practicing. His sword stayed in his hand, but the goblin's sword flew through the air, landing by the body of the giant. Flinging its shield upward while stepping backwards, the goblin managed to deflect Javin's sword that came slashing in. The deflected sword bounced off the shield and into the shoulder of the goblin, who screamed a high-pitched scream of pain. Smoke rose from the burned shoulder of the goblin. Javin's sword had cut through the scale armor the goblin wore like it was cloth, instead of steel.

The fight with the goblin went on while Javin's other sword was continually deflecting the attacking gorm axe. The now injured goblin rolled backwards out of Javin's sword range, leaving Javin both his swords to deal with the gorm. He deflected the gorm's axe one last time, before going on the attack. His right sword swung sideways toward the gorm's head, while the left sword came in from the other side toward the creature's stomach. The gorm made the only move it could, axe met the sword coming at his head, while his small buckler shield met the sword coming in lower. Javin pulled his swords back in front of him. He spun his swords through his fingers one time before lashing out again. Both swords were blocked a second time.

Javin's whole body twisted in a spin. Coming out of the spin, both swords came in sideways from the same direction. The gorm easily got his axe up to protect his head, but the shield had to come all the way across his body from where it had deflected an earlier blow. The gorm was too slow. The sword blew right through the chain mail, cutting into the gorm's side; through muscle and ribs. Javin then quickly spun his whole body back the opposite way, ripping his left sword out of the gorm's side. He spun hard and fast. Both swords crashed hard into the opposite side of the gorm. Again, the swords cut through the chain mail and buried themselves into the ribs of the gorm. This time, Javin ripped the swords out of the gorm by stopping his spin and rolling sideways. He came out of his roll, spinning around in a crouch to face the gorm and the goblin.

The gorm was still standing, but he had both axe and shield lowered to the ground. The goblin was pulling his short sword out of the gorm's chest. Blindly, the creature had stabbed hard with his retrieved sword toward Javin's back, but Javin was no longer there. The gorm had taken the sword meant for Javin right through the heart.

The fight was over for the gorm. He collapsed onto the field, smoke rising from his body. The goblin stood there, his eyes moving between the gorm and Javin. The goblin's shield arm was hanging useless by his side, due to the muscles that had been severed by Javin's sword, earlier. Fear flashed in the eyes of the goblin as Javin stepped forward.

The goblin screamed and leaped forward, his sword stabbing toward Javin's stomach. Javin turned his body slightly, causing the goblin sword to slice through nothing but air. Both of Javin's swords stabbed past the goblin's sword, straight into the goblin's good shoulder. The goblin sword fell from his nerveless hand into the grass. A squeal escaped the goblin's lips. Both arms were now injured and useless. Javin stood facing the helpless goblin.

"Go, your life is spared," Javin said, waving his flaming sword toward the goblin's army. Instead, the goblin rushed right back at him with teeth barred. The broadside of Javin's sword crashed into the knee of the goblin, breaking a knee cap and burning its leg. The creature fell to the ground. It managed to stand back up again, wobbling on his one good leg. The severely injured goblin hopped toward Javin.

"Go!" Javin yelled, his flaming sword pointing toward the enemy lines. The goblin barred its teeth and continued to hop. Javin's foot kicked forward, hitting the goblin square in the chest. The goblin fell back to the ground where it struggled to regain its feet.

"He fought bravely, he does not deserve to die like this," Javin yelled over his shoulder toward the sixteen foot giant and the magic user. The sickening thought crossed his mind that he was going to be forced to kill the helpless goblin. Then, a brash command issued from the giant commander's mouth. The goblin gave Javin a last look filled with utter hatred as it regained its feet. He turned and hopped back toward the enemy lines.

Javin's breathing was labored and he felt completely exhausted. The only noise he heard was the flapping of the flag in the swirling breeze. He stood up straight and raised both his swords straight towards the sky. Blood red flames danced around the blades of his swords. Silently, he thanked God for giving him the victory over his foe. He turned to face the giant commander and the mage that were standing twenty paces back from the flag. He let his raised swords burn with fire for several long seconds. A thunderous cheer erupted from the fort behind Javin. Re-sheathing his swords, he turned away from the giant and walked over to join Thunderfall and the officer.

Thunderfall shook his head once Javin joined them. "Both of them? Are you out of your mind?" Javin could hear the amazement in the dwarf's voice.

Before Javin could reply to Thunderfall, the officer cut in. "That is the craziest thing I have ever seen."

"I felt the peace of God come upon me and I knew, deep in my heart, that the victory would be mine."

Shaking his head, Thunderfall led Javin and the officer back into the fort.

****

"We found one, and only one," the captain reported while standing in front of the all too familiar table that Licheaon used for his paper work. Licheaon looked up from his work as the captain dropped *The Guide* on the table. Picking it up, he absently flipped open the pages without really looking at them. He had been forced to change plans once word came down to him that Fort Outlands was facing an invading army. Instead of going north to do the next show, he had turned back south toward the capital, picking up smaller towns he had bypassed earlier. Farm Circle had taught him to make no assumptions based on the size of the town. No assumptions, so he paid to send everyone working for him involved with the show to a party at a local inn, while several of the guards searched everyone's belongings.

"Where was it?" Licheaon asked as he absently played with *The Guide*.

"It was in the clothes chest of the hair and makeup artist girl."

"Dismissed, go ahead and go over to the party at the inn. Make sure that you and the other guards keep quiet. Do you understand me?"

"Yes sir," replied the captain, "I will make it very clear to the others what is expected of them, and what will happen if they blab their mouths." With that, he left the tent.

Licheaon got up and walked out of the tent. He walked quickly away from the town until he came upon a large bonfire, circled by wagons. Preveshawl soldiers were busy setting up the camp. The guards let Licheaon through, without any questions. He walked over to the largest tent and past the guards that stood at the entrance way.

"Good evening, Commander," Licheaon said as he ducked into the tent. The commander was about to take a bite from the plate of food in front of him. Instead, he put his fork down, anger clearly on his face.

"What do you want now, Licheaon?" His stare made Licheaon flinch. This commander gave him chills. Not many men did that to Licheaon.

"I am sorry to bother you. I need you to take care of a minor problem for me before leaving in the morning for Farm Circle." Licheaon tossed *The Guide* over to the commander, who caught it with one hand in midair. "This was found in the chest belonging to one of my employees. I would like the problem to disappear."

The commander glanced at *The Guide* briefly before tossing it back to Licheaon. A cold, uncaring expression surrounded his face. "Tell Sergeant Thegeth that I am ordering him to go with you and bring your problem back to me. He is by the main fire." Licheaon started to thank the commander, but the commander had already returned to his meal, ignoring Licheaon. He turned around and rushed out of the tent and to the fire to find the sergeant.

****

Chellell and Lily sat in Chellell's tent, talking and laughing. They both had enjoyed a good time at the inn.

"I am going to go ahead and retire for the evening," Lily told Chellell, giving her a hug. "See you in the morning, beautiful."

"See you in the morning," Chellell replied with a yawn.

Lily left Chellell's tent and strolled through the maze of tents. Taking a deep breath of the cool night air, Lily paused and tried to clear her head. For some reason, she was getting slightly nauseous whenever she spent time with Chellell. The nausea was even worse with the other magic users that were Chellell's assistants. Feeling a little better after a minute or so of deep breaths, she continued through the maze of wagons and tents. While walking, she whistled one of the songs she had heard at the church several weeks ago. This had to be the happiest Lily had ever been in her life. Ever since asking God to save her, she had felt like a new person. The emptiness inside was gone. Joy now filled the emptiness that had once controlled her heart.

Seeing her tent, she ducked under the entrance flap. Instantly, she felt something was wrong. She turned to leave when a large man stepped from the side of the entrance, blocking her exit. Before she could scream, Lily hit the floor. Her whole face and head throbbed with intense, sharp pain. Lily moaned from the floor of the tent. When her hand touched her face, it came away covered in blood.

"You didn't have to hit her that hard, you idiot," Lily heard someone above her say.

"Do not try to scream again." This voice was different, gruffer, Lily realized. She slowly started to rise when pain exploded inside her head. Moaning, she managed to sit up. Blood was running from her nose and mouth, staining her blouse. Overwhelming fear filled her body.

"What... Why?" she started to say but bit back her words when the huge man standing over her raised his fist.

"Pick her up," a voice ordered. Lily now recognized the voice as belonging to Licheaon. Rough hands grabbed her under her arms, lifting her off the ground. Lily would have fallen back down except that the large man kept his grip on her. He roughly spun her, to face Licheaon. Through tear-filled eyes, the blurry image of Licheaon came into view.

"Is this yours?" He asked while holding up *The Guide*. A lot of thoughts went through Lily's terrified mind.

"Yes," was all she managed to whisper.

"Why Lily, why?" Licheaon crossed his arms and fixed his eyes on her. "You know owning this book is outlawed." She gave no answer. She hung her head and looked toward the ground.

"You know we can pretend this never happened." Licheaon paused, looking hard right at her. Lily still had her head hung low, blood seeping into the blond hair that was hanging over her face.

"If you can answer a few questions for me, and answer them correctly, then we can pretend you had a nasty fall and life can go on. Do you understand me?"

Lily raised her head up; shakily pulling her hair back from her face. She nodded toward Licheaon.

"Good. The good sergeant here will let you know if you have answered correctly or not. First question: Who is the Lord of the Stars?"

Fear came over her, but she quickly decided to be brave and speak truthfully. "God," Lily answered. As soon as the word left her mouth, she felt the blow to the side of her head. She would have fallen down, but the man behind her held her up with his other arm. Pain exploded inside her head again.

"Wrong answer, Lily; I warned you the sergeant would let you know when you gave a wrong answer." Lily saw Licheaon's evil smile. She hung her head down again, not answering.

"Let me help you out," Lily felt a hand on her chin, lifting her head up. She was inches from Licheaon's face. When I ask you who the Lord of the Stars is, you are to say a prophet, a good man, a teacher; any answer will work except the one you gave. Now, who is the Lord of the Stars?"

"God," she whispered without hesitation. Lily felt herself flying through the air; the last thing she remembered before blacking out was horrible pain from hitting the mirror and her makeup dresser.

"You are wasting my time," hissed the sergeant. "I am going to take her to the commander, as ordered. He can make anyone change their ways."

Licheaon looked over at the crumpled form of Lily. Blood was pooling around her head. Broken glass covered the floor. Her once angelic face was shredded almost beyond recognition by the broken glass. He sadly shook his head, but his mind was already on where to get his next makeup artist. The sergeant picked up the crumpled form of Lily. Without saying a word to Licheaon, he threw her roughly over his shoulder and walked out of the tent.

****

Lily woke up, with the sun blazing overhead. Confusion filled her mind. She was not in her tent or her bed. She was lying on hard wood, bouncing around. Every bump made it feel like a hammer was hitting her head. She tried to move her hands from behind her back, but couldn't. They were tied with rope. She managed to roll over with a groan. The hot sun was beating down hard; sweat covered her clothes and skin. She saw her own blood pooled around where her head had been lying.

Looking around, Lily recognized that she was in the back of a wagon that was moving down a bumpy road. Trying to move her feet, she found they were tied as well. Tears started flowing from her eyes. As they touched her lips, she realized how thirsty she was. Thirsty and hurting, her mind relived the nightmare she had gone through, was going through.

Tears kept coming, but she found comfort as she relived her experience at the church. She remembered back to the few parts of the passages of *The Guide* she had been staying up late to try and read. Barely able to read, Lily would spend an hour on one page of *The Guide*. In her mind, a passage gradually appeared, as if she was reading it. *But those who suffer he delivers in their suffering; he speaks to them in their affliction*

Feeling comforted, she remembered another passage, *for which I am suffering even to the point of being chained like a criminal. But God's word is not chained.* The words calmed her, and Lily did the only thing she could think of, she prayed. She knew she wasn't as good in speech like the

138

man at the church, but she prayed through the pain she felt. A last verse came into her mind, *fear not them which kill the body, but are not able to kill the soul: but rather fear Him which is able to destroy both soul and body in hell.* While praying, peace overcame her, and the pain melted away. Lily fell into a deep sleep.

****

Lamar was leading a patrol of militia soldiers made up of individuals from Farm Circle. Most were retired soldiers, earning a living now, as farmers. Three of the men with Lamar's patrol were once members of the famous Wolf Troop, the special operations unit Lamar commanded during the Ogre Invasions.

The elders of Farm Circle had heeded the warning from Jewla, after they found out what her cat had heard in Licheaon's tent. Concerned for the safety of all the Farm Circle families, the elders had started using militia patrols and naturalists to keep a watch around the Farm Circle area.

"The wagons and the soldiers are southwest of us," Jewla said to Lamar. She opened her eyes, breaking contact with her falcon. "They have stopped and are setting up camp where Eagle Creek meets the road."

"How many?" Lamar asked while he waved the patrol with him to a stop.

"Two, maybe three dozen," Jewla replied while glancing over at Lamar. Surprise registered on his face.

"That is not nearly the number I expected." He seemed deep in thought, for several long minutes.

"Follow me," he called out, swinging his horse southwest through a hay field. Twenty Farm Circle militiamen turned their horses and followed him. Lamar had expected two to three times more soldiers than the number Jewla had told him. The fact that there was only thirty or so soldiers changed Lamar's plans.

Once darkness had settled in, Lamar had the men crawl slowly on their stomachs through the tall grass. The lesser moon was out at three quarters, providing Lamar barely enough light to see into the camp from the bushes he was hiding behind. Everyone with him was sprawled flat down in four foot high grass twenty feet behind him. Lamar watched, analyzing the guards' movement and counting the number of soldiers. Jewla had been correct, there were thirty soldiers. By their uniforms, Lamar determined that it was a regular infantry squad plus a half-squad of a special operations unit. "Not well trained cither," he thought, "they should never have allowed anyone to get this close." He was amazed to see the entire special operations unit lounging around with weapons on the muddy ground.

Lamar was analyzing the soldiers, when the main tent flap opened. A large, muscular man strolled confidently out of the tent. Lamar recognized him as a commander, a very high rank to be out with such a small group. As he continued to watch, he saw the commander give an

139

order to a soldier, who proceeded to grab a thick pole, driving it into the ground by the fire. The commander briskly walked to a wagon, jumping nimbly into the back of it. A bundle then flew out over the side of the wagon, landing and rolling on the ground. Something red was flying around on one end of the bundle. It was red hair. A woman! The bundle was a woman! Jumping from the wagon, the commander grabbed the woman's hair, and dragged her across the ground, toward the fire.

Lamar initially had no intention of attacking this group. He had wanted to determine their motive for being out so close to Farm Circle. He did not want to attack his own country's soldiers. If these soldiers had evil plans for Farm Circle, then he would attack, if fighting could not be avoided. However, watching this woman being treated so roughly was changing his plans. Lamar quickly crawled backwards to one of his men.

"Bows ready; get within ten paces. Do not fire unless I signal. Pass the word along." By the time Lamar had settled back behind cover, the woman was tied to the pole. Using the grass as cover, he started moving closer to the camp. While crawling, he heard the commander start screaming at everyone around him. He gritted his teeth in anger and crawled a little faster. When he reached the edge of the camp, Lamar heard the commander screaming wildly at a sergeant.

"She is nearly dead! I told you to bring her to me alive." The commander was standing next to the girl tied to the pole. He had a long whip in his hand. "I would have had her denying her God and cursing him within minutes, you imbecile." The commander was waving the whip in the air in frustration. Lamar glanced back, and saw the grass moving. His men were not in position yet. Looking closer at the woman, he noticed that she was completely limp. Anger was rising in Lamar, stronger than anything he had felt in over twenty years. These were not soldiers. This was a group of thugs in soldier uniforms. Glancing back again, he saw maybe a quarter of the men were now in position behind him.

The commander reached over to the pole, grabbing a handful of very long hair. He started screaming fanatically at the limp figure. "Why hasn't your God saved you? Where is He? Where is this Lord of the Stars?" The commander stepped back, brutally striking the limp woman's face with the handle of the whip.

Lamar had seen and heard enough. Forgetting to give the night owl call, he drew both his swords. "You want to meet God, commander? I will introduce you to Him this day," Lamar called out as he walked into camp. "It will be a meeting you will have an eternity to regret."

The commander spun around, shock registering on his face at the stranger walking right toward him through his soldiers. Soldiers started frantically grabbing weapons. Arrows rapidly filled the air as the Farm Circle militia started firing. Chaos erupted in the camp while Lamar calmly strolled straight toward the commander.

****

Lily saw herself tied to the pole. She saw soldiers falling to the ground as arrows hit them. Men were running through the grass, engaging soldiers sword to sword. She saw a man calmly walking toward the pole, where she saw herself tied up. It was Lamar! She heard the screams of men and the sounds of steel striking steel. She saw this from above, as a bird would see things.

All at once, the sights and sounds were gone and a bright light surrounded her. She felt awesome power from the light. Love and power by an extreme measure, greater than anything she had ever felt, emanated from the light. A man appeared beside her. He was dressed in pure white robes that blazed in holy light. A golden girdle was around his waist, holding a pure ivory white sword. Lily knew this was a being of immense power.

"Am I dead?" She asked, but for some reason, she really did not care if she was dead. "Are you the Lord of the Stars?"

Not expecting a reply, Lily was surprised to hear the powerful man answer. "No. I am one of His servants." A smile showed on his face, which gave great comfort to Lily. "My name is Lochemel. The Lord of the Stars sent me to instruct you on what you are to do in the days ahead."

"Then I am not dead?" Lily's confusion was obvious.

"You are dead, but only for a brief time. The Lord of the Stars holds the keys to death and life. For you, He has decided to restore your mortal body and life." The angel then took Lily by the hand. "Come; walk with me while I give you instructions from the Lord of the Stars."

****

Lamar's short sword clanged into the commander's long sword. The sound rang through a now quiet camp, because all the Preveshawl soldiers had surrendered. His second short sword stabbed in toward the commander's chest, but the commander leaped backwards, avoiding the stab. Lamar felt the rage burn in him as his swords whistled in and out toward the commander, who was backing up while deflecting Lamar's swords. The short swords kept pushing forward. A short sword slashed in sideways, past the shield held by the commander. The shield flew from his hand. Howling in pain from the cut in his hand, the commander again leapt backwards. The mail armor gauntlet was the only reason his shield hand was still attached to his arm.

Lamar saw fear in the commander's eyes, but that did not stop the rage, as he slowly and purposely pressed forward toward the Preveshawl commander. There was nothing that Lamar despised more than a man who abused women. Absolutely nothing! Especially an abuser that served in an army that he once commanded; an army sworn to protect its citizens.

Desperate, the commander stabbed his sword right toward Lamar's chest. Lamar calmly drove the commander's long sword down to the ground with one short sword while swinging the second sword as hard as he could into the hilt of the commander's sword. The commander's long sword fell to the ground.

Unarmed before Lamar, the commander easily could have been

killed by Lamar. Instead, Lamar flipped his swords into their sheaths and punched the commander with all his might, right in the face. He could hear the crack of the nose as the commander fell back, unconsciousness. Grabbing the commander by the boots, he dragged the unconscious man until they were next to the pole. By this time, the commander was moaning and starting to regain consciousness. The girl was no longer tied to the pole. Looking around, he saw her lying on the ground, with two of his men standing by her. One of his men was shaking his head.

"Sorry, Lamar, we were too late." Lamar walked the few feet over to the body and looked down at a girl he knew, Lily. He fell down beside her. Though he was well acquainted with war, he could not remember ever seeing a face in such bad shape. Bloody cuts and deep gashes covered what used to be an angelic face. Blood covered her whole chest. Her hair was no longer blond, but stained red from blood. Lamar stared at Lily's mangled face. Eyes were open, but unseeing. His mind flashed back to her laughing while chasing chickens at his farm. Even more rage filled him, so much so that tears started running down his face. Lamar stumbled to his feet, burning with out-of-control-anger.

"Tie him to the pole," Lamar coldly ordered his two men standing by Lily. He picked up the whip that the commander had held in his hand. Rage filled his soul as he prepared to administer justice to a woman-abuser, and murderer.

****

"You are to tell Lamar and the elders of Farm Circle that Thunderfall knows where they must go. If you and Gevi lead, then the elves will show the way. They are all to go to the ancient city of the Linkrins," Lochemel instructed Lily as they walked through the grass. Lochemel continued, "You will meet the King of the Elves. When you do, deliver the message The Lord of the Stars has placed in your mind. When you see his face, the words will flow freely. Until then, you will not remember any of it." The scene abruptly changed. They were now walking alongside a bubbly creek. Lily could see the camp in the distance. Lochemel stopped walking and looked at Lily. "I see something is heavy on your mind. If the Lord of the Stars permits, I will answer whatever you ask."

Lily thought about the light she had felt before Lochemel had appeared to her. The fearsome power and love coming from the light was something she would never forget. She knew she had felt the very presence of God, in a very intimate and intense way. She instantly felt sorry for her new best friend, Chellell.

"My concern is for Chellell. I am so confused. She grew up in church, but now she has no interest in God, though I think she still kind of believes there is a God."

Lochemel paused, but before he could answer, words filled Lily's mind. *"Not everyone that saith unto me, Lord, Lord, shall enter into the Kingdom of heaven; but he that doeth the will of my Father which is in heaven."* Surprise showed visibly on Lily's face.

"You are indeed blessed," Lochemel said, laughing in a deep, baritone voice. "The Lord of the Stars has given you the answer. I am instructed to explain further." The angel stopped laughing, his face becoming serious again. "Know this Lily. It is not given to mankind to know the hearts of others. Because they hear and sit in a church, does not mean they listen and obey. Instead, as *The Guide* says, *you shall know them by their fruits.* Chellell sat in church hearing the truth, yet she refuses to accept the truth. Her fruit reflects her true beliefs."

"The knowledge of God's plans concerning His creation is rarely revealed to men. His ways will always be mysterious. Mankind is required to operate by faith alone. However, the power of prayer has been given to His children. Pray for Chellell. Prayer can move God into action. The prayer of His children is a joy to Him, and answering His delight."

"I will remember to pray for her," Lily said, concern in her voice.

Lochemel's response was instant. "Good. As for Chellell's future, The Lord of the Stars will deal with her as He sees fit, and in a time when He sees fit. If you want to influence the outcome, make sure you remember to pray for her. Now, it is time for you to return, but I want you to remember what *The Guide* says: *"Judge not, and ye shall not be judged: condemn not, and ye shall not be condemned: forgive, and ye shall be forgiven."*

"I will remember," Lily said, though confusion showed on her face as to why she should remember this.

"You think so?" Lochemel replied, "Repeat it to me." Lily repeated it. He had her do it again, and again. Ten times in all. "Now, I want you to shout it as loud as you can." He faded from view as Lily began to shout the words as loud as she could.

****

Lamar held the whip the commander had planned to use on Lily in his hand. The rage still boiled in his blood as he pulled the whip back over his head. "No soldier under my command would ever have touched a woman without severe punishment, commander. For her death, you will be..."

"Judge not, and ye shall not be judged: condemn not, and ye shall not be condemned: forgive, and ye shall be forgiven." A woman's voice spoke so loud, it seemed to echo through the camp. Lamar spun around, whip still in hand. Lily was sitting up on the ground, a dazed and confused look on her face. *"Judge not, and ye shall not be judged: condemn not, and ye shall not be condemned: forgive, and ye shall be forgiven,"* she screamed out again before collapsing back to the ground.

Lamar dropped the whip and ran over to Lily. She was breathing, and alive! Unconscious now, she kept murmuring, *"Judge not, and ye shall not be judged: condemn not, and ye shall not be condemned: forgive, and ye shall be forgiven."*

The rage left Lamar, like water from a leaky bucket. As the rage left him, he moved his gaze off the bloodied and mangled face of Lily and onto the commander. A fight brewed inside his soul. It seemed from what Lily was shouting, that she wanted him to forgive. Yet, this commander and his soldiers did not deserve forgiveness. "No one should treat a woman like this and live," he thought to himself as he slowly drew a dagger from his boot. "I would be justified sending him straight to God right now." His mind continued to fight with what the commander deserved and the passage from *The Guide* that Lily yelled out.

In a motion so swift the eye could barely see it happen, the dagger flew from Lamar's hand. It stuck right into the wood post, inches above the commander's head. "Untie him," Lamar said, pointing at the commander. "Take the soldiers down the road. Have them strip down to their under shorts, then let them go. Gather their boots and clothes and burn them." Lamar turned and walked over to the commander, who was being untied by one of Lamar's men. Fear still showed in the commander's eyes. "From the God you blasphemed, this girl," he pointed toward Lily, "has ordered me to forgive you and spare your life. Strip to your shorts and run, before I forget what she did for you." The commander stripped to his shorts and ran barefoot, from the camp.

Chapter 13

Be ye therefore followers of God, as dear children. – The Guide

The twenty-four-hour truce given by the opposing army was only an hour old when Javin arrived at Thunderfall's shop, after he and Thunderfall had picked up Gevi at Crystal Cave. Along the way, Thunderfall had explained to Javin that the giants had an extreme system of honor. As evil as they could be, the giant commanders were bound by their customs.

To help Gevi and Thunderfall, Javin decided to go back to the shop and help pack. They hurriedly packed up a wagon with blacksmithing tools and personal items. Once done, they headed to Ledia's house. Mac had just made it back, though he was upset that he had missed the Hero Challenge that the soldiers were talking about.

Saying his good-byes, Javin was planning to return to Farm Circle and his family. Much to his surprise, the other four had decided to go with him. Thunderfall told Javin that everyone from the church was now at the ruins, or on their way. Farm Circle, along with Javin's family, would need all the help they could get. Gevi was overjoyed to be helping Javin and his family. They departed as fast as they could, south away from the invading army.

While traveling, Gevi noticed something had changed with Javin. "You are not stuttering!" Thinking back, he realized he had not stuttered the whole time they were packing. Everyone was in such a rush, they had not noticed.

Surprise showed on Javin's face. "You are right! The stuttering is gone."

Thunderfall looked curiously at Javin. He, Gevi, and Javin were sitting together in the front of the wagon. "Do you know how you got healed?"

The strange man Javin had met on the road came back into his memory. He had nearly forgotten about this strange encounter. The man's prophecy, "On the day you put on the full armor of God, and swords of flame devour the enemy of God that He has raised up to judge Preveshawl, then you will stutter no more," came back to Javin's mind. Now, he understood. In the battle at the fort, He had stood on the wall, in the armor Thunderfall had made him, with flaming swords, which he had used to destroy the enemy. He had not stuttered since that time. Javin told Thunderfall and Gevi about the strange man of God he had met, and what the man had told him. He also told them what the old man had said about the barbarian princess, "For your second weakness, only partial healing will be granted. A barbarian princess, known as the Slayer of Giants, will be given the power from God to give you partial healing. In turn, you will lead her people into war."

Javin quickly regretted telling Gevi about the barbarian princess. The rest of the ride to the Crossroads was filled with her teasing him about a gorgeous barbarian princess romantically healing him. Javin insisted that because she was a barbarian, she would probably smell like animal leather and have enough muscles to break him in half. He tried to convince Gevi that the barbarian princess would be un-bathed, smelly and wild, like he envisioned barbarians to be. Gevi would not listen, insisting that Javin would fall madly in love with this foreign beauty, and leave Preveshawl to live in her castle, somewhere in the far North. She continued her unmerciful teasing until they reached the Crossroads.

****

The five companions reached the Crossroads as night fell. The main army from the capital city of Preveshawl Castle had arrived at the Crossroads. Soldiers were busy digging trenches and setting up large catapults and ballistae.

The Crossroads was the last strategic spot that an effective defense could be set up against a large army, until the great river was reached. From this point on, the land was largely flat grasslands and farms, allowing any army to move freely in any direction. If the invading army got through the Crossroads, they could follow the road west to Bear Tree City, east to Farm Circle and the farmlands, or south to the river.

Javin and his friends were allowed to pass through the guard post. The soldiers recognized Thunderfall as the dwarven hero who had slain the giant. He was constantly being congratulated and asked about the Black Knight with the flaming swords who had defeated the gorm and goblin heroes. As they traveled through the camp, Javin asked his friends not to tell anyone he was what they were now calling, the "Black Knight".

"Your identity as the Black Knight will be the worst kept secret in all of Preveshawl," snorted Thunderfall. "A great swordsman that uses two short swords is so rare, your name will have to come up. Besides, the officer and Kevinan both know it was you under the armor."

Javin had to agree with Thunderfall's assessment. Still, he would rather people not know it was him. Attention was something he really did not desire.

They carefully led the pack horses and wagons through the maze of tents and soldiers. A captain came up to the group and informed Thunderfall that the general over the army was requesting his presence in the command tent. Thunderfall went to see the general, while the others settled around a campfire. Off-duty soldiers gradually joined them and they quietly ate a supper of bread and cheese while listening to the gossip.

"Not only do we have the filthy monsters coming down from the north, but I hear that commander Firdac got his tail beat by a group rebelling against the king east of here." Javin's ears tuned in to the soldiers across the fire from him, making sure he heard the whole conversation.

"That must be why we shut the road down going east, but what is east of here?"

The soldier that started the conversation replied to his fellow soldier, "Nothing but farmers, I hear."

146

Another soldier piped in, "I saw a group of soldiers come into the camp this morning, wearing nothing but their shorts. Their bare feet were so cut up they could barely walk."

"I guess once we send these gorms running back north, we will have to settle the pitchfork rebellion." The group of soldiers started laughing.

Javin listened on as the soldiers joked about farmers with pitchforks sending this particular commander back to the army in nothing but his shorts. Gevi glanced over at Javin with a worried look on her face. Javin smiled back, trying to put her at ease. He knew trouble had already reached his hometown and his family. An hour or so was spent listening to the soldier's gossip, while waiting for Thunderfall. Javin had to bite back a laugh at the Black Knight stories, which seemed to be growing and growing.

"He jumped over the thirty foot fort wall?" whispered Mac to Gevi, astonishment showing on his face.

"No," she whispered back, "he flapped his arms and flew." Mac stared at Gevi for a second, until Gevi burst out laughing. He frowned at her, realizing he was being made fun of.

"I can't believe I missed all the fun," he replied in disgust. Thunderfall picked that moment to show up.

"The general got my report. Let's get the wagon and get going," Thunderfall said. He was obviously in a rush to get away from the Preveshawl army camp. They were not allowed to go East, so they headed the wagons south instead.

Well into the night, they turned off the South road and circled back East through abandoned farm fields. The wagons moved very slowly. Several times, the men had to dig out wagon wheels stuck in the rich, black, mud that made these farms so productive. Finally, they reached the east road, on their way to Farm Circle. An hour past midnight, Thunderfall gave the order to stop for the night. Javin was so tired, that he did not bother to set up his tent. He rolled out his bed roll and fell asleep on the ground.

****

"How is she?" Lamar asked while standing by his wife outside the hospital building.

"It looks like the healing potion you found in that commander's tent has her face back to normal, save for a few scars." Annba replied; her voice tired from spending so much time in the hospital. "She was really blessed that you found that potion. It was hard, watching her go through the pain caused by the healing potion, but she is a strong girl. You can go in and talk to her now, if you want; she woke up a little bit ago."

"She was dead, Annba, dead!" Lamar said. "I was going to beat that commander to death for what he had done, when Lily started screaming a passage from *The Guide*."

"The Lord of the Stars had a hand in these events. Why He decided to return the young lady back to life is something we may never know. We can be thankful that He did. Why the Lord of the Stars stopped you, is obvious." Annba looked at Lamar, who was frowning.

"To be honest, every time I think about how Lily suffered, I wish I had not let him go."

Annba grabbed his arm and started dragging him into the hospital. "Then you would have to spend the rest of your life knowing you ignored God's orders to forgive someone. Sometimes forgiving is the hardest thing a follower of our Lord must do. Go see Lily, maybe that will ease your mind." She kept a grip on his arm and pulled him over to a bed in the corner of the hospital.

Lily was in the bed. Her eyes were closed with *The Guide* lying opened on her chest. A gasp escaped Lamar's lips when he saw Lily's face. It was back almost the way he remembered it, when she was laughing and chasing chickens.

There was a scar running across her forehead. Another scar went from her nose to the corner of her lips. A third one ran from her left ear to the bottom of her eye. Her face was still as beautiful as ever, as far as Lamar was concerned. Her hair had been washed and cleaned, golden blond wrapped around her sleeping body. She was breathing, peacefully.

"How did you repair her nose?" Lamar whispered in amazement. Lily's nose had been broken in at least three places when he brought her into the hospital. It had been a horrible mess. Now Lily's nose was only slightly bent to one side. Lamar understood that bones had to be set back in place before a healing potion was used, otherwise they would heal still bent.

"Nose cartilage is tough, but I got it the best I could," Annba replied in a hushed whisper.

Lamar reached a hand down and placed it on Lily's cheek. As soon as he touched her, her eyes snapped opened.

"Sorry, I must have fallen back to sleep. That healing potion really tired me out. I think the pain from healing..." She abruptly stopped, taking a deep breath.

"How do you feel? You sure look a lot better," Lamar's replied, still amazed at the how good she looked. He had seen healing potions before, even though they were rare in Preveshawl. Still, he could not believe that it had restored her face like it had.

"Tired. Very tired. Annba warned me that extreme pain, followed by exhaustion, is expected after a healing potion is used on you. By the way, thank you for rescuing me, even though I was dead."

Lamar glanced over at his wife, with an 'I told you so' look.

"How do you know you were dead, Lily?" asked Annba. She slid into a chair beside the bed, putting her hand on top of Lily's hand.

"I know, because I left my body. I saw a light radiating awesome power and love, as well as one of the servants of the Lord of the Stars. Oh, that's right; I was supposed to give you and the elders a message from The

Lord of the Stars." She looked at Lamar, before struggling to sit up in the bed.

"Stay down Lily. You need to rest," Annba gently pushed Lily back into bed. "He is right here, go ahead and tell him your message."

"I was told to tell you and the elders that Thunderfall knows the way they must go. If Lily and Gevi lead, then the elves will show the way. They are to go to the ancient city of the Linkrins." Surprise showed on Lamar's face, his mind racing in thought. Lily's eyes slowly closed as she fell back to sleep. Quietly, Lamar and Annba left her to her sleep.

"I saw your look. Something she said caught your attention," Annba said as she stood with her husband outside the hospital building.

"I believe her when she said the message is from The Lord of the Stars. There is no way she could understand what she said. Thunderfall is a dwarven prince, by far the strongest and gruffest dwarf you will ever meet. His brother is the king of the Dwarven Nation. Thunderfall was leading the group of dwarves that joined up with me in the frozen wastelands during the Ogre Invasions. He is the one that killed the giant commander. He was different from the other dwarves, serious and very large. He had a temper that made him dangerous." Lamar seemed lost in thought. "He was extremely honorable, even for a dwarf. I suspect he was more than a prince to the dwarves. They treated him differently from any dwarf royalty I ever met, including the Dwarven King himself. There is no way Lily would have any knowledge of Thunderfall."

Annba waited for a minute to see if Lamar would say anything else. When it was clear he was finished, she asked, "What about the rest of what she said?"

"Well, the elves live northeast of us, in the Elven Forest. Everyone knows that, but they do not allow humans in their forest. I have no clue about the Linkrins, or their ancient city. That is a mystery to me." He paused, deep in thought again. "I have no idea who this Gevi is either. Let me go talk to the elders; maybe they will know something."

Annba gave him a quick kiss, "I will be here. Oh, by the way, we will be ready to release the last of the injured soldiers you captured later today." Lamar was already walking off, but replied back to her over his shoulder.

"I'll send someone over to you around noon to take care of the details. I already got the information from them I need." His voice hardened, "Their orders were to murder every man, woman, and child of Farm Circle and the surrounding farms. They were not here to take prisoners." With that, Lamar headed on over to the meeting hall.

****

Someone was shaking Javin's shoulder. "Come-on youngster, we need to get an early start today, so we can have you home by noon." Javin barely opened his eyes, to see a bearded dwarf right above him. It was still pitch dark.

"The sun isn't even up yet," he moaned while slowly getting up and

149

wiping the sleep from his eyes. "What's that smell?"

Thunderfall smiled, "Gevi's cooking breakfast over the fire, or trying to." Javin moaned again, but was smiling as he fell back onto his bedroll.

"I heard that. If you don't like it you can..., oh, oh, oh, ouch!" Gevi started yelling, in obvious pain.

"That cat caught something, I'm going to go see if I can steal myself some of it for breakfast," Thunderfall said, making sure he said it loud enough for Gevi to hear. "I think I saw where he hid it."

"Fine," said an agitated Gevi, "but I will not be cooking it. Kitty will get your share of breakfast." Javin went ahead and sat back up. Gevi was fighting with a frying pan that she was trying to hold over the fire. Javin got up and sat by the fire, joining Mac and Ledia. They were already eating what looked like eggs, with something that was round and black.

"I scrambled them a little bit ago," Mac said while pointing over to a pan holding the scrambled eggs. "Gevi wanted biscuits to go with it." Mac smiled while holding up his blackened, round biscuit. Javin heard Gevi yell again as she jerked the pan back away from the fire. Shaking his head, he scooped himself some scrambled eggs. Gevi set the pan down, using a cloth to get the biscuits out of the pan. She promptly plopped two blackened biscuits on Javin's plate without even asking him if he wanted any.

"Scrape them a little," she said with a grimace. Javin blew on one to cool it down. He then removed the black top and took a bite. It was so hard, he barely could break a piece off with his teeth.

"Not bad, not bad at all," he told her as he tried to chew the bite he took. Gevi was biting into one of hers, but she quickly spat it out.

"You are sweet, but a liar," she growled, tossing both her biscuits over to Kitty. Kitty sniffed the biscuits before going back to chewing on a bone that was left over from his kill.

"It's bad if the cat will not even eat them," commented Thunderfall as he scooped up the last of the eggs. Gevi glared at her father.

"You are doing a good job, Gevi," Ledia said as she put her plate aside. "Cooking over a fire is much harder than on a stove." She looked over at Thunderfall and Javin. "If you two think you can do better; there is the flour and the pan. Get busy." Ledia smiled sweetly toward them. Javin decided to give it a try. He got up and started mixing the recipe he remembered his mother doing, although he remembered his mother using milk instead of water. Ten minutes later he threw his burned brew into the fire and stuck his burned hand into a bucket of water.

"Aren't you going to even try your biscuits?" Gevi smirked. "Not so easy, now is it?" Javin grimaced and pulled his hand out of the bucket. He hoped he would have a day or two before having to use a sword. "I am sorry. I hate to admit it, but yours turned out better than mine."

"Enough fun you two," Thunderfall grumbled as he finished his eggs and stood up. "We need to get going."

"Wait," Ledia ordered, "Kitty smells humans, northeast of us." Javin saw that Kitty was ignoring his bone now, nose sniffing in the wind.

"Everyone in the grass," Thunderfall commanded. Everyone took cover, with Ledia keeping Kitty beside her. A short time later, a lone figure walked into the camp, bow in hand. Javin recognized him and called out. "We come in peace, Elder Johanom; it is I, Javin, son of Lamar." The man spun around, startled. When he saw Javin standing a short distance from him, he lowered his bow.

"Nice to see you, Javin; your parents will be overjoyed to see you." Elder Johanom gave Javin a hug while fifteen more men joined them in the camp. Kitty got a lot of stares, but everyone from Farm Circle was used to naturalists and their animals.

"Are you Thunderfall?" Elder Johanom asked the dwarf.

"Yes," replied a puzzled Thunderfall, who was not sure how this man knew his name.

"The elders will want to see you as soon as we get back to Farm Circle," Elder Johanom said.

"See Daddy, I told you your good looks were famous throughout the land," chimed in Gevi while she patted him on his bald head. Thunderfall's face started to turn red. "It's not every day a dwarf with a face as pretty as yours appears in their town, so they want to meet the famously handsome dwarf, named Thunderfall."

Javin tried to choke down his laughter as Thunderfall's face turned a darker shade of red. He failed and started laughing, joining Mac and several of the men from Farm Circle.

"Stop that," Thunderfall said as he glared at Javin. "And why are you trying to completely humiliate a poor old dwarf who's only failing in life was not spanking his daughter when she needed it?" His glare was now on Gevi. More of the group started joining the laughter.

"We will see if you ever make fun of my cooking again, now won't we, Daddy?" said a smug Gevi as she put her arm around him and kissed him on the top of his head again. The dwarf started sputtering and stammering so hard that everyone started laughing.

****

They finally arrived at Farm Circle around noon. Javin's three sisters were outside playing, and they were the first to spot him. Javin was almost taken to the ground as the three ran to him giving him hugs and little girl kisses on his cheek. His youngest sister, only five years old, saw Gevi, standing next to her brother, grinning ear to ear.

"Wow. You're pretty," she said once she let go of Javin, "almost as pretty as Chellell."

Gevi went down on one knee in front of the little girl. "Why thank you, and you have beautiful brown hair."

"I love your eyes," Javin's youngest sister said, staring at Gevi's arched eyebrows and bright emerald green eyes, "They are definitely way prettier than Chellell's eyes. How do I get my eyes to look like that?"

151

"The only way to get eyes like this is to have a mommy or daddy that's an elf." Gevi replied as she sat the little girl on one of her knees. "Who is Chellell?"

"When I get bigger, I am going to find me an elf to be my mommy, so I can get eyes like that," the little girl said, matter-of-factly. She ran a finger over Gevi's eyebrow. "Chellell's mommy isn't elven."

"Well, you just do that then," Gevi gave Javin's sister a squeeze. "Now tell me, who is this Chellell?"

"I can explain latter," said Javin while trying to disengage himself from his other two sisters. He reached over to pull his youngest sister away from Gevi. Gevi swung the girl around on her knee, putting her back toward Javin.

"Ignore him," she said. She ran her hand through the little girl's curly brown hair. "Now tell me about this beautiful girl, Chellell."

"Chellell is Javin's girlfriend," the girl said with a serious expression on her face. "They are going to get married, you know. Javin told me I could dress up and throw flowers at him and Chellell at their wedding."

Javin groaned, "ex-girlfriend, and we are not getting..."

"Why don't you tell me all about your brother's girlfriend?" Gevi interrupted while focusing on the little girl on her lab. She smiled a mischievous smile over at Javin, "He told me about you and your sisters, but he never mentioned a girlfriend."

"She was here last week. She made fire come out of her hand and people float in the air." Javin's sister was swinging her arms like she was doing magic. "She even vanished in a puff of smoke."

"Really? I know someone who wishes he could vanish in a puff of smoke," Gevi said, looking over her shoulder at Javin. Seeing his discomfort, she gave him another big smile. Javin had to agree. He wished he could disappear right now.

Javin's middle sister, who was nine years old, cut in. "Chellell and her friend came over to our house for dinner with Mom and Dad. She was hoping to get to see you, Javin."

Javin's oldest sister, who was thirteen years old, and actually knew a lot of what was going on, decided to help her big brother, who certainly looked like he needed it. "Javin and Chellell have not been friends since they went to the Guilds."

"We are still friends; it's just that..."

"Still friends," Gevi said interrupting again with a wink, "I see."

"See what little girls to do your life, Javin," Thunderfall said. He had been standing behind them watching the whole thing. "I hope you take this lesson to heart."

Gevi ignored her father, "So, Chellell and her friend came over to your house for dinner. I bet she didn't forget to tell her friend about Javin."

"Chellell's friend was hurt by bad people. Daddy found her a couple of days ago." Javin's youngest sister said, still on Gevi's knee. "She is in the hospital, but Mommy made her all better." That statement caught everyone's attention. They focused in on the little girl. The people from Farm Circle they had met at the camp told them about the encounter with the soldiers and about the girl. None of them mentioned the connection to Chellell.

"Mom is at the hospital?" Javin asked, forgetting his embarrassment. All three sisters nodded yes. "Go on and play. Gevi and I better go on to the hospital."

"They want me in the meeting hall; I'll catch up with you kids later." Thunderfall turned and started walking over toward the meeting hall. "Don't do anything else to embarrass me," he called back toward Gevi. Gevi absently waved a hand his direction.

"Does Jewla the naturalist still live here?" Ledia asked as she walked up to join them. Javin was thankful she didn't hear Gevi's and his sister's conversation.

"Yes, over there," he pointed to a house on the other side of the small town.

"Come on, Mac. She was one of my Guild of Nature teachers when I was at the Guilds." With that, Ledia, Mac, and Kitty, headed off toward the house. Javin's sisters stared at Kitty as he trotted away.

"Let's go to the hospital. You can meet my mother," Javin said to Gevi, who still had his sister on her knee.

"I'll be over in a minute," she replied to Javin while adjusting herself to sit cross legged on the ground. She patted the ground next her, "have a seat girls, we are going to have a woman only talk." The two older girls started giggling as they sat down on the ground with Gevi. "I want you to tell me about Chellell, barbarian princesses, and all the other girlfriends your brother seems to have conveniently forgotten."

"There is no other..."Javin stopped mid-sentence because Gevi obviously wasn't interested in listening.

"Javin used to always sit by Chellell in church," the middle sister said, grinning up at Javin. "He would hold her hand secretly, like this." She reached over and grabbed Gevi's hand. Gevi heard Javin gasp. He was trying to say something, but nothing was coming out.

"Really, why don't you... Excuse me, woman talk only." Gevi said sternly to Javin. He stood there, not sure what to do. Finally, he decided he better make a quick escape. He started walking toward the hospital.

Javin abruptly stopped and spun back around to face his sisters. "I order you to say nothing else. It's not fair that I can't tell my side of the story."

"Women are never fair; are we ladies?" Javin's sisters started giggling again. "Now go away. This is a woman only talk." Javin rolled his eyes before trotting off to the hospital. The last thing he heard was Gevi telling his sisters that since she was a woman, she could overrule his order not to talk. Javin knew that he was in big trouble.

****

The meeting of the elders was fast and decisive. They listened to Thunderfall's description of the ruins, and about the two routes to the ruins that wagons could travel on. One route went through Fort Outlands, which was now controlled by the gorms. The second route went through the Elven Forest, where elves had forbidden human entrance for over a hundred years, due to a long dead Preveshawl king, and his logging attempts. Elders in the meeting discussed the approaching gorm army, which would meet the full Preveshawl army at the Crossroads in a couple of days. It was concluded that no matter who won at the Crossroads, Farm Circle would be targeted next. The gorms would want the Farm Lands, and Preveshawl's king was determined to wipe out the followers of the Lord of the Stars. In a 12-0 vote, the elders decided to relocate. They would present their plans at the town meeting, and let every family decide for themselves whether to stay, or go to the ruins to start a new life.

****

"Step forward. Cross your swords high to catch the pole of my halberd. Then step in and strike with your knee while sliding your crossed swords down the pole," Lamar instructed. In slow motion, Lamar brought the halberd down toward Javin's head. Following his father's direction, Javin crossed his swords, catching the pole of the halberd. He slid his crossed swords down the pole and raised his knee toward his father's stomach.

"That is how you counter an overhead strike from a halberd," Lamar explained as he lowered his weapon and looked around. "I see our audience has left us."

"They went back inside the house, right after our practice when we both used short swords. I saw them leave after you got through my defense and struck me in the chest."

"You are getting better, Son." Lamar looked closely at his son. Javin was getting better, but he still was not fast enough to be the great, undefeated swordsman everyone talked about. Someone should have been able to defeat him in an arena fight. "Maybe the quality of fighters has gone down since I was at the Guild of Warriors," Lamar thought to himself.

"I don't think I will ever get used to you not stuttering. Your healing is a miracle from God. That old man you told us about, I would love to know who he is."

"All Gevi wants to know about is the barbarian princess, called 'Slayer of Giants," Javin said while rolling his eyes. "It was the strangest encounter I have ever had with anyone, but his words were true. He did warn me to stay humble. Practicing with you, Dad, will sure keep me humble."

Lamar gave a short laugh, putting his arm around his son. "Come on, let's put the weapons up and get our stuff out of the house. Your mom wants women only in the house at night. Men get the barn."

Father and son walked toward the barn, where Lamar kept a

special locked room for weapon storage. "Javin, I am very proud of you," Lamar said as they entered the barn. "I saw you and Gevi studying *The Guide* together under the old oak tree after supper. She is a beautiful girl. I am very happy you found someone that has a strong belief in God, and who loves to read His Word."

Entering the weapon locker, they hung up the halberd and their practice swords. "I really love her, Dad," Javin said nervously. "But I think she is still upset with me. I never told her about Chellell."

"Well son, I think she cares deeply for you. If you grow spiritually together, then you will survive the problems every relationship encounters. Take your lesson to heart. It is better to tell someone something up front from you, than to let them find out from somebody else, like your little sister."

Lamar and Javin exited the weapon locker and the barn, walking toward the house. "That armor and swords Thunderfall gave you are amazing. Gevi's ingenuity with making the swords flame up and shoot balls of fire is something I have never seen before. You are very fortunate, Son. She's smart, beautiful, and a disciple to the Lord of the stars." Javin nodded his agreement. "We better go get anything we want out of the house now, before your mother decides not to let us in for the night."

****

"Goblin and gorm?" Lamar asked Thunderfall later on that same night. They were sitting together outside the barn. "He challenged a goblin and a gorm hero, and beat them both, simultaneously? He is my son, and I love him, but he is not fast enough yet with those swords to win a fight against the best heroes the gorms and the goblins have."

"Humph," replied Thunderfall. "He is a lot faster than you are. He is a lot faster with those swords than you were twenty years ago, when we fought the ogres together." Surprise showed on Lamar's face, but he listened to what Thunderfall had to say. "Gevi and I watched you two earlier. She made the same observation I did. He is slowing down when he practices with you; slowing down considerably. I think you have a son who deliberately, or sub-consciously, will not outdo his father. He has too much love and respect for you. I've seen him fight, Lamar; he could beat you, easily. I am sure you know a lot of tricks with the sword that you can teach him, but as for pure speed and swordsmanship, I have never seen anyone Javin's equal."

Lamar leaned back, surprise showing clearly on his face. Thunderfall was the best fighter Lamar had ever seen in combat. He heavily respected the dwarf's opinion. A slow smile spread across his face as he thought about what Thunderfall was telling him. Stories coming back to Farm Circle about his son's skill in the arena through the years now made sense. The quality of fighters had not gone down since Lamar was at the guilds. His son's skill with the swords had outdone them all. Javin just could not bring himself to beat his father in practice. A warm glow spread through Lamar as he thought about how great a man Javin was growing up to be.

****

"I think you should let Daddy sleep inside with us. He always complains about how old he is. Sleeping outside can't be helping his health any," Gevi said the next morning. She placed a big pan of biscuits down on a long table they had set outside on the porch for breakfast.

"Humph, sharing a house with one girl is what made me so old," Thunderfall said between bites. "Must be nearly a dozen of you under this roof; I think I'll take the tent."

"These biscuits are actually good," Javin said to Gevi. He smothered another biscuit with gravy. Gevi glared at him from where she had seated herself across the table from him.

"What?" Javin reached a hand under the table to rub his shin that she had kicked. It wasn't a hard kick, just enough to get his attention. "You didn't make the biscuits, did you?"

She gave him a sweet smile, "What makes you think I didn't make these biscuits?"

"Enough, you two," said Javin's mom. "No kicking under the table." Gevi actually looked embarrassed. She hung her head down and concentrated on her plate.

"Chellell never kicked you, did she?" Javin youngest sister asked him. Gevi's head snapped back up. Javin pretended to not hear anything, concentrating instead on his food.

"Well?" Gevi had a smirk on her face. "Are you going to answer your sister?"

"Now, now," Kelley said. "My daughter and Javin were..."

"I am only going to say this once. Here is the whole story." Javin put his fork down and looked at his younger sisters who were sitting by him. "Yes, Chellell and I were best of friends growing up. Yes, we talked about a future together. That ended when she chose to enter the Guild of Magic. Yes, I handled things badly three years ago. Yes, we patched things up over a month ago. We are now friends. She deserved that. No, she never kicked me, even though she should have, at times." Javin looked around at everyone at the table, "I hope this settles the matter." He lowered his head and started furiously eating.

It was quiet, but only for a few seconds. "So, who cooks better?" Gevi was smiling teasingly at Javin.

"Both of you are such wonderful cooks. I don't think I could decide. If you ever meet Chellell, then I will happily let you have a cooking contest."

Thunderfall looked over at Lamar, "You have raised a wise son." That comment made everyone start laughing, including Gevi.

Lamar started to gently bang a spoon on the table. "Let me have your attention. As everyone knows, we leave here in six days. That is not much time to get a fully operational farm with livestock loaded and moving. I will have to harvest all the vegetables I can before we leave. "

Lamar pointed over to four empty wagons, "We will need to load up

156

our wagons, and Annba is in charge of making sure we take what we absolutely need. Two wagons will hold nothing but crops. We are taking the animals, which I will bring into the front pasture today."

Lamar then looked over at Gevi, "Gevi, I want you to take Lily shopping today for clothes and anything else she needs. Have the stores put it on my account. Javin, take your sisters and go with Gevi; I have a shopping list for you as well. Get what you can, since almost everyone will be looking to stock up for our journey." With that, everyone finished breakfast and went to their assigned chores.

****

"We were attacked! Fort Outlands has fallen!" Chancellor White's face was twisted with a mix of fear and anger.

"Attacked? Really?" Ambrissan's image asked from the mirror. "Who attacked Preveshawl?"

"Giants, goblins, and gorms; reports say over ten thousand of them."

"Hmmm," Ambrissan seemed deep in thought. "My castle I am currently in is not too far from the homeland of the giants. I will have to check into your claims."

"They are not claims! This is real. There were reports of a magic user riding some kind of flying monster that blew up half the fort." Chancellor White was pacing around in front of the mirror on his desk.

"Rest assured, I will check into it and find out what I can for you. The magic user claim actually does not surprise me. All the magic users outside Preveshawl are much more powerful than you are. They are not restricted by the presence of the followers of The Lord of the Stars." Ambrissan leaned in closer toward his mirror, so that Chancellor White could see only his face. "I suggest you start eliminating the cause of your weak magic, so that you can use your magic to fight this army with their magic users. Otherwise, you will be licking the boots of a goblin general, as his slave." Ambrissan paused, a serious look on his face. "I was trying to warn you your kingdom has grown weak. It looks like the giants found that out as well. I cannot help you, yet. I am not willing to have my magic weakened. Eliminate the followers. When I sense my magic will be strong, I will come to your aid."

Ambrissan ended the magic that caused his image to appear on the mirror. He also ended the illusion of a castle wall behind him. He exited the house at Fort Outlands, a house he had claimed as his own until the army marched again. "This is too easy," he said to himself. "The imbeciles in Preveshawl were only helping him."

The followers of the Lord of the Stars did weaken your magic. That was a truth revealed to him from the Linkrin familiar that possessed him. Magic would be stronger, once the followers of the Lord of the Stars were eliminated. Once these people were gone, then nothing would stop him.

Chapter 14

And ye shall know the truth, and the truth shall make you free. – The Guide

Chellell really missed Lily, but she could not blame her for leaving in such a hurry, considering the sad news Lily had gotten from her mother. Licheaon had shown her the letter written by Lily's mother that informed Lily about her mother's grave illness. Chellell had hoped to see Lily one more time, but Licheaon informed her that Lily had left that minute with a guard. He had ordered her stuff packed and sent to her home.

After leaving Bear Tree City, the company passed a large army, marching down the road from the capital toward the Crossroads. As the army marched past them, half of the guards with the magic show were ordered to join the army. Both of Chellell's magic assistants were also taken, forced to join a group of magic users in the army.

At first, she had been terrified to learn that Fort Outlands had fallen. Relief came when she learned most of the people and a lot of the soldiers had evacuated. Figuring that Javin was fine, she decided she would send a letter to his house at Farm Circle. Surely, that is where he would go. She was worried about her mother and their neighbors in Farm Circle, but the soldiers were confident that the invading army would be stopped at the Crossroads. Chellell grew more confident, knowing that the Preveshawl army had magic users.

Upon arrival at the royal palace in the city of Preveshawl Castle, Licheaon announced a week off for everyone with the magic show. After the week off, they would travel to the southern cities of Preveshawl. They would stay in the southern cities until the end of the year.

Chellell remembered that Lily had said she was from the capital. It was a gigantic city, but she was going to do her best to find Lily and see how her mother was doing. She started asking around about Lily and where she lived. She would have asked Licheaon, but he was in constant meetings. An idea finally came to her, so she checked in with the palace beauty parlor. Sure enough, Lily had worked there before being assigned to the show. She got directions and a map to follow to Lily's last known address. She slept that night, happily knowing that she would see Lily the next morning.

Chellell was amazed at how big and crowded the city of Preveshawl Castle was. With Sanatarial on her shoulder, she left the palace early in the morning and started walking through the crowded streets. Eventually, she came to a section of the city she was unfamiliar with, but it was near Lily's home. The street was a dirt road, with trash everywhere. Shacks made out of whatever bits of brick, stone, or wood that people could find lined the street. Chellell had rarely even seen a barn that looked as bad as most of these shacks. The smell of sewage made her want to gag. Crowds of people eyed her, making her feel nervous. She knew her nice clothes didn't help either. Making a connection with Sanatarial, Chellell felt magic flow into her body as a group of young men approached her.

"Can we help ya?" the biggest of the bunch asked. "I'm thinking ya must be lost." A couple of the boys with him snickered.

"I am looking for the house where a girl named Lily used to live." Chellell responded nervously. Glancing around she noticed everyone on the street was making a noticeable effort to ignore her.

"Well, you're in luck. It'll cost ya though." A big, rough looking boy held out his hand.

"How much?" she asked, not liking where this was heading.

"Well, o'l Lily hasn't paid her protection fees to us in months. I figure she owes us ten copper. It will be another ten for us to show you the way."

Chellell knew that this was outrageous, but decided to hand him the twenty copper pieces to avoid any problems. Sure to their word, they led her to a little hovel built of wood planks. She knocked on the door. A woman's voice called out from inside the shack, telling her to enter. The door was a big piece of wood, which she slid out of the way to enter. An older woman was washing some clothes in a pan that was sitting on the dirt floor.

"Can I help ya?" She barely even looked up at Chellell.

"Yes Ma-am. I am looking for the home of a young lady named Lily. Is this her house?"

"It was. We put her out several years ago. Done right fine for herself ever since though. She came by a month or so ago, said she was going to get to travel. Lucky girl. I knew her looks would get her better than I got." The lady kept on scrubbing clothes as she talked. Several children unexpectedly burst into the house, sliding to a stop when they saw Chellell.

"Git outta here. Don't come back till supper time, ya hear?" the woman yelled. This time she did look up. "And go find your Pa; he's probably passed out again at the Shady Lounge." The children stared at Chellell for a second before running back out the door. Chellell saw they were dressed poorly and were very dirty.

"Are you Lily's mother then?" Chellell asked, even though she knew the answer.

"Yep," was her reply.

Chellell waited a few seconds before asking. "Is Lily around?"

"Nope. Like I said, haven't seen her since she left with that show thing."

Dread overcame Chellell. Lily didn't make it home. Yet, the letter said Lily's mother was gravely ill. "Lily left the show several days ago. She got a letter from you that said you were gravely ill and that you wanted to see her."

"I doubt that. I can't read nor write, and I obviously ain't sick. Hadn't been sick in years." Lily's mother continued doing clothes, not looking at Chellell as she talked.

The dread she was feeling was now slowly being replaced with a cold anger. "Thank you, Ma-am. I will take my leave now." Chellell turned and headed for the door.

"Tell Lily I said howdy, next time you see her," Lily's mother said as Chellell reached the door. One of the children who had run in earlier stepped into the doorway and stopped Chellell.

"The worm gang is going to get you," he said with a sincere face. "I heard em talking after they brought you to our house."

Chellell reached into her pocket and took out the last of the coins she had on her, handing them to the boy. "Thank you," she said coldly. She again restored her contact with Sanatarial. Magic power flowed through her as she walked through the slums. Sanatarial was perched on her shoulder, his wings slightly spread and tail moving slowly side to side. Sure enough, the same group of boys approached her. The large boy that addressed her earlier stepped right in front of her, blocking her progress.

"We decided you need to pay Lily's dues in advance, seeing she's still gone and all." the boy stated. Several boys behind him were chuckling.

"I'm not paying any more," Chellell icily replied. She stepped sideways and took a single step forward, but the large boy again stepped in front of her.

"If you don't pay, then you will need to come with us until we can make an agreement on payment," the large boy stated. "I think we can..."

"You and your friends have one last chance, I strongly suggest you take it," Chellell snapped as she took a step backwards away from the young men. Sanatarial was now standing on her shoulder, head stretched out and hissing.

"Cute lizard, Lady; I guess we do this the hard way then," the boy replied as he reached out toward Chellell. The hand never reached her. Chellell's right hand came out in front of her. A compressed ball of air shot from her hand directly into the boy's chest. His feet left the ground as he flew backwards into two of his friends. All three hit the ground rolling. The remaining five stared in shock at their leader, which allowed Chellell to back up several more feet. The large boy quickly rolled back to his feet, anger flashing wildly in his eyes.

"Get her," he growled. Long knives were drawn and three of the young men started to move toward her. They didn't even come close to touching her. A ball of fire hit the boy closest to her. Flame exploded across his whole body, throwing him backwards into the group of boys behind him. Chellell was no longer the focus of their attention. Several of the young men were now on fire. The boy who had been hit with the ball of fire had enough sense to roll to his right into a large mud puddle, saving his life. He lay there moaning; smoke rising from his burned clothing. Three others were beating the fire off their clothes. Chellell stood facing them, a deep anger showing on her face. A small ball of fire was balanced on an outstretched hand.

"Do you want to keep playing?" Chellell said acidly. The small ball of fire in her hand was now bouncing up and down. She got no reply.

Instead, the boys ran in various directions, leaving their friend moaning in the mud puddle. Chellell instantly put the fire out and pointed to the large boy who was the obvious leader of this worm gang. The young man's whole body instantly froze. He fell hard, sliding to the middle of the dirt road. Chellell calmly walked over to where he was lying face down, and tore the money pouch off his belt that held the coins she had given him earlier. She then used magic to flip him over. She was not gentle. He rose up off the ground, flipped over, and dropped back to the ground flat on his back. A wild, terrified gaze met her own, calm eyes.

"I warned you," she said, smiling down coldly at the completely paralyzed boy. "Here are the new rules you will follow. Rule one: You and your gang will not harm Lily or any of her family. You will no longer take money from them. Rule two: You and your gang will never again try to harm a woman." The ball of fire appeared in her hand. She held it above his face where he could feel the heat of it. "If you break the rules I gave you, I will personally roast you alive in the street. If you think I will never find out, then you are one who does not understand the power you are dealing with. Am I clear?"

The fire in her hand disappeared. The boy's eyes were still showing extreme fright. "To help you remember, I will give you a sign." Chellell put her finger to his cheek. Chellell saw the boys eyes change from fear to pain as her finger burned into his flesh. She jerked her hand back away from his face. She had planned to burn the Preveshawl symbol of magic into his face, as a lesson he would never forget.

"What is happening to me?" Chellell thought to herself as she fought the rage burning inside her.

"Do it!" the voice of Sanatarial said in her mind. "Make him pay for what he has done. Revenge makes you strong: forgiveness only shows your enemies you are weak."

Chellell remembered back to her time as a youth sitting in church. Forgiveness was always stressed in the teachings. Fire was on the tip of her finger again as she struggled internally between revenge and forgiveness. She wanted to teach this boy a lesson he would never forget. Revenge was what she desired.

Again, pain flashed in the paralyzed boy's eyes as she burned a circle on his cheek. The lightning bolt inside the circle was halfway burned onto his face when Chellell looked into the boy's eyes, again. They were eyes filled with pain and terror. Chellell jerked her flaming finger back.

"Finish it!" Sanatarial hissed out loud. "Then kill him." Chellell saw unimaginable terror in the boy's eyes. He was completely paralyzed, but he could still hear what her familiar had hissed.

Chellell stood back up and stepped back. With a wave of her hand, the large boy was free. A horrible, howling scream escaped his lips that could now move. His hand flew to his cheek where Chellell had burned the half completed symbol for magic. She walked off, leaving him rolling in the street, screaming in pain.

"You should have killed him. You should have killed all of them," Sanatarial hissed. The coldness of his comment shocked Chellell out of her anger. Chellell was furious, and using that fury, she had come close to seriously hurting or even killing that boy. Something in her was changing, Chellell realized. What kind of person was she becoming?

"Maybe I am getting stronger," she thought to herself. Out loud she said, "They learned their lesson."

"You must be strong and not show forgiveness or mercy to the weak who oppose you," Sanatarial hissed out. "The stronger you are, the stronger your magic becomes." Chellell kept her thoughts of revenge versus forgiveness to herself as she briskly strolled back to the palace.

Back at the palace, Chellell went straight to the office of Licheaon, only to learn that he was at a tavern near the palace. Anger mixed with worry over Lily filled Chellell's mind. She left the palace again and walked the short distance to the tavern.

Once inside, her senses were assaulted in every way possible. On stage, a band played loud, squealing music. The smell of alcohol and wood smoke clogged her nostrils. Eyes watering from the harsh smoke, Chellell wormed her way through the crowd, looking for Licheaon. She finally found him, sitting in a corner booth by himself. The table in front of him was littered with glasses and bottles. She slid into the booth directly across from him. Blood-shot eyes stared across the table at her.

"What happened to Lily?" Chellell demanded, not bothering to greet him.

"Well hello, Chellell," Licheaon slurred, "Can I buy you a drink?"

"No thanks," Chellell said in disgust, "I never touch the stuff. What happened to Lily?"

"Who is Lily?" Licheaon took another drink while giggling to himself.

"You know Lily, the make-up artist. What happened to her?" Chellell shouted while banging her fist forcefully down on the table.

"You saw the letter from her mother. I think it was self-explanatory." Licheaon said, getting even more slurry. Chellell looked over at him, not bothering to hide the disgust that showed on her face.

"I met Lily's mother. There was no letter. She can't even write; time to tell the truth, Licheaon." Chellell leaned across the table as she said this, looking him right in the eyes.

Licheaon tried to sit up straight, but he was having a hard time. "Fine, you want to know the truth, I will tell you the truth." The alcohol was making him say things he would never say to her, if he were not under its influence. "Your little show and all the magic tricks are nothing but a way to find those who are a danger to Preveshawl, because they are followers of the Lord of the Stars." Licheaon giggled again before taking a big drink. "After we leave a town or city, soldiers arrest the men, women, and children that set off anti-magic detectors. Having such a reaction to magic is a sure sign they are followers of the Lord of the Stars."

Chellell listened, horrified, realizing that Farm Circle had been one of the shows. "I am asking one more time, Licheaon; what happened to Lily?" she asked in a cold, demanding voice.

Licheaon became angry, his voice rising. "Lily was found with *The Guide*. She refused to deny that the Lord of the Stars is God, so I had her arrested. She would be in jail now, except your friends at Farm Circle rebelled against the king and rescued her. Soon, the king will destroy that town, and kill everyone there. After he deals with the gorms, that is."

Chellell started to connect with her familiar. For the second time today, her anger reached a boiling point. With no warning, Licheaon abruptly passed out on the table. Angrily, Chellell gripped the back of his hair pulling his head up. He was out cold. She let go of his hair, letting his head fall back onto the table.

****

Night was starting to fall when Chellell decided to look for a place to stop. Even though it was only a half-day's journey to Farm Circle, she was too exhausted to continue on. She had been on the road for two days, traveling toward Farm Circle. Two days with Sanatarial constantly nagging her. After leaving the club and Licheaon, she had gone straight to her room and packed her travel gear. Using the last of her coins, she bought a horse and rode it out of the capitol city.

Anxiety and fear had driven her to ride hard with almost no food. She had to warn Farm Circle that they were in extreme danger. "This is my fault," She thought to herself. Anger again bubbled to the surface of her mind as her exhausted horse continued on down the road. "My magic show was never meant to show people the usefulness of magic," She mumbled bitterly to her horse. "It was meant to find followers of the Lord of the Stars."

Finally, she saw several small wagons and a campfire off to the side of the road. Chellell decided to see if she could join whoever it was that was there. When she came up to the camp, she saw Preveshawl soldiers sitting around the fire, cooking a meal. Relieved that this would be a safe place to camp, she reined her horse over and climbed down.

"Greetings," Chellell called out. "I am looking for a safe place to stay the night. Do you mind if I share your fire tonight?"

"No problem," a soldier called back. "Just tie your horse up with the others." He pointed to a tree over by a wagon. "You are just in time to share supper." Chellell led her horse over to the other horses, but noticed a horrible smell coming from one of the wagons as she walked by it. It stank like a latrine. She staked her horse fifty feet from the camp in a grassy area, near where the soldiers had most of their horses. She watched her horse stick its nose into the ground, coming back up with a mouthful of sweet, green grass. Giving the horse a quick scratch between its ears, Chellell hurried back toward the camp.

"Miss, do you have any food to spare?" Chellell looked toward a wagon where the voice had come from, and saw a man looking out of a set

163

of bars in the side of the wagon. Sanatarial was moving around on her shoulder, obviously uncomfortable.

"I don't..."

"Leave the prisoners alone," yelled a soldier over by the fire. Chellell turned from the wagon and quickly hurried over to the fire. Looking around, she noticed several more wagons with bars on them. Sitting down on a log by two female soldiers, Chellell eagerly accepted a bowl of soup with some bread. The growling of her stomach was a reminder that she had barely eaten the past two days.

"So where are you going?" One of the female soldiers asked, but before Chellell could answer, she spoke up again. "Hey, I recognize you; you're from that magic show. You are the magic user. That was an awesome show. I saw it in Bear Tree City. So what are doing out here by yourself? My name is Heaterch. What is your name?"

"You talk too much," said the second female soldier. She looked Chellell up and down for a few seconds. "Yep, you're the lady magician. The lizard on your shoulder is a dead giveaway."

"Yes, that's me," replied Chellell. "My name is Chellell, by the way." She was silent after that, not really wanting to say anything else.

"So what you doing out here by yourself? Shouldn't you be performing or something?" The first soldier said again, slurping noisily on her soup.

"We were given a few weeks off, so I decided to go visit my mother. She lives near Farm Circle." Chellell noticed both soldiers stop eating and look at each other.

"Don't think so," said the second female soldier. "They say there is a rebellion out there against the king. The Crossroads is closed to Farm Circle."

"Really?" replied Chellell nervously, "I did not know that. I guess I will talk to the officer in charge at the Crossroads and see what can be done."

"Good luck with that. The gorms will be there within days." The second female soldier finished her soup and was now concentrating on her bread.

"So why are people locked up in those wagons?" Chellell asked, looking intently at the more talkative of the female soldiers.

The first soldier answered eagerly, "They violated the king's law concerning The Guide. We are..."

"You need to learn when to keep your yap shut, Heaterch," interrupted the other soldier. "Eat, and no more talk." Heaterch glared at the other women. In a huff she got up and finished her supper elsewhere in the camp.

Eventually, everyone started going to sleep, so Chellell got her bedroll and laid it out by her horse, away from the soldiers. She was far enough from the wagons that she could not make out anything being said, but close enough to hear people crying, including children. She was extremely restless, because the thought kept coming to her mind that these people were now prisoners because of her show. Sanatarial was gone, which did not surprise her. He often disappeared at night, but would come if she called. She did not call.

Quietly, she slipped over to the wagons. Scared to death, she stopped right at the back of the first wagon. A scream almost escaped her lips when she saw a man looking through the bars right at her. It was the same man she had seen earlier.

"Are you going to help us?" he whispered. Chellell nodded her head, swallowing down the terror she felt inside. "You are an angel," he whispered. "Get that axe behind you that they were using to chop wood, and hand it to me through the bars." Chellell nodded her head. She looked back and saw the axe halfway in a piece of wood. It took her a minute to work the axe free. Seeing no soldiers, she slipped the axe through the bars to a grateful young man.

"Are you going to bust the door down?" She asked, thinking about the noise that would make.

"Yes. Then we are going to run for it. I wish I could get to the other wagons, the two with the children inside." The young man paused. "I will try to rescue the others later, if I escape."

"Hold on, I have an idea," Chellell whispered. "The soldier's horses are straight behind this wagon in a little pasture. If you get to them, follow the Azak star northeast a half-day ride until you find Farm Circle. Ask for Lamar or Javin, if they are there. They will know what to do."

"Got it; I am going to start swinging in five minutes. Get on your horse and get going toward Farm Circle. Maybe you can get us help if we fail. Those who escape will follow you. I will tell everyone in the wagon willing to make a run for it, so they can also head toward Farm Circle." Chellell nodded and ran back to her horse. She was shaken so badly that she fell right off her horse seconds after she had mounted it. Climbing on again, she kicked her horse hard in the side. The horse took off at full gallop, weaving through the farm fields toward Farm Circle.

Guilt was her constant companion while she rode toward Farm Circle. According to Licheaon, those arrested were in the prison wagons because of her magic show. Amazingly, the man did not recognize her. "Must have been too dark to really see me," Chellell thought to herself.

After thirty minutes, she reined her horse to a stop. Anxiety filled her as she looked back to see if anyone had escaped. The faint moonlight gave her an answer within a few minutes. Two horses running at breakneck speed were coming toward her. Chellell worried that they might be soldiers, so she summoned Sanatarial. He appeared right as she saw that the two on horseback were escaped prisoners, not soldiers. One was the young man she had given the axe to.

"What have you done, Chellell?" The voice of Sanatarial screamed in her mind, stunning her. His claws dug painfully into her right shoulder. The pain brought her out of her stunned state.

"This isn't right!" she screamed right back. The two escapees halted their horses in confusion. She was using her hands trying to push the familiar off her shoulder. Feeling a sharp pain, she jerked her hand back knocking her familiar from her shoulder. Sanatarial had bitten her! Blood from the vicious bite ran down her arm and between her fingers.

"Keep going," Chellell screamed at the two prisoners who were staring at Sanatarial. "Find Lamar or Javin!" One of the prisoners took off, but the one she gave the axe to stayed put.

"It looks like you need some help," he called to Chellell.

"There is nothing you can do. This is a magic issue," Chellell yelled back with a voice that was breaking with overwhelming emotion. "Go! I will catch up later. Do not stop or wait." The young man looked troubled, but he nodded before racing after his friend.

"You need to decide if you want the joy and the power of magic, or if you are going to help the followers of the Lord of the Stars," Sanatarial said in her mind as he hovered overhead. "Your decision should be an easy one."

Chellell sat down on the ground and looked up at him. "This has gone too far, Sanatarial," Chellell said as her voice broke, tears started running freely from blue eyes. "I agree their belief is wrong, but taking people off to prison is too much." The words barely came out from Chellell's lips as sobs racked her body. "Magic is to help people, not harm them. Do you remember saying that?"

"You help people by doing what is best for the majority. The demise of the followers of the Lord of the Stars will increase the influence of magic," hissed the dragon coldly. "You must learn to accept what is the greater good. The king knows the killing of a few will greatly benefit all."

Chellell abruptly stopped sobbing. The shock of what her familiar had said reverberated through her numb mind. She looked up in disbelief into the night sky at the hovering dragon. "Killing! The decree said 'prison', not killing."

Sanatarial was silent, not saying anything. The only sound was the sound of his bright red wings flapping furiously. Finally, he spoke up. "They will be given a chance to change their ways, and the young ones a chance to be enlightened. But if that fails, you must do what is best for Preveshawl."

Shocked, Chellell could only sit there, staring at her familiar. How could this be the same creature she had summoned years ago at the Guild of Magic in the Summoning Ritual? Peace, love, and prosperity were promised to those who kept to the path of magic. Yes, it was a ritual where the existence of higher deities was denied over and over in ritual chants. The ritual also included the denial that the Lord of the Stars was God. It blamed Him for all the evil in society. The ritual promised riches and power for all in society, as long as they followed the enlightened path taught by familiars.

There were many elements to the ritual that Chellell refused to think about, or remember. She only participated in them because a familiar, along with its powerful magic, would not come until you proved you were free from any moral or religious bondage. Now though, her familiar was talking murder.

These thoughts went racing through Chellell's confused brain, until suddenly a single thought came to the front of her mind. "Farm Circle did not rebel. They were attacked." She said this as she jumped back to her feet and stared accusingly at Sanatarial, her finger shaking as she pointed it right at him. "They set off the magic detectors at my show!"

"We're going to attack them," hissed the dragon with more hatred in his voice than she had ever heard from anything in her entire life. "They decided to attack first, and rescue your little traitor friend, who was polluted with the teachings of the Lord of the Stars at that church you took her to."

Chellell was so shocked she was completely speechless. She struggled for words while gazing into the burning eyes of Sanatarial, eyes that shined with utter hatred. "I don't need this. I certainly don't need you!" Chellell turned and jumped up on her horse. "Magic is not worth someone's life. Have a good life Sanatarial; I hope I never see you again."

Kicking her horse into a gallop, Chellell headed toward Farm Circle. She did not see the flash of lightning that came from Sanatarial. The bolt hit her right between the shoulder blades. She fell off her horse, unconscious before even hitting the ground. Sanatarial smiled wickedly to himself. He hovered over Chellell, waiting for several soldiers that had come into view.

****

"The few humans who remain now understand the tax levied on them and what must be brought to the fort as payment," a small gorm with glasses said from across the table of the Grand Leader. "They were given a copy of the new laws they are to live under. They understand that they can live in peace under you, Grand Leader, as long as they pay their taxes and follow the laws." He absently pushed his glasses up on his nose, eyes fixed nervously on the massive giant in front of him.

"That is good, very good," replied the giant. "I hope everyone in this room understands that wealth will come from ruling these humans, not killing them. And you, General," he stared hard at a gorm general sitting off to his left, "better make sure that your troops understand that pillaging and killing will not be tolerated. Is that clear?"

"Yes, Grand Leader. I have already whipped several soldiers in front of everyone, and made them pay for damages."

The Grand Leader nodded toward his gorm general. "I know you gorms believe that the soul of every person you kill strengthens you. Tell your troops they will have fighting and killing in the days ahead. That should keep them happy."

The Grand Leader turned his attention away from the gorm general and addressed everyone in the tent. "Tomorrow, we march toward the

167

main Preveshawl army. This battle will either break us, or break Preveshawl." The giant made sure to make eye contact with everyone at the table. His large fingers squeezed the armrest of his chair so hard the wood overlay creaked. With a grim voice, he announced, "We march at dawn." Everyone around the table started talking, planning the mobilization of such a large army. The Grand Leader motioned for the mage Ambrissan.

While Ambrissan approached, the Grand Leader fought to contain the anger that was overwhelming him. The Black Knight had humiliated him by defeating two of his heroes, simultaneously. Forcing him to spare the life of the goblin had greatly reduced his honor. He despised showing mercy to anyone, and being forced to show mercy in front of his whole army had been overwhelmingly humiliating.

The Grand Leader had lost honor for the first time in his life because of the Black Knight. Even now, he could sense the giants in his army thinking less of him. If he was going to remain Grand Leader, then he would have to restore his "honor", and restore it quickly.

The giant race was extremely evil. They valued personal strength above all else. Part of a giant's strength, was their honor. Anytime a giant was insulted or showed weakness, then their "honor" was damaged. The only way a giant could restore his honor, was to return the insult one hundred times, or kill the one who dishonored them.

Showing mercy and forgiveness was a sign of weakness that greatly reduced honor, for the giants. The Grand Leader had been forced to show mercy to end the greater insult the Black Knight had given him by taking on two of his heroes at the same time, and easily beating them. That insult and reduction in honor grew worse when the Black Knight started toying with his goblin hero, refusing to honorably kill the injured creature. The Grand Leader spared the goblin's life, before his honor was hurt even more than it already had been.

Now, the Grand Leader needed to restore his honor. If he did not, then the giants would lose respect for him, eventually replacing him with another Grand Leader. There were two ways the Grand Leader could restore his honor. He could insult the enemy army the Black Knight fought with by somehow forcing the humans to show mercy. If the Grand Leader could somehow force the humans to show mercy, the humans would be greatly insulted in the eyes of the giants, restoring the Grand Leader's honor. The second way the Grand Leader could restore his honor would be by killing the Black Knight. That would show the giants that the Grand Leader was stronger than the Black Knight.

"Have you learned anything more about the Black Knight or the dwarf?" Anger was very clear in the tone of the Grand Leader's voice as he addressed Ambrissan.

"The dwarf is a blacksmith that showed up twenty years ago. He has a half-human half-elf daughter. Neither the Black Knight or the dwarf were soldiers in the army." Ambrissan was silent after stating what he knew about the dwarf.

"And the Black Knight?" asked the Grand Leader. He could feel the anger bubbling up in him thinking about that knight.

"The Black Knight is a complete unknown to every human we questioned," Ambrissan replied. A smile spread across his face. "However, I am certain I know who this Black Knight may be, and where he will be in the near future." He looked at the Grand Leader who was listening intently.

"Two possibilities for who the Black Knight is: A young man, who is a legend at the Guild of Warriors, fights with two short swords. It could be him. The other, Grand Leader, is someone you know very well. A certain general that killed your father, also fought with two short swords."

The Grand Leader's eyes narrowed. Even though twenty years had passed, he still remembered that day. As a young officer under his father, he had sworn vengeance when burying his father.

"No one I know of, knows General Lamar's location, or if he is even alive," Ambrissan said. "However, the young fighter, named Javin, is known to be from a small farming town east of the Crossroads. I have several wolf riders that are highly skilled assassins. A goblin naturalist with a bird could scout the whole area for someone wearing black armor. If we find him, then we could assassinate him."

"Do it," snorted the Grand Leader. "I want him dead, by my command."

The giant paused for a second, deep in thought. "After you send out your two-headed wolves, I want you to have wanted posters put out for the dwarf and the Black Knight. You can claim the reward for the Black Knight if your hunch is correct. Do a wanted poster for the dwarf's little girl as well. Make sure that her poster says wanted alive. Sometimes the best way to get a father is through his children. Make sure the picture of them is accurate. Use magic if you have to, and spread them throughout the army."

Chapter 15

Teach me to do thy will; for thou art my God: thy spirit is good; lead me into the land of uprightness. – The Guide

Javin wolfed down his breakfast while listening to the conversation and plans for the Farm Circle departure the following morning. In a few minutes, he and Mac would have to leave for their last patrol duty. No trouble was expected, but the town was still keeping a careful eye on the surrounding areas. Javin was clearing off his plate, when Ledia and Gevi strolled up to the breakfast table. Javin looked curiously at the two, noticing both were dressed in their full leather armor, with bows slung across their back. Gevi carried her staff, while Ledia had a small bird, known as a Pygmy Falcon, on her shoulder. She had purchased the animal from Jewla, who had been training it as an aerial scouting bird.

Kitty followed the two women out the door. The tiger stared at the bird, before giving a low growl and walking over to the edge of the porch. He sat with his back toward Ledia.

"Why you...! Now that was not nice, Kitty," Ledia said with a huff. She spun her bandana so that Kitty's red jewel used to communicate with him was no longer on her forehead. "He keeps sending me images of himself eating my new bird," explained Ledia to Gevi as the two woman took a seat at the table. "Like a typical male, he is jealous when he is not the center of attention."

Mac gave a choking cough. "Sorry," he said when Ledia glared at him. "Food went down the wrong way."

"Kitty has refused to eat anything since I got the falcon," Ledia continued. "Like all males, he pouts when jealous."

Mac coughed again, but did not look up at his wife this time.

"I don't think all males..." Javin started to say, but Mac cut him off.

"After twenty years of marriage, Javin, I have learned when to keep my mouth shut," Mac said in between bits of food. "There are times you just agree with whatever the woman says." Kitty picked that moment to give another growl toward Ledia. He walked off the porch and out of sight around the house. Ledia glared at the back of her departing tiger.

"You better listen to this wise man," piped in Gevi. She gave Javin a wink.

Javin was about to say something, but Mac gave him a swift "no" motion with his hand. Sighing, Javin changed the subject. "Are you two going somewhere?"

"There is nothing left to pack or do around here, so we will be joining you boys on patrol today," Ledia explained while looking at her husband. Mac shrugged, but kept his attention on his plate. Javin actually was happy to have them along because patrol had been extremely boring lately. However, he saw two problems.

Javin looked over at Gevi. He was always amazed at how beautiful she looked in her travel leathers. It was the same outfit she had worn when they had fought the gorms in the mountain meadow. For some reason, Gevi looked better dressed like this, than she did wearing a formal dress. "Your dad would not approve."

"Daddy knows I am big enough to make my own decisions. Besides, he told me and Ledia this morning he approved, as long as the patrol captain agreed."

"You have another problem. What are you going to ride?" Javin asked as he stood up and buckled on his sword belt.

Gevi looked at him with a puzzled expression, "My horse, of course."

"She threw a shoe yesterday, or did you forget that?" Mac commented. "Lamar has not had time to re-shoe her."

Javin noticed the disappointed look on Gevi's face. "You can ride with me if you want. My stallion can carry both of us." Gevi's face beamed with happiness. "Just don't eat a big breakfast. He can only carry so much weight." He ducked the wooden spoon that flew well over his head in an obvious deliberate miss from Gevi.

****

Gevi was really enjoying being outdoors with the fresh breeze and the sunshine this pleasantly warm morning. She didn't even notice that Javin had steered the horse away from the others, though the patrol was in sight and still relatively close. To her surprise, Javin nervously asked, "Did you mean what you said on the day of the Hero's Challenge?" Gevi was riding behind him on the horse, hands gently holding his shoulders while the horse walked through the high grass. She moved her arms down around his chest and gave him a squeeze from behind, before moving her hands back to his shoulder.

"I meant what I said, Javin," she replied. She paused a few seconds before going on. "Growing up with Daddy near the fort, I have had soldiers asking me on dates since I was an older teenager. They were all gentleman, especially after Daddy took care of those soldiers in the tavern. I always refused them. Do you know why?"

"No," answered Javin in an anxious voice.

Gevi started laughing, making Javin relax and smile as well. "I wasn't sure either, but none of them interested me. No matter how good-looking, tough, manly, or anything most girls would like, I was not interested. The first night we met, you used those swords like nothing I had ever seen any soldier at the fort do. But honestly, I could care less. What really impressed me was the fact that after you thought we were asleep, you sat up and read from *The Guide,* and prayed."

"I do that every night," replied Javin, "or almost every night. I only want to learn; it is not a big deal."

"You are wrong. It is a big deal. I love studying and discussing *The Guide* with you. That means so much to me. I said I loved you at the Hero's Challenge because I was so scared I would never see you again. I love you still, because you are my best friend, and you have a deep love for God that melts my heart. I have never met anyone, besides my father, who really has the devotion to God that you do." With that, she put her arms around his waist and leaned her head against his back. Several quiet minutes passed while the horse munched on some grass.

Javin allowed the horse to have a quick snack, his mind swirling with confusion over what to say to Gevi. "You're not upset over Chellell?"

Gevi started laughing again, "No! I was having fun with you, like I did with the barbarian princess story you told us." She leaned her head back, enjoying the clouds and the breeze. "I realized quickly, while talking with your sisters, that something happened between you and Chellell a few years ago. I could not resist giving you a hard time and having some fun. I still can't believe you never even mentioned her to me, so you deserved everything you got. Seriously though, I believe it is important to trust. If I didn't think I could trust you, I would not have let our relationship develop as far as it has."

"It is hard for me to..." A yell made Javin stop what he was saying. "Hold on," he shouted as he spurred his horse into a run back toward the patrol group. Gevi held on tight. They were back with the patrol in less than a minute.

"Ledia's falcon has spotted two riders riding hard towards us. They are a couple of miles southwest," Mac told them as Javin pulled his horse to a stop.

"Everyone slow gallop southwest," ordered the patrol captain. "I want to intercept the riders, but keep our horses fresh in case we have a need to move fast. Ledia, you and your cat stay by me. Have your bird stay overhead and give me direction changes as needed." Javin put on his helmet before glancing back over his shoulder.

"I guess I was wrong, Gevi; there may be some fun after all on this patrol." Gevi tightened her grip on Javin as he kicked his horse into a gallop.

****

Javin listened to the story of how a young lady with flaming red hair had helped the two escaped prisoners, and how she was last seen fighting with a small dragon. He kept his worried thoughts to himself, but from the description of the girl and the small dragon, he was certain that it was Chellell. If it was, Javin promised himself he was going to kill her familiar, if given a chance.

Jarold, the patrol captain, spoke up, after the two riders explained how they escaped. "Why were you two in a prisoner wagon? What kind of crime did you commit? "

"No normal crime!" one of the escaped men explained. "Soldiers came to my house in Bear Tree City. They arrested me, my wife, and my daughter, after searching our house and finding *The Guide*. Everyone with us was arrested for the same thing, possessing *The Guide*. The girl that rescued us told us to head this way, and ask for Lamar or Javin. They would help us and rescue our families. Someone has to help us!"

"I am certain Lamar would order us to help," Javin said from behind his black, chain mail face cover. He directed his comment toward the patrol captain.

Jarold made a split second decision. "We will help. The girl that rescued you sounds like Chellell. You two have no armor or weapons, so I want you to continue on to Farm Circle. We will rescue your families, and everyone else in the prisoner wagons." Jarold focused his attention on a person standing near Mac. "Thorb, I want you to guide them to Farm Circle, and bring back reinforcements. Everyone else, follow me."

****

"Gather around, everyone," the patrol captain said. The patrol circled around him. Gevi was squeezing in hard against Javin on their shared horse, obviously nervousness. "They have three wagons and twenty soldiers. Mac, Ledia, Gevi, Travier, Gefamin, and Kitty will circle over to the west of the wagons. The sun will be going down, which will make it hard for them to see you. The rest of us will come up behind them in full force, demanding the release of Chellell and the other prisoners. They will be allowed to leave in peace, as long as they meet our demands. They outnumber us two to one, but hopefully they will not realize that, if we act like we have the advantage. If fighting does break out, I want everyone to try not to kill. Our objective is freeing Chellell, and any other innocent prisoners, not killing people. Are there any questions or comments?"

"Yes sir," Gevi spoke up from behind Javin. She pulled a small cylinder from her belt, and held it up for the captain to see. "I made this a couple of months ago. It launches a ball that will break open and emit sleeping gas. Anyone that breathes in the gas will pass out in seconds. If you make sure we get within twenty feet, I can launch it if fighting starts."

The captain thought about what Gevi said before responding. "It's worth a try, but get it near their archers. They will be the most dangerous to us. I want you to be careful young lady. I fought with your father, and Javin's father, during the Ogre Invasions. I do not want to face Thunderfall's wrath if something happens to you. Travier, you are to stay close to Gevi at all times."

****

The sun's rays lingered on the horizon as Jarold spoke, "We have you surrounded. If you surrender your prisoners peacefully, then you will be allowed to leave in peace." A group of ten Preveshawl soldiers with drawn bows was kneeling in formation, facing the patrol from Farm Circle. Another ten soldiers were behind the archers, holding spears or swords with shields.

"This isn't going very well," Javin thought to himself as his horse pranced around on the hard packed road.

The squad commander was the only one mounted on a horse for the Preveshawl soldiers. His horse paced behind the formation of soldiers as the commander looked nervously to the right and left side of the road. Seeing no threat, he gave the signal to fire.

"They're firing! Off the road and engage," shouted the patrol captain as he wheeled his horse sideways toward the side of the road. As soon as the words left his mouth, a thunderous explosion boomed out. A thick, grayish smoke started spewing out of a canister in the middle of the Preveshawl formation. Javin charged his horse forward. Several arrows were launched toward him, but the ones that hit bounced off his armor.

Confusion overcame the Preveshawl soldiers; several collapsed into unconsciousness, while the rest were running in all four directions, trying to escape the sleeping gas billowing out amongst them. Javin drew both swords. Deep red flames danced across the blades.

Like a joust of the ancients, the Preveshawl captain turned his horse to face Javin, who spurred his horse into a charge. At that moment, Kitty leaped from the side of the road. The tiger took both the squad leader and his horse down to the ground. The scream of the horse, mixed with the scream of the squad leader, who was pinned under his horse, told Javin that the Preveshawl squad captain was out of the fight.

Javin did not see what Kitty did next because he leaped off his horse in order to save Mac from a spear thrust. Before his feet touched the ground, Javin's sword hacked hard into the spear of the soldier engaging Mac. The spear shattered. Javin saw the shocked look on the soldiers face as he swung his second sword broad side into the side of his helmet. The soldier buckled, falling unconscious to the ground.

With a nod of thanks to Javin, Mac yelled, "Between you and that mangy cat, I'll be lucky to even get to swing my sword!" He turned and ran toward a group of soldiers regrouping by one of the wagons.

Javin spotted another heated fight going on between the Farm Circle patrol and Preveshawl soldiers. Within seconds, he was beside his two comrades. A long sword stabbed straight toward his chest, but was knocked sideways by Javin's right sword. His left sword cut sideways above the soldier's shield. The soldier stepped back, causing Javin's sword to slice through empty air. A tiger yowl echoed through the battle as Javin pushed his advantage. Quick as a flash, he dropped to his knees while swinging both swords broadside with lightning speed, into the knees of the soldier. The soldier cried out and dropped to the ground.

Javin flipped back onto his feet as a long sword crashed into the ground where he was seconds before. The long sword broke in half as Javin's flaming sword smashed into it. His left sword swung hard into the wrist of the soldier. At the last second, Javin turned his sword so that the flat of the blade hit the wrist. The bone snapped. Javin knew this soldier was done fighting.

With no one near him, Javin took a second to survey the battle. He saw that the Farm Circle Patrol was winning the fight. However, there was one soldier that was handling his blade really well. Javin watched this Preveshawl soldier stab one of his friends in the shoulder. A foot then flashed out, kicking the man from Farm Circle to the ground. Javin charged.

The Preveshawl soldier saw Javin coming and spun around to meet him. Saber and flaming short sword met. Javin's left sword flashed in from the side, but the soldier nimbly danced backwards, before lunging forward a split second later, after Javin's sword whistled through the air. Javin deflected the saber aimed at his heart and stepped back.

With the fastest moves Javin had ever seen, saber strikes started coming at him. He worked his swords to deflect the saber while watching his opponent closely. Finally, Javin saw what he was looking for. As the saber stabbed in toward Javin's chest, the handle was exposed for a brief second. Javin's right sword slammed into the sword handle while his left sword forced the blade sideways away from his chest. The saber was ripped from the hand of the shocked soldier, spinning through the air toward a wagon.

Javin twisted his sword and swung it hard broadside toward the soldiers head. Eyes registered fear, giving Javin his first look into the soldier's face; the face of a woman. Javin lifted his sword swing, passing his sword over her head. He stepped back, confused over what he should do. The female soldier saw Javin's hesitation, and lunged for her saber. She grabbed her saber in one smooth motion and rolled back to her feet. Before Javin could gather his thoughts, she was attacking him again.

Javin deflected the sword strikes while nimbly dancing out of range. His mind was racing the whole time. He could not hit a woman. In all his matches at the guilds, Javin had never faced a woman. He continued to deflect her saber as a plan formulated in his mind. Once again, he disarmed her when she exposed the hilt of her sword. He turned the flames of his swords off and placed the tip of one sword to her chest.

"Surrender," he ordered. The female soldier started to slowly raise her hands when she suddenly threw herself backwards. Once again, she came up with her saber in hand. Javin furiously deflected her strikes, but it was becoming obvious to the female soldier that he was making no attempt to hit her. After a minute of Javin fiercely defending himself, he managed to disarm her again.

"I said surrender!" Javin demanded, the tip of his sword resting gently on her chest. He saw that no else was fighting, but a lot of the Farm Circle soldiers were circled around, watching his fight with this soldier.

Calmly, the female fighter grabbed the blade of Javin's sword and pulled it away from her chest. Her other hand flashed out, slapping Javin across the face. Smiling, she turned and slowly walked over toward her sword. Bending down she picked it up and turned to face Javin.

"So the Black Knight is chivalrous," she spat out mockingly. She calmly walked back toward Javin with her saber weaving a pattern in front of her. "Like the knights of old, you can't hit a woman, can you?" She didn't give Javin time to respond. "Well then, I guess we keep playing this game, until you make a mistake."

She lunged toward Javin, saber twisting as she stabbed toward his chest. Instead of dancing back after her stab, she fell forward. Javin dropped both his swords and caught the woman in his arms. She was out cold.

"I, personally, have absolutely no problems hitting a woman," Gevi said with a grimace. Her staff was coming back to rest in her hands. "You are going to pay for this staff, Javin, if it's broken." She gave Javin a brilliant smile. Inside, her respect for him just grew tenfold.

Ledia jumped forward and took the woman from Javin's arms. She was moaning as she started to regain consciousness. Her hand was rubbing the back of her head, where Gevi's staff had left an impressive bump. Ledia had her bound with rope before she completely regained consciousness.

"Thank you Gevi. Thank you Ledia," Javin said with relief.

"No, Javin," Ledia replied as she handed the female soldier over to Mac, to be taken to the other prisoners. "Thank you. In this time of fighting and violence, it is so nice to see a young man keep his honor and treat a woman with respect. You held your honor, even though she had no honor as a woman, and took advantage of you. You impressed me, young man."

"If I have broken my staff, it was well worth it," Gevi said as she glared at the back of the female soldier Mac was leading away. "I should give her another whack across the head for the slap she gave you."

"Gevi, you and Ledia go check the prisoner wagons, while I go talk to the captured soldiers," the patrol captain ordered. Use your healing potion on anyone that needs it, and then bring it to me. Mac, go with your wife. Keep everyone in the wagons. Get those wagons moving toward Farm Circle as fast as possible." The patrol captain spun around, walking over to the captured Preveshawl soldiers.

"You will all be free to go after we leave and after you burn your boots. We will take your horses, and release them a couple of miles north of here." The patrol captain said to the captured soldiers.

Gevi joined the patrol captain a half hour later. "Only one prisoner needed the healing potion, along with two soldiers from our patrol," she reported while handing the last of her healing potion to the patrol captain. The captain gave the potion to the Preveshawl soldiers to use on their wounded, and ordered everyone to mount up.

Gevi was holding Javin's hand, but she let go when they found his horse. She jumped on it ahead of him, taking control of the reins. Javin smiled, and leapt up behind her, letting her guide his horse as they rode away. The prisoner wagons, loaded with prisoners, led the way.

****

The greater moon was out full while the lesser moon was on the horizon as a half moon, lighting the way for the wagons. Javin rode behind Gevi this time, holding on to her shoulders. He was so tired he could barely keep his eyes open. He could tell Gevi was exhausted as well. For the first time since he had met her, she was not talkative.

At midnight, the patrol captain gave the order to stop. "We need to let the horses rest. Two hours rest, then we will be riding again. No fires."

Gevi and Javin both slid off the horse. Gevi went straight to the ground where she curled up and went fast asleep. Javin got his horse water and oats before staking him to the ground. Pulling a blanket off the horse, Javin gently covered Gevi. He stood there, watching her for several minutes, admiring how beautiful she looked. Carefully, Javin bent down and gave her a light kiss on the side of her head.

Giving Gevi one final look, Javin headed over to the wagons. Adults with children were coming out of the wagons, making beds on the grass. Javin walked up to a man holding a child in each hand.

"Have you seen a young, red-haired woman, who would have been placed in the wagon recently?" Javin asked.

The man pointed off to his side. Javin could see the flaming red hair spread out on the grass. "Looks like she's asleep already," The man replied.

"Thank you," Javin replied. Emotions welled up in him, but these emotions were different from the emotions he had felt the last time he had seen Chellell at the guilds. Instead of pain, it was relief and joy. He took one last look at her before walking back toward his horse. He found a spot near to his horse. Removing only his helmet, he soon fell fast asleep.

Javin felt like he had just closed his eyes when someone shook him awake. "Captain says it's time to mount up again." Javin groaned as he jumped to his feet. His neck was sore from sleeping on the ground. His horse nickered at him in disbelief as Javin threw the saddle back on him and walked him over to the still sleeping Gevi. He shook her shoulder, trying to wake her, but ended up jumping back when a leg kicked out at him.

"Leave me alone," she moaned. She curled right back up and fell back to sleep. Javin again shook her shoulder.

"Captain says..."

"I will catch up with you later," she murmured before rolling over and facing away from him. Javin smiled as he reached down and grabbed her under her arms, lifting her off the ground. "Come on sleepy-head, you wanted to come on patrol with us. We ride together. No soldier will be left behind!"

"I'm not a soldier. Unhand me, you grunt!" Gevi shook herself free of him, wide awake now. Javin smiled as he jumped up on his horse and reached a hand down toward her. She glared at him for a few seconds, before ignoring his hand and climbing up on the horse behind him. Several minutes later, they were riding alongside the wagons. Javin was thinking of a good way to tell Gevi that he had seen Chellell, when he felt her arms wrap around his neck and her head rest against his back. Within minutes, he knew she was fast asleep. He sighed to himself, so tired he was actually jealous of her. Javin made sure to keep the horse away from rough terrain as much as possible, so she could sleep.

"Javin, you and Grahem go relieve the east guard patrol," ordered the patrol captain several hours later. The captain's command startled Gevi awake. "Gevi, you can lie down in one of the wagons, if you need to."

"I'll be fine, captain," Gevi replied, "I feel a lot better now." She stretched her arms and repositioned herself on the saddle behind Javin.

The captain nodded and rode back toward the front of the caravan. "Stay in sight of the caravan at all times," the captain called back toward Javin and Grahem. Javin spurred his horse past the caravan, toward the eastern guards.

Another hour quietly passed as Javin's horse walked slowly through the grasslands. Javin could barely see the caravan off to his right side. He turned his horse back toward the west because he did not want to get too far from the caravan. Grahem, who was riding twenty feet behind him, turned his horse to follow. Taking a deep breath, Javin decided to bring up a subject he would rather avoid.

"I saw Chellell." This was all Javin said. He felt rather awkward not saying anything else. There was silence between him and Gevi for what seemed like an eternity.

"Is she injured?" Gevi finally asked. Javin heard sincere concern in her voice. "I don't remember seeing her when I checked on the prisoners. Then again, I have no idea what she looks like."

"The description the escaped prisoners gave us was probably accurate. Her familiar must have turned on her, and gave her up to the soldiers. That's how she ended up in the prison wagon."

"Oh wow," Gevi explained. "I bet she was overjoyed to see you."

"Well I, I...." Javin stammered.

"I haven't been around magic users much, but I do know they have a very tight bond with those dragon things. I can only imagine how the poor girl must feel. It would be like your best friend turning on you, and becoming your enemy. After dedicating a large part of your life to something like magic, it must really hurt when in the end, it leaves you nothing. That's so hard!" Gevi paused for a second. "So did she feel any better after getting to see and talk to you?"

"Not really," Javin murmured, "I haven't been able to talk to her yet. She doesn't know..."

"You mean you haven't bothered to see her?" Javin could hear surprise and dismay in Gevi's voice. He was glad he could not see her face right now.

"It's complicated, Gevi. I didn't want to upset you by..."

"Upset me! You just did that!" Javin could feel the heat in her voice. He knew she was angry. "You don't seriously think I would be jealous because you talked to someone who happened to be a childhood girlfriend? I thought we were past that. I can't believe you think so little of me, Javin." There was silence between them for several minutes as the horse continued to plod across the ground.

"You're right Gevi, I am sorry," Javin finally said. "I guess I'm acting like an idiot."

"I don't think you need to guess," Gevi huffed, obviously still angry.

"I will go see her first chance I get. But there is something else you need to know, something even Chellell is not aware of." Javin took several nervous breaths before continuing. "You know how some people get noticeably uncomfortable around magic users?" Javin did not wait for Gevi to answer. "Well, I am one of those people. I get extremely sick. Ever since Chellell started using magic, I get violently ill every time she gets too close to me."

"Javin, she is your friend, and she is in desperate need of a friend like you right now. And that still doesn't change the fact that you thought we would be rolling around on the ground pulling each other's hair out over you."

Javin couldn't help himself; he started laughing, which made Gevi even angrier. She let go of Javin's shoulders and jumped off the horse.

Javin stopped the horse and spun it back around to face the furious Gevi. She turned and started stomping off toward the caravan. It wasn't until later; she realized that jumping off the horse, saved her life.

Javin was looking at Gevi when he felt several sharp blows to his back and side. He also felt several pricks. like somebody was pinching his back. His horse jerked beneath him, throwing him from the saddle. Both swords were in his hands before he hit the ground, feet first. Another arrow bounced of the top of his helmet, followed by the pinching sensation in his chest.

Javin glanced at his chest while running toward the source of the arrow fire. A small needle was stuck in his skin over his right lung. The little needle was small enough to fit between the rings of his armor and sharp enough to penetrate leather.

A two-headed wolf rose out of the grass. A goblin sprang out of the grass beside the wolf, leaping onto its back. Deep red flames engulfed both swords as Javin charged toward wolf and rider.

A flash of lightning, followed by an earth-shaking boom, sounded off behind Javin. The shock of the blast was clear on the face of the wolf rider in front of him. However, the wolf was unfazed. Wolf and fighter closed on each other. Javin side-stepped as wolf jaws snapped at him. He felt teeth ripping his armor on his back as he rolled forward. In the middle of his dive, Javin plunged his right sword into the side of the wolf. Rolling quickly to his feet, he spun back around. The two-headed wolf, known as a Fenris Wolf, was thrashing around on the ground, dying. Its goblin rider was sprawled out in the grass, struggling to regain his feet.

"Look out!" screamed Gevi. A second Fenris Wolf was in the air, leaping toward Javin. Powerful wolf jaws snapped toward Javin's throat. Reflexes took over. One sword deflected the wolf's jaw while his body flew sideways. The Fenris wolf's momentum carried him past Javin. Two-headed wolf with goblin rider slid to a stop, spinning around to face him.

Both heads of the wolf snapped viciously in the air toward Javin, while its goblin rider lowered a spiked lance. Flaming swords were spinning in Javin's hands as he waiting for the inevitable charge of the wolf. The Fenris Wolf started to charge, when an arrow plowed into the side of the wolf. The wolf collapsed, rolling head-over heels toward Javin. The goblin rider flew over the two-headed wolf, landing on his back at Javin's feet. Flaming sword flashed down, ending the goblin's life. Leaping over the dead goblin, Javin plunged his flaming sword into the mortally wounded Fenris Wolf.

"Something must be wrong with Gevi's staff," Javin thought to himself.

Pausing, he glanced quickly around. He saw Gevi kneeling behind his dead horse, notching an arrow to her bow. His thought was confirmed. Her staff was on the ground by her side. In horror, Javin saw another Fenris wolf and rider charging hard at Gevi. The goblin had its lance lowered. There was no way Gevi could fire an arrow in time. Javin yelled out a warning and sprinted toward Gevi.

Gevi threw herself behind the horse's body, when suddenly, a yowl filled the air. A Great Northern Tiger crashed into the Fenris Wolf. The wolf rolled through the grass, while its rider flew through the air. Instantly coming to its feet, the goblin drew a short sword and turned to face Javin. Closing quickly, Javin brushed the goblins short sword aside with his right sword, while his left cut deep into the goblins chest, dropping the creature.

Meanwhile, Kitty and the Fenris wolf were viciously fighting. The Fenris wolf had one head hanging limply, destroyed by the massive paw of Kitty. Its other head was snarling at the Great Northern Tiger, who was circling the injured wolf. Roaring, Kitty charged toward the wolf with slashing claws and flashing teeth. His paw slapped the remaining wolf head with unbelievable speed, followed by teeth slashing into the back of the wolf. Spinning away from the tiger, the wolf snapped its jaws into Kitty's shoulder. Kitty ignored the bite and threw his great weight into the wolf, throwing it onto the ground. Teeth and claws started ripping into the Fenris Wolf as the two massive animals rolled around on the ground. Finally, the wolf became very still. Releasing his jaws from the neck of the dead wolf, Kitty raised up from the ground.

Looking around, Javin saw no more two-headed wolves, so he extinguished the flames on his swords. Taking several deep breathes; he turned around to check on Gevi. She was sprinting toward Grahem. Everything looked a little blurry to him. His head was also starting to throb. He started to walk over toward Grahem when Gevi rose up and met him. Kitty was at her side, sniffing the air for more intruders.

"Grahem is dead," Gevi said when she reached Javin. Tears were running down her face as she slid into Javin's arms. He stumbled, a wave of nausea overcoming him. "What's sticking out of your back?" Gevi spun around behind Javin to see four needles in his back. She jerked them out of his skin, throwing them to the ground. She stepped back around in front of him, this time looking closely at him. Sweat was pouring off his face, and his eyes had a vacant look in them. Seeing the single needle in his chest, she ripped it out, causing Javin to wince in pain.

"I think I need to rest a minute," Javin groaned. He sat down in the long green grass. Gevi looked toward the caravan, relieved to see horses heading toward them at a full gallop.

"Lie down and relax," Gevi said, trying to hide her anxiety. She knew he had been poisoned. As Javin lay back in the grass, she picked up one of the needles she had thrown down and carefully put it in her pack. Feeling his head, Gevi grew even more worried at the fever that was burning him up.

The patrol captain arrived within minutes. Gevi was relieved to see that Ledia was with him.

"What happened here, Gevi?" Ledia asked as she started quickly checking Javin's heart rate and breathing. "Get me some water," she yelled back to one of the soldiers. The soldier quickly dismounted and brought her his water bottle.

"Grahem is dead, and I think the gorms poisoned Javin," Gevi replied with a shaky voice. She pulled the needle out of her pack and held it for Ledia to see. Ledia was carefully pouring the water on Javin trying to cool his body down. Javin was actually talking, but nothing he said made any sense. Ledia then took the needle from Gevi and examined it closely.

"Rumel Root," she muttered. She tossed the needle back toward the gorm bodies. "A healing potion won't work with Rumel Root!" She stood up and looked around the landscape. Her eyes locked unto a small grove of trees north of them. "Is there water near that stand of trees?" she asked as she pointed toward the grove.

"That's Cold Spring Grove," replied the patrol captain, who had come to stand beside her and Javin. "There is a spring inside the grove."

"Get him on a horse and over to the spring," Ledia ordered. "Gevi, immerse his whole body into the water, and pray it gets his fever down. Rumel root will cause the body to produce an out of control fever. His body will burn itself up if you don't keep him cooled down. I am sending my falcon to Annba with a note. There is an antidote for rumel root, and she should have it or can quickly make it. She can attach the antidote to my falcon. Keep Javin cooled down until we get the antidote."

Ledia wrote a quick note before releasing her falcon. "I am going back to the caravan; I may have something in my bags that will reduce his fever, temporarily." Ledia jumped on her horse while Mac and the patrol captain lifted Javin, and put him across the captain's horse.

****

After everyone left the area, a vulture circling overhead turned and flew east. Several miles later, the bird landed on the shoulder of a goblin. The red gleam of a jewel flashed on the goblins forehead. Smiling wickedly to itself, the goblin jumped onto the back of his two-headed wolf. His mission was accomplished. Costly in terms of how many wolves were lost, but successful, in that the target would soon be dead.

Chapter 16

If you forsake the LORD and serve foreign gods, he will turn and bring disaster on you and make an end of you, after he has been good to you. – The Guide

"I'm too old for this," Mac said, just before exiting the ice cold water. He had been in the spring of water with Javin. Javin's body was almost completely submerged. Mac kept his hands behind Javin's neck, holding his head above water so Javin could breathe.

Gevi jerked her foot out of the icy water. "Whoa!" she exclaimed.

"Hurry up, Gevi!" Mac called out between chattering teeth. He was soaking wet and shaking from the cold water. Gevi put her foot in again before jerking it back out. Shaking her head, she jumped in. Water came up to her chest. A startled yelp escaped her lips as the cold hit her body, but she positioned herself behind Javin to support his head.

"Javin will probably be fine, and we will die of pneumonia!" chattered Mac. He started quickly gathering up sticks for a fire, which he had going a few minutes later. "This hits the spot," Mac said to Gevi, "a nice warm fire to dry you out." Gevi glared at Mac, her teeth now chattering. Her hand moved to Javin's forehead, which she noticed, had actually cooled down. The next hour was spent with Mac warming back up, Gevi freezing, and Javin slipping in and out of consciousness.

Mac was about to replace Gevi, when a slim young lady with long red hair came through the trees on a horse at nearly full gallop. She reined the horse to a stop before jumping off.

"Javin!" Chellell yelled as she ran up to the spring. "Is he…"

"He is doing a lot better than he was," explained Mac. He was not sure who this young lady was, but it was obvious she knew Javin. Javin started muttering about how he wanted to go play with Chellell, and why was his mother not allowing him to go?

Mac stood up and walked over to stand by Chellell. "I'm Mac, by the way, and the young lady who thinks she is freezing to death, is Gevi." Gevi rolled her eyes and once again glared at Mac. "He was poisoned, causing his fever to rage…"

"I know," Chellell interrupted while looking toward Javin with concern. "I think your wife will be here shortly, Mac. She told me everything. She said her falcon should be here in half an hour."

Mac stepped one foot in the water, before jerking it back. "Alright Gevi, I will take a turn."

"I got him," Chellell said. She jumped into the water, right before Mac could jump in himself. Her breath rushed out of her lungs as the shock of the cold water hit her. She moved behind Javin, taking his head from Gevi and holding it above the water. Mac smiled, shaking his head. He helped Gevi get out of the water and over to the fire.

Gevi was finally starting to warm up, when Ledia and several Farm Circle soldiers arrived at the spring. Following Ledia's orders, the soldiers pulled Javin and Chellell out of the water. Chellell made her way over to the fire, while Ledia poured a fluid down Javin's throat. Chellell sat, shaking with cold. Gevi slid over to share a horse blanket with her. She noticed that Chellell had several bad scratches on her neck, traveling down toward her shoulder and back. The blouse Chellell was wearing hid the rest of the damage.

"You must be Chellell," Gevi said trying to start a conversation. "I'm Gevi, daughter of Master Thunderfall, to whom Javin was apprenticed." Within minutes, the two girls were deep into conversation, talking about Javin and the things that had been happening through the summer. Their conversation finally stopped when Javin was moved over by the fire.

"Looks like he will be ok," Ledia commented, when both girls looked earnestly at her. "The medicine is working. I am not moving him tonight though, so I sent the two soldiers back to get us our camping supplies." Relief showed on both girls' faces.

****

Ambrissan stood by the Grand Leader on a barren hill, overlooking the Crossroads. A clear bubble surrounded the pair, making them invisible to those fighting below. They watched in silence while goblins broke past the trenches and embankments defended by Preveshawl soldiers. It had cost the Grand Leader a lot of his goblins, which he had put on the very front lines. But the goblins had served their purpose, and freshly rested gorms were now ready to enter the battle. This was day five of the battle at the Crossroads. The Grand Leader's army had pushed the kingdom soldiers back to their last line of defense, but both sides had lost several thousand soldiers each in the conflict, so far.

"Tell my giants to form up, execute operation back lines as planned last night," the Grand Leader said to his magic user. Ambrissan held both arms out, using magic to form a bubble that slowly appeared in his hands. He spoke into the bubble before tossing it into the air. The bubble flew down toward the Grand Leader's army. Ambrissan turned his attention back to the battle and saw lightning, mixed with balls of fire, blast into the goblins. The Grand Leader turned toward Ambrissan, looking down at the balding, skinny man in black robes.

"Magic users," said Ambrissan before the Grand Leader could even ask. "Looks like maybe two dozen of them." Fires were springing up on the battlefield as more balls of fire flew into the goblin lines. "They must be getting desperate, having magic users enter the conflict." Inside, Ambrissan felt no remorse killing these magic users. Their familiars were eternal and would find other humans to teach magic to. Besides, they were so weak, he barely even considered them magic users.

"We will put an end to the magic users, shortly," the Grand Leader replied. He watched Preveshawl soldiers charge behind the latest blast from the magic users, mixed with anti-personnel shot from human catapults. Magical explosions ripped across the battlefield. The charging Preveshawl soldiers smashed into the devastated front lines of the Grand

Leader's army. They regained their entrenchments and pushed the goblins back up the road. The humans abruptly stopped their advancement, quickly retreating back to their trenches and embankments. From the back of the Preveshawl camp, catapults fired again. Fist sized rock rained down on the goblins.

"Order catapults to fire two rounds at the locations of the magic users, to fifty paces back," ordered the Grand Leader. "Have them fire sand soaked with fire water. Tell them to hold their fire until the magic users start casting fire spells. Order the gorms to enter the fight."

Ambrissan gave a laugh while he formed several more bubbles, sending them toward the Grand Leader's army. His attention went back to the fighting.

Humans were defending their trenches with spears facing outward, when the gorms attacked. Intense fighting caused the Preveshawl soldiers to buckle. They tried an organized retreat, but fear caused it to quickly become a riot as the soldiers ran back toward the lines held by the magic users.

Again, the Grand Leader's army pushed toward the line that the Preveshawl army was holding with the magic users. As balls of fire were cast toward the Grand Leader's forces, clay pots started falling from the sky, hitting the ground and spraying out firewater soaked sand. Fire from the magic users hit the sand soaked with fire water. A chain reaction of explosions blew skyward, killing every magic user, instantly. Several hundred Preveshawl soldiers on the line with the magic users died as well. The sand soaked with fire water sparkled and burned across the battlefield.

The gorms and surviving goblins charged as soon as the explosions stopped. Human soldiers rushed forward, only to be knocked back by the gorms. Ambrissan could hear the screams of dying soldiers as the two armies fought. He was really enjoying this battle.

All of a sudden, giants in a wedge formation marched onto the battlefield. A war cry went up from the mouth of the giants as they charged. The giants easily broke through what was left of the human lines, running full speed, with large, giant strides.

Meanwhile, like two waves crashing into each other, humans fought with gorms and goblins. The two forces moved back and forth, viciously fighting in violent combat. The clash of steel on steel echoed through the hills.

The running giants did not engage any of the Preveshawl soldiers. Instead, they ran straight for the catapults at the very back of the human lines. Their purpose was to use their massive clubs and swords to destroy the catapults and engineers that operated the machines.

"Pull the gorms back. Have our catapults fire three shots each, anti-personnel loads. Tell the gorm commander to hold the line and charge again after the third shot." Ambrissan sent the messages off while the Grand Leader laughed loudly. The giant seemed very pleased with himself.

Several trumpet notes sounded, causing gorms and goblins to disengage from hand-to-hand combat, retreat, and take up formations.

Several minutes passed, with Preveshawl soldiers scrambling to find cover. They knew what was about to happen. As expected, the sky started raining fist-sized rocks. Damage inflicted on the Preveshawl army was devastating. No catapult fire could be returned from the human side. The giants had finished their destruction of the war machines, and were now locked in combat with the Preveshawl soldiers at the rear of the camp.

More anti-personnel volleys fell amongst the humans. As soon as the third volley struck the ground, the gorms charged. Preveshawl soldiers jumped out of their trenches to engage the enemy, but they were now completely disorganized. The humans started giving ground.

From the east end of the human war camp, the Grand Leader saw a gleam of metal moving toward the battlefield. One hundred knights in shiny plate mail armor, riding plate-armored war horses, galloped onto the battlefield. They moved into formations, with half the knights facing the gorms, while the other half faced toward the giants at the back of the camp.

"The prized Preveshawl Knights of the Silver Order," commented the Grand Leader. "No surprise; they always wait until the battle is almost over before they fight. Credit for the victory always goes to them because they are the last ones to fight. But the human generals have waited too long this time."

"Order the gorms to retreat and muster into formations. My giants can hold their own, but the gorms will get slaughtered by the knights," the Grand Leader said. "Bring in your Fenris Wolf riders. It is time to let them have some fun. Do you want to let your gryphon in on the fun as well?"

"I don't want to risk my gryphon," Ambrissan replied. A message bubble flew from his hands down toward the army. "However, my wolf riders desperately want to fight."

A few minutes later, a hundred Fenris Wolves, carrying goblins, rode onto the battlefield. The gorms moved into formations several hundred feet behind the wolves, while the human soldiers all moved eastward toward their tents. The human officers were yelling out orders, trying to get their demoralized soldiers organized into formations while the knights were on the field of battle.

Knights in gleaming armor stood patiently in formation in the middle of the battlefield. Several minutes passed, when suddenly a trumpet blew from amongst the Preveshawl knights. Lances snapped down in perfect unison amongst the knights. A second trumpet blast a short time later, and the knights charged, half toward the wolves, and half toward the giants.

A howl went up from the wolves. Goblin riders snapped their lances down and charged toward the oncoming knights. The collision sounded like a peel of thunder on a stormy night. Lances snapped as man and goblin screamed in pain. Horses kicked and bit while two-headed wolf jaws snapped. The knights that managed to stay on their horses continued riding past the wolf riders. Like every combat they had been in before, they would ride past their encounter with the enemy, turn back around in formation, and charge again. This time, things were different.

The Fenris Wolves spun around and chased after the knights. As the knights were turning their horses to again charge an enemy they thought was well behind them, the wolves struck. Wolf jaws grabbed armored legs, pulling the knights from their horses. Knights tried desperately to use their maces, but close quarter combat did not favor them. The kicking hooves of the war horses were the only thing hurting the wolves, but their goblin riders were using razor sharp short swords to stab into the gaps of the horse's armor.

The group of knights that charged the powerful giants did even worse. Lances splintered on the shields of the giants. Massive clubs and two-handed swords crushed the knights. Every knight facing the giants was down within minutes, while only a handful of giants were injured or killed by the knights.

"Have the gorms charge," the Grand Leader ordered with glee in his voice. "The battle is won."

The gorms charged into the fray with the wolves and the remaining Preveshawl Knights. The knights were quickly overwhelmed by the numerous gorms and the vicious two-headed wolves with goblin riders.

The Grand Leader continued to watch while Preveshawl soldiers started surrendering. As ordered, the gorms and the giants accepted the surrender. Some humans managed to escape, but the vast majority of Preveshawl's army was either dead or captive. Thousands of goblins and gorms lay dead on the battlefield as well, but the Grand Leader wasn't concerned. He had won the battle, and was pleased to see more humans down on the battlefield than goblins, gorms or giants.

"Let's go meet our new slaves," the giant said to his magic user. A very pleased Grand Leader strolled quickly off the hill toward the battlefield.

When the two arrived at the northern edge of the battlefield, the Grand Leader called one of the gorm generals over to him. "Gather the wounded, both sides. If they cannot walk, kill them. I am not interested in running a hospital for the weak." The gorm general turned and started barking orders. "Allow the soldiers to loot as they will, but inform them that if any fighting breaks out, both parties will be executed." The gorm general nodded before barking more orders toward his officers.

The Grand Leader continued through the camp, followed closely by the mage. Finally, they arrived at a holding area for the captured Preveshawl soldiers. A hundred giants were guarding five hundred human survivors.

"Bring the high-ranking officers forward," the Grand Leader ordered a giant. Seven men were forced forward. The Grand Leader instantly noted from the uniforms that two of the humans were generals.

These two were quickly questioned, while the other five were returned to their fellow prisoners. One was a lower ranking general from the Fort at Bear Tree City, the other, a full general from Preveshawl Castle.

"Hold them," the Grand Leader ordered. Two giants instantly grabbed both generals, holding them tightly in place. Neither man showed fear; both expecting to meet their end at the hand of the conquering Grand Leader. "Ambrissan, do your spell," the Grand Leader ordered. He smiled gleefully as Ambrissan cast his slave spell on both generals.

"On all fours; bark like a dog," the giant ordered. Both generals fell to the ground, barking and yapping like dogs. The giant laughed, before ordering them to do even more humiliating things, right in front of the human captives. After having his fun, and while the generals licked his muddy boots, the Grand Leader spoke in a great bellowing voice. "You get to make a choice. When you are brought forward, you can stand before the mage and have this spell put on you and serve us as slaves the rest of your miserable lives, or you can stand in front of one of my giants, who will end your miserable life for you. However, I will let all of you go free right now, if one human can step forward and defeat one of my giants in a Hero Challenge."

A murmur went up through the human captives. Several tried to make a break and run, only to be squashed by the giants that surrounded them. Disappointed that all the humans were cowards, the Grand Leader started walking away.

A large human stepped forward. He was nearly seven feet tall, heavily muscled, with long blond hair that went down to the middle of his back. "I'll fight one of your giants," Merion called out, "if you give me back my sword and shield." Turning back around, the Grand Leader eyed the young man. Impressed with the young man's courage, the Grand Leader ordered one of the giants to take him over to the pile of weapons collected from the humans. Merion returned with his long sword and shield a few minutes later. The Grand Leader had an area cleared, before ordering a thirteen foot giant to fight the young human.

Merion stepped a foot into the circle, shaking with fear. His eyes focused on the red bearded giant, but his thoughts were on the men behind him, who depended on him for their freedom. The giant bellowed and charged as soon as Merion's second foot stepped into the circle. He thrust his sword upward to block the giant's sword coming down toward his head.

That mistake almost cost Merion his life. Nobody he had ever fought was stronger than him. Like Javin, they were often much faster, but not stronger. As the swords collided, Merion barely managed to dodge sideways as the giant sword crushed his sword right back toward his head and into the ground. Remembering a move Javin did to him in one of their many contests, Merion spun his body, whipping his sword around with lightning speed. His sword smacked hard into the side of the giant. The sound of sword striking armor rang out as Merion rolled sideways, away from the giant. He sprang back to his feet and faced the giant. Pain showed on the giants face for a split second. Merion's sword had done some damage to the giant. However, the giant was able to get his sword and shield back into position.

The next half-hour seemed like an eternity for Merion. Blows were constantly exchanged, but neither was able to hit the other. The exhaustion Merion felt was beyond anything he had ever endured. He knew that he would have to do something soon, or the giant would win this fight. The giant looked just as exhausted, but he came at Merion again.

Merion decided to go for all or nothing. He unexpectedly rushed the giant, swinging his sword as hard as he could toward the side of the giant. His sword met the shield of the giant, like he expected. Merion then spun with all his might, hoping his sword finished the giant before the giant's sword got to him. His sword struck with a powerful blow right into the side of the giant, the same place he had struck earlier in the fight. At the same time, the giant's sword brushed the side of his helmet in a powerful down swing. Merion heard the giant roar in pain as his own head exploded in blinding pain. He felt his sword fly from his hand as he fought off the blackness overtaken him. Fighting his way back to consciousness, Merion opened his eyes to see the giant standing over him, his sword pointed straight at his chest. Blood was running freely from the side of the giant. A good hit, Merion realized, but not good enough. His helmet was broken, lying on the ground next to him. Merion realized that if he had taken a full hit from the giant on his helmet, he would be dead right now.

"At least let me stand and take my death like a man," Merion growled at the giant from his back. The giant growled and raised his sword over his head.

"Hold," the Grand Leader ordered. He saw a way to restore his honor. The giant looked over at the Grand Leader, confusion mixed with anger on his face. Fear of his leader won out. The giant stepped back and lowered his sword.

"Because the Black Knight refused to kill my goblin champion, I refuse to kill you. You will not be allowed an honorable hero's death." A mumble of approval went up from the giants. The Grand Leader stepped forward to stand right in front of Merion. Merion looked up to see a hand extended toward him. He held his hand out, clasping the much larger hand of the enormous giant. The Grand Leader pulled Marion to his feet. This was a sign amongst the giants that their Grand Leader was stronger than the defeated human in front of him. Approval again was voiced from the giants.

"You see these human cowards standing behind you?" the Grand Leader said to Merion. Merion quickly looked over his shoulder at his fellow captives before turning back to the giant. "They chose to surrender as cowards with no honor. I will give you a choice. On your word it will be done. They can come forward one at a time, and I will order a giant to give them an honorable death, so that they do not have to live their lives as cowards and slaves. Or, you can choose one hundred of the cowards, and I will free them with you. They will be forced to live a life knowing they are cowards, and the only reason they live is because you decided to have mercy on them. The rest will be my slaves, licking my feet until they drop dead. You decide their fate."

Merion stood before the Grand Leader, completely confused, as a howl of approval came from all the giants. Why would this giant make such a strange offer? How would death restore anyone's honor?

"I choose to have one hundred of my companions freed," Merion said calmly to the Grand Leader. A smile spread across the face of the Grand Leader as the howl of the giants grew in volume. His honor was now completely restored.

"Get your sword; you are free to go. You may take one hundred soldiers who are not officers with you. I will give you one hour to pick and be gone from this battlefield. The rest of these stinking human cowards will be our slaves till they drop dead from their miserable existence."

After Merion had picked one hundred enlisted soldiers and left the battlefield, the Grand Leader ordered one of his largest giants to bring ten soldiers to Ambrissan. The Grand Leader briefly watched as the spell to enslave them was cast. "Such pitiful creatures," the Grand Leader mumbled to Ambrissan. "There is greater honor in death." The next group he did not bother to watch, instead he ordered the lesser general from Bear Tree City to follow him.

****

"You know that the slave spell can be broken," Ambrissan said as he walked with the Grand Leader through the destroyed human camp, after the last human was enslaved.

"How so? The Grand Leader asked.

"If someone reads to them from *The Guide,* and the slave believes what they hear, then they are freed from their life of slavery."

The Grand Leader started laughing, "Preveshawl outlawed *The Guide.* Ironic that their only path to freedom is now outlawed by their own king, isn't it?" Ambrissan secretly smiled to himself.

****

As night fell, the Grand Leader was again approached by Ambrissan. The Grand Leader spoke first. "I sent the general from Bear Tree City back to his city, with a story of how he escaped capture." Ambrissan looked curiously at the Grand Leader. "When our army arrives at Bear Tree City in a couple of days, the general will surrender to me." The Grand Leader paused for a second. "Fighting is so much fun," he sighed, "but we took some heavy losses these last few days. We will need the soldiers we have for the future."

Ambrissan was impressed with the Grand Leader. This giant would have Preveshawl on its knees before this war was over. He would have to be careful, and make sure the armies were evenly matched. Ambrissan did not want to help the humans of Preveshawl, but it looked like the intelligence of the Grand Leader would force him to provide some kind of aid to the humans. His plans were for the two armies to destroy each other, along with the dwarves and elves, if possible.

Ambrissan decided it was a good time to give the Grand Leader some good news. "It seems the Black Knight will no longer trouble us," Ambrissan reported. The giant turned his attention to the magic user. "He killed all my wolf riders, with the exception of the naturalist. The naturalist reported that the Black Knight was struck down by poison darts. He lay dying in the grasslands. Unfortunately, we could not get you armor, swords, or a body as evidence. He had too many friends around him."

The Grand Leader smiled. His honor was now fully restored, so he did not need evidence of the Black Knight's death. He was overjoyed to hear about his death though. Looking at Ambrissan, the Grand Leader noticed that the mage looked troubled. "What's wrong?" he asked. The magic user realized that his worry was obvious to the Grand Leader, but he did not want to say too much.

"It's nothing," Ambrissan replied. "The surviving goblin also reported that the Black Knight was accompanied by a magic user. From the descriptions they gave, she is somewhat of a powerful magic user." Ambrissan decided not to mention the fact that he also knew that this person was very different from him and his fellow magic users from the Kingdom of Preveshawl. This woman did not have a familiar.

Ambrissan knew his goblin would think it was magic, but magic was only possible with familiars. Something else very powerful had created the reported lightning blast that killed a wolf and rider; something similar to the flaming swords of the Black Knight. Not magic, but something else very powerful. This woman and her staff were the key to this unknown power. Ambrissan was determined to find out how those swords flamed, and how a staff could cast lightning bolts without a familiar's aid. This power would be his. Even with all his knowledge from the Linkrins, Ambrissan had never heard of anything like this. For now though, it served his purposes to let the Grand Leader think that the Black Knight was accompanied by a powerful magic user.

****

Chancellor White sat at a large, black marble, round table with the rest of the Advisory Council. His elbow was on the table while his hands supported his head.

The king had thrown his wine glass and exited the room in a rage, but not before threatening to execute everyone at the table. Like spilled blood, red wine was dripping down a white marble wall, reminding everyone that their very lives depended on the outcome of this meeting. He was worried; he had been unable to contact Ambrissan.

"How fast can we get the southern army?" A richly dressed, middle aged woman that was part of the fifteen group council asked. Silence followed, until a heavily built advisor from the Guild of Warriors, seated to Chancellor White's left, replied that it would take two weeks for the southern army to reach the capital. Chancellor White listened while the council discussed and wrote down their recommendations. They discussed dropping the bridge over the main river, forced army recruiting, and what the invading monsters were likely to do next.

"Maybe we should compromise and get the dwarves to help us out. Surly we would win if..."

"And what do you mean by 'compromise'?" Chancellor White raised his head up from folded hands to glare at the advisor who had made that suggestion. "I vote for you to be the one, to go tell the king that he must humble himself before the Lord of the Stars." He started laughing when he saw the man's face across the table turn ghostly white. "That was the demand from the dwarves, if they were to join this fight." Chancellor White leaned forward, looking the man in the eyes who had made the suggestion. A sickly smile was on his face. "That's right; you would have a meeting with the gallows."

"Maybe we can temporarily suspend the law to get the dwarves' help," an older woman chimed in. "Or somehow convince the dwarves things have changed, even though they have not."

Chancellor White slammed his fist down on the table, anger clearly showing in his face. "How you simple minded imbeciles got on this council is beyond me," he roared across the table. *"But rebel against the commandment of the LORD, then shall the hand of the LORD be against you."* The mockery could be heard in his voice as he quoted the verse from *The Guide* put in the message from the dwarves. "I would rather be a slave, licking the feet of a goblin, before acknowledging the Lord of the Stars," Chancellor White roared. Insane rage covered his face. "Preveshawl's defeat at the Crossroads would have happened with or without us worshiping this Lord of the Stars. I doubt a few, superstitious, dwarven soldiers, fighting with us, would have made any difference. The fact is, we live in a world where the strong survive, the weak die, and the intelligent rule. Religious superstitions only lower the intelligence and the strength of a kingdom. I believe we are stronger and smarter than any gorm, goblin, or giant. So let's use our superior intellect that got at least some of us on this advisory council, and save Preveshawl! Using intelligence, we won't need a god!" The silence lasted for a long time, once Chancellor White stopped his ranting speech.

"I may have an idea," said a young man sitting across the table from Chancellor White. "What if the invading army thinks that the dwarves and elves are attacking them?" Chancellor White leaned over and looked at the youngest member of the council, a cousin to the king from one of the southern cities.

"Go on," prompted Chancellor White, curious now about what this young man was thinking.

"I was thinking that we could sneak a hundred of our troops past the gorm army, and use magic to make them look like elves and dwarves. If these spelled soldiers did a lot of hit and run attacks, making a general nuisance of themselves, then those monsters would turn their attention to the homelands of the dwarves and the elves. No army likes enemies at their back."

"And suppose the pitchfork rebels joined up with these dwarves and elves," Chancellor White replied with a smile. "Magically, it is possible, though it would take some work." He paused in thought for a minute.

"I think this is the best idea of the day," another advisor chimed in. "It's the kind of thing that the king would love and it would definitely keep us from the gallows."

"Agreed," replied Chancellor White. "I say we make this the number one recommendation for the King."

****

"So, do you know a spell that will make a human look like a dwarf or elf?" Chancellor White asked the image of Ambrissan.

Ambrissan was impressed with this plan, though he doubted Chancellor White came up with this plan, as he claimed. "Yes. I want you to watch me closely. I will show you three times, so that you won't forget." Ambrissan stepped back from his mirror so that Chancellor White could clearly see him. "I will probably have to show him the spell ten times," Ambrissan thought to himself as he started the illusion spell.

It would be marvelous if the Grand Leader decided to attack the elves and the dwarves. Knowing how smart the Grand Leader was, the giant would probably send just enough soldiers to take care of the job. Either way, it fit perfectly into Ambrissan's plans. His plan to restore the Kingdom of the Linkrins, with himself as king, was quickly coming together.

Chapter 17

This I say then, Walk in the Spirit, and ye shall not fulfill the lust of the flesh.
- The Guide

Javin sat, reading from *The Guide*. The wagon he was riding in bounced so much that he was having a difficult time focusing on the words. The whole town of Farm Circle was now several days into its journey toward the Elven Forest.

Sighing to himself, Javin put *The Guide* down and thought about what he did manage to read. *Now to the one who works, wages are not credited as a gift but as an obligation. However, to the one who does not work but trusts God who justifies the ungodly, their faith is credited as righteousness. Blessed are those whose transgressions are forgiven, whose sins are covered. Blessed is the one whose sin the Lord will never count against them.*

He thought about dwarves and their tradition of debt. Thunderfall explained that the dwarf's belief about debt was meant to honor what the Lord of the Stars had done to pay our debt. *The Guide* taught that works without grace left you a reward of only debt to God. But to those that believe in Him, debt is erased. You can never, in an entire life time, do enough good works to reach God. Only by grace is salvation earned.

The wagon slowed and came to a stop; Javin picked up *The Guide* and started reading again, only to have his mother crawl in through the back of the wagon.

"You're officially released from our care," his mother said as she sat down beside him.

"From your prison," Javin replied, but he was smiling as he said it.

"It was only three days of rest and relaxation; you made it four, by sneaking off to practice your swordplay."

"I would still like to know who tattled," Javin grumbled while he pulled on his boots.

"The tattler was Kitty. Good luck getting even with him." Annba smiled at Javin, before slipping out the back of the wagon.

After climbing out the back of the wagon, Javin felt stiff and sore. His muscles needed a good workout from being laid up for so many days. To combat his sore muscles, Javin decided to take a hike through the camp, and see what everyone was doing. This was somewhat strange behavior for Javin, because typically, he stayed away from groups of people. As Gevi and Javin's friendship grew, so did Javin's desire for social interaction.

While moving through the camp, he spotted the un-mistakable red hair of Chellell, with a group of young women. Javin casually walked over to her. As he approached, he felt someone wrap their arms around him from behind.

"I see they finally set you free, or are you trying to sneak out again."

Javin tried to turn around but Gevi held on tightly. "I was granted

193

my freedom."

Gevi released him and grabbed his hand. She had one of the brightest, happiest smiles on her face he had ever seen. Her green eyes were sparkling with joy. She pulled him toward the group he had seen Chellell with. Javin went along willingly, noticing that Lily was there as well.

"I've been meaning to ask you, Gevi, did you ever find out what was wrong with your staff?"

"The ground stones for my second and third shot got knocked out of place when I whacked that woman over the head. It was an easy fix." Javin nodded, and continued to walk hand-in-hand with Gevi.

Once they reached the group, Gevi let go of his hand. "Meet me back here in an hour," she ordered while giving him another quick hug. "The girls and I have this class here we are taking. The elders have different classes set up for anyone interested in learning new skills after the wagons stop in the evening." She walked over to stand by Lily and Chellell.

A plumpish, older woman that Javin knew used to run the only inn at Farm Circle addressed him, "Are you here for the lady's cooking class?" Several of the girls started giggling, including Gevi.

"No, I only..."

"Javin, right?" The older woman didn't even wait for his reply. "Come back in an hour and you can judge which lady makes the best pie." Javin quickly glanced over at Gevi, who was beaming ear to ear at him. A mischievous smile slowly spread across his face.

"Well ma'am, I would love to, but I only recently recovered from being poisoned. I don't think I could handle being poisoned again so soon." The words had barely left his mouth when a ball of wet dough smacked him right in the side of the head. Laughing out loud, Javin decided to make a quick exit. "I'll be back in an hour." Gevi somehow managed to give him a bright smile as she glared defiantly at him. The older woman stood facing the girls, hands on hips. Javin nearly fell over laughing when he heard her address the young women.

"Now that was very unladylike," she said in a scolding voice. "No matter how rude the men are, you always act like a lady. Encourage men to become gentlemen by pleasing their stomach, not by throwing food at them. Now everyone get a bowl off the cart. She fixed her eyes on Gevi. "You will need to get flour to remake the dough you wasted on that poor, dear, boy."

Javin did not hear the rest, but he could feel Gevi's glare burning through the middle of his back. He wandered around the camp for the next hour, getting a lot of handshakes and hugs from people who were glad to see him doing well. He did return to the cooking class, as promised.

Having no idea who had made which pie, he ended up judging Lily's as best and Chellell's as second. The three girls, along with Javin, left to head back towards their wagons for supper. Each girl carried the pie they had made.

"I can't stand you Javin," Gevi said with irritation in her voice. She interlocked her arm through his arm and gave him a teasing pinch on the forearm. "Every time I get even with you, my actions come back on me tenfold! I pour a little bit of water on you, because you insulted my cooking, and I end up having to sit with you in freezing ice water for an hour."

"A little bit of water?" Javin stared at her in disbelief. "You dumped an entire bucket over my head." Javin clearly remembered the soaking Gevi had given him for making fun of her cooking back when the dwarven troop came to Thunderfall's shop.

"We almost froze to death in that spring, because of you," interjected Chellell, who was walking right beside Gevi.

"And the whole time we cooked, we had to listen to lectures on how to behave like ladies," Lily said. She glared playfully up at Javin from his other side. "Getting lectured is your fault. You provoked poor, innocent Gevi, into throwing dough at you." Lily interlocked her arm through Javin's free arm.

"Ladies are to take care of their men and always act like ladies, no matter how bullish the men act," mimicked Chellell. She almost sounded like the woman teaching the cooking class.

Javin tried to say something, but the three girls kept on scolding him.

"Throw a little dough at a rude and impolite male, who was begging to have a frying pan thrown at him, and we have to listen to how unladylike we are all class." Gevi said, continuing to hold Javin's arm.

"To end our session, that very same brute of a man comes back to judge which one of us ladies was best able to satisfy his poor, empty stomach," Lily said with mirth in her voice. She was really enjoying this.

"You had the nerve to not pick my pie for the top three," Gevi replied, her bright green eyes flashing at him. She whipped her straggling hair out of her face with her hand in fanned disgust.

"I saw him make a grimace when he tried your pie, Gevi," Chellell said with a sly smile.

"Well, I know us men folk are very happy that someone is trying to teach you women how to cook and become proper ladies." Javin finally managed to speak up between the women's scolding. "I think I will suggest to your instructor that maybe I should judge who is the most ladylike while they cook." Javin smiled at Gevi.

Gevi pulled him to a stop. She was about to say something, but Lily beat her to it. "Tell me Javin, how ladylike is this?" Next thing Javin knew, his whole face was covered in pie because Lily slammed her first place cooking right into his face. He freed his arms from Lily and Gevi's grasp, reaching his hands up to wipe warm fruit pie out of his eyes. Gevi's pie came down on top of his head while Chellell's pie hit the side of his face.

"Ok, Javin, which one of us do you judge to be the most ladylike now?" Gevi was laughing so hard she could barely get the words out. The other two girls were laughing just as hard. Javin stood there in shock, trying to wipe pie out of his hair and off his face. The three girls laughingly joined arms and walked away from Javin toward their wagons. He followed them, wondering where he was going to be able to take a bath tonight.

"You know I didn't raise her, I just survived," Thunderfall grumbled when the three girls, still laughing, sat down by the fire for dinner. Javin had come in right behind them, the red fruit from the pie still dripping from his hair and clothes. Ledia looked over toward Javin from her seat between Thunderfall and Mac. She rolled her eyes and continued her quiet conversation with Mac. Javin's sisters started giggling when they saw him.

"Having problems, son?" Annba commented when she set a large tray of meat down by the fire. Lamar followed with a similar sized tray, filled with farm vegetables and fruit. With the exception of Javin, everyone lined up to fill their plates. Javin grabbed a bucket of water with a cloth and proceeded to try and clean himself.

"I want you to know that I did not raise her with such manners," Thunderfall said to Annba, hanging his head in shame as he spoke. "Maybe it is something she picked up in school, or..."

"What makes you think I'm the one responsible?" Gevi asked while she loaded up two plates with meats and vegetables. "Maybe Javin is clumsy and fell on a bunch of pies." Chellell and Lily both broke out giggling again.

"It's as obvious as the two moons in the sky that you are behind this," snorted Ledia. She turned her attention to Thunderfall. "You know her behavior did not come from my schooling. If anything, it comes from a home life with an ill-mannered, gruff dwarf that..."

"Actually, I started it," said a giggling Lily. The adults stared at her in surprise. Lily had been the quietest and best behaved of the three girls since they started hanging out together.

"And I finished it," said Chellell as she smiled over toward Javin.

"Chellell!" her mother said, with exasperation in her voice. "That is not how a young lady should behave. Did the guilds..." She was interrupted because the three girls burst out laughing.

"You're right Mom; my behavior was very unladylike, don't you agree, Javin?" Chellell spit out between giggles.

"He deserved it," Gevi said. She handed Javin a plate of food and sat down beside him. Grabbing a washcloth, she proceeded to help Javin get the pie off himself.

"My daughter is ruining these sweet, innocent girls," Thunderfall moaned. Gevi looked away from Javin to glare at her father.

"Give me your shirt after you are finished eating," Lily said while she ate. "I have laundry duty tomorrow anyway."

Javin sat his plate down and pulled off his long over shirt, exposing the silver crown on his mesh armor. He tossed the shirt toward the girls, where it landed squarely on Lily's head.

"Why are we expected to act like ladies, around this brute?" Gevi said as she put her arm around Javin's shoulder.

"Gevi, you need to find a gentleman training class, and sign him up," Chellell said.

"He would fail," retorted Gevi. She gave Javin's shoulder a squeeze and proceeded to eat her supper.

"This is an example of how you should not behave when you grow up," grumbled Thunderfall toward Javin's three sisters. They started giggling again.

"Oh, I almost forgot," Gevi said to Javin. "Chellell wants her sugared fruit bread tomorrow for dinner." Chellell chocked on her food, spitting a bite out to the side.

Javin seemed confused for a split second, before he remembered the bet he had made with Chellell at the guilds before they went their separate ways. He turned bright red with embarrassment and glared at Chellell. Chellell had to set her food down beside her, she was laughing so hard.

"A bet is a bet, Javin," Lily said, smiling sweetly toward Javin. "You clearly lost, Sweetie. So you need to pay up."

Javin continued to glare at Chellell. "Is there anyone you did not tell? Did you go to the elder's meeting and blab everything to them as well?" It had been a long time since Chellell had laughed so hard. She was enjoying Javin's discomfort.

"I personally think Chellell lost the bet," Ledia said. "I was told by Lissae that the bet was that Javin would show up with a pretty farm girl on his arm. Gevi is pretty, but not a farm girl. She is an educated, sophisticated lady." Javin turned his stare on Ledia, shock showing on his face that she had learned about the bet from someone Javin barely knew. Gevi burst out laughing again, when she saw Javin's expression.

"Well, I have to disagree, Dear," replied Mac. "Farmer Mattle told me about the bet. We both agreed that since Gevi can milk, gather eggs, and knows how to raise a garden, that she qualifies as a farm girl. You are a farmer dear, and you are highly educated." Ledia, Mac, and the other adults continued to argue over whether Javin or Chellell won the bet, concerning Javin showing up with a farm girl on his arm. Javin decided that this had to be tops for the most embarrassing thing that had ever happened to him.

****

After supper, everyone went to bed, except Chellell. It was a beautiful night, the kind of night that Chellell needed to be alone with her thoughts. At least somewhat alone because Kitty had appeared from what seemed like nowhere. Chellell was laughing quietly to herself while the Great Northern Tiger walked along beside her. It had taken her several minutes to get over the fright the tiger had given her.

While meandering around slowly in the silver moonlight, with knee high grass tickling her legs, Chellell's thoughts swirled through her mind. Four years of studying magic and graduating near the top of her class at the guilds had been all for nothing. She thought about summoning

Sanatarial, so she could feel the power of magic once again. Fear instantly overcame her when she thought back to her last encounter with her old familiar. She also remembered how sick she had been, sick all the time. One inescapable fact was that ever since she had avoided Sanatarial, she was feeling a lot better.

Chellell sighed while pulling her bow off her back. Besides magic, archery was the only other thing she had done every year while at the guilds. "Four years of my life wasted with magic," she thought to herself again. An arrow came off her back, which she fitted to the bow. Scanning around the grasslands, she saw a small scrub bush sticking out of the grass twenty feet from her.

"You know Kitty, there is a God out there, isn't there?" Kitty gave a yawn and sat down on his haunches in the grass. Chellell drew her bow string back and fired in one smooth motion as she had been taught. The arrow struck the bush, disappearing inside it. "The Guild of Magic always said there was no God. Thinking back, I always hoped it was true. Deep inside, I knew there really was a God. But if God is so powerful, Kitty, then why has he never listened to me?" Chellell fired a second arrow, again hitting the bush. Tears started to slowly fill her eyes as she fitted a third arrow to her bow. The arrow struck true into the bush.

Clearing her eyes, Chellell retrieved her arrows. She spent the next hour firing at various targets, talking to Kitty the whole time about God and her life. Finally, she sat down beside the Great Northern Tiger and wrapped her arms around him.

"For a male, you are a great listener, Kitty," Chellell said as she buried her face into the fur of the tiger.

Her arm was draped over Kitty, when his purr turned into a growl. The tiger's eyes were looking skyward. Chellell followed his gaze upward, to see a hovering Sanatarial. A mixture of fear and regret flooded Chellell's body.

The temptation of once again having the power of magic and everyone's respect filled Chellell's mind. It would feel so good to once again be powerful with magic. However, other strange thoughts starting flowing into her mind, thoughts of being sick all the time and the memory of Sanatarial casually discussing murder.

"Are you going to force me to murder my mother and my friends?" Chellell asked in a challenging voice. "They are not changing their beliefs in God. If I refuse to attack someone or help someone that happens to believe in God, are you going to turn on me again?"

"It is too late for you Chellell," hissed the familiar. "You are in way too deep on our side in our war with the Lord of the Stars. You must destroy everything He stands for, or He will destroy you. I, along with my magic, am the only thing that can save you. You made yourself an enemy of the Lord of the Stars, by summoning me. Without me, you will be weak, and He will destroy you."

"Wait a minute," responded a confused Chellell as she put her arm around the growling great northern tiger. Kitty was closely watching the hovering Sanatarial, his flashing teeth very visible. "You always said the Lord of the Stars was a fantasy god and that belief in fantasy gods blocked the mind from using magic. Now you are saying He is real?" Chellell shook her head in disgust, bright red hair flying around her face. "What is truth and what is a lie, Sanatarial?"

"As I said, Chellell, you are in too deep now to back out," hissed Sanatarial. His eyes glowed a bright red. Chellell could physically feel the hatred emanating from her familiar. "It is kill or be killed. I am going to send you straight to this Lord of the Stars that your friends love so much, if you side with them. You will understand, too late, the dire consequences of this meeting. Summon me again, Chellell, or die."

Chellell hesitated. This was not what she expected from her familiar, who had always promised help and guidance. Sanatarial saw the hesitation.

"In time, we will meet again. Enjoy eternity in Hell, Chellell." Lightning blazed out from Sanatarial toward Chellell and Kitty. Chellell screamed, falling back to the ground. The lightning did not hit her. Instead, the lightning bounced off an invisible shield several feet above Chellell.

"Shielded!" screamed Sanatarial in dismay. "Who is praying for you?" the familiar glared down at Chellell, who was pushing in tight against a highly enraged tiger. "This is not over, Chellell! I will be back." Sanatarial vanished into thin air.

Chapter 18

Pride goes before destruction, and a haughty spirit before a fall. – The Guide

Gevi and Javin rode side by side. The two rode down a trail that meandered up and down through the grasslands. Small patches of trees peppered the grasslands. These groves were increasing in number and size the closer they got to the Elven Forest. A light misty drizzle had started to fall. It had rained almost continually since they had left the caravan. The caravan had departed Farm Circle six days ago. With only a few days of travel left to reach the Elven Forest, the elders had decided to send a patrol ahead to the Elven Forest. They were on that forward patrol. In fact, they would be at the edge of the forest any minute now.

Javin looked over at Gevi and frowned. Her black hair was soaking wet and plastered across her face and back. She looked absolutely miserable. The patrol had ridden nearly twelve straight hours this day. She looked completely exhausted. "Tired and wet," Javin thought as he shook water out of his hair.

It was hard for Javin to believe that he had met Gevi a little more than two months ago. Two months that had dramatically changed his life. Every night, he thanked God for her, and prayed that he would not mess up their relationship that was growing with each passing day.

About to say something encouraging to Gevi, Javin stopped when they abruptly entered a small, circular clearing in the trees. The trail ended against a wall of thick, vine covered trees. A person could squeeze through, but horses were going no further.

The whole patrol dismounted while Thunderfall and Lamar discussed how to proceed from here. Lily limped over toward Gevi and Javin. Lily and Gevi were included on the patrol because of the message from the Lord of the Stars. "If Lily and Gevi lead, then the elves will show the way."

Knowing she was not used to such hard travel, Javin suppressed a laugh when he saw the grimace on Lily's face every time she took a step. "Remind me to get Gevi to invent a saddle as soft as a down-filled pillow," Lily moaned as she limped past Javin. "And, I need to find a horse that does not ride so rough."

"Make camp, everyone," called out Lamar. "Put the horses in the southeast part of the clearing." Javin pulled his pack off his horse and unsaddled him. He started to lead his horse off, when he saw Lily struggling with her saddle.

"Let me get it for you," said Javin. He walked over and pulled her bag off the horse.

"Thanks, Sweetie," Lily said with relief in her voice. Javin started unsaddling the horse. "I think I would rather run alongside the horses, like Master Thunderfall," Lily said while rubbing her sore backside. "I won't be able to sit for a week."

"Only a dwarf can run like that all day," Javin replied. "Gevi has some muscle balm that should help." He pulled her saddle off the horse, placing it on the ground.

Lily groaned and sat down on the saddle, "I'm willing to give running a try. I'm sure I would not be as sore as I am now." She absently wiped soaking wet blond hair out of her face. Javin smiled, before walking both horses over to the corner of the clearing.

While tying up the horses, Javin's mind went back to the conversation he had with Chellell right before he had left with the forward patrol.

"You know that even without magic and the religious thing coming between us, we were only going to be friends," Chellell said to Javin. They were standing together, watching Gevi teach a class on technology. The class was packed full of curious teens and adults. Her staff and Javin's swords had fascinated the elders so much, that they set Gevi up to teach for an hour every evening after the wagons had stopped for the day. "I will always cherish our friendship. Every time we talked about a future together, I was scared to death, and I'm the one who brought marriage up to you. I only did that because I craved your friendship. I couldn't bear to lose another man in my life. To avoid being lonely, I was going to marry you, Javin. My reasons were the wrong reasons. I figured if anyone was loyal, it was you. I can't picture you ever leaving somebody."

Javin spoke with a look of concern on his face. "I am so sorry for..."

"Stop." Chellell interrupted. "We are friends, and the past is the past. We both made mistakes. For once, I am telling you the truth. You are blessed to have someone like Gevi." Javin nodded his head, agreeing with Chellell.

"Here is what I have learned in my young life; I will never let a man do to me what my father did to my mom. You will teach me how to use a sword, once we settle down at the ruins. I want to be able to defend myself, should the need arise."

Javin stared at Chellell silently, concern for her growing in his heart. Chellell's expression was stone cold as she stared back into his eyes. "Why don't you go over there and sit in on Gevi's class? It would mean the world to her." Chellell finally smiled again, sensing Javin's concern.

"Yes, Gevi and I have talked about you. She was really worried about me; the rest is girl talk and none of your business. Go sit in on her class. Showing a woman how much you respect the things she is good at will make her love for you stronger." Chellell spun around and started to walk away from Javin.

"You know I have never been good at expressing my feelings, but I'm glad you're my friend." Javin said loudly enough for Chellell to hear.

Chellell stopped and turned back around. "Understatement of the year," she replied with a hint of sarcasm. "Look Javin, I know you are unable to express your feeling. Believe me, Gevi figured it out a long time ago."

A voice brought Javin back to the present. "Lamar wants us to go get firewood," Gevi told Javin. She had already staked her horse off in the corner. "Where we are going to find anything dry in this swamp, is beyond me."

"It's not a swamp," Javin replied, but Gevi brazenly walked on past, ignoring him. Javin staked Lily's horse, but took his horse back with him to load up with firewood. Looking around, he saw Thunderfall grumbling and complaining about the weather while he worked on setting up tents. Lily looked miserable, sitting on the saddle with Gevi standing beside her, obviously in a bad mood.

"I'll get the wood," Javin said to Gevi. He grabbed a hand axe from out of his pack.

"No, I will come along," Gevi sighed. Javin led them away from the camp. He spotted a fallen tree almost immediately. Pulling an axe off his horse, he started working on the rotted tree, while Gevi gathered smaller pieces of wood. Javin was working up quite a sweat, chopping pieces of wood out of the old rotten tree. The inside part was somewhat dry, which would make it easier to burn.

Each piece was loaded into the sack slung across his horse. Gevi walked up with an armful of wood, but dropped it as she looked past Javin. He saw the look in her eyes and instantly spun around with both swords out. A tall, thin, man was standing on the log Javin had been chopping at. He stood well over six feet tall and had large pointed ears. Long blond hair flowed down his back. Arms and legs showed smooth, pale, cream-colored skin. The eyes were arched like Gevi's, but the color was brown instead of emerald green like Gevi's eyes. The man was dressed in clothes that were forest green in color. Slung across his back was a large bow.

An elf, Javin realized. This was a real elf! Javin felt Gevi come up behind him while he watched the elf sit cross-legged on the log. Eyes stared coldly at him and Gevi.

"Put the swords away," she whispered in his ear as her arms circled around his waist. Her chin was right on his shoulder. Javin knew she was trying to make sure he didn't attack.

"I never attack first," Javin whispered back while putting his swords away. Gevi let go of him and stepped around to stand beside him.

"Tell me. What are a bunch of humans and a dwarf doing on the edge of our forest?" The elf asked this while staring straight at them.

"We are refugees from Preveshawl," Gevi replied, quietly grabbing Javin's hand. "We only seek passage through your beautiful forest so that we can reach our destination, the Ruins of the Linkrins." Javin's hand was being squeezed really hard. The elf stared at them for nearly a minute. Javin and Gevi exchanged glances. Javin was getting nervous.

"Humans are not welcome in our forest," the elf replied with a voice that conveyed boredom. "There is another way to the ruins, as I am sure you know, since humans have been at the ruins the last couple of weeks."

"The army of gorms and giants is blocking the other route," Javin replied. "In fact, the whole northern half of Preveshawl has fallen to the gorms."

"And Preveshawl is persecuting the followers of the Lord of the Stars," added Gevi. The elf slowly stood up, his long, pure, blond hair flowing down to the middle of his back. Javin was impressed with how smooth the movements of the elf were.

"This is not our concern," the elf said with distain. "You may go or stay, I really do not care. You will not be entering our forest." The elf stood and turned his back. He managed a couple of fluid steps toward the direction of the Elven Forest when Gevi unexpectedly let go of Javin's hand and leaped toward the elf. Javin tried to grab her but his hand slipped off her moving shoulder. Reaching for the elf, Gevi grabbed and violently spun him around to face her. A face enveloped with rage was inches from the elf's face.

"My whole life, I've dreamed of meeting my father's people," she screamed right in his face. "Now I am ashamed that such arrogant blood runs through my veins." A shocked look covered the elf's face. Javin put his hands anxiously on both his swords; worried things might get out of hand.

"We will find another way to the ruins, you arrogant elf," Gevi screamed before spinning him back around and pushing him toward the trees. In total shock, Javin watched as Gevi kicked him as hard as she could, right in the backside; so hard he fell flat on his face on the muddy ground. The elf sprang back to his feet, turning to face them. Gevi turned her back on the elf, coolly walking back toward Javin. Rage covered her face. Mud now stained the clothes of the elf. Javin's swords were back in his hands.

"Wait," the elf said when he saw Javin's swords. His demeanor showed anger, kept carefully in check. "Are you elven?" Gevi spun back around to face him, tears of rage running down her cheeks. Her emerald eyes flashed with deep anger. She pulled her hair back to show her ears.

"No! I cut them this shape myself," Gevi replied sarcastically. "While I was at it, I stitched these eyebrows to stick up like this for fun. I thought the humans would like me better if they mistook me for an over-prideful, arrogant elf." The elf gingerly sat back down on the log. His eyes, blazing equal anger, fixed on Gevi. However, after a deep breath, a stone cold, emotionless expression took over the elf's face.

Having seen her angry plenty of times, but never this angry, Javin walked slowly up to Gevi and slid his arm through her arm. She tried to pull away, but he held her arm securely.

"Peace, elven girl," the elf said, "What is your name?"

"I am called Gevi," she replied angrily. She finally stopped trying to pull away from Javin. She was still extremely tense though, with anger.

Relaxing his grip a little, Javin gave Gevi a concerned look. He had never seen her like this before. There had to be something deeper going on. Something from Gevi's past.

"My real name is much longer than that, I think. I was real young when my parents died."

"Our laws state all elves, and their guests, may enter the Elven Forest. Unfortunately, I am bound by our laws." The elf gave Gevi a cold, emotionless look. "In the morning, you will find that your trail continues on north through the Elven Forest. In half a day, you will be at our city. You and those with you will be welcome." The elf bowed his tall, skinny, six foot frame almost in half. "Prince Thunderfall," the elf said while bowing, "our king will most certainly want to see you, as well as this elven girl."

Javin glanced back to see Thunderfall, Lamar, and a couple of soldiers standing behind him. He realized that Gevi's screaming at the elf must have been heard back at the camp. He turned back toward the elf, in time to see the elf's back, disappearing into the trees.

Jerking her arm free of Javin, Gevi turned and walked off down the trail away from the camp. Javin started to follow, when he felt a large hand on his shoulder.

"Let her go." Thunderfall told Javin. "She needs to be alone for a little bit. I will go talk to her once she has time to settle down." Javin started to reply, but knew that Thunderfall had Gevi's best interest in mind. Javin nodded and started picking up the wood that Gevi had dropped. They all returned to camp.

While Javin struggled to get the fire going, Thunderfall slipped out of camp. It did not take the dwarf long to find Gevi. She was right off the trail, sitting on the ground with her back against a tree. Her head was resting on her drawn up knees. Thunderfall sat down next to his daughter.

"You alright, Girl?" Gevi lifted her head and looked up at him. Even though there were no tears, it was obvious that she had been crying.

"That was not how I envisioned meeting my father's people," she replied as she slid sideways over to Thunderfall. She put an arm around him and rested her cheek on top of his head. "He was so cold, unfeeling."

"That is how most elves behave toward strangers," replied Thunderfall as he put his arm around his daughter. "Elves only show warmth and feeling towards family members, and then, only behind closed doors. To all others, including other elves, they act cold and unfeeling. It is the way they are. Also, remember that your real father did not come from this forest or tribe of elves."

Gevi sighed, "I guess I had always imagined lots of hugs, crying, excitement, and a big party for me, since I am at least distantly related. Instead, I get an arrogant elf, telling me I am not welcome."

"You have the look of the elves, with the exception you're shorter and have black hair with green eyes. Those must have come from your mother. Other than that, you look like an elf. However, you have the emotions and personality of a human." Thunderfall gave her another squeeze. "I think you've got the best of both worlds." Gevi smiled at her father. Her hand was absently stroking his long beard. She hadn't done that since she was a child. Her actions caused Thunderfall to choke up. When he first brought her to his home, she found comfort, playing with his beard.

"I don't think the elves think much of my personality," Gevi said absently.

"What makes you think that Gevi?" Thunderfall asked.

"Because I kicked him as hard as I could in his arrogant behind." she replied." Gevi gave a sigh. "I really need to learn to control my temper."

Thunderfall sat there for several long seconds, digesting what she said. As the image of his daughter's foot kicking the elf's behind ran through his mind, he started chuckling. Next thing he knew, he was roaring with laughter. Finally, he caught his breath.

"All this drizzly rain that won't stop, and the long ride, already had me in a tiny bit of a bad mood," Gevi said. "Then that arrogant elf had to push me over the edge."

"Now, now, be honest with your old dad. As a dwarf, I know grouchy. You were grouchy enough to make the oldest dwarf in the mountain proud. You could have chewed a rock and spit out pebbles, before you even saw that elf."

Gevi started giggling. "Fine! I was as grouchy as a dwarf. And since you want me to be honest, I am not a bit sorry I kicked him so hard he went face first into the mud. I would do it again if given a chance."

"Gevi, you are no longer a child. Just as you said, you must learn to control yourself," Thunderfall said as he stood both of them up. "A lot of people are depending on us to get them through the Elven Forest."

Gevi smiled down at her father, "What you are really telling me is that kicking arrogant elves is not the best diplomacy. Is that right?"

"Yes," replied Thunderfall. "That is exactly what I am saying. The elves are very prideful on the outside. Remember that on the inside they are like you or me. It's their culture and their way, to act like this in public. If you remember this, you will understand them." Gevi took Thunderfall's hand and the two started slowly walking back to the camp. "You should also remember one of the laws of God. What you look like on the outside has nothing to do with who you really are on the inside. You may look like an elf, but on the inside, you are Gevi. Because the elves look like you, you expected them to be like you. Your ears, nose, or even the color of your skin will never dictate what you are on the inside. Man tends to judge based on what he sees, on the outside, but God judges by what he sees in the heart."

The pair silently walked back toward the camp. As they entered the camp, Gevi saw Javin still struggling, trying to start a fire. "You know Javin will never let me live this down," Gevi sighed to her father. She let go of his hand and joined Lily over by the horses. Lily was hugging her horse, trying to convince the animal to ride smoother, come morning.

****

A small ball of purple light formed over the magic user's hand. The light followed her hand as she gently put the ball of light over the soldier standing at attention in front of her, engulfing the soldier with its purple brilliance. Instead of a human soldier, a long bearded dwarf now stood before the mage. An illusion spell covered the soldier. The soldier was still human, but all eyes would see a dwarf.

The transformed soldier ran over and grabbed an axe off the back of the wagon before returning to the formation line. Several rows down, another magic user was transforming soldiers into a tall, skinny, fair-skinned humanoid with long, pointed ears. These soldiers, now elves, were arming themselves with longbows. Another group of soldiers were dressed in a style typical of Preveshawl farmers. They carried older, rusty swords, or farm tools, they would use as weapons.

Half a dozen magic users finally finished the illusion spells on the hundred and twenty soldiers. A commander that looked like a farmer started calling out squad leaders with ten soldiers in each squad. Four groups were formed, each group made up of ten dwarves, ten elves, and ten farmers. They then marched off toward their assigned attack areas. Hit and run raids broke out around the Crossroads on gorm caravans. Word of the elves and dwarves joining up with the humans quickly spread through the invading army.

****

When the army arrived at the Bear Tree City, terms for surrender were sent to the fort general. As the Grand Leader had ordered him to do after his capture, the enslaved general surrendered the fort, without a fight. At this moment, the enslaved general was cleaning the floor of the Grand Leader's new throne room. Everyone entering the presence of the Grand Leader saw the general in full uniform on his knees scrubbing the floor. They all understood this would be their fate, if they crossed the Grand Leader.

The Grand Leader was listening to various reports from his new local rulers of Bear Tree City when a giant came lumbering into the Grand Leader's new throne room. Humans, gorms, and goblins filled the elegant room. The Grand Leader waved the giant over to his large, marble throne, where he was comfortably seated.

"Grand Leader, I must speak with you in private," the new giant said as he approached the Grand Leader. The Grand Leader raised his hand, causing all conversation in the room to cease.

"Follow me, General," the Grand Leader replied. He walked over toward a door, attached to the side of the room. Both giants had to bend to get through the doorway, designed for humans. The Grand Leader closed the double doors behind him. They were standing in an outdoor garden, right next to a beautiful fountain, decorated with various marble fishes and dolphins.

"I have received several reports of dwarves, elves, and human farmers attacking supply lines and scout patrols around the Crossroads area." The giant general spoke quickly and to the point. "Hit and run raids, it seems."

The Grand Leader sat down on a marble bench next to the

fountain. Nothing was said for several minutes. The giant general stood still as a statue, waiting for his leader's orders.

"Attack and run?" the Grand Leader asked his general. The general nodded his agreement.

"That is the way of the elves, but not dwarves. Dwarves charge in groups, like rampaging ice mammoths. They never run." The Grand Leader paused in thought. Finally, he spoke again, "I will have Ambrissan send out wolf riders to track down these hit and run groups. Then we will know the truth. Someone is trying to deceive us, but it does not matter. Ambrissan suggested to me yesterday that we go after the elves, and he is right. It is time for us to deal with the elves."

"Continue the army operations in the takeover of the small towns and farms north of the river as we planned. However, I want you to pull two gorm legions and three squads of giants from Bear Tree City, and attack the Elven Forest. That will give you two thousand soldiers. The elves will only number a quarter of that. Kill every elf you find, and destroy the Elven City. I don't care if you have to burn down the whole forest, though I would prefer it if you did not, because it would be a good source for lumber." The Grand Leader started laughing as he thought about cutting down the elven trees.

"What about the dwarves and the humans?" the giant general asked.

"Kill any of them you run into, but your objective is the forest. Once the elves are destroyed, return here. Even if real dwarves are involved in these hit and runs, which I doubt, the dwarves will crawl into their holes up in the mountains, once they think they may be attacked. You would lose an entire army digging them out. The humans are farmers rebelling against Preveshawl. My spies learned this a week ago. They should be easily neutralized if they are also involved in these hit and run attacks." The Grand Leader sat back down. "You will leave in two days."

The giant general realized he was dismissed, so he turned around and started to head out the door. "One more thing," the Grand Leader called out. "We have new magic users with us. Ambrissan is certain they will be loyal to us and not Preveshawl. Have him send two or three with your army."

"Yes, Grand Leader," replied the giant general.

Chapter 19

Godly sorrow brings repentance that leads to salvation and leaves no regret, but worldly sorrow brings death. – The Guide

When the Farm Circle scout patrol woke early in the morning, they saw that the trail no longer stopped at the wall of trees. It continued north. With elven permission, Tree Nymphs had moved to reveal the trail. Javin was in complete awe to see Tree Nymphs. These gentle, grass eating creatures, looked like medium sized fruit trees. Tree Nymphs were gentle, but they did have a "cousin", that was not. Death Oaks were large, carnivorous monsters that looked like a giant oak tree. Though even rarer than Tree Nymphs, Death Oaks were rumored to also live in the Elven Forest.

The group followed the trail. Close to half a day passed while they rode through the forest. Large, thickly clustered trees, full of birds, surrounded them. Animals were everywhere as well. Javin saw deer, elk, bear, and a lizard that was twice as big as a horse. No one saw any signs of the elves or of the Elven City.

"So yesterday you were a boy, but today you're a man," Gevi teased, while riding beside Javin and Lily. Javin smiled back at her. He was certainly glad to see her in a better mood! Gevi had been upset with him earlier because Javin had said nothing about his birthday. She found out this morning, from Lamar.

In Preveshawl, the eighteenth birthday of every person was greatly celebrated. A person that turned eighteen was considered an adult. All laws meant for adults now applied to them. They were now required to pay taxes and attend government meetings. They could marry and enter into legally binding business transactions. With all the fighting and action Javin had seen this past summer, this birthday really did not mean a lot to him.

"Maybe now I will get some respect from you two." Javin changed his train of thought. He was curious about the way the elf had greeted Gevi's father. "By the way, did Thunderfall explain that prince thing?"

"We will show the same respect we always have," replied Gevi with a grin, "As for Daddy, he grumbled something about having twelve brothers and that one of them happens to be the king of the dwarves. The elves therefore call him a prince."

"You think he isn't telling you something?" Lily asked. The way she rode on her horse showed that she was still very chafed and bruised from the long ride yesterday.

"I know he isn't telling me something," snorted Gevi. "He gets to really grumbling and subject changing when he wants to hide something." All three were forced to stop their horses. The whole patrol had halted

"Oh wow," explained Lily, awe showing on her face.

Gevi had a very similar look on her face. They were on a slightly elevated hill, with the Elven City spread out below them. Trees that were as

big as three or four houses, at their base, filled a large valley in front of them. These trees reached several hundred feet up into the sky. Wooden houses and shops were spread along the ground and up into the large branches of the trees. Walkways filled the spaces between the trees. The abundant green of the huge leaves, foliage, and grass, mixed with the sapphire blue water, was breathtaking. A hundred foot sheer cliff to the north stretched across the whole valley. Pouring over the cliff was a spectacular waterfall. Water pooled at the bottom of the waterfall, before forming a river cutting through the middle of the Elven City. A watery mist covered the whole city. This mist, mixed with the sun shining down through the leaves, created a colorful rainbow, shining from one end of the city to the other.

The patrol started again, winding down a trail toward the city. Everyone was silent, in awe of the beautiful city. Javin could not take his eyes off the massive trees. Absently, he put on his helmet and latched the face chain in place. When he looked back toward the city the image was changed. The great trees had ugly, purplish spots all over them. The leaves were a dull yellow. The water in the river was brownish black. He unstrapped the face chain and took off the helmet.

"Gevi," he said. She looked over sideways at him. Javin held the helmet out toward her. She took it from his hand, looking at him curiously. "Put it on and look at the city." Gevi at first thought he was joking, but seeing the seriousness on his face, she put the helmet on her head.

"It doesn't fit me very well; my head is not as big as yours."

"No; look at the city," he said, ignoring her teasing. She looked back at him, her face puzzled.

"What do you want me to see?"

"Doesn't the city look strange?" Javin asked.

"No," Gevi said with obvious confusion. She looked back toward the city. She loved the rainbow that sailed across the city.

"Maybe it is more than the helmet," Javin thought to himself. He unstrapped his weapon belt while Gevi was taking off the helmet. "Hold on," he told her. She pulled her hands down from off the helmet and took the weapon belt from Javin. Guessing what he wanted she put on the weapon belt. She turned back toward the Elven City. This time she saw the ugly, purplish spots on the trees, and the blackish, brown, muddy river. She starred at the city for several minutes, while her horse navigated the trail. She took the helmet and belt off and handed them over to Lily. Lily struggled getting the armor on, and staying on her horse. Once she accomplished this, she saw the dirtiness and the disease of the city. She took off the armor, looking at the silver cross on the helmet and the silver, open book symbol, on the belt.

"Salvation, combined with Truth, leads to true sight," Lily commented. She handed the helmet and belt back to Gevi, who passed it back to Javin.

Javin rode his horse up the line of the patrol toward his father. The patrol stopped while Lamar and Thunderfall looked through the helmet at the elven city. He returned back beside Gevi and Lily once the patrol started up again.

"Lamar and Thunderfall will talk with the Elven King privately," Javin told the two women. "They will borrow my helmet and belt, so the king can see what we are seeing. Lamar wants to continue on. The elves need to see for themselves and understand what God is showing us."

Two elven guides met them once they entered the outskirts of the city. They left their horses with a couple of elf horsemen and proceeded on foot. The elven guides curtly ordered Gevi and her bodyguard, Javin, to follow right behind them. The elves informed Gevi that her companions were to follow behind them.

"I think you are enjoying this too much," Javin whispered to Gevi after the guides insisted he lift Gevi over a tree branch lying across the path.

"Yes, yes I am. Almost as much as you enjoyed judging who baked the best pie."

"But..." Gevi didn't let him finish.

"Yes Javin, this is a little much. Believe me, I am not really enjoying the fact that they think I am better than you and the others because I have elven blood in my veins. The only thing I could think of even sillier is if they thought skin color made you superior to others." She looked deep in thought for a second. "Still, you need some humbling." She gave him a teasing smile and a wink.

The patrol followed the guides through the bustling city. Not used to strangers, Elves were coming in and out of shops onto the crowded streets, while elven children ran in and out of the crowds in their play. Every elf they saw, man or woman, had long blond hair. The women's hair went down to the back of their knees, while the men's hair stopped mid-back. The men were over six feet tall, while the elven women were slightly less than six feet. Javin was astonished to see every elven woman wore a naturalist stone on her forehead. As they were in the forest, animals were everywhere. Each animal had a red gem on its forehead. A lot of the elven women had large eagles riding on their shoulder.

A light, misty rain started to fall again as they followed the guides up a ramp into the gigantic trees. One of the guides did hand Javin a small umbrella. It was obvious to Javin that he was expected to hold it over Gevi. With a shake of his head, Javin held the opened umbrella for Gevi.

"I guess a little rain will ruin my beautiful hair," Gevi whispered mockingly while tossing her hair with her hand. It was clear to Javin that Gevi was barely able to keep from laughing at the ludicrous predicament

"Actually Gevi, you have beautiful hair," Javin said in a serious tone. "I do not mind holding an umbrella for you."

Surprise showed on Gevi's face, "Why thank you, Javin." She gave him a beautiful smile and reached her hand out behind her. Fingers intertwined with Javin's fingers. Javin realized that he and Gevi enjoyed playing and teasing in their relationship. However, there were times he should be a gentleman, and treat her like a lady.

They reached a second wooden ramp that spiraled further up into the trees. Houses and shops lined the sides of the walkway, which was wide enough for four or five wagons to travel side by side. Lush grass covered the walkways, with rows of red, yellow, and purple flowers lining its sides. No dirt or stone could be seen anywhere. To Javin's eyes however, everything looked sickly yellow and wilted.

As they were on the ground, elves were everywhere up in the trees. Most were tending to hanging gardens that had been erected amongst the branches; all had various crops growing on them. Some Javin even recognized from his father's farm.

The spiral ended at a platform facing north, giving a spectacular view of the waterfall and a castle. The large castle was actually carved into the largest tree Javin had ever seen. The base of this tree had to be several hundred feet in diameter. To the east, a second tree, nearly as big as the castle tree, had a large church building carved into it. The tree with the church building in it was by far the sickest tree Javin had seen.

Finally, they entered the castle and were led to a large throne room. The room was filled with dozens of richly dressed elves. Some were standing in groups talking while others were sitting at small, round tables. At the far end were two large chairs, covered in green vines, seating the King and Queen of the elves. The chairs were on a solid white dais, so finely polished that the shine nearly hurt the eyes. The walls around the throne room were some sort of natural brown wood. Green, leafy vines, blossoming with white flowers, flowed from the ceiling and down the walls. Various paintings of plants and animals adorned all four walls of the throne room.

Several elves stood near the King and the Queen, but one of them caught Javin's attention. He wore a long, purple robe with an elaborate head piece, made from white silk. He carried a large wooden staff that ended in a silver cross. Through the eye slits of Javin's helmet, the staff looked like rotten wood.

As they approached the elven royalty, the room slowly quieted down until all was silent. The King and Queen both watched while the two guides led the party toward the thrones. The guides stopped them at the steps leading up to the dais where the thrones where located.

One of the guides walked up the steps and gave a short bow before the king. A long winded, elegant address flowed from the lips of the guide to the king. Lily had been looking around with wonder at the splendor of the throne room, until her eyes met the eyes of the king. Both stared at each other. In an instant, Lily's memories were freed and the message from the Lord of the Stars, for the Elven King, was ready to be delivered.

"Your majesty," the elven guide said after a pause from his long speech. "I would like to present to you Prince Thunderfall of Clan Spewrock of the Dwarven Nation. Also your majesty, at this time I would like to present Gevi, thought to be Geviasaracaila from the Northern Elves, along with her bodyguard and companions."

The king pulled his gaze off Lily, raised his hand, and stood up from his throne. The guide making the presentation looked confused and abruptly stopped speaking.

"Bring the blond girl forward," the king ordered. Lily did not wait for the guard that was moving toward her. She climbed up onto the dais, curtseyed before the king, and waited for the king to speak.

"A week ago, I had a vivid dream," the king explained in a loud voice so that everyone in the throne room could hear. "In my dream, I was in an elf sized balancing scale being weighed. Large, ugly, and filthy packages fell from the sky into the other cup of the scale. As they dropped, that side of the scale lowered to the ground and the cup I was in raised skyward. The filthy packages kept falling until the cup overflowed and they spilled out onto the ground. The smell of these packages rose into the air, choking me with the stench. All of a sudden, a thunderous, booming voice proclaimed 'enough', and the filthy packages stopped falling."

The king paused, but the room stayed silent. "Then, a figure appeared, shining like the sun. His features I could not make out because of the brightness of the light. I felt completely insignificant before this figure, like an insect before one of our trees."

A gasp went out from the elves in the room. For their king to say he felt insignificant before anyone else was a shocking revelation. "The figure began to speak and said, 'maybe if we send them one last warning, they will listen.' The booming voice agreed. Then the figure turned toward me, while I stood in the cup of the scales. My eyes were blinded by his brilliance, but his voice was clear to my ears."

The Elven King looked around the room, making sure everyone was paying attention. "The figure said 'A human girl with golden hair, the same as an elven woman, will be sent to you. Heed her words.' Instantly, I woke from my dream." The Elven King fixed his eyes on Lily. "What are your words for me and the Elven Nation?"

Lily took a deep breath, calming herself. "Your majesty, I know this dream because the same dream was shown to me. This is what your dream means. The balancing scale you were on symbolized the scales of judgment before God. You, oh King, represent all the elves. The filthy packages represent the evil pride and wickedness found in these same elves. The booming Voice is the Voice of God the Father. Your nation's sins have grown to such a weight that the scales of judgment have overflowed from their burden. The stench you smelled is these sins coming before God and how He views these sins. God the Father has had enough, and has decided to destroy the elves and their city."

A gasp came from the elves around the room. The elf king, again, raised his hand, bringing the room to silence. "Go on," he prompted. "We are listening."

Lily took another deep breath and continued. "The figure that was so bright you could hardly look upon Him is the Lord of the Stars. He spoke on behalf of the Elven Nation, and God the Father agreed to give the elves one more chance."

Lily quickly scanned around the throne room. All eyes were fixed on her. Saying a quick prayer for courage, she continued speaking before the king. "The message from the Lord of the Stars to you and all elves is this:"

"These people honor me with their lips, but their hearts are far from me. You have forgotten the truth given to you. The elves worship in vain, with traditions that bear no fruit. You are proud, beyond arrogant. Your church leaders are as wolves, leading the sheep to slaughter and refusing to accept the offer I give to free them of their debt. In turn, they add to your debt and cause you to ignore your debt before God."

"You say with your lips what is right and good, yet in your hearts, you think it is foolishness. You claim you know me, yet I deny knowing you. Without repentance, I will destroy the elves. Every tree shall be cut down and consumed with fire and the river will overflow with the blood of the elves before the fullness of the great moon. Humans will refuse to farm this land for seven generations, and the gorm shall call it cursed for three. Courageous dwarves shall cast lots, with the loser entering this land, with great trembling."

"Yet, because of the love your kings had for me in times long past, I will grant one last chance. Search and understand, seek wisdom. What turns aside the wrath of God? Did I not say *Draw near to God, and he will draw near to you. Cleanse your hands, ye sinners; and purify your hearts, ye double minded. Be afflicted, and mourn, and weep: let your laughter be turned to mourning, and your joy to heaviness. Humble yourselves in the sight of the Lord, and he shall lift you up.* Judgment is upon you, for who can escape my wrath? Yet to the humble will I show mercy, to the weak will I give strength. Heed the words of My maiden, for your time is short."

It was deathly silent in the throne room when Lily finished speaking. She hung her head and looked at the floor in front of her feet, golden hair hiding her face.

"Read every word she said, for everyone to hear," the king said, pointing to an elf that was documenting everything in a book. The king's face looked very troubled. An elf with glasses stood up, holding his large book in front of his face. His voice boomed out through the throne room.

"Your majesty, I know this dream because, the same dream was shown to me. This is what your dream...."

When he concluded her testimony, the elf with the long purple robes began to speak. "The true God has spoken to me, and He has called this human female a liar and a blasphemer." His large staff that had a tip of a silver cross was pointing directly at Lily. Extreme anger showed in his face and eyes.

Standing strong in her faith, Lily lifted her head, locking her eyes on the elven priest. "Your church of idolatry is no more," she said in a low, meek voice. As soon as she spoke, the ground shook. For several long seconds, the throne room swayed back and forth. A loud, crashing noise reverberated through the throne room, followed by a thunderous boom that echoed throughout the Elven City.

Mayhem broke out in the throne room, but Lily's commanding voice carried over the noise. "All your fellow priests this minute are taken to the grave where they now and forever will reap the reward of their idolatry, pride, and foolishness," Lily's eyes were now flashing with anger. Her hand was pointing at the elven priest. "Not only has your church of idolatry and pride been judged, but you, false priest, have been judged as well." Purple splotches appeared on the hand of the elven priest. The splotches spread up his arm, covering him from head to toe in seconds. "The pride and wickedness you helped spread among the elves diseased these trees. Now, you will carry the same disease in your body, until you are claimed by the grave."

It took the Elven King several minutes to restore calm. He had his guards remove the priest, who was screaming and scratching at the purple splotches that covered his body. While the guards were dragging the priest out of the throne room, several more guards ran frantically into the throne room. They bowed before the king.

"Your majesty," one of the guards said, completely forgetting any protocol that was required. "Our great tree holding the Grand Church has fallen. The church is destroyed and the priests are dead."

"Was anything else damaged? Were any other lives lost?" The Queen asked calmly from her throne, where she had remained calm through everything that had been going on in the throne room. "That tree is second in size only to the one we are now on. The tree falling in any direction would cause massive damage in the city."

"No, my Queen," replied the guard. "The tree fell straight down to the ground. I saw it with my own eyes. The tree trunk literally disintegrated and the tree fell on itself. Nothing else damaged, no one else hurt." The Queen nodded to herself, leaning back in her throne.

"Take a patrol, completely survey the damage and bring your report back to me."

"Yes, my Queen," the guard replied to the Queen's command. Both guards leaped to their feet and ran from the throne room.

Lily had quietly returned and was now standing by Chellell. Her head once again was bent toward the floor. She was visibly shaking. Chellell was trying to comfort Lily, but she was shaken to the core of her being. She had never seen anything like this. At Lily's spoken command, a massive tree had fallen and a priest from the elven church was now stricken with disease. This was way beyond the power of magic. This had to be the Hand of God! This display of awesome power was terrifying.

"Read again every word that this young woman said," ordered the Elven King a second time. He sat on his throne, listening to the message from the Lord of the Stars. He ordered the message read three more times. Lily had to leave the throne room after the second reading because she was sobbing so hard. Chellell led her out of the throne room, where she sat with Lily in the hallway, underneath a glorious painting of a star filled sky.

The throne room was completely silent after the final reading. The Queen of the elves rose and whispered into her husband's ear. No one could hear what they were saying, but they conversed for several minutes in whispers before she elegantly returned to her throne.

While the king sat on the throne, deep in thought, no one said a word. The humans stood at the bottom of the dais, as quiet as all the elves. The king's eyes were closed, deep in thought. Finally, he raised his head. Tears were falling down the king's face.

The king stood up and began to speak. "Send the heralds out into the city. I declare a royal decree that every elf will start fasting and praying tomorrow at sunrise. The heralds will declare that God has found the elven nation proud and sinful. They will read the words this human girl spoke. As a nation, we must humble ourselves in order to receive His blessings and escape this judgment." He pointed to a couple of elven scribes sitting at a round table. "Copy the girl's words and post them throughout the city. The king hung his head for a second, before looking up again. "I pray that my people will sincerely repent and humble themselves before the Lord of the Stars." The king then looked over at his Queen. They both stood up from their thrones simultaneously. Hand-in-hand, they walked to the edge of the dais.

"If anyone wishes to join us, we are going to the city square for prayer," the king said to the elves that were gathered in the throne room. Together, the two walked down the dais and out of the throne room.

Lamar got Javin's helmet and belt from him. With Thunderfall, the two left the throne room. They wanted the King and Queen to see the disease of their city as seen when wearing the armor.

****

The elves spent several days fasting and praying. Posted everywhere were the words Lily had spoken to the king. Elves from all corners of the forest were making a pilgrimage to view the collapsed tree that had once held their church. The evidence it provided the elven people was impossible to ignore.

Javin was really surprised at the complete change in attitude among most of the elven people. A humble spirit was very evident among them now. It was obvious that they had taken the warning from the Lord of the Stars very seriously.

****

Javin and Gevi walked around the city looking at the goods for sale in the shops that had recently reopened. The shops had been closed during the time of fasting and prayer. Gevi steered Javin out of the trees, toward a field adjacent to the elven city. It was part of the large meadow that contained hundreds of horses. To Javin's surprise, the Elven Queen, and Thunderfall, were standing by a large barn. Beautiful, sleek horses graced the inside of the barn.

216

"I heard you lost your horse in an ambush," the Queen said once Javin and a smiling Gevi joined her and Thunderfall.

"Why anyone would want to ride these smelly beasts is beyond me," grumbled Thunderfall from behind his long, thick beard. "God gave us perfectly good legs to use." The Queen smiled and then gestured toward the barn. An elf came out of the barn, leading a tall, solid black stallion. The Queen reached up and rubbed the nose of the stallion.

"Javin, meet Nightwind." Javin stared at the horse, which was saddled up with a black and silver saddle that matched his armor. "He is a little spirited at times, but I understand that should be no problem for you," the Queen said. She handed the reins over to a speechless Javin.

"I don't know what to say," Javin finally managed to say while he eyed the horse. "I don't think I can afford such a nice...."

The Queen's laughter interrupted him, "Nightwind is yours, a gift from the elves." The Queen's eyes were sparkling with laughter. "Jump on. Take him out through the pastures and let me know what you think." Not knowing what else to say, Javin jumped into the saddle, steering the horse out into the fields.

"This is the best horse I have ever ridden!" exclaimed Javin once he returned. Excitement showed in his voice. "But why would you give a farm boy a horse fit for a king?"

"I am not giving the horse to just a farm boy," the Queen replied. "I am giving it to a knight of the Lord of the Stars." The Queen focused on something beyond Javin.

"Now, time for the real reason for our private meeting," the Queen said, glancing over at Gevi. A group of strange-looking elves and humans were walking towards them.

Introductions were made, and everyone sat in the lush grass near the horse barn. Gevi was sitting really close to Thunderfall, nervously holding his hand. The visitors consisted of four elves and six humans.

The visiting elves' hair was whiter than the blond of the Elven Forest elves. They also had their hair cut much shorter. They did have the same tall, skinny build common to all elves. The difference in these elves could only be seen through the eyes of a trained warrior. These elves' movements were fluid. Their eyes were sharp and intense, like that of a hunter. They had a look that showed they were used to combat, and were not afraid to fight. They wore leather armor covered with white fur. Bows even larger than the ones the local elves used were slung across their back. Long swords hung at their hips.

The visiting humans looked like Gevi. They had the same striking, deep, black hair, with bright, emerald green eyes. Each human wore a single feather clipped to the back of the hair. They were dressed in the same white furs as the elves. Their arms showed many scars from combat, and a vast array of weapons crisscrossed their bodies. Like the elves with them, they moved with a confidence one would only see in a well-trained warrior.

One of the visiting human males called Erik, spoke in a low, gravelly voice, breaking the silence. "I see you have grown into a beautiful woman Geviasaracaila. Our tribe would be proud..."

"The girl remembers almost nothing about her parents or her people," Thunderfall interrupted. "Why don't you start by telling Gevi why you are here, and what you know about her past?" Erik nodded agreement toward Thunderfall.

Gevi was cuddled in tight against Thunderfall. It was obvious to everyone she was frightened. She had dreamed of a moment like this for years, but now that it was happening, she was afraid. "Why?" Gevi asked herself. "Why am I so afraid?" She couldn't rationalize it in her mind. "What if my parents were bad people; or what if their death was my fault, and I blocked out that memory?" Thoughts like these raced through her mind, causing her to squeeze in tighter against her father. He had always been her rock of security since adopting her.

"Several months ago, when the sun grew long in the sky and the ice and snow started to melt, I was preparing with my tribe, The People of the Raven, for the summer battles. We noticed that the gorm tribes were unusually small in number."

"Probably because they are here in Preveshawl," commented Javin.

"That is what we found out," responded Erik. "Over the next couple of months, we took advantage of their absence and attacked a gorm tribe that has always been too close to our borders for comfort. The elves came to us during this time, asking if we wanted to accompany them on a journey to the southern Elven Forest. With the gorms at their lowest number in decades, such a journey was possible. One of the elves wanted to look for a son thought to be dead, and a granddaughter that disappeared nearly twenty years ago. We agreed. The elf that disappeared was married to a woman of our tribe. We knew she had died, but were unsure of the fate of their child."

Gevi kept a straight face, keeping her eyes focused on the visitors without showing any emotion. The scared expression she had earlier was gone, though she still was pushed up tightly against Thunderfall.

"We found this, with a band of gorms we killed," Erik said as he passed some parchments over to Gevi. Gevi stared at a picture of herself. It was a near perfect picture of her, standing with her staff. It was a wanted poster that offered a reward if she were captured alive. She stared at the reward offer in amazement.

"I see I am loved," Gevi murmured before passing the flyer to Thunderfall, who stared at it in disbelief.

"We found rewards for Thunderfall as well, and for a human known as the Black Knight. He wears black armor and carries flaming blades. The image on the flyer makes him look like some kind of demon or guardian." Gevi glanced over at Javin, giving him a quick wink.

"Since Gevi is half-elf, I assume elves and humans far north of us interact and intermarry," Thunderfall commented.

"Unlike our elf cousins here in the south, our people and the people of the tribes can freely intermarry if they so wish," an older elf sitting next to Erik said.

"Actually," the elf Queen spoke up. "There is nothing prohibiting elves and humans from inter-marrying here. It never happens, because the elves stay in the Elven Forest and humans were not allowed to enter. I think that will be changing very soon, as long as humans no longer try to cut down our trees."

"The custom among the tribes is that the woman makes the marriage offer to the man," Erik continued. "Once she and her chosen man sign a marriage contract, they will be married after one year. The one year waiting period before the marriage is meant to be a time they can get to know each other and grow in friendship. During this time, the man and woman may decide marriage is not meant for them, and they peacefully can go their separate ways. A peaceful separation happens most of the time, but not all the time. Some tribes are very prideful. When a man or woman breaks off the contract with someone from another tribe, sometimes war breaks out. If a woman wants to enter into a contract with an elf, then that is her right. The elves respect the marriage contracts, and honor them."

Erik paused, looking toward Gevi with penetrating eyes. "This marriage contract has relevance for you. So let me back up and tell you how a marriage contract caused you to end up in this land as a child." Gevi stared at Erik, curiosity covering her face.

"Over twenty years ago, an elf named Asaracaila was sent to the Tribe of the Raven as an ambassador. While there, he fell madly in love with the chieftain's oldest daughter. Her name was Liosa. Liosa in return, fell in love with Asaracaila. However, Liosa had recently ended a marriage contract six months into the waiting period with the chieftain's eldest son from the Tribe of the Crow. Something happened between Liosa and the warrior she was contracted to, causing Liosa to mourn for many months the contract she had signed. Finally, she terminated the marriage contract. Shortly after that, she met the elven ambassador, Asaracaila, and entered into a marriage contract with him."

"The chieftain's son, from the Tribe of the Crow, convinced his father to declare war on the Tribe of the Raven. These two tribes were by far the most powerful of the northern tribes. Vicious fighting broke out. Liosa's only sibling, her younger brother, was killed in the fighting. It was the worst fighting my people have ever been involved in. Our people have to constantly defend our lands from gorms, goblins, giants, and even ogres, but this war with the Tribe of the Crow was far bloodier."

"After a year, Liosa and Asaracaila were married. They moved into the forest with the elves. Liosa was distraught that so many men were dying over her decision to not marry the Chieftain's son from the Tribe of the Crow. Finding out about her marriage to an elf, the Tribe of the Crow convinced the Tribe of the Hawk to join forces with them. Then, they declared war upon the elves. Now, the Tribe of the Crow and the Tribe of the Hawk were fighting the Tribe of the Raven and the elves. Asaracaila joined the elven forces while Liosa lived with the elves. During that time, Liosa learned she was pregnant. Her child was born while Asaracaila was off fighting."

"They named the child Geviasaracaila, though everyone called her Gevi," an older elf said, interrupting Erik. "After the custom of the northern elves, her name contained her father's name."

"That's why I only remembered Gevi, though I knew there was more to my name than Gevi", Gevi said as she leaned away from her father. Excitement could be heard in her voice.

"The war went on for years," the older elf said, taking up the story from Erik. "Geviasaracaila and her mother lived with me. I only saw my son, Asaracaila, when he was home between battles." It was obvious to everyone that this older elf was Gevi's grandfather. "When Geviasaracaila was three years old, Asaracaila was brought home, gravely wounded. He survived, but because of the damage to his arm, he was no longer able to fight."

"Several months short of Geviasaracaila's fifth birthday, Liosa and my son decided to take their daughter, and leave. Liosa wanted her daughter to grow up in peace. They saw no end to the war. The gorms were continually taking advantage of this war, raiding the elves and the tribes. Many men were dying. Liosa hoped that if she vanished, then there would be no cause to fight and the war would end. They decided to travel south, promising to send word back once they found a place they could live in peace."

The older elf seemed to struggle to speak, tears coming to his eyes. Finally, he managed to finish, "I never heard from them again."

Javin looked over at Gevi. Tears were flowing down her face. She got up and sat beside her newly found grandfather, embracing him. After several minutes, Gevi finally spoke, through the tears.

"I remember the snow and the trees, as well as the faces of my mother and father. The last clear image I have of them, was coughing heavily in a room we were staying, in after weeks of walking. I tried to wake them the next morning, but..." Gevi dissolved into sobs, worse than anything Javin had ever seen. She had never mentioned to him trying to wake her parents, but being unable to.

"There was a horrible plague going through Preveshawl at that time," Thunderfall said.

Javin could hear Thunderfall's voice breaking. Tears came unbidden to Javin's eyes, which he wiped away with his hand.

Finally, after she had calmed down, Gevi returned and sat by Thunderfall.

"I grieved my son's death many years ago," Gevi's grandfather continued. "He would have found some way to get word back no matter what it took. After not hearing anything for several years, I knew he had died."

"We also grieved for your mother," replied Erik. "We knew she was dead, because her heart stone shone no more." Eric passed over to Gevi a necklace. It had a square, pink stone hanging from a gold chain. "Every woman of the tribes receives this stone. The stone will faintly glow, if the woman it is bonded to is alive. The stone also gives a general location of the person it is bonded to. The top of the stone glows if the woman is north and the bottom glows if she is south. The woman will often give the stone to the man they marry. Her husband will always know if she is alive, even if he is out hunting or at war. He will also know if she is located north, south, east, or west of him."

"The stone in your hand is your mother's stone. She left it so that we would know that she lived. The stone glowed south for several weeks. Then the glow abruptly vanished."

Erik stopped talking. Javin could tell that the man wanted to say more, but was unsure how to proceed.

"You need to tell her the rest, Erik," another man said that was seated near Erik.

"Well Geviasaracaila, there is more to the story. After your mother and father took you South, five more years of war went on. It turned out that your mother was just an excuse to start the war. The man she had initially contracted to wanted to rule all the northern tribes. He killed his own father shortly after the war started, becoming a chieftain. He was so arrogant that he freely admitted he impressed your mother, so she would give him a marriage contact, and then caused her to end it, so he could start a war. He died by my hand in combat, ending the war."

"Our victory made your other grandfather chieftain over all three tribes until his death last year. He had no surviving children. Your mother would have become queen over the three tribes upon his death, with her husband becoming chieftain, but she was dead. However, she had a daughter. That daughter, if still alive, would be our queen, and her husband, or future husband, would become our chieftain. You, Geviasaracaila, are the last surviving family member of a long line of chieftains that has ruled our tribe for centuries."

"Gevi is the Barbarian Queen!" Javin sputtered out. He looked toward Gevi with astonishment, only to see she was equally as shocked.

"We go by the People of the Tribes, with each tribe named after a bird. True, to all other races, we are known as the Northern Barbarians."

"She is very young Erik," Thunderfall said with concern in his voice. "She is too young to take on a responsibility like this."

"We agree," replied another of the barbarians. "His name was Keln. "We all agreed earlier that the circumstance with Geviasaracaila is different; so different the laws and customs of our tribe do not apply. If she was found alive, then we would have to consider that she grew up in a strange land, never knowing the Tribe of the Raven. Erik is our acting chieftain. We all agree that he will remain our chieftain, for now.

Geviasaracaila will be our queen. If she wishes, she can return to our tribe at any time. If she returns, and if she marries, then Erik will step down as chieftain and Geviasaracaila's husband will become our chieftain. If she ever wants to rule our people, it needs to be because she wants to, and in a time when she feels ready to do so. Our people would love to continue the family line of chieftains we have had for centuries, but forcing someone into that position would only weaken our tribe, already weakened by the war with the Tribe of the Hawk."

Thunderfall and Gevi had been listening intently. Relief dawned on both their faces. "Thank you," said Thunderfall. "You are obviously a wise people. I think given the circumstances, you and your tribe have shown great wisdom with my adopted daughter." Gevi nodded her agreement, though she was still overwhelmed with everything she was learning about herself, and her parents.

"Thank you, Good Dwarf," Erik replied to Thunderfall. "Our people are very grateful you have taken such good care of our queen. Geviasaracaila..."

"Gevi, please," Gevi said, interrupting Erik. "I have gone by Gevi my whole life."

"Gevi it is then," responded Eric. "We brought with us several gifts from the three tribes. If it is acceptable to you, then we will present them to you at this time." Gevi nodded her agreement. She stood up, as Erik came forward to stand in front of her.

"The first gift is in your hand," Erik said. Gevi looked down at her mother's heart stone necklace. "If you put one drop of your blood on the stone, the stone will bond to you. It will glow as long as your heart is beating, and indicate the direction you are located if someone else has the stone."

Erik reached into a pack he was carrying, and removed three feathers. "The feathers from the Raven, the Crow, and the Hawk are yours to wear proudly." Erik gently turned Gevi around, and clipped the three feathers into the back of her hair. The feathers hung down against her back. "Each feather represents one of the tribes under your care."

Erik pulled a long, fur cloak out of his pack. He held it so Gevi could see the picture stitched into the back of the cloak. It was a picture of a raven, a crow, and a hawk. "This is a cloak worn only by a queen of our tribes. Stitched into the back are the symbols for each tribe under the queen." He folded the cloak back up, and handed it to Gevi.

"It is beautiful," Gevi said with awe. "Thank you."

"I hope it keeps you warm in the cold of winter," replied Erik as he dug back into his pack. He removed a leather parchment and a sharp writing quill. He handed the items to Gevi. "This is a marriage contract and its quill." Gevi's face showed surprise, as she stared down at the leather parchment in her hand.

"Do not worry," Erik chuckled when he saw her expression. "You are not required to marry because you have a marriage contract. It is a custom amongst the tribes to give every woman a blank marriage contract like this, upon her eighteenth birthday. If the woman decides she wants to marry, she takes this quill and signs the contract. She then gives the contract and quill to the man. If he wants to marry her, he signs it and they enter into a one year waiting period. Should he decide he does not want to marry the woman, he returns the contract to her unsigned. Please, we beg you, be careful. The Tribe of the Raven does not want another war if you break the contract in the year of waiting."

Gevi gravely nodded her head, signaling she would indeed be very careful.

The rest of the day was spent visiting. Gevi sat with her grandfather, getting every detail she could about her parents.

****

"The giant and his army will not attack again until Spring," Ambrissan said in a calm, assuring voice. Chancellor White looked visibly relieved. "Have all the soldiers spelled to look like elves and dwarves return to Preveshawl Castle. I made sure my goblin wolf riders did not harm any of your magically disguised soldiers, when they found them. The Grand Leader is attacking the Elven Forest with a large force of gorms, so there is no reason to chance having your soldiers, which are spelled to look like the enemy, found out."

Ambrissan paused in thought, before looking hard at Chancellor White. "I can already sense that my power would be stronger in Preveshawl, but you still have a long way to go. You have all winter to eliminate the followers of the Lord of the Stars. Tell your king that if you do that, and he pardons me for past alleged crimes, then I will fight for Preveshawl at the bridge of the City of the Guilds." Ambrissan gave Chancellor White another calming smile. "I will bring my magical army that serves me with dozens more magic users." The lie came easily to Ambrissan's lips while he kept a sincere face.

Chancellor White sat back in shock. "A magical army?" he thought to himself. Now that was something he wanted to see and be a part of.

"As I have been telling you," Ambrissan continued after he saw the look on Chancellor White's face. "My magic is not limited, like yours is. Do you feel yourself growing more powerful every day?" Chancellor White nodded toward the mirror in enthusiastic agreement, as Ambrissan abruptly vanished.

Chancellor White hurriedly stood up. He could not wait to tell the king that finally, a strong ally was coming to help Preveshawl.

Chapter 20

For God hath not appointed us to wrath, but to obtain salvation by our Lord Jesus Christ. – The Guide

While Gevi was meeting her long lost people, Lamar and Annba were enjoying the warm summer day by walking through the Elven City. They had left a clothing shop when Chellell and Lily joined them. Together, the four continued on through the city.

"Chellell, you are awfully quiet today. Is something bothering you?" Lamar asked after they had left a shop selling bows and arrows.

"No, nothing's wrong. Well, maybe, do you think I could talk to you sometime? Whenever you have some free time, that is. It isn't important, so whenever..."

"No time better than the present," Annba replied. "Lily, why don't you come with me?" Annba took Lily by the arm and steered her toward a store, selling shoes. "You two can catch up to us later," she called back toward her husband.

Chellell allowed Lamar to guide her to a bench off to the side of the walkway. They sat silently for several minutes, watching two squirrels running through pink flowers gathering nuts.

"You were right about familiars," Chellell said, breaking the silence. There was a long pause, as Lamar waited for her to keep talking. Realizing she was not going to say anything else, Lamar decided to keep the conversation going.

"It's a case of old age and experience. Honestly Chellell, I did not expect you to believe me, or heed my warning." Lamar leaned back on the bench. "You are like a daughter to me, Chellell. I had to warn you of the dangers. I had to tell you the truth."

Chellell looked over at Lamar, who continued to watch the squirrels. "You have been like a father to me." Lamar could hear the pain in her voice. "I wish my father had been around for me and my mom, like you have been for Annba and your kids." Lamar started to say something, but Chellell continued on. "God never answered my prayers. My father never returned. Why did God ignore my prayers as a child? Why did God allow my mother and me to suffer? If God is so powerful, why did he allow all that to happen?" Chellell abruptly stopped. Lamar looked into her eyes and saw a mix of pain, anger, and confusion.

"Tough questions, Chellell," Lamar replied with a sigh as he put his arm around her shoulder. "They are questions men have been asking since their creation." Lamar paused a minute to gather his thoughts and to say a quick, silent prayer for the right words to say.

"To answer this, you have to go back to the very beginning, to creation itself. God created a perfect world in six days, full of plants and animals. On the sixth day, he created the first man and first woman. The first man and first woman were created sinless and perfect. However, God created them with the ability to choose. In the garden where he placed mankind, he placed two trees. One of these trees, he ordered them not to eat of, or they would die. God's Nature desired for man to choose to love Him, to serve and obey Him, because they wanted to. He warned the first man and woman what would happen if they choose to disobey him, but he allowed them to make their own decision." Lamar glanced over at Chellell, seeing he had her full attention.

"Now, back up a little bit. Sometime during creation, powerful servants called angels were also created by God. Like man, angels were created with the ability to choose or reject their creator. The most powerful of these angels chose to reject God. One out of every three angels followed this powerful angel in rebellion, choosing to reject God. They made their choice and God rejected them. No offer of forgiveness was ever made to these angels. God created a place of eternal punishment for these powerful beings, a place of eternal suffering and fire. A place these angels know, without any doubt, they will be cast into, for eternity, once God decides to end this world and enter into judgment." Chellell instantly remembered her last encounter with her familiar. Sanatarial had said, "In time, we will meet again. Enjoy eternity in hell, Chellell."

Lamar again glanced at Chellell, pleased he still had her attention. "The most powerful of angels who rebelled against God decided to try and get back at God. He approached the man and woman God had created and loved, and tempted them with the fruit of the tree God had commanded them not to eat. The first man and woman listened to this powerful angel and took the fruit God had forbidden them to eat. God created mankind with the ability to serve or reject him, and they rejected him. The powerful angel had succeeded. God's special creation, whom He loved, was now condemned to join the devil and his angels in the eternal Hell that was created not for man, but for sinful angels."

"They chose to disobey God, so why does that affect us today?" Chellell asked. "We did not eat of the fruit, they did."

"By eating the fruit, the desire to sin and rebel against God was implanted in mankind. The first man and woman passed on to their children two things, the right to choose or reject God, and the desire to sin. From that day on, this deadly combination doomed all mankind; for as *The Guide* says: *all have sinned and fallen short of the glory of God.*"

"Now this evil, powerful angel thought it was over for mankind. He knew God's perfect Nature would never allow sinful man in His presence. He thought he had given God a black eye, by dooming His special creation to Hell, as he was doomed. But God had a bigger plan."

"Unlike the angels, God decided to offer mankind forgiveness. He sent his only Son, to die on a cross. While on the cross, God poured out his wrath on his only Son, who was taking our place, receiving the punishment meant for us. Once the Son of God rose from the dead three days later, our sins could be forgiven and removed from us. However, mankind still has the created ability to choose, and God has never removed that capacity. All mankind has made the deliberate choice to sin and head down the path to Hell, but God has offered a lifeline to rescue them. The choice is ours to make. God will never force anyone to accept His offer of salvation. Mankind must choose to accept the Son as Savior, or continue down the path the evil, powerful angel, started them on.

Chellell's eyes were fixed on the ground, but Lamar could tell she was listening. "Now, you asked why bad things happen around us every day. Well Chellell, it is because mankind has the right to choose right or wrong. Look at the tree that held the Grand Church." Chellell's eyes rose, looking upon the ruins of the tree. Lily's words, "Your church of idolatry is no more," flooded back into her mind. The tree had fallen as Lily spoke. Shivers ran up and down Chellell's spine as she thought about the power she saw displayed.

"Did you notice something, Chellell, in the message from the Lord of the Stars? The elves had to make a choice. Listen and obey God, or refuse, and keep doing what they were doing. God did not force them to become humble. They had to make that decision themselves. It is the same with your father. When you prayed, God would have put your father in positions to make decisions. Obviously, he decided to continue down the road he chose, and not return to you or your mother. God will never force your father to change, but prayer for him will cause God to force him to make decisions. Hopefully, one day, he will make the right decision."

At that moment, an elven child, around four years of age, ran up to Chellell. The little girl handed Chellell a beautiful, purple flower, before running back to her mother. Lamar recognized this was a good teaching opportunity. "Can you, Chellell, force that child to love you?"

"No!" Chellell said with exasperation. "A child loves you, because you show the child love, first."

"Exactly," replied Lamar. "God showed us His love, first, through the sacrifice of His Son. As *The Guide* says, *we love because He* (God) *first loved us.* A parent shows a child love; in return, the child loves back. Parents cannot use force to make a child love them. God showed us love, but He is not going to force anyone to Love Him in return. God wants mankind to choose to love. The Lord of the Stars has put the decision before you. Like your father, He will not force you. You can decide to love and serve Him, or to continue down your road of unbelief. You have seen His power demonstrated through the elves. He does love you, Chellell, and wants you to be a part of His family."

Chellell stared at the fallen tree and the ruins of the Grand Church that displayed God's power and the decision the elves were required to make. Images of her last encounter with Sanatarial flooded her mind. His words again, came back to her, "It is too late for you, Chellell. You made yourself an enemy of the Lord of the Stars by summoning me."

Chellell burst into tears. She turned and put her head on Lamar's shoulder. She cried and sobbed, while Lamar held her. Finally, Chellell settled down, holding on to him silently.

"There can never be forgiveness for me," Chellell whispered in a barely audible, shaky voice.

Lamar thought he heard her right, but he wanted to make sure. "Sorry, Chellell, can you repeat what you said?"

"I said, God will never forgive me," Chellell said a little louder. "I willingly participated in the Ritual of Summoning. Sanatarial told me God is now my enemy." Her voice dropped back to a low whisper. "The Lord of the Stars will never forgive me for what I said and did."

Lamar reached into his shirt pocket, pulling out a small book. "Fallen angels like Sanatarial are liars. Before you decide what our all-powerful, Holy God will and will not forgive, I want to read you the words of God, Himself, on that subject." Lamar flipped through the pages, until he found the passage he was looking for. "*Wherefore I say unto you, all manner of sin and blasphemy shall be forgiven unto men: but the blasphemy against the Holy Ghost shall not be forgiven unto men. And whosoever speaks a word against the Son of man, it shall be forgiven him: but whosoever speaks against the Holy Ghost, it shall not be forgiven him, neither in this world, neither in the world to come.*"

"I want you to understand, Chellell, what is being said by our Lord here. He was talking to men that had just seen an amazing miracle done, by our Lord. They refused to believe, and attributed the miracle to a demon. They were hardening their hearts, even though overwhelming evidence was in front of their eyes."

"All sin, all blasphemy, even against the Son of God, Himself, is forgivable. The Son said that. The only sin not forgivable is blasphemy of the Holy Spirit. You see, Chellell; the Holy Spirit convicts all men of their sins. As *The Guide* says of the Holy Spirit, *and when he is come, he will reprove the world of sin, and of righteousness, and of judgment.* He convicts the heart when men hear how they need to be redeemed by the Son of God, and that there is no other way to be saved. Those that reject the Holy Spirit and His message will never be forgiven, once they pass from this world. These are people that refused the message from the Son of God. There is a danger that people can reject the Holy Spirit often enough while they are living, that the Holy Spirit withdraws from their life and no longer reproves them of sin. Without the Holy Spirit, a person will never seek God, and they will be hopelessly lost. That is what the Guide means when it says *neither in this world, neither in the world to come.*"

"Everyone that listens to the Holy Spirit and receives the Son as their Savior will be saved. Those that blaspheme the Holy Spirit by refusing to listen to God's offer of salvation, they will never be forgiven. They will spend eternity in Hellfire." Lamar looked over at Chellell. She had her head down, resting on her knees. "I know the Ritual of Summoning, Chellell. It is very blasphemous, with extremely wicked and evil things occurring. That is why the familiar demons are attracted to it. But nothing happens in that ritual that God cannot forgive. In fact, the Lord of the Stars wants to forgive it. The decision is yours." Lamar put his arm across Chellell's back, trying to comfort her.

"Thank you," she finally whispered.

"What are you going to do Chellell?" he asked.

"I don't know," she said with a sigh. "I need to think." She wiped her tear streaked face and gave Lamar a smile. "Thank you, for taking time to talk with me."

****

When the rest of the Farm Circle refugees arrived later that day, the elves opened the forest, allowing them to pass through. The Ruins of the Linkrins were only two days travel from the Elven Forest, though it was going to be a tough two days due, to the rough mountain trail.

The elves invited their human guests to stay for a couple of days. The elders of Farm Circle agreed, pitching a large camp in a field next to the Elven City. For the first time in centuries, elves and humans intermingled freely.

Gevi spent as much time as she could, with her grandfather and the barbarians. But the time was short. They needed to get back to their homes in the North while the way through the land of the gorms was still open. The high mountain trails of the Dwarven Mountains were only passable during a single summer month every year. They gave Gevi maps to show where they were located, but warned her never to come North without a lot of protection. Thunderfall ensured them that Gevi would be protected by the dwarves, if such a trip was ever made.

Gevi said a tearful good-bye to her elven grandfather, and watched them depart the Elven Forest. Thunderfall gave her a kiss on the cheek before leaving to go meet with the Elven King. She was standing alone, when Javin walked up behind her, taking her hand into his hand. Turning towards him, Gevi wrapped herself in his arms. After several minutes of Javin holding her, she pulled away from him, wiping tears from her eyes.

"They're tears of joy, Javin," Gevi said as she once again took his hand into hers. "Grandfather told me how beautiful my mother was. He told all about her life, and the life of my father. I barely remember them, but now I feel like I know them again."

Silently, the two walked, hand-in-hand, through the Elven City. Together, they sat on a bench, near a field. In front of them, dozens of elven children were playing a game that involved hitting a small ball with a stick.

"I guess you were right about the barbarian princess." Javin said, breaking the silence. "You said I would fall madly in love with this gorgeous barbarian princess. You were absolutely right."

"You better think I was right," snapped Gevi, as she gave his hand a squeeze. "You said the barbarian princess would be ugly and smelly."

"You were right; the barbarian princess is gorgeous. And she has healed me. The old prophet on the road told me, a barbarian princess, known as the slayer of giants, will be given the power from God to give you partial healing. In turn, you will lead her people into war."

"It still has to be another princess. I am certainly no slayer of giants. No one will ever call me a giant slayer."

228

Javin decided to ignore her giant slayer comment. "Yesterday, I was walking through the Elven City. Inside a weapons shop, I realized that I did not feel uncomfortable. The place was crowded, but the usual funny feeling and the fear that starts to overcome me from crowds, wasn't there."

"I know you don't like crowds," Gevi replied. "But that isn't a sickness, just a preference."

"Not with me, Gevi. It goes beyond that. I tried very hard to hide it from you the few times we were together around a lot of people. The fact is crowds used to terrify me. The more people around me, the worse it was. I barely survived the City of the Guilds. I had a quiet place in the forest nearby, where I could escape. Being alone there, helped me keep my sanity. Arena crowds were a nightmare to me, only overcome by my love of the swords, and concentrating on fighting. There were times in my life that I just wanted to go into a forest, and never come back. The only thing that stopped me was my love of God, my family, and my swords."

"So you are getting comfortable around people," Gevi said. "But I had nothing to do with that."

"Yes, you did," Javin replied. "I do not understand it, but your presence and your friendship is helping me. I still feel somewhat uneasy around crowds, but it's not nearly as bad."

"I guess a barbarian princess is good for something," Gevi said with a smile. "She put her head on Javin's shoulder, taking comfort in being near him. "I wonder though, about the giant slayer and the lead her people into war part. Honestly, I think you are mistaken. Just promise me, that when the real barbarian princess finds you, that you will not fall in love with her!"

****

The trail was extremely steep and winding as the caravan of Farm Circle refugees left the Elven Forest. Horses struggled to pull wagons, forcing many stops along the way. They had set up camp the first night, when a group of elves rode into camp. Javin's curiosity was roused when the elves gathered around a fire with the elders of Farm Circle.

The next morning when everyone with Lamar's group was eating breakfast, Lamar told them that the elves had brought news that several thousand gorms were marching toward the Elven Forest. They would reach the southern boundary of the forest within three days. Lamar paused when Gevi walked up and sat down beside Javin. Javin reached toward the fire and put a couple of meat strips and eggs on a plate. Lamar smiled when he saw his son hand the plate to Gevi.

"Thanks," Gevi said. She took the plate from Javin before fixing her gaze on Lamar, "Dad left last night for the Dwarven City." Lamar nodded, no surprise showing on his face.

"He will have the dwarven forces here in a week, maybe a day or two less," Lamar replied back to Gevi. Lamar glanced around at the group of family and friends. "The elders have put me in charge of leading a fighting force from Farm Circle to help the elves defend their homeland, while the caravan continues on to the ruins. Anyone who wants to volunteer, needs to pack at least ten days of supplies and then meet over by the last wagon, two hours from now." Lamar sat down and proceeded to quickly eat breakfast. Javin only ate half his breakfast, before getting up to go pack.

****

The giant general that the Grand Leader had put in charge of destroying the elves stood on top of a hill, surveying the Elven Forest. His army was making camp a half hour ride from the edge of the forest. A wicked smile crossed his face, as he thought about the elves he would be killing in the days ahead. His smile slowly faded when he observed a strange, dark cloud rising from the Elven Forest. The cloud slowly left the forest, heading toward his army. Looking off to his left, he realized his army was unaware of the approaching cloud. He focused again on the cloud, watching the dark mass move and swirl with chaotic randomness.

"It is too small to be a cloud. No cloud I've ever seen moves like this," the giant commented to himself. As the cloud moved closer, the giant's frown deepened. Not a cloud, he realized, but a large flock of birds. Gazing toward the sky, the Giant Commander could now see the birds were carrying something in their claws. The flock reached the front lines of his army when he noticed that the birds had small nets in their claws, nets loaded with fist sized rocks. The giant watched in amazement as rocks rained down from the sky, landing on his army. Screams and shouts filled the air as the rock missiles struck the gorms. Several of the larger eagles carried firewater in hollowed-out clay balls. The explosions were deafening.

Gorms started firing arrows up into the sky, trying to bring down the large eagles. Very few hit, but many more gorms died from the deadly barrage of arrows that came crashing back toward the ground. The three magic users traveling in the gorm army had better luck. They had air shields protecting them from falling rocks, while their lightning blasts killed a handful of the eagles. The eagles turned and flew back toward the forest, allowing gorm officers to regain control of their soldiers. Returning from the hill, the giant commander walked through the camp. He did not even bother to glance at the wounded and the dead. The report he got in his tent later that night confirmed his thinking. Nearly two hundred dead or severely wounded enough that they could not fight.

"Have the magic users brought here, immediately," the giant general growled at the officer that had brought him the report. "Tell them to think of some way to make sure this never happens again, while they are on their way here."

Chapter 21

*Why do the heathen rage, and the people imagine a vain thing? The kings of
the earth set themselves, and the rulers take counsel together, against the
LORD, and against his anointed, saying, Let us break their bands asunder,
and cast away their cords from us. He that sits in the heavens shall laugh:
the LORD shall have them in derision. –The Guide*

The flock of eagles crashed into an invisible wall in mid-flight. Birds
started falling out of the sky, along with the rocks they were carrying.
Violent explosions ripped the air when a ball of fire flew up from the ground
and into those birds that were carrying the firewater. En masse, the
surviving eagles turned and flew back to the forest.

"Well, it worked once," whispered Javin, who was watching events
unfold from behind a tree. Gevi heard his whisper. She was crouched
behind a bush, right beside Javin's right foot.

"Those poor birds," Gevi whispered back. "I knew the enemy magic
users would not allow the same thing to work twice."

"Come on," Javin whispered again. "We need to..."

"Wait, something is happening." Gevi handed a long spy glass to
him that she had been using. Javin took the spy class, putting it to his eye.
"Look at the east side of their camp."

Javin saw what she was talking about. A large part of the army was
leaving camp and marching east.

He kept watching, trying to determine the number moving out. The
image through the spyglass was crystal clear, better than any spyglass he
had used in the past. It was another item made by Gevi.

"Tell Willow to report to Lamar that seven hundred are heading
east. They are following the edge of the forest." Gevi nodded and crawled
backwards into the grove. "Have Grange and Trevor relieve us," Javin
called quietly after her. She turned back, giving him another nod before
crawling back through the brush.

After several days of fighting at the border of the Elven Forest, the
elven commanders had sent Lamar and his Farm Circle soldiers to a thick
grove of trees southwest of the enemy army. The plan was for Lamar to
sting the enemy with night attacks and raids. Lamar had formed eight
groups of ten. He had kept three of the groups with him, at a spot north of
Javin. The other five groups were spread around the edge of the grove, to
watch for gorm scouts. Each group had an elf assigned to them as guides,
because elves always knew where they were in the trees, never getting lost.
Lamar was also using them to keep communications flowing in an effective
manner.

Lamar had made the decision to put Javin in charge of one of the
patrols. The Farm Circle soldiers had a deep respect for Javin's fighting
ability. To offset Javin's youth and inexperience, Lamar made sure to
assign experienced fighters to him. He put Gevi with Javin, as an extra

safety factor for both of them. Her staff, and whatever else she carried on her, would come in handy if Javin got into trouble. Lamar realized that Javin was fast becoming a man and a renowned warrior. As a father, he did not want to put his son in harm's way. As a general, he knew his son was ready to lead. The general part of him, assigned Javin as commander of a patrol group. The father part made, sure to assign his most capable and experienced fighters to Javin's group.

"Everyone try and sleep," Javin said after being relieved from guard duty at the edge of the grove. "We shouldn't see much action until night falls. Guard change every three hours, as I assigned this morning." Javin's men started unpacking bedrolls and laying them out. Gevi, Mia and Willow had a side of the small clearing reserved for them, since they were the only women with the group.

****

A massive tree branch reached down. Claws at the end of the branch snatched a gorm up into its branches. The gorm was sent flying through the air, a second later. A second gorm was swinging an axe wildly at the tree trunk, only to have another tree claw rip into him from above.

"I will never get used to this," sighed Mac, as he watched the Death Oak rip the gorm apart. Death Oaks looked exactly like trees, but they were actually flesh and blood animals; slow moving animals, but very powerful. In the wild, they ate anything that came to close. Animals seeking the shade of the giant creature they thought was a tree, would end up as a quick lunch. This Death Oak was one of several, controlled by the elven naturalists.

Mac pulled his eyes off the tree monster. Spotting a group of a dozen gorms carefully moving through the trees toward his position, Mac drew back his bow. As he was about to fire, a pair of bears roared and launched themselves into the gorm patrol. The bears were followed by two badgers and several eagles, dropping out of the trees. The gorms were dead within seconds. "Nope, I will never get used to this." Mac sighed as he lowered his bow.

He watched to see if any more gorms would show up, before ordering the hundred elves with him to follow him. A large division of gorms with several giants were reported to have entered the Elven Forest, just west of his position. Mac aimed to have them running back to their camp before the sun set. Mac and the elves slipped quietly through the trees, closing in on their foe.

****

Javin had a terrible time falling asleep. Not only was it the middle of the day, but his anxiety with being in command and the fighting sure to come, kept him wide awake. To pass the time, he read from *The Guide*.

He had finally fallen asleep, when someone shook his shoulder. "Your turn," the man said quietly. "Javin sat up, wiping the sleep from his eyes. He glanced over to see Gevi, still curled up in her blanket. She was his partner on watch.

"She is tough to wake up, and super grouchy," Javin warned over his shoulder to the man that was now trying to wake Gevi. Sure enough, the poor man was hopping around on one leg as the words left Javin's mouth. Gevi curled back up in sleep, not even aware she had kicked someone right in the shin.

Javin shook his head and crawled toward the guard post at the edge of the grove. He replaced the guards and started his watch standing behind a tree. He became wide awake when he saw the edge of the Elven Forest on fire. Pulling out the spyglass that Gevi had loaned him, he focused in on the fire. The bodies of many gorms, along with a couple of giants, could be seen scattered along the edge of the forest. Hundreds of gorms were moving into the forest between the fires.

Javin seriously doubted the fires would spread too much. The Elven Forest was way too wet for fire to be effective. Magic had probably been used to get the fires they had. He put the spyglass back into his belt reluctantly. As much as he would love to watch the action, he had a job to do. Besides, he knew Mac had been put in charge of an elven fighting battalion. Mac was probably already engaging the enemy. Knowing Mac, the enemy would shortly be on the run.

Scanning the grasslands, Javin remained alert and watchful for gorm patrols. He saw several, but they seemed content to patrol in a tight area around the main army camp. A few minutes later, Gevi slid up beside him. Javin was thankful for the chain mail across his face that hid his smile. She was soaking wet.

"You put them up to this," she hissed in an accusing voice. Javin almost started laughing at the glare she was giving him.

"I had nothing to do with it. I learned my lesson last time I tried to wake you." He pulled Gevi's glass back out and started scanning the grasslands again. This time, he saw something. "I think we may have visitors soon." After a few minutes, he handed the spyglass over to Gevi. She pointed it in the same direction Javin had been looking. A gorm patrol was slowly riding toward the grove of trees. Her anger from being wet disappeared. "Keep watch," Javin said, giving her wet shoulder a squeeze. "I am going to get the others." With that, he left Gevi and headed back toward their camp.

****

Javin allowed the gorms to stake their horses near the grove and enter it. When the gorms started exploring deeper into the grove, he sent Willow along to shadow them. She was to warn another patrol if the gorms got close to them. If the gorms didn't find any traces or spot any of the humans, then Javin planned to let them leave, unharmed. Their goal was stay undetected until late tonight.

While his men hid, Javin, Gevi, and Grange, moved to the edge of the grove to keep an eye on the two gorms guarding their tethered horses. After several minutes, a Gorm War Pig, covered in spiked leather armor, trotted out from the circle of horses. Its snout was sniffing the air.

"Oh no!" Gevi whispered. The war pig was slowly moving toward them, while sniffing the air. Carefully, all three slowly drew their bows. Sniffing the air, the war pig closed the distance towards them. Grunting, the war pig lowered its head and charged right toward them.

"Shoot the guards!" Javin yelled.

Arrows flew from the edge of the grove, killing both gorm guards. Drawing both his short swords, Javin leaped out from behind a tree onto the edge of the clearing, making himself visible to the pig. Without slowing down, the war pig charged toward him.

The monstrous pig was covered in leather armor, with wicked looking spikes sticking out in all directions. Javin's right sword swung hard toward the gleaming white tusks. The sword crushed into the War pig's mouth while he dived sideways. The impact of the sword spun the Pig's head around, its momentum carrying it past Javin and causing it to crash hard to the ground. Javin quickly rolled back to his feet. Several more arrows flew from the grove and into the war pig. It ignored the arrows that barely punched through the thick leather armor, and spun back around to face Javin. The war pig had a large, bloody gash across its mouth from Javin's sword.

The thought of flaming the swords crossed Javin's mind briefly as the pig started to charge back toward him. He instantly rejected the thought. He might be spotted by the enemy camp off in the distance. The pig rushed in again as another arrow struck its armored back. Javin jumped toward the war pig, both swords striking forward, as man and beast collided. The left sword went straight into the eye of the war pig while his right went deep into the neck. Air exploded from his lungs when the head of the pig hit him full in the chest. The impact launched him backwards onto the ground, the war pig landing on him. The dying war pig snapped several times into Javin's black mesh armor, but the result was only broken teeth. Javin saw the light of its one good eye fade as the pig died, right on top of him.

He was rolling the War Pig off himself when Gevi and Grange rushed out of the grove to help. "You're going to get yourself killed," Gevi hissed at him while helping him off the ground. Javin gave her a breathless smile. When he reached his feet, a strong, horrible odor, made him gag. It came from his right arm and from one of his swords, which was covered in blood from the War Pig. The stench was unbearable, making his eyes water while he tried to keep the contents of his stomach from coming up. Gevi stood right by him, holding her nose as tightly as she could.

"Serves you right for playing hero," Gevi smirked. She stepped further away from him while covering her nose. "This breed of pig that the gorms use has the worst smell on the planet, when their blood is exposed to air. But I guess you know that now, don't you?"

Javin glared at Gevi. "A hug would make me feel much better," Javin gasped, while reaching his arms out toward her. She quickly stepped away from him, horror clearly showing on her face.

"Until you take several baths, I would rather hug a gorm," she retorted. The stench of the War Pig was quickly overpowering him. Gasping, Javin returned to the grove.

The rest of Javin's patrol gathered around him, waiting for further orders. They kept as much of a distance from him as they could, their noses visibly twitching. War Pig blood had to be one of the worst smells Javin had ever had the misfortune to be around, let alone have on him. He drew on every bit of strength he had, to keep from throwing up, right in front of his patrol.

"Ok everyone, spread around and take cover, as we planned earlier, if the gorms discovered us. When the gorms return, we need to make sure none make it out of the grove. Grange, go ahead and hide in the middle of the gorm's tethered horses. Kill any gorm that manages to get past us."

Javin paused while Grange made his way over toward the gorm horses. "Mia," a middle aged woman, holding a large bow, stepped forward and looked straight at Javin. "You're really good with that bow. Join Grange. Shoot any gorm that pokes its nose out into the clearing." The woman nodded and followed after Grange.

"Won't your smell give us away, long before the gorm's get near us?" Gevi asked with a sly smile on her face. The other soldiers started snickering, continuing to cover their noses.

"I'll worry about my smell. Everyone into position and under cover," Javin ordered ignoring the snickering of his soldiers. "Gevi, I need you right by me. In fact, I need you to stay really close." The soldiers started chuckling even louder.

Gevi glared at him while holding her nose tight with her hand. Knowing the smell would warn the gorms something was wrong, Javin made a command decision. "Miller, you're in charge until I get back." Javin grabbed his backpack and ran through the grove toward a nearby creek.

****

Fear shone from the eyes of the gorm, as Mac's sword ended the creature's life. Forcefully, he pushed forward, taking a mace hit into his shield. While he fought, an elf grabbed a fellow wounded soldier Mac was protecting, and dragged him to safety. Flashing his sword forward, Mac disposed of the gorm with the mace. A roar from a lion caused Mac to disengage from a third gorm. He turned and ran back into the cover of the overgrown Elven Forest.

"Six elves wounded, one dead," an elf soldier reported to Mac once they had regrouped. Mac scowled. The gorms had the numbers to take the heavy losses that Mac and his men were given them. The elves did not. "Get the wounded on the way to the hospital," Mac ordered, giving Kitty a scratch behind his ears. The tiger was his constant companion. "Short rest; then we move again," Mac called out to his elven soldiers. "Meghan, have your naturalists set up a guard perimeter." An elf woman wearing a red jewel on her forehead started giving orders to a group of elven women, all wearing similar jewels. Mac sat down against a tree trunk, trying to regain his strength. With the animals guarding the perimeter, Mac and his men could get a much needed rest.

The strategy Mac was using was to hit the gorms, then retreat. Over and over, all day, his battalion had constantly been on the move. His strategy was working, somewhat. The gorms had slowed their advance through the Elven Forest. However, Mac had lost twenty of his men so far today. He estimated they had killed nearly one hundred gorms, but that number was hardly having any effect on the enemy army. Word that Mac had received was that the other four elven battalions were having greater losses than he was.

He hated to admit it, but the animals with the naturalists were the only reason the gorms had not reached the Elven City yet. Looking off to the side, Mac saw Kitty cleaning himself. The Great Northern Tiger was now sitting with a group of ten Forest Wolves. Kitty and the wolves, with their speed and power, had been especially deadly with Mac's hit-and-run strategy. "Get me up in thirty," Mac called out to Meghan. The elf naturalist nodded her head as Mac closed his eyes. Exhaustion had him asleep in seconds.

****

"You still smell, but it is a lot better," Gevi commented once Javin slid in beside her. Willow was also with Gevi. "You are right on time. Willow says the gorms will be here any minute. The patrol is in position around the trail." Both women had their bows out and loaded.

"Ladies," Javin whispered. "When I touch your shoulder, fire the first shots."

"No problem," Willow replied. She focused her attention toward the small game trail the gorms were following. Gevi did the same. Javin drew both swords and waited.

"Remember, Gevi, under no circumstances, can you use your staff. That boom will be heard all the way to the Elven Forest." Gevi rolled her eyes and gave Javin an expression that told him he really didn't need to remind her. Ignoring her reaction, he took a deep breath and waited.

Kneeling in front of him, the two women watched carefully through the bushes for the gorm patrol. Their wait was short. The gorms thought no one was in this grove of trees. They were arguing loudly with each other in their guttural language, making no effort to conceal themselves.

Javin waited until the entire gorm patrol came into view. He put his right sword on Willow's shoulder and his left on Gevi's shoulder. Willow's arrow flew straight and true, killing the War Pig at the front of the gorm patrol. Gevi's arrow flew into the side of the gorm that was leading the pig. Arrows flew out from behind trees and bushes into gorms that were diving for cover. Javin flamed both his swords, pushing past Willow and Gevi. Both women threw their bows down, arming themselves with sword and dagger to follow Javin.

Javin's orders had been one barrage of arrows and then attack with hand weapons before the gorms could regroup. Soldiers jumped out from

236

hiding and attacked the gorms. Javin's flaming right sword went under an axe and into the chest of a gorm. The gorm burst into flames, falling backwards against a tree trunk. Looking around, he saw one of his soldiers drop because a gorm had struck him with a flail. The gorm was raising the flail to deliver the killing blow to the fallen soldier, when a flaming sword cut through the chain, holding the spiked ball to the flail. Javin's other sword sliced the gorm through the neck a fraction of a second later.

Meanwhile, Gevi and Willow were fighting off a second War Pig. Their backs were against a large tree. Javin could see that they were barely keeping the pig at bay. He ran hard toward the back of the war pig, closing the distance within seconds. Right as the snarling pig leaped toward the girls, Javin's right sword plunged into the back of the creature's neck. His left sword slammed into the side of the neck so hard, its spiked collar was sent sailing through the air. The war pig died in mid leap. Its momentum knocked Willow backwards while pinning Gevi to the base of the tree.

Javin glimpsed Gevi struggling to get out from under the nearly decapitated pig. Javin moved a step forward to aid Gevi, when he saw something behind him out of the corner of his eye. He barely had time to drop to his knees. A large battle axe whistled through the air where his head had been an instant before. Reflexes took over. Both of Javin's swords stabbed backwards over his shoulders while angled upwards. They stabbed through the leather armor of the gorm and into his chest. The gorm fell backwards, his axe flying out of his hands and into the bushes. Smoke rose from the burn holes in his chest.

Leaping back to his feet, Javin saw only two gorms remaining. Both were backed against a tree fighting for their lives. Javin's whole patrol was circled around the two gorms. It was over before Javin himself could get involved. Glancing back over his shoulder he saw that Willow had pulled Gevi free from the body of the war pig.

An involuntary gasp escaped his mouth. She was covered head to toe with blood. His shock was replaced with relief once he realized it was from the War Pig, and not her own blood. Turning away, he quickly took count of his patrol. It only took seconds for him to account for everyone. The only soldier who was injured was the one hit by the flail.

"Give me a count of the gorms," Javin ordered. The count came back to him within seconds. Ten gorms along with two war pigs were dead.

"That should be all of them," commented Javin. "Still, we need to make sure. Partner up and search the area carefully for the next hour. Make sure you stay quiet and under cover. Willow; go check on Grange and Mia." Javin paused, sniffing the air. His face turned sour. He turned to see Gevi standing beside the nearly decapitated pig, a look of complete and absolute horror on her face. The horrible stench of the pig blood assaulted Javin's nostrils. Soldiers started pairing off and heading out into the grove as quick as possible, escaping the disgusting odor.

"Willow, hold on a second," Javin managed to gasp. "Go with Gevi to the creek..." Javin bent over as the smell hit him full on. His eyes watered while he gagged and tried to regain his breath

"This is the most horrible thing I ever..." Gevi turned and ran for the bushes. Javin could hear retching sounds coming from the bushes.

"I'll run to our camp and get her a change of clothes and some soap," Willow said. Javin stood back up and waved her on. A few minutes after Willow left, Gevi reappeared. Her face was pale.

"Willow will be back with your clothes in a few minutes, then you can go to the creek." The smell assaulted Javin again, causing him to cover his nose. Even with Gevi's situation, Javin remembered that he was in command. He kept a careful ear for fighting or yells that would signal a gorm had been found. So far, no sounds had been heard.

"You had to slice that sticking gorm pig through the neck while it was jumping at me," Gevi growled at Javin. She fell to her knees on the ground. Javin turned his head, but he could still hear Gevi gasping and retching. "A second earlier and the pig would have died in front of me, instead of on me." Gevi gasped to Javin between breathes. "A second later, I would be dead and not smelling like a goblin garbage dump. This is your way of getting me back for having a little fun when you got a tiny bit of the stench on you." Gevi raised her eyes to glare accusingly at Javin.

Javin stared defiantly back at her, wondering about her logic. "You know Gevi, you are right. I planned to use you as a weapon against the gorms. With you leading us and smelling like that, victory would be ours. The gorms would all pass out, once they came within a hundred feet of you."

Gevi jumped up from the ground, her green eyes flashing angrily. She started to step toward Javin, but her stomach forced her to turn and run again into the bushes. A retching noise soon followed. Feeling guilty because of losing his temper and knowing firsthand how miserable she felt, Javin started to walk over toward the bushes. Gevi reappeared first. Javin held out a water bottle, which she angrily ripped from his hand. He paused to listen again, but no fighting noises came from the grove.

"Sorry Gevi," Javin said with a sigh. He sat down across from her. Using every bit of strength he had and holding his breath, he managed to keep a straight face. "Willow should be here any minute now. Stench or no stench, I hope you know that I would hold you right now, if I did not have men under my command that need me on the battlefield." Gevi's face softened as she heard the sincerity in his voice.

"I know you would, but right now, I wouldn't hold myself!" she whispered while giving him a forced, agonized smile. Willow picked that moment to return. Gevi jumped up and followed Willow to the creek.

****

When Lamar had asked for volunteers, back when the elves had informed them an army was heading toward the forest, Chellell and Lily had also volunteered to help. Lamar was hesitant about Lily. Taking him aside, Annba told Lamar that Lily had expressed interest in learning the art of healing from her. She suggested to her husband that he assign Lily and Chellell to the elf healers. If Lily still showed interest in healing after having to deal with the horrors of a hospital during a time of war, then Annba would consider apprenticing her. Lamar thought it was a good idea. He assigned both Chellell and Lily to the elf healers. Annba would have been a great asset for the elves, but they still had three young girls to take care of.

Lily finished rubbing a cream on an elf soldier's back shoulder. The elf twitched in pain while Lily tended to the jagged, open wound. Reaching for the bandages, she covered the wound like the healers had shown her. The elf soldier took the treatment better than most patients she had. Typically, injured soldiers had to be held down by her male helpers while she applied the salve that prevented infections. Once she finished, Lily helped the wounded elf roll over onto his good side. She placed several pillows underneath him to make him comfortable. Reaching into her pocket, she pulled out a small, purple leaf, which she handed to the wounded soldier.

"Put this in your mouth and chew on it, whenever the pain starts to bother you," Lily said as she rose up from the side of his bed. "It will help with the pain for several hours if you chew. Don't swallow it. It won't kill you, but it will not help the pain anymore. The last soldier that didn't listen to me got a horrible belly ache to add to his miseries." Lily reached down and ran her fingers through the elf's medium length hair. "Don't worry; you'll be back up and on your feet inside a week." She turned to leave, but the elf reached up and gently grabbed her arm.

"Miss..." Lily turned back around, her bright blue eyes locking onto his slanted brown ones. "If you don't mind, when I get well, I would like to take you to dinner one evening." The elf soldier started to stammer something more, but Lily's eyes and bright smile stopped him.

"I would love to go to dinner with a brave, handsome soldier," Lily replied. The young elf's face lit up. She placed his hand in her hand. "But the general has ordered no dating the nurses until the war is won." The elf's face went from happy to downcast. "After the war, if you find me, and I am not married to another brave and handsome soldier, then I would love to have dinner with you."

Lily gently put his hand back onto the bed, smiling at him the whole time. "Rest; your job at the moment is to get better." The soldier smiled and put the leaf Lily gave him into his mouth.

Lily walked away, once the soldier closed his eyes. Passing Chellell, Lily held up seven fingers and mouthed the word "seven" silently. Chellell scowled at Lily, before walking over to a moaning elf soldier who was waiting for treatment.

****

After finishing a twelve-hour shift at the hospital, Chellell and Lily sat at a table in a large, crowded tent. Though very tired, they always made time to eat supper together, before going off to their shared tent with eight other nurses.

"You cheated," Chellell huffed while she carefully cut a slab of meat with her knife. Number nine only asked you out so you would stop flirting and he could get some sleep."

"Now, Sweetie," replied a smug Lily, "jealousy doesn't look good on you. You're very pretty, but we know now, that elven soldiers prefer blondes over redheads." Lily tossed her hair with her hand, causing Chellell to smile. She was really glad to have a friend like Lily.

"I had several soldiers ask me on a date. One offered to marry me," Ledia huffed as she sat down with the two girls. "Their eyesight must get blurry from the medicine they give them to ask a woman as old as I am. Of course, I informed them that I was already married to a soldier." She took a quick bite of a red fruit that filled her plate.

Chellell quietly wondered to herself how Ledia always knew what people were talking about. "Young men in the army never change; they will flirt with any woman, even if a woman like myself is old enough to be their grandmother," Ledia said between mouthfuls. "Dwarf, elf, or human, they are all the same." Chellell and Lily both started laughing. Ledia had impressed both girls. Even though she was working a full night with the elven naturalists, she still worked half a day in the hospital. The conversation quickly turned serious, when Chellell asked how the battle was going.

"Not so good, right now. You noticed the flood of wounded." Both girls nodded. "Their magic users have found a way to stop the eagles. They also caused havoc on the front lines with fire spells. Part of the invading army split from the main group and attacked the forest a half day's ride east of here. The elves were forced to relocate soldiers over to that side of the woods. It's a good thing elven women are naturalists. The animals fighting for us are the only reason the Elven Forest hasn't fallen yet."

Chellell looked sick while Ledia was talking. Deep inside, she wished there was something she could do to help. Ledia noticed Chellell's face, and signaled for the girls to lean closer toward her. "This stays with you. No blabbing, understood?" Both girls nodded their heads. Ledia stared hard at both of them for several seconds, making sure they understood. Finally, she started whispering as quietly as she could in the noisy lunchroom. "I am joining with Kitty an hour after midnight. I sent him to Lamar a couple of hours ago. Lamar and his group are going after the magic users."

Lily stomach churned. "Gevi?" she asked. Chellell said Javin's name at exactly the same time.

"The battle report I saw, stated Gevi and Javin already got into it with the gorms," replied Ledia in a hushed whisper. "Kitty saw them, so I know they are fine. I am confused though, why Kitty keeps carrying on about how horrible the two kids smell." Ledia saw the looks of alarm on the two girl's faces. "They are uninjured; Kitty just thinks Gevi and Javin really stink." Ledia said. "Take some time to pray hard for them, before you go to bed tonight." Ledia stopped eating and concentrated on the girls.

"By the way, do any you know a seven-foot-tall, young man, who is built like an ox, with hair as blond as Lily's?"

"No," replied Lily.

"Yes", came from the lips of Chellell. "That sounds like Merion. He is the number two fighter at the guilds. He and Javin faced each other in the final round, four years running."

"I thought I heard the name Javin from him, though he is delirious and hard to understand," Ledia replied.

"How badly is he hurt?" asked Chellell, concern in her voice.

"He is worse than hurt. He is seriously wounded. His condition will be touch-and-go for a while. He wandered into the forest from the east by himself and ran into a gorm patrol. The elves rescued him, but not before he received several arrowheads in his back. He has lost a lot of blood."

"You said we need to pray tonight. Why wait? Can we pray now?" Lily asked.

Ledia nodded and bowed her head. With her head bowed, Chellell thought about how she could help fight. Without magic she felt helpless. While Ledia prayed and Chellell pondered how to help, a powerful, foreign thought suddenly invaded her mind. "Prayer is more powerful than magic, Chellell."

Confusion filled her mind, while she bowed her head and listened to Lily pray. Confusion was replaced by skepticism as Chellell listened to Lily ask for the impossible in prayer. She asked God that no elf or human die this night, and that the battle would end this very night, with a victory for the elves.

Ledia was surprised at the power and the depth of Lily's prayer. For a new believer, this young woman had an amazing amount of faith. "Have your stuff packed and with you at the hospital, in the morning," said Ledia "If we have another day like today, the gorms will be in the Elven City before nightfall, tomorrow."

****

Lamar watched happily as dark clouds completely hid the moon and stars. He looked over at his three companions, praying silently for their safety this night. Last time he tried a maneuver like this, over half his men died.

These men had survived with him. Lamar jerked his mind back to the present, away from the Ogre Invasion of many years past. Even though they were much older now, Lamar trusted nobody more for an infiltration attack like this. "The wolves again are going to howl and draw blood this night," he thought to himself. He drew both short swords, holding them out toward the three men with him. They drew their swords, placing them on top of Lamar's swords. Each sword blade was etched with a wolf. The infamous special force unit known as the Wolf Troop was reunited in combat, once again; reunited, after twenty years.

****

"I still smell like a goblin sewer." Gevi had her mouth right on

241

Javin's ear, while kneeling right behind him. Her voice was so low, it carried no more than a foot from them. Her right arm was tangled around his body, but her left arm kept a firm grip on her staff. Her body was pressed up against his back. They were both watching the gorm camp fires from behind bushes outside the exterior of the gorm camp. Kitty was right beside them, pressed into the high grass.

"Kitty thinks we both stink," Gevi whispered while giving a quick glare sideways toward the tiger. Kitty had both his paws on his face, covering his nose.

Javin twisted his head back until his mouth reached Gevi's ear. Her hair was blowing in his face. "To me, you will always smell like a summer rose," he whispered back. In a daring moment, he kissed her lightly on the cheek. She still smelled, but not as bad. Then, he glanced down at the sand glass near his foot. Only a few minutes left. His stomach started to tighten with fear.

Gevi was shocked speechless by Javin's light kiss. He had never done anything like that before. "Shy to a fault," she thought to herself, as a warm glow spread through her body. She squeezed him with her one arm and put her lips by his ear again. "You're a liar, but I love you for it." She kissed him back on the cheek.

Javin smiled, while Gevi's hair blew again in his face. After a minute or two, Javin pointed down to the sand glass. The sand would be in the bottom of the glass in less than a minute. Seeing their time nearly up, Gevi gently reached over and strapped Javin's face guard back into place. Javin turned his head back, to whisper one last thing to her. "You go left and center; I go right. Stay back at the edge of the camp with your bow and pick off whatever enemy you can."

Irritation flashed through Gevi. This was the third time he had given her the same instructions for the attack. She had no time to make a retort though because Javin was drawing both swords. The sand had run out of the glass. Together, they stood up. Gevi's staff was pointed toward a campfire with a small group of gorms sitting around it. Javin's sword was pointed right toward a group of patrolling gorms.

"Three, two, one," Javin said so quietly only Gevi could hear. Lightning crackled from Gevi's staff at the same time as a ball of fire flew from Javin's sword. Neither watched the destruction they caused. Instead, they turned toward their next targets. Lightning and fire flashed again, destroying a medium sized tent and a group of gorms around a cooking campfire. Both lightning and fire flew over the heads of the Farm Circle soldiers, who were running full speed toward the gorm encampment.

Gorms screamed when the swords from Farm Circle soldiers cut into their bodies. Eighty Farm Circle soldiers met little resistance. Once they got near campfires, the soldiers started grabbing burning logs. As Javin had ordered, the soldiers started burning every tent and flammable thing in sight. Meanwhile, Kitty disappeared into the darkness. The only sign of his progress was the tiger's roar which was always followed by a gorm scream. Eventually, gorm guards, in full armor, started entering the combat.

Javin's flaming right sword cut through a gorm's armor and deep into his elbow, causing the gorm's axe to fly from his now numb hand. His left sword went out sideways, directly into the stomach of a second gorm. Javin twisted away, avoiding the sword that flew from the grasp of the gorm he had just killed. The gorm with the mangled arm turned and ran. Javin let him go, his attention now on a giant that was lumbering his way.

The giant stood ten feet tall. He was carrying a two-handed sword nearly as long as the giant was tall. Javin's blood ran ice cold. The giant smiled wickedly at him. Javin wished with all his heart, Thunderfall was here now. As the giant raised his sword, his chest exploded.

Javin stared at the giant in complete shock. The giant stood there, looking at the big hole in his chest. He slowly fell forward, landing at Javin's feet. Looking over his shoulder, he saw Gevi grinning at him, bow in hand. Shaking his head, Javin started to go after a fleeing gorm when a loud boom sounded off in the grasslands behind them. He quickly turned and ran toward Gevi. Together, they both ran from the gorm camp, back into the grasslands.

Farm Circle soldiers gathered around the two men that had stayed behind to set off the boom stick Gevi had given them. They had set it off when the sand had run to the bottom of the glass. Javin counted every soldier as they arrived. He was surprised to learn that all eighty were accounted for, and no one was seriously injured. He sent two men back to the grove, with minor injuries, before quickly moving on to their next location. Ten minutes later, they were in position at the rear of the army; an army that was now wide awake.

"What did you do to that giant?" Javin whispered once they settled down again with the soldiers lying flat in the grass behind him. This time, Gevi was to his right, behind a much bigger bush.

"I made more explosive arrows, after they successfully blew up the monkey-man statue. These arrows are one of the reasons you need to stay close to me. I'll protect you when big, bad giants try to chop off your head." Javin rolled his eyes and made a mental note to try not to be so overprotective of Gevi. She was probably more dangerous than anything he was going to meet in this battle.

****

Lamar and the other three 'wolves' moved, as soon as the first lightning flash from Gevi's staff went off. Following the shadows, they crept toward their target, a tent in the middle of the camp. The elven naturalists had used high flying eagles to locate the tents where two of the magic users stayed. Hearing a grunt, Lamar glanced back to see one of his men pull a sword out of a gorm, before vanishing into a nearby shadow. The distraction Javin and the Farm Circle soldiers had given them helped, because a lot of the gorms were rushing toward that end of the camp, where the fighting was going on.

Lamar's wolves were so skilled, that only two other gorms had to be dispatched while they snuck through half the camp, before arriving at their target location. Sensing no magic, Lamar realized that the magic users were not in the tents at this moment. Waving toward his men, two of them went into the tent to Lamar's right. Lamar was about to step into the other tent when he heard a shrill clanging noise.

Spinning around and grabbing the soldier next to him, he saw that bars had slammed into place around his men in the other tent. "A trap!" Lamar realized. The two of them dived for cover, amongst a pile of barrels. They were fully concealed when a dozen armed gorms surrounded the tent. They yanked the tent canvas away, revealing the two soldiers trapped in the cage.

Lamar and his companion watched from their hiding place while the gorms disarmed his soldiers. He knew his wolves were highly trained and experienced, but right now two of his wolves were in deep trouble. The gorms were poking spears through the bars, tormenting his men. One of his men was bleeding from a deep scratch one of the gorms had put across his back. The gorms were laughing and grunting as they toyed with the humans in the cage.

Finally, two humans approached the cage. One had a snow white familiar on his shoulder, while the other one had a familiar that was deep purple. Both dragons were hissing at the men in the cage.

"Bring them out," one of the magic users ordered. Both men were led out of the cage, gorm spears held to their backs. "Which one of you is General Lamar?" One of the men instantly stepped forward. Spears snapped forward toward the man's chest, stopping him from advancing any further.

"So, the infamous Lamar tried the same tactics he did twenty years ago," the second magic user said snidely. He had a white beard with gray hair, much older than his fellow magic user. "Yes, I remember the truth of what really happened during the Ogre Invasions. When I learned there was a good chance you were involved with the pitchfork rebellion, and were allied with the elves, I figured you might try the same trick again." The magic user started laughing and wheezing.

The real Lamar slowly pulled two small knifes from his boots, one for each hand. "I decided I would think like you, Lamar," the older magic user continued after he regained his breath from the wheezing laughter. "If I was facing this army, I would try to assassinate the magic users. Therefore, we would go to our tents in plain sight of your spying birds, and then teleport to our real tents." The magic user broke out in laughter again. He wheezed so hard it took several minutes for the older man to regain himself.

The younger magician was starting to grow impatient. "Take them to the general; he will hang them in front of the elves, come morning."

"Wait a second," the older magic user ordered, stopping the younger one from sending the gorms away with the captives. "I want Lamar to know that we know where his men are outside the camp. They will be dead before he reaches our general."

The mage's maniacal laugher was cut off by the blade of a knife that had embedded itself into his chest. The mage looked down in disbelief at the knife that was ending his life. His familiar screamed a high-pitched, blood curdling scream, which sent the gorms to their knees. The older magic user crumpled, falling on top of the younger magic user who was already dead from Lamar's second knife. His white familiar screamed even louder than the first familiar. Both vanished into thin air.

The captive men took advantage of the downed gorms, exploding out of the circle of gorms, hitting the ground, and rolling to their feet. They retrieved their swords before leaping back into the fray. Lamar blasted into the gorms with both short swords swinging. Swords and bodies collided. Two gorms managed to flee, screaming through the camp. The others lay dead, at the feet of Lamar and his wolves. Without a word, the four men turned and headed south through the camp, toward Javin and the rest of the Farm Circle soldiers. Still keeping to the shadows, they moved at a fast pace. With the other Farm circle soldiers in danger, the third mage would have to wait for another day.

****

Javin waited while the sand in the sand clock slowly fell to the bottom glass. They were to wait one hour at the south end of the enemy camp before starting the next attack. They had thirty minutes to go. Yawning, he watched the torches from the gorm patrols moving through the west and north grasslands.

"What is that?" Gevi asked. She pointed toward the East. Clouds had been moving from east to west all night, shading the light of a half moon and a quarter moon. What they were seeing was different. This looked like a solid wall of clouds, from ground to sky. Lightning was flashing throughout the ominous storm cloud. The wind was picking up speed throughout the camp.

Across from their hiding place, Javin was starting to get alarmed with another development. A whole gang of gorms, with three giants, were moving into fighting formations. A human with a familiar on his shoulder was standing with the giants. An order was quickly barked out by one of the giants, causing the enemy to charge toward Javin and his group. Javin had to make a split second decision, run or fight.

"Get the magic user!" The words had barely left Javin's mouth when lightning flew from Gevi's staff into the magic user. There wasn't much left of the poor man. All three giants, along with a couple of gorms, were on their backs, blown down by Gevi's blast. Two of the giants leaped quickly back to their feet, but the third was lying very still. One of the giants bellowed and charged behind the gorms. Javin jumped up, both swords drawn and flaming. He and his men charged forward, colliding with the gorms.

Javin's swords were lashing out in all directions, sinking into gorm flesh and deflecting gorm weapons. Flaming swords, with pitch black armor, made for an ominous sight. Kitty was protecting his back with slashing claws and gleaming fangs. Several gorms screamed out, "The Black Knight" in their guttural language, before fleeing the fight.

Smoking gorm bodies littered Javin's path. His right sword blazed downward, cutting a spear in half. The left stabbed forward through leather armor into the chest of another gorm. Javin nimbly jumped sideways, crashing into a gorm and knocking the creature to the ground. A massive, spiked club crashed into the ground that Javin had vacated. He flicked his right sword out sideways and downward, finishing the gorm he had knocked to the ground. His eyes, however, were focused on the giant who had tried to smash him.

This time, Javin felt no fear. Adrenaline flooded through his body, and he prepared himself to finally fight one of the fearsome giants. As the giant raised his spiked club, an arrow pierced his jaw. The arrow immediately exploded, causing the giant's head to fly in a direction away from its body. Javin turned around to see Gevi shrug her shoulders, in an "I told you so" movement.

The wind started to blow even harder, but the fight continued. Roaring wind was drowning out the desperate battle between gorm and human. The strange, black cloud Gevi had pointed out earlier was closing in on the gorm camp. In amazement, Gevi watched as trees started snapping in half before being sucked up into the cloud.

"Retreat," Javin screamed. He stabbed forward with one sword while swinging sideways with the other. One gorm got it in the stomach, the other in the wrist. Javin spun and ran back toward their original hiding place, diving to the ground beside Gevi. The men of Farm Circle disengaged and followed him. All of them diving for cover, wherever they could find it.

The fast moving, spinning cloud crashed into the east end of the camp. Tents and other equipment in the camp were ripped off the ground and sucked up into the cloud, along with hundreds of gorms, and even a few giants. Nothing was spared that was in the path of the dark, spinning cloud. Powerful blasts of lightning flashed into the ground with violence. Javin rolled himself on top of Gevi as debris from the camp started raining down around them.

It was over as fast as it started. Javin rolled off Gevi and saw that the strange cloud was heading West, out through the grasslands. The gorm army was devastated. A path of barren earth over one hundred feet wide, went right through the middle of the gorm army camp. The fierce wind had even pulled the grass from the ground. Debris was everywhere. Not a single tent was standing. Javin stared in pure disbelief at the chaos he saw. The gorms they had been fighting with took off running back into the camp, leaving the last giant, standing alone.

"I got this one," Gevi said as she rose up from the ground. She pulled a strange looking arrow from her quiver. She twisted the tail of the arrow until it clicked and then set the arrow to her bow. Drawing the arrow back, Gevi aimed the arrow toward the giant, who was staring straight back at her. She had never seen fear in a giant before, but this one clearly was afraid. The giant spun around and started running. Two giant steps were taken before the arrow struck his lower back. The explosion threw the giant through the air, where he crashed and rolled into an overturned wagon. "That's what you get for trying to squash my man," said Gevi loud enough so the soldiers around them could hear. Javin pretended not to hear the snickering of his soldiers.

****

Ledia's eyes snapped open. Mac, along with his elven battalion, surrounded her. Ledia's attention fell on her husband. "We need to attack, now, with everything we've got." She said this in a quiet, matter-of-fact voice. Mac looked into her eyes, and saw everything he needed to see.

"Get everyone up and ready to hop," he ordered the elf sitting next to him. Mac was moving through the elves, shouting orders. He ordered another elf to report his intentions back to the commanders in the main camp, while sending others out to the other four battalion commanders, not too far from Mac's location. Mac and his men were a mile from the edge of the forest. He wanted to move as fast as he could to the forest edge.

A short time later, Mac was surveying the enemy camp through a spyglass. As he focused in on the camp, the clouds cleared, leaving the enemy camp bathed in moonlight. He sat the glass down beside him, giving Ledia an astonished look. She smiled knowingly back at him. Turning to the elf on the other side of him, he gave a final order. "We charge on my command." The elves started relaying Mac's orders through the ranks.

****

Lamar crawled out from under the tent that had blown on top of him. Looking around, he saw the other wolves were with him. Amazingly enough, none of them were hurt.

"What in the world was that?" asked one of Lamar's men. Several gorms ran by, completely ignoring them.

"Worst storm I've ever seen in my life," commented another one.

"Enough chit-chat; let's move," ordered Lamar. With that, he started moving through the darkness toward the location Javin was supposed to be at. The small group almost reached their destination, when Lamar abruptly stopped.

Chapter 22

Evil shall slay the wicked: and they that hate the righteous shall be desolate. – The Guide

Thunderfall picked himself up from the grass. "What was that?" the dwarf next to him asked. He was sitting up and pulling grass out of his beard.

"Make sure everyone is alright," Thunderfall ordered. The dwarf jumped to his feet and ran back through the dwarven lines behind them. The large cloud had barely missed them, passing north of the marching dwarves. Ripped up grass and dirt had rained down on the dwarves. Thunderfall brushed dirt out of his beard while stomping around impatiently. Finally, his brother dwarf returned with the word no dwarf was injured. "Form up!" roared Thunderfall. Dwarves fell into a rectangular formation behind Thunderfall. The spacing left to right, front to back, was exactly the same for each for the three hundred dwarves. "Move out!" Three hundred dwarves started jogging in perfect formation.

A short time later, along the edge of the Elven Forest, the dwarf battalion came to a complete stop. On the horizon, Thunderfall could make out activity. A dwarf came up and handed him a spyglass before returning to formation. Thunderfall silently focused in on what he saw. A few minutes later, he brought the spyglass down.

"Ironhand," Thunderfall called out. Ironhand came forward out of formation. "Take seventy-five brethren into the forest. Circle around until you find the elves that are fighting these gorms I see up ahead. Make your services available to the elves."

"Aye, Battlelord," Ironhand replied. He spun back to the formation. A couple of sharp commands and a group of dwarves disappeared into the Elven Forest.

The next half hour was spent with dwarves hiding in the grass between the sparse tree cover that bordered the Elven Forest. The spyglass was to Thunderfall's eye the whole time. Finally, he put it back down to his side.

"Let's battle, brothers," he called out behind him. The dwarven army started running in perfect formation straight toward the gorms gathered ahead at the edge of the Elven Forest.

****

"Gevi! Gevi! Gevi!" the men around Javin started cheering. The bodies of the giants and the mage Gevi had killed were laid out on the edge of the camp, in front of the men. The area in front of Javin was empty now, with the exception of a handful of gorms.

All of a sudden, Kitty leaped up, and with a yowl, bounded down toward the gorm camp. It only took the Great Northern Tiger a few seconds to cover the ground. With a swipe of his paw, Kitty knocked down a gorm preparing to launch an arrow. Another screamed as Kitty pounced on him, biting down before jumping to his next victim. Before Javin could even think about what to do next, Gevi spoke up.

"We should attack now, Javin," Gevi said while she lowered herself back into a kneeling position beside Javin's prone body. Javin had to agree. The enemy camp was in pure chaos. Saying a silent prayer that his father was spared from that wild windstorm, Javin leapt to his feet.

"Attack!" he yelled while flaming both swords again. The men around him jumped to their feet and followed Javin down into the gorm camp.

Both flaming swords spun slowly through Javin's hands while he stepped over a gorm that had actually tried to attack him. Most of the gorms ran as soon as they saw the Black Knight. Javin realized that the great windstorm that had destroyed the gorm camp had not dropped any rain. The Hand of God had to be behind tonight's events. His thoughts were interrupted when a screaming gorm ran toward him with Kitty only several feet behind him. With a roar Kitty launched himself into the air, hitting the gorm square in the back. It fell dead at Javin's feet. After a quick head rub from Javin, Kitty was off again.

"Even swords; odd bows," Javin called out. His men gathered behind him, half with bows drawn while the other half held swords. Javin led the eighty Farm Circle soldiers toward the middle of the camp, hoping to find more gorms. Every few seconds, Javin would hear a bow string twang from his men, shooting at panicked gorms.

"Give me your arrows," Gevi said, after she fired her last normal arrow into a gorm off to Javin's right.

"Take them all," he replied with a smile.

"She is one dangerous woman," Javin thought again to himself. Gevi took the arrows off his back. In the darkness, Kitty's yowls filled the night, causing even greater panic throughout the camp.

They continued to slowly move forward. Out of nowhere, a giant surrounded by a group of armored gorms, came into view. Arrows flew from Javin's men into the group, dropping several of the gorms. The Giant roared and charged right toward Javin and his soldiers. Javin's men moved to engage the enemy.

Steel clashing with steel rang through Javin's ears, followed by an earth shattering explosion. "Gevi must have gotten the giant," Javin thought to himself while his left sword stabbed into the gorm in front of him. Stepping forward, he blocked a mace while slicing into the neck of the gorm with his other sword. He was about to strike a third gorm when Kitty's paw crashed into its head. Javin barely was able to change the direction of his sword, missing Kitty by a hands width. The Great Northern Tiger started spinning, fangs and claws lashing out in all directions at the unfortunate gorms around him. They had seen enough. Gorms started running, only to be dropped by Javin's men waiting behind the fight with bows drawn.

"Mac is right. You take all the challenge out of fighting," Javin muttered toward the cat that was already chasing down one of the fleeing gorms. Moving forward, he saw the dead giant lying on the ground, confirming his earlier thought. Gevi's explosive arrow had hit the giant, right in the heart. "Between Gevi and Kitty, it's a miracle I even get to swing a sword. Might as well walk around selling cookies, and let Gevi and that cat take care of the fighting," Javin said to the soldiers next to him.

The soldiers responded by cheering "Gevi! Kitty! Gevi! Kitty!" Javin joined in with the rest of his men, enjoying Gevi's embarrassment as the excited soldiers cheered.

"Five giants to, let's see, oh yeah, to zero," said Willow as she put her arm on Javin's shoulder. "Now that the power of a woman!"

Several men chuckled. "Don't forget the magic user," one of them called out. "Gevi! Kitty! Gevi! Kitty!"

They continued to cheer, although they kept their eyes open for any gorms or giants. Willow then turned to Gevi who was blushing with embarrassment. Gevi raised her bow and fired a quick shot into a running gorm. "You know Gevi; we elven women have a saying for unmarried women. Don't outdo the man your chasing too often, or he will find a woman he can outdo. You should let Javin have one giant every once in a while, maybe a small one." Gevi turned even redder, but Javin burst out laughing so hard, tears came to his eyes. Finally, he got control of himself.

"Enough." he yelled while wiping tears on his sleeve. "We have unfinished business to take care of."

****

"I am getting too old for this," Lamar thought to himself once he rolled back to his feet. The giant's two-handed sword was stuck a foot into the ground, in the spot he had vacated. With lightning fast speed, the giant general ripped the sword from the earth, causing chunks of dirt to fly skyward. Lamar started to lunge forward, but was forced backwards when the giant's sword whistled sideways through the air.

"Run while you can, little man," the giant general over the army spat through his long, black beard. His giant two-handed sword was held easily out in front of him. "Run, before I squash you like the bug you are."

Lamar stayed silent, slowly circling around the giant general. The giant's thick armor left him few open spots, but he knew he would have to get his sword into one soon. He was starting to tire from the constant dodging. A noise distracted both combatants, though they still kept one eye on each other.

The north end of the camp, closest to the Elven Forest, erupted in elven war cries, mixed with wolf howls and other animal noises. The moonlight illuminated gorms that were running away from the attacking elven army.

"Cowards!" screamed the giant in rage. He lunged angrily toward Lamar. The wild swing of the giant's sword crashed into the ground. This time though, Lamar barely moved sideways to avoid the sword. Both short swords lashed out toward the hand of the giant. One sword rang out as it slammed into the steel of the giant's gauntlets. The second sword cut into

250

a gap right at the giant's elbow. Blood flowed down the arm of the giant.

Lamar continued his movement forward, swinging both swords as fast as he could toward the giant's knee. Each sword bounced harmlessly off the giant's armor. The giant stepped back several steps, trying to get his sword back into position. With one arm injured and bleeding, the giant struggled with the weight of his sword. Pressing the advantage, Lamar stayed close to the giant. Whistling swords slammed into the giant's armor.

The giant's return strokes with the sword were too slow now to concern Lamar, but he could not find an opening through the giant's armor. His right sword bounced off the giant's thigh when he spotted what he was looking for. The giant's chain mail hung over a bulging stomach. There was a gap of several inches between the giant's hips and his stomach.

Lamar lunged into the giant. He stabbed upwards with both swords right before his collision with the giant. Swords went through the gap in the armor, piercing deep into the giant general's abdomen. The giant jerked back with a roar of pain, spinning to the ground. A great leg crashed into the side of Lamar, sending him flying through the air. He landed with a thud, pain shooting through his wrist. Glancing at his twisted, broken wrist, Lamar slowly pushed himself up from the ground. Preparing to fight with only one hand, he looked toward the giant. He was lying face down on the ground.

He knew reinforcements had arrived when he heard a voice yell, "One giant for Lamar; five giants for Gevi!"

Lamar struggled for a few seconds to catch his breath and clear his mind from the pain in his wrist. He wondered how Gevi had taken down five giants. His answer came a few seconds later. A ten-foot giant appeared, and charged right toward Lamar's men. Gevi's arrow exploded into the unfortunate giant's chest, before anyone else could even react.

"One giant for Lamar; six giants for Gevi!" Willow yelled out

"Split into your former groups of ten," Lamar ordered with a shake of his head toward Gevi. Javin saw his dad's wrist, but decided to keep his questions to himself. The men quickly formed up into the groups he had organized them into earlier. "The gorms are running, and I aim to keep them running. You hunt gorms until the morning light and then head for the command tent in the Elven Forest." A tiger's yowl interrupted Lamar. "See who can get more gorms than that cat," Lamar said while focusing on Gevi. "You are also to get more giants than Gevi. How many, Gevi?"

Gevi slid behind Javin, using his body to hide her embarrassment from Lamar. Javin held up six fingers, while smiling ear to ear.

"Six giants, one mage, and dozens of gorms!" Willow shouted out.

Lamar was relieved to hear the last mage was taken care of. "Let's see if anyone can beat Gevi's six giants then. Get going!" Everyone headed out looking for gorms, but Lamar stopped Javin and his group. "Javin, take your group North to the elven command tent in the forest. Tell them I think they should press the gorms out in the plains for the next couple of days, so that they don't have a chance to regroup. Set up a nice camp for everyone. They are going to be tired when they get there in the morning. Have a good breakfast waiting." With that, Lamar gathered his group of ten, while Javin and his group started heading toward the Elven Forest.

"Javin, make sure someone besides Gevi cooks breakfast," someone from Lamar's group yelled back to them. Gevi froze in mid-step beside Javin. Spinning around, she pointed her staff toward Lamar's group.

"Who said that?" she yelled back. The embarrassment from her face was gone, replaced by anger. Javin grabbed her before she could march toward Lamar.

"Whoa, Gevi," said a laughing Javin. "You can get your revenge at camp in the morning. I will let you cook breakfast for Lamar's group."

Gevi stopped pulling against Javin. "You men are jealous, because a woman got more giants than you could get, even in your dreams." She yelled this toward Lamar's group, who were laughing as they marched away. She spun back on Javin, with her bright, green eyes flashing. "And I will cook breakfast, for everyone, just to show you a woman can fight, and cook!" She pulled free of Javin's grasp and started marching toward the Elven Forest.

"Is she really that bad a cook?" one of the men asked Javin in what he thought was a low voice.

"Be careful how you answer that, Dear," Gevi called out without looking back. Javin gave the man a wink and hurried to catch up to Gevi.

****

The giant captain over the battalion that had split off from the main army was relaying an order when a deafening roar filled his ears. Spinning around in alarm, the giant scanned the grasslands for the source of the noise. He had never heard anything like this before. His alarm grew when he saw a wall of charging, roaring dwarves, coming straight at him.

Gorms started screaming and running for the safety of the Elven Forest. Lowering his spear, the giant captain set his feet, in preparation for the charging dwarves. A dwarf crashed into the spear with his shield, running at full speed. The spear shattered with such force that both giant and dwarf were flung to the ground. Jumping to his feet, the giant roared as two more dwarves slammed into his knees. He flew through the air, landing flat on his back. The giant looked up, to see a dwarf calmly standing above him, with a black steel, two-headed battle axe raised toward the sky. It was the last thing the giant ever saw.

"Into the forest," ordered Thunderfall. He easily ripped his great axe out of the giant. "Not a single gorm is to make it out of the forest, alive."

Meeting little resistance, the dwarves advanced rapidly through the Elven Forest. Finally, word came to Thunderfall that a large pocket of gorms was trying to escape the forest. Thunderfall pulled fifty dwarves with him to take on this gorm formation. The rest continued northward, fighting gorms as they found them.

252

Spying a large log on the ground, Thunderfall stopped the dwarves. He ordered four large shields secured to the end of the log. The dwarfs were known worldwide for their ingenious engineering. Within minutes, the shields flared out around the log. Half a dozen dwarves easily lifted it up onto their powerful shoulders, before marching toward the enemy location. Dwarf and gorm spotted each other at the same time. With a roar, the dwarves charged, without a single word from Thunderfall.

The gorms would have buckled and run, but a sharp command from their officer kept them in a square formation, with spears sticking out behind small round shields. It would have been better if they had run. Dwarves, with their homemade battering ram, crashed into the formation. Shields, mounted to the log shattered the gorm spears. Charging dwarves, following right behind the log, plowed into the gorms, sending them flying backwards. Axes started swinging.

Thunderfall's mighty axe was swinging at amazing speed, piling up gorm bodies around him. Neither Gorm sword, nor shield, nor armor, offered any protection against Thunderfall and his battle axe. One swing would break a sword, and then bust a shield, before blowing through the armor of the unfortunate gorm. It was over in minutes. Thunderfall stepped out of the pile of gorm bodies around him. Six dwarves were wounded, but none were dead. He ordered several dwarves to stay and help the wounded; the rest continued the hunt for gorms.

****

"I knew we should have marched faster," grumbled Thunderfall. The dwarf was sitting by Gevi on a sturdy log, in a clearing on the northern edge of the Elven Forest. Gevi smiled contentedly as she put her head on his powerful shoulder and wrapped an arm around him. All week, Thunderfall had complained because the dwarven army had missed the majority of the fighting. Gevi knew that her father was more upset over the fact he had missed how God, Himself, had handed the elves a victory with the great windstorm.

"Daddy, are you going to tell me why the dwarves have been calling you Battlelord? They never called you that before! I would remember that."

"They were under strict orders to only call me Thunderfall," the massive dwarf grumped. "But I will tell you everything, if you promise not to tell anyone, except Javin." Gevi lifted her head off Thunderfall's shoulder, looking at him with a puzzled expression. "I have my reasons. Do you agree?" Gevi nodded her head in agreement.

Unwrapping herself from him, she repositioned herself to face him. Thunderfall sighed and looked squarely into Gevi's emerald green eyes. "The dwarves have a king, my brother as you know already. However, the Dwarven King is not the same in power as the human king. Dwarven kings rules the Dwarven City and the mines. The dwarven kingship does not pass down through a royal family. A son does not become king when the father dies, nor is the king elected by vote of the people."

"Then how did your brother become king?" Gevi asked.

253

"Well, every one hundred years the dwarves have a huge feast and festival. All officials in the dwarven government resign, including the Battlelord and the King. A wrestling match is held. Dwarves spend decades training for this match, especially those who want to be Battlelord or King. The last match was over ninety years ago. Dwarves wrestled. One loss meant the dwarf was out. The top twenty places are marked for official positions. They wrestle until only two undefeated contestants are left. Nearly a century ago the undefeated were myself and my oldest brother."

"So he out-wrestled you and became King, while you became..."

"No Gevi, I won. I chose to be Battlelord of the dwarves. My brother then chose to be King. Number three chose what he wanted, and so on. You see Gevi, a king rules the city and the mines, but the Battlelord is not under the authority of the king."

"Basically, the Battlelord is never bothered with ruling, taxes, mining, and other things of everyday life that the king deals with. The Battlelord rules the armies of the dwarves. He can call every dwarf, including the King, out of the mines for war. Every dwarf, young or old, male or female, is required to fight, should the order ever come from the Battlelord. The Battlelord is focused outside of the mines and the city, watching the gorms, giants, humans, elves, and so on."

"Why did you never tell your own daughter this? Why the secrets?" For the first time, Gevi had a look of hurt on her face.

Thunderfall sighed. "There are several reasons, but mainly because the humans of Preveshawl did not need to know who I was while I lived among them to repay the debt."

"Another reason for the secret was you. Once you were in the picture, and word got out about who I was, then your life would have been in grave danger. Imagine a giant or a gorm getting their hands on the daughter of the Dwarven Battlelord! Ogres and goblins would love to get even with me as well. Your safety depended on them never knowing who I was. Over the last century, very few of these creatures ever saw me as Battlelord and lived. No one would ever suspect a dwarf metal smith living with humans to be the Dwarven Battlelord. Even the elves had no idea who I really was. You noticed they called me by the title of prince."

Gevi looked thoughtful before bending forward to give Thunderfall a hug, "I love you Daddy," she whispered, her face disappearing into his beard. "I guess your secret makes sense." Thunderfall returned the embrace. Gevi let go of the embrace and leaned back, a sly smile on her face. "Still, I want to go on record as saying that using wrestling to pick your government leaders is extremely silly."

Thunderfall started chuckling, "you know, Girl, the older I get, the more I have to agree with you. Think about it though, it is no sillier to use wrestling than methods other kingdoms use. The richest, the best speaker, the best looking, or who your father or mother is. Because you can wrestle or speak charmingly does not mean you can rule or lead. One day, maybe, the dwarven tradition will change. We will have to wait and see."

Thunderfall was silent for several long seconds. "You know something else? If the truth be known, the happiest time in my life was being plain old Thunderfall, the smith. Let's keep it that way."

"My lips are sealed," replied Gevi. "You know Daddy; it was quite a celebration this morning, wasn't it?" Gevi inquired as she looked up into a night sky full of stars. Thunderfall nodded his head in acknowledgement while Gevi's fingers gently stroked his long beard. The elves had declared a big feast of thanksgiving and praise, thanking the Lord of the Stars for the victory he had given them.

"May we join the Great Giant Slayer?" Javin asked. He was with Lily and Chellell. The three sat on a log across from Gevi and Thunderfall. He returned Gevi's glare with a smile. Giant Slayer was the new nickname all the elves were calling Gevi, much to her dismay.

"What did the Dwarven King want?" Chellell asked Gevi. Gevi pulled her glare from Javin, but Thunderfall spoke up before she could reply.

"My brothers seem to want some of those fancy, exploding arrows, from Gevi." Thunderfall ran his hand over his axe that was leaning against the log they were sitting on. "I told him a real dwarf uses an axe."

"A real dwarf can be squashed like a bug by a real giant," Gevi huffed. "Uncle Hardstone offered me a gold piece per arrow, for one hundred arrows. The dwarves will supply the materials I need to make each arrow."

"Paying too much for them, I say," grumbled Thunderfall, but he gave Gevi a gentle squeeze as he said it. The pride on his face was obvious. Gevi didn't say anything; instead, she gave him a big squeeze back. Thunderfall unwrapped himself from Gevi and stood up. "I'm getting too old to stay up this late. You kids better get to bed soon yourselves; we've got to leave at first light for the Ruins of the Linkrins."

They wished Thunderfall a good night before he left. The four remaining friends got off the log and sat in a circle on the grass.

"I hear a certain elf prince has been taking a certain red-haired girl out to dinner every evening this week," Gevi said smugly. Chellell's face turned bright red.

"I heard that he pulled rank on several elven soldiers who were going to take her up on her offer of a dinner date," Lily said giggling. "She agreed to go to dinner with any of her patients that asked."

"Lily!" exploded Chellell, her face still red. "You started the whole contest about who would get the most soldiers to ask us for a date. And you are one to talk! You've gotten a free dinner every day this week."

"I may have had more soldiers ask me out, but you won the prize," Lily replied with a smirk. If possible, Chellell's face turned even redder. "Besides, I made it clear to all that asked this week, that I only wanted to be friends. They still took me to dinner."

"Ledia told me about that incredible prayer you prayed, Lily; asking God for no one to be killed and for the battle to end that night. How did you know He would answer you?" Gevi asked.

"I didn't," Lily replied. She was silent for several long seconds. "But I think the Lord of the Stars wanted to teach us how powerful prayer is."

"And God wanted to teach the elves that He is their strength and their deliverer." A tall elf with long, blond hair stood behind Chellell. "He wanted to teach the elves that strength comes from humility, and not from pride." Chellell turned; her face lighting up when her eyes met the eyes of the elven prince, Yehowana. Gevi looked embarrassed as the elf sat down beside Chellell. She hung her head down, refusing to look at the elf.

"I think God is now teaching someone a lesson concerning her temper," Javin said as he started laughing. Gevi playfully punched him in the shoulder without even raising her head.

"I think someone needs a lesson in keeping his mouth shut," Gevi retorted.

"Peace; no need to give her a hard time," the elf prince said to Javin who was still laughing at Gevi. "I deserved what I got that night."

Gevi noticed the questioning look from Chellell and Lily, once she lifted her head. "We had a slight difference of opinions, one night," Gevi explained.

"Slight!" Javin started laughing even louder.

"I met Gevi and Javin while they were gathering wood, when their patrol first arrived at our forest," the elf prince said to Chellell and Lily "I arrogantly told them they would not be allowed to enter our forest. Gevi let me know that she did not appreciate my pride, and that she did not appreciate the fact that I would not let them into the forest."

"Not appreciate!" gasped a laughing Javin.

Gevi shoved Javin backwards to the ground and jump on him. She was trying to cover his mouth with her hands. A few minutes later, the two settled down and sat back up in the grass.

"When I first met Javin, I could not get him to talk. Now he won't be quiet!" Gevi snorted. "When I get to Heaven, I am going to ask God why He allowed men to talk," She gave Javin an irritated look, but she was putting her arm around him and her head to the side of his shoulder. Looking at Chellell and Lily, Gevi gave a sigh. "I will tell both of you about how Prince Yehowana and I first met, when there are no obnoxious men around." She gave Javin's shoulder a squeeze.

"Obnoxious men!" Javin replied in amazement. "Do I need to remind you which woman refuses to acknowledge that a certain man was correct when he identified her as the Barbarian Princess called Slayer of Giants? She still refuses to believe, even though all the elves call this woman, 'Valk Usefid', which is elven for Slayer of Giants."

"Fine," retorted Gevi, "you were right all along, Javin. If that is what you have been waiting to hear, then you have heard it, with witnesses present. Javin was right about the Barbarian Princess, Gevi was wrong."

"Gevi!" Chellell had a shocked look on her face. "You just broke the Woman's Code of Conduct. Never admit a man is right about anything!

Especially that man," she pointed right at Javin. "His pride will swell, and he will never let you forget that you said he was right."

"Chellell is right, Gevi," Lily said. "The Woman Code of Conduct requires you to twist past events so that you were right all along, while constantly insisting that the man was wrong."

Gevi laughingly wrapped her arms tightly around Javin. "You two are right. Let's get together, after no men are around, and decide how past events really happened. We can't allow Javin's head to get any bigger than it already is."

Javin rolled his eyes and looked toward the elven prince for support. Seeing no support coming from the elf, Javin sighed and gave Gevi's hand a squeeze. "There is absolutely no winning with women," he said toward the elven prince. I guess I just follow the Man's Code of Conduct and say, Yes Dear, you are right."

Another hour passed, with the friends enjoying each other's company. Finally, they got up together and headed for their beds. Before going to bed, Chellell pulled out her childhood copy of *The Guide*, and started reading. *Keep on, then, with your magic spells and with your many sorceries, which you have labored at since childhood. Perhaps you will succeed, perhaps you will cause terror. All the counsel you have received has only worn you out! Let your astrologers come forward, those stargazers who make predictions month by month, let them save you from what is coming upon you. Surely they are like stubble; the fire will burn them up. They cannot even save themselves from the power of the flame. A flame that is not coals for warmth; nor is it a fire to sit by!* In her heart, conviction grew. This passage was speaking directly into her heart.

In the middle of the night, Chellell left her tent, returning to the solitude of the forest. At the base of a tree, she fell to her knees.

With head bowed, a prayer issued from her lips. "Lord, I am so sorry that I ran from You, and denied You for so long. I know now that You are God, the Lord of the Stars. Please forgive me for all I did. I did great evil. If You will, please forgive me for the Ritual of Summoning." Tears started flowing freely down her face. "I know I am not worthy, but please, save me. You are the Son of God, who died and rose for me. Please, save me from my sins."

An hour later, Chellell entered the tent she was sharing with Gevi and Lily. Not waking the others, she crawled into bed and fell into a deep sleep.

Chellell dreamed. She didn't normally dream, or at least have dreams she remembered. But this dream was crystal clear. It was like she was there, like it was real. Chellell found herself in the most magnificent throne room you could imagine. Thousands of warriors, radiating awesome power, stood around the throne. In the center of the room was a gigantic throne, made of solid gold. Around the throne was flooring, so clear, it looked like crystal glass. No walls could be seen anywhere. Instead, brilliant stars, in numbers greater than she had ever seen, surrounded the entire throne room.

Chellell was looking around when suddenly, the brightest light she had ever seen appeared in the middle of the throne. Immense, Holy Power radiated out from the throne; enough power to fill the entire universe.

Chellell was on her knees bowing toward what she knew, without a doubt, to be the Presence of God. She saw the powerful warriors around the throne were on their knees as well. Finally, she felt a hand on her shoulder.

"Rise, young one," a deep, bass voice said to her. Chellell rose with the help of the warrior who spoke to her. "Stay here and watch." The warrior stayed right by her, but did not say another word. The warriors were all dressed in white robes, with golden sashes holding swords. As Chellell watched, two men approached the throne. They also radiated power, but it was different from the Holy Power she had been feeling. It was a power she recognized. A light went off in her mind. This was the same kind of power she used to feel when she used magic. The two men stopped before the throne.

"What is it that you seek, oh fallen ones?" A voice boomed from the throne. The voice, though not loud, was so powerful, it shook the entire throne room!

"We seek a girl that belongs to us, but you now protect," one of the fallen ones replied. "We seek to reclaim that which is ours."

"And why do you think this girl belongs to you? Is she not my creation?" boomed the voice from the throne.

"Your creation, true, but I want you to see what your creation has done." One of the fallen ones waved his hand, causing a large screen to appear off to the side of the throne room. In some strange way, you could see the screen, no matter where you stood in the throne room. Chellell gasped in absolute horror as the Ritual of Summoning played out on the screen. Every word and blasphemous thing she had said played in crystal clarity. The things she did with the other magic users that were extremely sinful and wicked at this ritual played in perfect color. Chellell was so horrified that she was paralyzed, unable to take her eyes off the screen. She remembered how she had wanted magic so badly that she was willing to do anything. Whatever was required to get that power, she willfully had done. The screen stopped playing right when it showed Sanatarial flying in and landing on her shoulder. Chellell felt so embarrassed she could die, right where she stood. She couldn't believe that these warriors, and God himself, had seen everything she had done.

"You have seen the evidence. The girl belongs to me and to Sanatarial." The man before the throne talking put a hand on the shoulder of the man standing next to him, indicating he was Sanatarial. Chellell gasped again, realizing the second man was actually her old familiar; a "fallen one".

"Besides, why would you want to have this girl? You saw what she said and the sinful things she did."

Just as the man finished speaking, another man stepped out of the immense light that surrounded the throne. Chellell knew instantly who this was. How, she did not know. But she knew, without a shadow of doubt, this was the Son of God; The Lord of the Stars. The Holy Power felt exactly the same as the Holy Power coming from the throne. Everyone around the throne fell to their knees. The warrior by Chellell again, helped her back to her feet a few minutes later.

"The girl is now mine," the Lord of the Stars said with the same kind of voice that emanated from the throne. It was different, but the same in power. "You, oh Lucifer, no longer have claim to her."

Chellell saw that the one called "Lucifer" seemed angry. He turned back to the throne. "Do I need to show you again what she did?" He turned to the Lord of the Stars. "Surely, Jesus, you do not want to bring someone like this into the Presence of your Father."

"Tell me, Oh Father, what do You see?" The Lord of the Stars boomed out, pointing a finger right at Chellell. The thousands that filled the throne room turned in one accord, eyes fixed on Chellell. Chellell stood paralyzed. Her eyes locked onto the Lord of the Stars. She could now feel the love He had for her, pouring into her body.

"I see absolute perfection," the voice of God the Father, from the throne, boomed out. "The girl I see is spotless, clean, and white as snow. She is sinless. She will be welcome in my Presence for eternity."

Chellell could see that her old familiar, along with the one called Lucifer, were staring at her with pure hatred, but she did not care. Her eyes were fixed on the Son of God.

The Lord of the Stars spoke directly into her mind. "My blood has washed you completely and totally clean. Your debt is paid in full. All is forgiven. Sanatarial will no longer be allowed near you, ever again."

Suddenly, the Lord of the Stars was standing right by her. "You desire the love of a father," he said to her. "Look upon the Father, and tell me what you feel."

Chellell looked at the throne. Intense love was directed out toward her. Joy filled her heart at this love, a love she had always sought. This was the love that had been missing most of her life.

"Chellell, Chellell, wake up. You are having a dream." Chellell opened her eyes, only to see Lily right above her face. Gevi was still asleep, but then Chellell knew that a charging bull couldn't wake that girl. She sat up, giving Lily a hug. They managed to finally wake up Gevi. That night, Chellell told them everything that had happened to her, and about her dream, with the Lord of the Stars.

****

"And so, your majesty, we think the Enlightened Church should stay as the only church for the humans," the two priests stated, standing before the Grand Leader. "The other churches need to be burned down, and the people that refuse enlightenment, put in to prison." The Grand Leader sat on his throne, deep in thought. His anger still burned at the news he received yesterday about his destroyed army. Several gorms had died by his hand that day, when they told him the details. Later in the morning, once he had calmed down, he interviewed dozens of surviving gorms and the one surviving giant. The picture he put together really troubled him.

This band of rebels from the Kingdom of Preveshawl and the elves were more trouble than he ever imagined. The Grand Leader looked down at the wanted papers in his hand. The picture of the gorgeous young woman, with coal black hair, holding a staff, was on top. The giant let his eyes linger on the woman before looking back up to the group in front of him. Ambrissan stood still, with his familiar wrapped around his shoulder. Standing behind him was another mage and two priests from the Enlightened Church.

"No one is going to touch any of the other churches, or hurt any member of them," said the Grand Leader in a statement that surprised everyone in the room.

Both priests angrily stepped forward toward the giant. The Grand Leader rose swiftly up from his throne, his huge mass towering over the humans. "They are not to be touched!" he roared.

The priests quickly moved backwards, angry expressions changing to one of fear. The struggle to contain his anger showed on the Grand Leader's face. "Dismissed; Ambrissan, I want you to stay." The second mage and the two priests bowed toward the Grand Leader, before quickly exiting the throne room.

Ambrissan came toward the throne. "What kind of magic user is this?" He handed the wanted posters to Ambrissan, Gevi's picture facing upward.

"She's not a magic user," Ambrissan said calmly.

"She single handedly destroyed my army," the giant roared again. His fist came crashing down onto the armrest of his throne. Broken pieces of wood and expensive cushion fibers flew into the air. "Many gorms that survived told me lightning and balls of fire flew from her staff at will. Magic arrows were thrown from her hands, killing my giants with explosions so powerful, the ground shook!"

The Grand Leader leaped up from his throne, his hands clenched in a fist. "She used magic to cause a great windstorm that killed a thousand gorms!" The giant turned toward the mage. Glittering, angry eyes locked onto the mage's eyes. "Another gorm reported her summoning tigers that appeared in the middle of the camp. One of the gorm captains told me she faced all three of your mages, turning them to ash before they could utter a spell." The giant stepped forward, bending down to look Ambrissan right in the eye. "And if you killed the Black Knight, then she raised him right back up from the dead," the giant said coldly. "Fighting by her side, he killed many gorms with those flaming swords." He gave another hard glare at the magic user, before returning to his throne.

Ambrissan kept the doubt he felt inside from showing. He knew that the gorms would say anything to save their lives. Still, his intelligence did confirm a great windstorm had destroyed the army. The girl's staff was also a known item of great power. What really puzzled him was that magic only came from the aid of familiars. This girl did not have a familiar. Her power came from another source.

"The Black Knight is obviously some type of summoned demon guardian for the girl. If you kill him, she will only summon him again. We kill the girl, and the demon will disappear," Ambrissan told the Grand Leader. This was a lie Ambrissan was sure the giant would believe.

The giant sat back down, his rage replaced with a sly smile. "I have a better plan, that I want you to execute before winter sets in. Find ten humans, females with a couple of males, and train them as spies. Once they are trained, I want them to join the churches that your priest friends asked me to destroy. I don't care what they have to pretend to believe, but they are to make themselves the best members in those churches. They are to be in these churches every time the door is open. Once they are accepted by the members, then I am going to outlaw these churches." The giant's smile grew bigger as he paused in his speech. "I will allow the churches to leave and head toward this rebel group up by the elves. I will be so kind; that I will even make sure they have wagons, horses, and food."

Ambrissan liked what he was hearing. This was the kind of thing he wished he had thought of. He would have to stop his secret assassins that he had planned to have murder everyone in a little church in Bear Tree City. "And once the spies find the girl, they befriend her, and then kill her," Ambrissan finished. An evil grin was plastered on his face at the thought. He had no intention of killing the girl, immediately, but he wanted the Grand Leader to think that he did. Whatever power it was she possessed, Ambrissan was going to make sure he was the recipient of her power. His smile vanished with what the giant said next.

"No, I want the girl brought back to me, alive. Knock her out, keep her out. Use herbs, or whatever. I don't really care how you do it, but make sure that the girl and the staff both get to me. Where she goes, the Black Knight will follow. Then I can have his magic swords." The giant started to laugh while he thought about his plans.

"Once I learn the secret of her magic, Preveshawl, the elves, the dwarves, and those rebels will kneel before me as their king." Maniacal laughter echoed through the throne room. The Grand Leader could barely contain his glee.

Ambrissan stood with an actor's smile on his face. He knew the girl had no real magic. She was extremely powerful from some source. Her power must never get to the Grand Leader. Ambrissan would make sure of that. Her power would belong to him, and he would rule all of Preveshawl. He quickly left the throne room to prepare his spies.

Conclusion

On the day when I act," says the LORD Almighty, "they will be my treasured possession. I will spare them, just as a father has compassion and spares his son who serves him. - The Guide

The refugees from Farm Circle arrived peacefully at the Ruins of the Linkrins. They were greeted by the few families from the church of Fort Outlands. With the help of these families already established, along with dwarves and the elves, the refugees quickly repaired old buildings, turning them into shops and homes. A council of governing elders was formed. They distributed land, houses, and shops to individuals and families as needed. The Elders decided to name their new settlement, Godspeace.

Javin received land near the fallen wall of the ruins, next to land given to his father and mother. He worked with his father to build his parent's house. Once his parents and sisters were established in a home, Javin built a small, one room cottage on his land.

Gevi was given a building to use as a shop, to make and sell her incredible items. Once Javin finished his house, he worked night and day with Gevi, to get her shop up and running.

****

Godspeace was in the full wrath of winter. Snow to the knee and howling winds punished the new community with bone numbing cold. Thick, gray clouds promised that another storm was about to blast the little community. Gevi's numb hand was holding Javin's hand as the two left her shop, walking to Thunderfall's smithy.

After knocking the snow off their boots, the pair entered the crowded shop, joining the other young people gathered for the study in *The Guide*. Gevi let go of Javin's hand, pushing her way to the blazing fire burning in an oversized fireplace. Javin sat down in a clear spot on the floor. As Thunderfall opened the Guide a few minutes later, Gevi, Lily, and Chellell joined him on the floor. Thunderfall read to everyone from, *The Guide.*

He finished his reading with this passage. *"He did much evil in the sight of the Lord, provoking him to anger."*

"It seems every time the ancient kings refused to follow God, God turned against that king and his nation," Lily commented.

"But, those that obeyed God, were blessed," Chellell said. She bent down to scratch Kitty's belly. The Great Northern Tiger purred contentedly, lying on his back at Chellell's feet with all four paws waving in the air.

Thunderfall set *The Guide* down and looked at the young people, sitting around him on the floor. Chellell, Lily, Gevi, Javin, and many others had been listening intently to Thunderfall, reading *The Guide.*

Walking over to a table in the middle of the group, Thunderfall drew their attention to something he had built earlier. Sitting on the table was a tower, made from blocks of wood. It was the same kind of blocks young children used in their play, to build play forts and castles. "This block tower represents a kingdom. How does the Great Dragon, the Fallen One, go about destroying a kingdom or a nation?" Many answers came at Thunderfall from the crowded room. After a minute or so of letting the young ones comment, he reached up and pulled a block off the top of the tower. "You can take blocks off the top, but the tower will not fall. Remember, this block tower represents a kingdom, protected by the Lord of the Stars. The majority of people in this kingdom are followers of God. God will not allow the Evil One to knock it down. So how do you topple this kingdom, if you are allowed to only touch one block at a time?"

"You have to start with the foundation," a young man spoke up that was seated right behind Lily.

"Correct," replied Thunderfall. "Now, give me some examples of what the foundation is for a kingdom or nation, that considers itself one nation, under God."

"God's Word, *The Guide*," Gevi answered from her spot between Javin and Chellell.

"Very good Gevi, God's Word is the biggest part of a kingdom's foundation. A kingdom must have a source of unchanging Truth. Now let's drill down and be more specific. The way the Great Dragon typically works is slowly, through deception. So how would you attack *The Guide?*"

"Creation," replied Javin instantly, smiling over at Gevi. His mind went back to her explosive arrow striking the monkey-man statue. "You say that God is not the all-powerful God that created everything from nothing, in six days." Thunderfall slowly slid a block out from the very bottom of the tower. The tower did not fall.

"You claim that our Savior, who died to pay our debt to God, was not God. He was only a good man, a prophet, or a teacher, but not God." Lily absently rubbed the scar that ran from her eye to her ear. A chill ran through her body as the face of Licheaon, right in front of her, ran through her mind. She could almost feel the impact of hitting her make-up dresser again. Shaking herself, Lily took a deep breath and watched Thunderfall remove another block. The tower still stood.

"Claim that *The Guide* contains many errors, because it is written by people. You would claim that it was not written by people under the powerful inspiration of the Holy Spirit." This came from a young man seated right by the table holding the tower. Another block slid out from the base of the tower. The tower swayed to the side, but quickly righted itself.

"Great examples on how to remove God's Word from the foundation; what else can the Great Dragon do to topple a nation?"

"Attack the education system," Gevi replied. Her arm was resting lightly on Chellell's shoulder. Start by removing *The Guide* from schools; then remove prayer, and finally, God Himself." Thunderfall slid another block out from the foundation. The tower swayed dangerously.

"Introduce false churches," a young woman called out from the back of the room near the door. "They can teach falsehoods like no Hell, or claim salvation comes from another source besides God's only Son."

"You could have a church where God is your magical genie granting your every wish," another young woman said. Another block came out. The tower looked like it barely was able to stand.

"Separate church and kingdom," Javin commented. "Make sure the rulers of the kingdom push an atheistic agenda on the people, under the claim that they in fact support no single religion." Another block came out from the base of the wooden block tower. The whole tower collapsed, scattering wooden building blocks all over the table and the floor.

"A nation under God has fallen, which is why we need to pray for Preveshawl," Thunderfall said in a very quiet and serious voice. "Three generations in a row of wicked kings, each worse than his father before him, has led to the situation we are now in. The foundation of Preveshawl is being destroyed." Thunderfall looked down to the ground, his thoughts troubled. "Still, God is a forgiving God. If the King repents of his sins and serves the Lord of the Stars, then maybe God will again bless Preveshawl. We can start to rebuild the foundation before the kingdom collapses."

"But as for me and my house, we will serve the Lord," quoted Gevi from *The Guide.* She leaned in closer to Javin, her arm leaving Chellell and going around Javin's shoulder.

"We need to pray for the king and the Kingdom of Preveshawl as Thunderfall said," Javin said. "Come this summer, we need to go down to the people of Preveshawl, warning them to repent and turn back to The Lord of the Stars." Thunderfall's head whipped around to face Javin, amazed at the wisdom of Javin's words. "We also need to help the imprisoned followers of The Lord of the Stars," Javin continued, not noticing Thunderfall's intense gaze on him. "They need to be set free, and given a home among us."

"The elves are a testament of what happens when a king and nation repent and rid themselves of false churches with false doctrines; obeying the Truth given by The Lord of the Stars," said a soft, monotone voice from the doorway. The group in one accord turned their heads to see the Elven Prince Yehowana standing inside the door. He was resting against the door frame; behind him, stood a massive human, Merion.

"How did he sneak in here?" Javin wondered. He stood up to greet his old friend from the guilds. Chellell jumped to her feet, weaving through the group, to stand by the elven prince.

"What are you doing here?" Chellell asked with a bright smile.

"A ragged group of half frozen humans arrived at the Elven Forest over a week ago," the Elven Prince answered. "It seems the giants are expelling the followers of The Lord of the Stars, and sending them to you. I decided to lead the first group up to you personally." He smiled down at Chellell the whole time he talked. "Geviasaracaila," the Elven Prince said in greeting upon seeing Gevi.

"Gevi, I prefer Gevi," Gevi said, but she was smiling at Chellell and the Elf Prince while she said it.

"Gevi then," replied Yehowana. He and Chellell sat down with the group on the floor. "It seems you, Gevi, and your Black Knight guardian, are becoming real popular among the people. I was asked a lot of questions about you two. Like the elves, the gorms are now calling you 'Giant Slayer'. The stories are growing and spreading amongst the humans." The smile left his face when he saw Javin and Merion stepping outside together.

Merion had a serious demeanor about him, he also seemed troubled. He paced around in front of Javin, kicking the snow away with his oversized feet. Finally, he stopped and faced Javin.

"I thanked the elves for rescuing and healing me," Merion said as he paced around in the snow. "I want to thank you and your people here as well. Real battle is a lot different than us crossing swords in the arena, Javin. I was at the battle of the Crossroads. It was horrible." Merion paused in the snow, his eyes going everywhere but toward Javin. Finally, he said what was really on his mind. "I know everyone here is rebelling against Preveshawl over this Guide and Lord of the Stars law, and that puts me in a tough spot." The large man started pacing again in the snow, ignoring the cold, biting wind. "We have always been honest with each other, so I will be honest now. I am loyal to king and kingdom, and I am not religious in any way. I would not fit in here, and would probably not even be wanted, but I have nowhere else to go." Merion stopped talking, but continued to pace around in the snow. Javin was about to reply, when he saw two women approaching them through the snow.

"Hi Merion," one of the ladies called out. They plowed through the snow, joining the two men.

"Oh, Javin, this is Lissal and Emna," Merion said, though he was obviously distracted and wanting to talk more with Javin. "They came up with me and the Elven Prince. They belong to one of those churches in Bear Tree City that the gorms outlawed."

"Do you know where we can find *The Guide* Study?" The woman Merion identified as Lissal asked, while looking at Javin. "The elders told us about it and said we could go to it and return to them later for a housing assignment." Javin pointed toward the door.

"Inside here?" Javin nodded his head. "Well aren't we blessed, finding it so quickly; can we go on inside?" Again, Javin nodded. The two women smiled sweetly, and went inside.

"Let's go inside, Merion, and I will hear your story tonight. You are welcome to stay with me as my guest as long as you want." Surprise showed on Merion's face. "Have no fear; the people here will welcome you as well. By the way, this land is outside of Preveshawl. Preveshawl law does not apply here." Javin put his arm on the massive shoulder of Merion. "Welcome friend, to the town and Nation of Godspeace."

Treachery of Magic, Coming September, 2013

www.ingramcontent.com/pod-product-compliance
Lightning Source LLC
Chambersburg PA
CBHW031939240626
47153CB00003B/793